RISE

RISE

JAMIE J. KEMP

LUMINARE PRESS
WWW.LUMINAREPRESS.COM

RISE

Copyright © 2021 by Jamie J. Kemp

Printed in the United States of America

Cover design by Melissa K. Thomas

Luminare Press
442 Charnelton St.
Eugene, OR 97401
www.luminarepress.com

LCCN: 2020913649
ISBN: 978-1-64388-391-5

For Dad

CHAPTER ONE

Change was in the air. Una could feel it on her skin as she raced through downtown Seattle to catch the bus home. It wasn't just the mist of the usual spring shower interrupted by bursts of sunshine that time of year, but a knowing deep inside that the comfortable life she had created for herself was about to be upended. She didn't fear it nor did she embrace it. She simply allowed the feeling to move through her, welcoming in the twists and turns that would shift her onto a new path in life. It was the one constant she could depend on in the last twenty-four years. This time would be no different.

She had another couple of blocks to her bus stop, but if she picked up the pace, she just might make it home to run a hot bath and shake off her busy day at the bakery. Just as she crossed Pine Street, making a slow run toward Pike, her phone began a slow slide out of the palm of her hand and slipped through her fingers onto the cold pavement below.

Had she not dropped her phone that day, Una would have made the bus on time, and the world would have remained in perfect balance as before. But the butter did leave a silky film on her hands over the course of a long, ten-hour shift. The last batch of cupcakes did take five minutes longer in the oven, and her coworker did wait out the extra four minutes in a long line at the coffeehouse to retrieve their usual order. All those delays resulted in a monumental shift on an otherwise ordinary day.

In a mad scramble to retrieve the phone, Una stumbled forward, forcing her backpack, recipe cards, notebook, and pencils to spill onto the damp sidewalk along with a freshly made latte. She came face-to-face with the pavement and started to laugh. For once, she wished someone had caught it on camera. It had to have been a comical display worthy of at least a thousand shares. She could taste a drop of French vanilla on her lips. The rest she would have to wear home on the front of her blouse and savor the smell under her nose for the few miles up to Capitol Hill.

Una scrambled to her feet just as a homeless man rolled up with a rusty, wobbly shopping cart. He reached for the notebook, thumbing through the scribbles of ingredients and pages covered in dry batter and butter stains. She had started the notebook just after leaving the culinary institute. It was her secret weapon, and she wasn't about to lose it.

"What the hell is all this?" the homeless man slurred as he held the book up to the fickle sunlight. There was a brief break in the clouds, a rare sighting on a typical dismal gray day. If the last month or so of weather was any indication, it certainly wouldn't last long.

"It's my recipe collection," Una answered rather loudly. She was concerned the old man wouldn't be able to hear her above the traffic noise.

She caught the stench of whiskey from six feet away. From the smell of it, the guy had enough to drink for everyone on the block. What a strange condition, to be drunk all the time, Una thought. She could barely manage on anything less than eight hours of rest, let alone operating under the influence for most of her waking hours.

"I hate cookin," he muttered and threw the now soaking book into a puddle. "I prefer to get my stores in drink, if you know what I mean."

He gently patted his so-called belly, masked delicately behind his full rack of ribs. The old man before her seemed more like a shadow than a human, a mere glimpse of the man Una imagined he used to be. She could almost see the darkness around him, a sort of life-force suck that seemed to plague all who found themselves wandering the streets these days. It was a life she was all too familiar with in her past. She wondered how he acquired his drink, much less where he slept or how he avoided the trouble lurking around every corner in this section of town.

"What about cupcakes? Do you like cupcakes?" she asked as she retrieved the book from the puddle. The sun began to hide behind another low-hanging cloud. She wished she had packed a few cupcakes to take home. The bag of bones before her could clearly use some.

"Are they soaked in rum?" he questioned back as he reached into the rusty cart.

Una instinctively checked for her phone. She had returned it to the pack's front pocket, an almost subconscious act at this point. She wanted to show sympathy, but she also needed to be smart. A phone would buy a decent amount of liquor for a homeless man on the streets of Seattle. At a minimum, it would keep his shadow aimlessly floating around in a fog for weeks.

"Cupcakes?" he considered. "I haven't had one in years."

"Well, maybe tomorrow I'll whip you up a batch. Will you be in this part of town tomorrow?" Una asked. "I pass by here just about every day."

"Don't know," he said as he began to turn the cart toward the alley. "Maybe…"

She watched him rattle and roll his way up the narrow opening. She felt an overwhelming sense of compassion for the man. He had to be lonely, she thought. No wonder he drinks.

"Watch your back today." His shout echoed through the alley. "You never know who or what will stab it."

As she passed the man in his lonely alley, the distinct smell of fish batter, sea salt, bitter coffee, and urine made the path to her nostrils. It was a combination that only Seattle could offer, and it was slowly growing on her. Like mold.

As she gathered her belongings and shoved them into her overloaded pack, she looked up to see her bus pulling away from the stop. She glanced at her watch to see she was a few minutes behind the usual schedule. The next one wouldn't be arriving for a while, so she pulled her hood up for some protection from the miserable clouds looming over Elliott Bay.

She sighed heavily and made her way toward the shelter. She wanted at least one thing to fall in place today. If the cupcakes had finished on time and she had taken time to scrub up a little more before leaving, she would be well on her way home by now. Everything happens for a reason, she thought. It's what she told herself anytime things didn't go according to plan. Lately, everything seemed to be going the opposite of plan, as if a chaotic storm was brewing just for her each day. Like now. She was hoping to duck into the shelter but noticed it was already full. She found a spot to settle in nearby and pulled the strings tighter on her hood as thunder rolled in the distance.

It was about that time that the rain began to fall again. The taps and drips touched the top of her head, reminding her of the fact the rainy season would stretch on for another four months. She was a Northwest girl through and through, but she was certain it rained more in Seattle than her hometown of Portland, a few hours south. She welcomed the bus delay. It was a chance to reflect on a very hectic week and all she had to do tomorrow.

She had spent the better part of the day putting together an enormous show of cupcakes for the Seattle Art Museum. The intricate display consisted of just over one thousand cupcakes for a fundraising event happening that afternoon. They all had to be baked to perfection in just under three grueling hours. The odd combinations of lavender, rosemary, and sunflower seeds were supposed to be reminiscent of the French countryside for the opening of a visiting Monet exhibit. She had thumbed through books at the library, getting reacquainted with the artist's work. The book was enormous, obviously meant for display on someone's coffee table. The edges of the pages were gold, furthering the illusion of opulence that one could only imagine in Monet's time.

She had needed some serious inspiration to pull it off, but Monet's serene settings did the trick. Somehow, she made the curator's list of ingredients work. The woman was relentless, demanding that Una use every ingredient on the list. There were days she wanted to curse the cupcake battle shows on television because everyone she encountered at the bakery door seemed convinced miracles could be achieved in under an hour, just like they saw on television. In reality, it took days to plan and a few more for good measure to perfect the recipe. Una seemed to have a magic touch though, reading into a client's mind and seeing exactly what needed to be achieved. She may have needed inspiration at times, but her displays always produced results.

She made her way to the bus stop bench, where an older, beautifully dressed woman sat quietly, eyes closed. Una couldn't tell if she was sleeping or just finding a moment to meditate or pray. Her long, gray hair was tucked neatly in a matronly bun. Like everyone else at the stop, she probably was longing to escape the crowded streets, noxious fumes, and overall grumpy tone that had become commonplace in the city as of late. Moods wouldn't lift here until at least mid-July, but along with the return of the sun would come more fumes and foot traffic.

Before long, others began to show up at the bus shelter. Some seemed put together, and looked as if they had worked their way up the corporate ladder toward a minimal raise and empty promises of a fulfilling white-collar career. Others were more typical of a bus ride east of downtown— single, smoking, and wearing an expression that said, rather loudly, "stay away."

An older gentleman sat quietly to the side, reading a copy of a fitness book called *The Four-Hour Body*. Una had to chuckle a little as she considered the man doing push-ups, sit-ups, and whatever else was required of a person to achieve physical perfection in four hours a week or whatever the timeline called for. He tore into a candy bar as he thumbed through the book, chocolate covering his fat fingers and staining the corners of each turned page. She didn't see him sticking to the program for long. It was just a hunch.

Inspiration can come from anywhere, she thought, as she reached for her phone. She hadn't checked in all day. As she waited for the app to load, she glanced at a young mom and son nearby. The mom bent down to nosy-kiss the boy and then pulled her phone from her bag. The boy squealed in delight as he maneuvered the screen, probably more of an expert than any adult there. Una liked him immediately.

A sort of man-child rolled up just then on a skateboard, earbuds jammed into his ears. He looked like a Southern California surfer who fell asleep on the northbound bus and found himself kicked off in a place called Seattle. The sound of death metal somehow found its way into the small crowd. Most of the people waiting didn't seem to care. The skater stared off into the distance. He might have been the only one there not looking at his phone.

The one thing all of the people gathered at the stop on Pike seemed to have in common was defeat. Defeat in their last encounters. Defeat at the end of a long day. Defeat in life. It was something she was seeing more often these days. Defeat, disgust, and overall dissatisfaction. As she watched the group scroll and search, she observed how quickly they smiled and scowled, and more importantly, how immediate the reactions were and how they would slowly fade away. It was sort of a kaleidoscope of faces, rotating to reveal one emotion to the next.

No one loved a phone more than Una, but these days she began to wonder how disconnected she had become from her friends: no longer meeting up for lunch but now texting or chatting through any number of apps. They communicated constantly, but the experience had gone from communal in school to virtual in the supposed real world. Not that she minded discovering her friends' likes, tastes, and disdain in every comment and share, but she secretly yearned for a tap on the shoulder, a tug of the arm. A human experience that technology just couldn't provide.

She often wondered if she was the only one who felt that way. The thought was only confirmed by glancing around at the group gathered around her. It didn't take keen observation skills to see how disconnected everyone was from each other. That's what her daily bus routes had become. It seemed to be an endless sea of long faces. They were all lost in apps, playlists, podcasts, or whatever other distraction was available to keep them from their own thoughts and feelings and each other.

The bus arrived ten minutes later, pulling Una back to reality just as the real rain came down. At least the driver was on time. She reached to the very bottom of her pack for her pass and quickly retrieved it before having to endure the driver's impatient look she had come to know so well.

The driver didn't bother to look up from his furrowed brows with the butt-crack line between them. His nose always seemed to be twitching in disgust at each stop, as if he were quietly judging everyone who boarded his personal bus. This time, he just nodded with no expression. Even though she had ridden this particular driver's bus at least two dozen times since the first of the year, Una still couldn't get eye contact out of the man. She had wanted to introduce herself every time but soon came to realize that, to him, she was just another daily rider in a sea of nameless faces.

After considering her seat choices, she saw the older woman she had encountered first sitting in the very last row. Una smiled as she took the seat beside her, putting the pack at her feet. She was always skeptical about setting her bag on the floor of the bus. She quickly chased the thought from her mind, determined to end her day in a positive frame of mind and not caught up in thoughts of all the germs that lurked below.

As the bus began to merge into traffic, the sun made a brief appearance from behind its gray curtain. The entire compartment was bathed in light. Each beam revealed the grimy layers of filth and fingerprints on the windows, railings, and handles. She lifted the bag back into her lap and shoved her hand into the abyss of its compartments. She felt her way through loose change, lip balm, nail clippers, and... yes...hand sanitizer. She applied it liberally and offered some to the woman she affectionately thought of as *abuela*. The woman politely declined.

Una had always wanted an abuela of her own. If she had a woman to call grandmother, then perhaps her mom would not have struggled as much as she did. The only constant in Una's world as a child was change. She could barely recall the early years that seemed to her an endless search for security. As a young child, she and her mom were consistently adrift in a sea of despair. It felt like they were constantly on the move, looking for a shining beacon that would be a night's rest in a homeless shelter. That's all her earliest memories would reveal, at least until age six or seven. The rest she likely blocked out of her memory bank for good reason.

Her mother worked daily to develop a plan for the evening. She talked to staff in the shelters over breakfast and gathered the information necessary to land a place that evening, preferably for women and children only. Shelter space was very difficult to come by, not because her mother was addicted. Quite the contrary. Had she walked in with tracks on her arms, they likely would have had a more permanent situation to offer her and her child. Instead, they would tell her that her case wasn't dire enough. Each one told her she was smart and resilient. Surely, she could find a job or a more permanent situation to fall back on during a troubled time. But who would watch Una while she was away? She didn't trust the cast of characters the agencies offered. The exchange played out like a worn-out recording as her mother's frustration grew. It was a moment-to-moment existence for a while, but they always found a way. More often than not, she could still feel her mom's sweaty hand in hers as the rain began to fall. It was a feeling of desperation Una would never forget.

The closest person to a grandmother Una had known was Bea, a larger-than-life woman who would shepherd souls in and out of Lamb's Door, one of the few women's shelters in Portland. Bea, short for Beatrix, didn't just greet you, she enveloped you. She was the heart and soul of the modest two-story saltbox in Southeast. It was one of the few women's centers that actually felt like any sort of "home" to Una and her mom.

Bea would welcome the duo with a wide smile and the smell of cinnamon and tobacco. "Got the spice from my mama and the bad habits from my daddy," she'd say with gusto and a giggle. Una would rush to her open arms, basking in a single, solitary moment of love and hope apart from her mother's presence. The sensation would move from her brain to her nose, as she took in the sweet smell of Bea's cookies. It was the first smell she identified with a home.

"You want one, baby?" Bea would ask, handing over the warm doughy goodness before Una could even answer.

She'd give her a wink and two more cookies for good measure. What child didn't love a haven with the constant scent of baked goods? Perhaps that was why Una had developed a love and passion for baking. Maybe it was her own way of providing people with the same sense of home.

She smiled for a moment, remembering Bea.

"You call me Bea or Honey Bea, but don't be callin' me Trixie," she'd say with a huff. "My mama called me that once, and I said, 'Mama, I ain't goin' by some horse's name!' Trixie just sounds like a horse name to me, or a dog. I ain't no dog, honey."

Una could picture Bea, her now graying hair pulled back into two neat braids, her glowing skin complemented by the bright colors she wore. Her clothing was modest in style but always seemed like it was picked from inside a rainbow. The color, like her personality, was simply captivating. Cheerful. Larger than life. That was Bea.

Una would watch Bea do something that few around the homeless ever did. She acknowledged their presence. So many strangers would look away or offer eyes soaked in sadness and pity. Bea knew everyone's name and considered every situation a series of unfortunate events. She didn't judge or preach. She simply listened, and mostly consoled. Her most effective technique, even with the worst of the downtrodden, was the ability to see humor in nearly every situation.

"Humor will see you through, honey," she would say, chuckling as she padded a shoulder or offered a hug.

Bea was such a force in Una's early years, teaching her everything she knew about baking, life, and love.

"Baking, like love, is a process, baby," Bea would say. "If you rush it, turn up the heat too fast, don't give it the time to bake fully or leave out a crucial ingredient? Well, baby, it will just fall on your plate like a hot mess and leave a bad taste in your mouth."

Una would shake her head at the thought.

Bea would offer these pearls of wisdom as she pulled a batch of Sweet Honey Bea Cakes from the oven, a recipe of her own invention and Una's personal favorite. Sweet cornbread made even sweeter by two cups of honey and a few M&M's placed on top for fun.

"That's for me, baby. Those bright colors catch their eyes and keeps them comin' back!" she'd say with a snap. "You gotta be pleasing with the eye while appeasing the stomach. That's how you keep these people off the street."

The recipe may have sounded disgusting on paper, but it looked beautiful on a plate and was pure perfection when the flavors danced on the tongue.

Bea always saw the good in every situation, and she and Una had connected on that virtue from the very beginning. Una, like Bea, had been blessed with a positive outlook, despite the circumstances that often surrounded her. She had a sweet disposition and was empathetic, considerate, and charismatic. In many ways, she was quite opposite from her mother, who was often wrought with anxiety and fear. As her now adult mind considered the enormity of their situation in her youth, Una certainly understood why her mother had felt the way she did a lot of the time.

Una would often wonder about her father and, upon asking, would get a shrug or shake of the head through her entire childhood. When she visited one weekend on a break from culinary school, her mother elaborated a little more about their encounter. She gleaned from the awkward conversation that her father was handsome and charismatic. He had instantly charmed her mother and drew her into his arms, as Santana played one night in a local bar.

Her mother had no intention of sleeping with him, but the magic of the evening led her straight back to the apartment she shared with a friend outside Buenos Aires. They spent the night enraptured, talking about their experiences in life up to that point and future plans in between rounds of passionate lovemaking. She said she felt like she had known him a lifetime in that night. In the morning when she woke, he left a candy on her pillow, one he had taken from a bowl at the bar. She never saw or heard from him again.

It was that same charisma that flowed through Una's veins, and seemed to draw people to her in her time at Lamb's Door. She would listen to so many stories of heartbreak and loss before gently offering the kind of wisdom only a child with special gifts could. Una had a simple view helped by a filter of innocence. Sometimes she would just offer her hand to a stranger sitting in the living room. Her touch alone was enough to comfort the most troubled souls. Some would grip so tight she would see the imprint of their fingers for days.

For years, Una passed through Bea's door, at first rather sporadically to stay, then later consistently after school. By then, her mom had a regular job as a maid in a local motel. The pay was terrible, but the room was free, and it was just a few blocks from Lamb's Door where Una would stay with Bea until her mother finished tidying up the endless row of rooms.

Bea was more than happy to have Una around. She just felt warm in her presence. Una was more than eager to try Bea's latest and greatest invention, her expression ever neutral even when the most appalling culinary "treats" passed her lips. Cakes made savory from saffron and pork pieces that were rarely found at the typical grocery store. Once, Bea added rosemary plucked from the garden out back and a few figs from a tree a few doors down; the pastry settled perfectly on Una's palette, and she smiled from ear to ear with approval.

Things changed again the morning her mother met José. Spring was slowly turning to summer, and that particular day was a suffering and sultry ninety-seven degrees. Her mom had just taken a slightly better job with a maid service, but the compact piece of junk she was given to drive around town overheated at the height of rush hour, and she broke down right in the middle of a freeway on-ramp.

Her fellow commuters were less than amused, offering honks and middle fingers rather than a phone call or push to the side of the freeway. José, who was passing by in a tow truck, pulled over immediately to help, and the rest, as they say, is history. He took her heart by the time the leaves fell and her hand by the New Year. Together, the two, along with Una, began the slow process of clawing their way back toward consistency, family, and a new normal.

Their first apartment together was a shabby one-bedroom in Gresham. José worked nights towing cars from lots downtown and would often take the couch when he arrived as the sun was rising, leaving the two ladies in his life to rest peacefully in the double bed. Yes, it was an aging complex and insects were commonplace, but the floors, sinks, and tub inside unit 4-B were spotless. Her mom, by then experienced in the "cleaning arts" as she called them, would spend days picking up after others and return home with renewed vigor, to scrub her own floors and tile with a toothbrush.

It was about that time that Una hit the double digits of age ten and would still trot the seven blocks to Lamb's Door after school to tackle a new recipe with Bea or just chit-chat about what was happening at school. It was the happiest time in her life. Fifth grade soon turned to senior year, and before long, Una was rushing through Lamb's Door with acceptance letters in hand, considering her future. Bea practically burst with anticipation as Una ripped open each envelope. Harvard, Yale, Brown, and Princeton all arrived at Unit 4-B, but it was a culinary institute that was secretly knocking at the door of Una's heart. Una finally shared her secret passion with Bea.

"Honey, I could have told you that years ago!" Bea shouted above the sound of the vacuum in the next room.

Bea caught Una's reflection in the mirror above the fireplace, watching as tears formed in the young woman's eyes. Bea stopped the vacuum and took Una into her arms.

"You gotta be true to you, girl," she said as her grip grew tighter. The oven timer went off just then. It was a good thing, too, because Una was about to pass out from the pressure.

"No sense trying to turn a cherry pie into shepherd's pie," Bea said, continuing the conversation into the kitchen. "Sure, they are both pies, but there's a big difference."

Bea pulled an enormous meat pie from the oven and hummed a brief tune as she set it on the table to cool.

"Here's the thing about pie and life," she said, looking Una squarely in the eye. "One has that big, meaty bite that settles into the gut. It makes the tough even tougher. Woof!" She barked for effect and gestured to the pie before her on the table, then made her way to a freshly baked cherry pie on the counter.

"The other pie is sweet but with just enough tart to keep a sweet tooth at bay," Bea said, dramatically gesturing to the beautifully baked concoction before her. Una seemed less than amused.

"You get what I'm saying to you?" Bea asked.

"I do, but Mom and José will be so disappointed in me," Una said, dropping her gaze to the floor. "This is their dream too."

"Girl, this ain't nobody's dream but your dream!" Bea shouted. "They love you and just want you to be happy."

"I guess so, but it's not glamorous or something to brag about to people they know. I don't think you understand the pressures of being an immigrant, Bea. It's on me to make our lives better. They expect that and it's hard to live up to sometimes."

"So what?" Bea shouted, throwing her arms skyward in another dramatic gesture. "Some of the most important work on this here planet is the least glamorous of all, honey. Ain't no fairy godmother up in this here joint, waving that wand over people. Probably make me a mess with all that dang glitter that I'm gonna have to vacuum up later!"

Una laughed at the thought. Oh, Bea. Always able to find the humor in the situation.

The news of her choice wasn't a shock to her parents at all. In fact, they were just happy she had finally settled on a future. Mom and José knew she was bright, and clearly gifted academically. But the idea of Una, a sweet and loving presence fully in tune with the feelings and actions of others, gracing the halls of institutions where competition was the norm and wolves waited at the door were what kept them up at night. Culinary arts seemed the perfect choice for their girl. It was hard work, for sure, but it was comforting to know she would be embracing her passion and, truth be told, living closer to them for a little while longer. She packed up an old Subaru José had found on Craigslist and made her way toward her future in Seattle.

The bus tire dropped into a pothole just then, snapping Una back from her reverie. She glanced over at Abuela. How the old woman managed to doze through such a jolt was truly amazing to her. Some people were like that. They could just sleep through anything. Sleep didn't always find Una easily, especially in the last two years, baking crazy concoctions for a vast clientele. She secretly envied the woman beside her, but she knew after this chaotic day she would definitely sleep tonight.

About that time, Una noticed her hands were sweating, much like her mom's in those early days in the shelter lines. Something felt…off. She could feel the hairs on the back of her neck and shifted uncomfortably in her seat.

She looked down the aisle to see the driver's reflection in the rearview mirror, sweat beading down his forehead. The other passengers seemed lost in their own worlds, but she could feel an unease among them. A few even looked up from their distractions, glancing at one another. Something bad was about to happen. She could feel it.

"Oh shit!" the driver shouted as he yanked the wheel to the right.

In that moment, it was as if the sudden movement set the world in slow-motion.

She could see the bus catapult into the air in one singular motion. Items that had seemed harmless just moments before suddenly turned into weapons. A purse came hurling toward her head, missing it by millimeters. Soda cans burst open, covering the cabin in corn syrup. Phones and books seemed suspended mid-air just waiting to be mechanized.

Then, impact. BOOM!

Looking back, it wasn't the moment of the crash itself, but rather the sound of metal sliding across pavement that stuck in her mind. It was like a combination of the worst sounds in her memory bank—nails on chalkboards, aluminum foil against teeth, dental drills—all colliding into a sound so horrific she wondered if it would ever leave her brain.

Quiet fell over the wreckage for a moment as the bus settled into position post impact. Despite a full rotation in the air, the bus somehow landed on the pavement in an upright position. All four tires were blown, and only a few shards of glass remained in the windows.

At first, Una thought her eardrums had burst, but then she heard ringing and a distinct hissing sound. Brake lines, she thought. It was an odd moment to realize that. She was suddenly flooded with memories of José combing through the parts of a car, attempting to teach her everything he knew.

She was lying in the center of the aisle, her small frame thrown onto her left side. Somehow, her body seemed separate from her mind, as if she were under some strange hypnotic spell. She was terrified to move anything.

As the hissing sound grew louder, she mustered up the courage to gently tilt her head back toward the sound just beyond her head, her eyes rolling up, straining to catch a visual. She could see steam rising from the bus engine out the windshield. Somehow, she had landed just a few feet from the front of the bus. Had she really been thrown this far forward? Her memory was fuzzy, but she vaguely remembered sitting somewhere in the middle, or maybe the back? How was she even alive?

For a moment, she thought about the worst-case scenario. As she did, she realized that the worst case would be to not be thinking at all. She closed her eyes and allowed feeling to seep back into her body, concentrating on her fingers and toes first. To her immense relief, they moved freely, but then, as if her nervous system reactivated, the pain shot through her upper back.

She rolled onto her stomach, reaching her right arm behind her back. Una could feel the edges of a large piece of glass, and it was deeply embedded between her shoulder blades. The realization of what it was made her shout out in agony.

"HELP!"

She was about to give it a quick yank but stopped when she felt a hand upon her shoulder. The pain she had felt suddenly disappeared, as her mind entered a strange state between consciousness and meditative trance. The calm moved through her core at first, then traveled up and down her body simultaneously. She felt such peace that she wondered for a moment if she were dead.

A sharp and intense pain brought her back to reality, as the triangular form slid through her skin. She moaned in agony as it was dislodged, barely finding her breath. She could feel a presence quickly covering the wound. She worried that it would cause her to bleed out.

"Don't worry," a voice spoke.

She turned her head to each side, looking for the person speaking to her. She didn't see anyone around her, other than a beautiful golden light. Within moments, the pain dissipated and the laceration seemed to rapidly disappear. Only a dull ache remained. Within moments, it too dissipated.

Aside from a distinct stickiness on her upper back and shirt, Una felt…normal. Beyond normal, really. Almost supernatural. She was instantly filled with energy from the light surrounding her. It was a feeling so intense that she burst into tears.

She was suddenly, almost abruptly, back in her body and began to examine her location and the situation around her. Una had flown the entire length of the bus, her back likely colliding with the windshield. She opened her ears to the noises around her as she attempted to stand.

"It's OK. You can heal them. Have faith," the voice whispered.

As if her hearing was switched on for the very first time, she heard the suffering all at once around her. Whimpers, moans, and sobs were coming from bodies that were seemingly dead. She looked around but couldn't link what was happening inside the bus to what she was hearing in her head. She started her long walk down the aisle, and as she passed, a different, distinct voice seemed to join the symphony of others in her head.

Only one voice remained silent in the chaos aboard. The fat man reading the fitness book earlier, clearly dead upon impact, was hanging headfirst out a window, his face and torso covered in blood. The book settled at his feet. There was no whimper or cry from beyond. No helping him, she thought, and kept moving.

Bodies littered the aisle and draped over the seats, but they were still suspended elsewhere, attempting to reach Una, some with frantic shouts and screams and others whispering silent prayers. People were scattered along the aisle floor, limbs bent awkwardly like demented Barbie dolls. She could feel them grasping at the very breath of life.

A small cry for help escaped from the woman on the stairs by the back door. Unlike everything else she was hearing, the old woman's voice seemed fully present, as if grounded in reality. She made her way to the old woman, weaving carefully through the maze of faces and limbs. She peered around the partition, bracing herself, not knowing the extent of the woman's injuries. Their eyes met briefly, and an expression of total calm seemed to overcome the old woman. She tried to speak, but a shard of glass had pierced her neck at the precise point of the vocal cords. A slow gurgling sound seemed to swallow up the small voice she had heard just moments before. A gurgle was all the woman could produce. Una looked around frantically for help, overwhelmed by the situation and what she could possibly do.

"PLEASE! Somebody HELP!" she shouted, wondering where the guiding presence she had felt before had gone.

"It's OK, Abuela," Una said as her eyes darted over the elderly woman's body, searching for other severe injuries. "Don't worry. I'll help you." She was deeply worried and not sure what to do.

"Act, don't react," the whisper said.

Una felt a sense of confidence as she looked over the woman's body. Within moments, it was as if an encyclopedia of knowledge filled her brain, a doctor's mind dropped instantly into her mind. She could see it was the memories of the old woman. She scanned through the images. The only woman in medical school, a prominent emergency room surgeon, a doctor experienced in trauma in the heart of Mexico City. It was as if Una herself held the old woman's medical knowledge in her head, and she quickly got to work. She somehow knew that the glass in her neck was the worst of it, though judging from the gash along her hairline, a concussion was likely.

Una pulled the piece of glass clean and quickly covered the woman's wound with her hand. Blood was pouring over her fingers. She didn't panic but rather began to whisper to herself softly, a sort of self-talk that had convinced her that even though the old lady would probably die, at least she was doing everything she could.

As if on instinct, she pulled Abuela into her arms. Tears were flowing from the old woman's eyes, as Una began to stroke the woman's forehead, rocking her back and forth. Una dropped to her knees and began humming a lullaby, one she could see flowing from the woman's mother when she was a child. It was all Una could think to do in that moment.

As Una's nimble fingers began to wipe away a sickening mixture of sweat and blood, something extraordinary began to happen. The gasping breath, the open wounds, the minor cuts, all began to disappear before her eyes. It happened slowly at first. So slowly, that Una thought her vision might have been affected by the crash and dismissed it for some sort of hallucination. But with each stroke of her hand, the old woman's broken body began to transform from one of emptiness and death, to life and hope. Una blinked her eyes several times in amazement.

The old woman reached for her throat. "Más mejor," she whispered as her eyes began to bulge in amazement. Her strength returned and soon the old woman appeared herself again, as if the crash had never happened. "Es un milagro," she whispered to Una. "Gracias." The tears began to flow as emotion flooded her face. Abuela threw her arms around her with the strength she must have had decades ago. Una just stared at the seemingly healthy woman before her, years erased from the timeline on her face.

With Abuela revived, Una scanned the cabin and reviewed the carnage before her. The cries and screams seemed to pierce through from the beyond. Another whisper overcame her.

"Touch them and bring them back to this world," it said.

Again, another download of information as she scanned the broken bodies before her. Some were draped over seats and wrapped around metal. She searched in panic for a face, any face, that appeared alive and coherent. Perhaps she had lingered too long with Abuela. She knew there was no time to waste.

Two rows ahead of her, she saw his head turn toward her. It was the young man with the headphones. Earbuds still stuck in his ears. He somehow found himself underneath the seats, his arm twisted around the metal footing. His breathing was shallow, eyes blinking rapidly.

"Help...me...," he said weakly to Una.

Glass cracked under her feet as Una walked the few steps toward him to assess the situation. It was clear his arm was badly broken, and as she scanned his body and landed her eyes on his face, she could see a small trickle of blood coming from his left nostril. She placed her hand on his chest, feeling his pounding heart on her fingertips. She closed her eyes, as if to retrieve him from the black abyss about to swallow him whole.

Within moments, air filled his lungs as the young man took a giant leap back toward life. Like Abuela, his health was immediately restored. He brought his arm forward, scanning every inch with his eyes. Una could tell by his expression that he was fully expecting to see damage of some kind. But it was just as before, and he closed his eyes in relief, almost laughing to himself. He opened his deep-set eyes and looked up at Una.

"Thank you," he whispered as tears streamed down his face.

She nodded a bit uncomfortably and moved on to the next person.

In a matter of minutes, Una made her way through the aisle, bringing souls back from the brink. Only two seemed out of reach, well on their journeys to the other side. As she walked by them, she could see each one within the confines of her mind, waving and giving nods of gratitude for her even considering saving their now dead bodies.

A few were hanging in the balance, lingering in a sort of purgatory that left them unsure of which direction to go. A simple touch restored a woman slumped in her seat. She then touched the child crumpled next to the woman. Within seconds, he gasped for breath as his mom cried in relief. On and on she went, retrieving at least ten lives on board from the brink. With each expression of gratitude, her power seemed to grow stronger.

As the living passengers stood one by one, brushing the shards of glass and debris from their clothing and skin, each one set eyes upon Una, completely incredulous of the power she bestowed. It was as if they collectively had the same thought: a living miracle.

Her focus turned to the last untouched victim. The survivors watched as Una slowly stroked the woman's forehead, wiping the gash just above her left eye. It only took a few seconds for the wound to disappear.

With the last surviving passenger revived, a quiet stillness overcame the space. Within seconds, a golden light appeared, and every inch of their bodies began to glow. Una was mystified as her own skin sparkled in gold. As quickly as it appeared, the light began to fade inside the bus. The remaining passengers looked around in a daze, all searching for the mysterious source of such an intense experience. The light began to change, and the color along with it, settling upon the scene like an image from an old black-and-white photo. Una felt a cold settle around her, as the tiny hairs on her arms began to spring to life.

"We have to get off this bus," Una ordered. "Now!"

As if on command, the group turned away from her and made their way over broken seats and twisted metal, and crawled their way toward the back door like spiders maneuvering a complicated web. Only two victims remained, along with the driver. His lifeless body hung over the warped steering wheel. As she pulled him back into the seat, Una knew it was too late. His eyes were glossed over, skin growing cold. There was nothing left to do but close the lids over his piercing green eyes. He looked almost peaceful, a very different expression from the one she saw when she first boarded the bus earlier.

She made her way to the back door, crawling through the bent metal frame and stepping down onto the wet pavement. The sight before her stopped her cold. There, to the side of the bus, sat an overturned garbage truck. She could see movement inside the cabin. A badly injured man dangled from a frayed seatbelt. He had a look of sheer panic on his face. He was tapping around the cabin with his hands, as if searching for something in the dark. He was still feeling his way around the bent steering wheel when Una rushed forward to the driver's side window.

"You OK in there?" she shouted.

"NO!" he answered. "I CAN'T SEE!" The man was clearly disoriented, and his condition was likely the cause of this horrific event.

"I'm a diabetic!" he said as he choked back a sob. "Please help me! I can't see! I need my shot!"

"It's OK," Una said, as she considered the situation. She could hear sirens far in the distance begin to drown out the small hiss from the brake lines.

"Help is coming," Una reassured him.

"I can hear the sirens," the man said, shaking as he reached toward the window opening.

"You are going to be OK, but you have to stay calm," Una said as she took the man's hand. "What's your name?"

"Jaxson," the man said shakily. Una's grip left behind a medicinal effect. The shaking stopped immediately.

"I'm sorry," he whispered. "Pease help me." Tears began to fall down his cheeks.

"It's OK, Jaxson," she said, looking around for a way out. This was an even bigger mess than inside the bus, thanks to the garbage from his load now spilling into the street. The smell made its way to her nostrils like a wave, leaving a feeling of nausea in its wake.

A crowd of survivors, phones in hand, began to gather around her. The young man with headphones approached with a metal bar he retrieved from the bus.

"Here," he said, handing it to Una. Maybe we can pry the door open."

"Look the other way, Jaxson!" Una shouted out the command.

Somewhere, deep inside, a strength she had never known before began to surface inside her muscles. With the skill of a trained first responder, she tore open the door and climbed in to release him from the seatbelt.

"I don't know…which way," Jaxson stammered.

"Shh," she said, placing her hand over his eyes, closing her own to tap in to what was going on. It was starting to feel like second nature now, accessing the source of the problem, downloading the information, then connecting the two as energy ripped through an elaborate matrix. She could see the pathways connecting, the very fibers of human existence. Seconds felt like minutes.

Sirens began to blare as emergency vehicles approached. Una began to lose her focus. She turned to see them arrive and saw a sea of by-standers filming her every move. She didn't give the attention a second thought, turning her focus back to the man in front of her. His medical issues were far beyond the confines of the accident. It was taking longer than the others.

"I can't...I can't SEE!" Jaxson cried.

"Hold on, Jaxson, we're almost there," Una said, as she made her way deep into the very strands of his DNA, repairing and reprogramming his physical form as quickly as possible.

She tried to release him from the seatbelt to ease his discomfort, but he was fighting her in some way. She couldn't quite access the reason why. The seatbelt dug deep into his torso and the physical pain was a block she couldn't lift inside him. She stopped to find the button, but in exasperation, tore it clean from the cab's wall. The belt broke free and Jaxson dropped down in a slump, no longer conscious.

She set him back on the seat and dropped down to the floor of the truck looking for a case, a bag, or whatever would hold his medication. Una could feel the glass fragments lodging into her skin as she desperately searched around for the packet. A distinct smell of gasoline filled the wrecked space.

She grabbed a soft case and made her way back toward Jaxson, fingers finding the zipper opening in the process. Inside were three syringes and a glass bottle marked "insulin." She closed her eyes, trying desperately to access what to do. Within seconds, the information appeared in her mind. She grabbed the supplies and went to work. She quickly pulled the fluid from the vile and jammed the needle into Jaxson's hip. No response.

Two first responders appeared behind her and reached around her sides before a third pulled her from the cabin in a single movement. She could see out of the corner of her eye, the other two carrying Jaxson away from the vehicle and setting him onto a stretcher. Una broke free of the firefighter's grip and raced toward him.

"Jaxson!" Una shouted. "Open your eyes, Jaxson!" No response.

"He's diabetic," she told the nearest firefighter. The woman nodded and reached in her bag for supplies.

"It will be fine," the firefighter said calmly. "You need to step aside and let us help this man."

"I'm..." She wasn't sure if she should say it. "I'm a... doctor, a, uh, medical student. I know where his injury is. Let me show you."

She knew if she hadn't said it, he may never return to this world. The responders made a hole, allowing her access to his lifeless body.

Una pulled forth her own medicine, as she hovered her hands over his form. She stopped on a large bruise on his neck, then finished by placing her hands on his face. Her eyes closed, and the scene grew quiet around her. She could see him on the edge of a cliff, a walkway into the clouds before him.

Please let this man live, Una thought to herself. It wasn't his fault.

Within moments, Jaxson's lids fluttered open and his body began to shake violently before quickly settling into a relaxed state.

"What...," he uttered as he took a deep breath. He began

Jamie J. Kemp

to look around, the environment somehow so much brighter than before.

He had never seen color so vivid. Even under the gray blanket he had come to know as the hue of Seattle, the world around him burst forth in greens, blues, but red most of all. A firefighter wiped the blood from his forehead but saw the gash quickly disappearing. Jaxson reached for Una's hand, taking the delicate fingers into his calloused palms.

"I can...see," he whispered. Tears began to roll down his cheeks. The quiet moment between them quickly disappeared, and the chaos of the scene emerged around them.

Cars surrounded the crash site as more spectators gathered on the sidewalks. Their phones were firmly fixed on Una, who had become the sole focus of a horrific scene. The change she had felt before now evident on every screen around her, and it all spread like wildfire across the digital divide.

CHAPTER TWO

The scanners came to life on the assignment desk at Channel 9 News. Most of the room had already been dispatched for the afternoon, working on the daily offerings that the team would conjure up from this slow news day. Not that those in the room particularly wished for something tragic to happen, but it would definitely make the time pass quicker and the work far more interesting. At least, that is what multimedia journalist Lucas Moore thought to himself as he heard the scanners come to life. Not only had it been a slow news day, it had been a slow news month. But that was all about to change.

Lucas was now a very different version of himself from the one born to the birth name Lukesh Mohanti. He felt the guilt every time he thought about it but then surmised that it was a hazard of working in the news business. Viewers always seemed to stumble on or completely butcher any name not commonly known, so he took the news director's simplified suggestion, and he ran with it. Signing off from a story still made him feel like a traitor to his own heritage. He secretly hated resigning his origin, but had learned to embrace the alter ego that now graced the airwaves every night on the evening news.

"Lucas!" the news director shouted.

The large open space made his voice louder than usual. Lucas could hear Joseph Stein's voice from across Lake Washington, without a megaphone. The reporters around him seemed to cringe in their seats at the prospect of a new assignment from Stein. The man thrived on assigning a challenge. Lucas, however, welcomed the opportunity. It beat the alternative of scrounging up some story that would be forgotten two minutes after it aired.

"You're on the bus crash," Stein said loudly, though the gap between them had closed. "It happened at Yesler and Boren, not far from I-5." He paused, then, to make sure Lucas was comprehending the area he was talking about. "Near the medical center?" he offered. "Harborview?"

"Oh yes," Lucas said. He remembered. Medical centers were always a good point of reference for him—something he knew, distance-wise, all too well.

"What do we know?" Lucas asked.

Stein dabbed his forehead with what appeared to be an already damp handkerchief. He was old-school like that—cuff links, striped ties—but his methods were surprisingly modern. He could have taught Edward R. Murrow himself how to report but seemed far more enthusiastic than most about the students coming out of journalism school today. He would constantly praise their high intelligence, digital prowess, and ability to multitask. But if you just looked at him, you'd never know it. It was almost as if Stein enjoyed throwing them off with the look of a bygone era when truth, typewriters, proper grammar, and smoke filled the newsroom but then reveled in watching their expressions when he dropped detailed knowledge of the analytics behind every piece of digital content the station produced.

"Sitting is the new smoking!" Stein would shout to the room frequently from his corner office. "We did an Instagram story on that last year, people, that garnered over thirty-two thousand shares!"

A heart event forced him to invest in a treadmill desk setup. There was usually a constant humming at his feet as he shoved Boston cream doughnuts into his mouth, while blowing through the countless emails he received on a minute-by-minute basis. Stein may not have been the fittest guy in the room, but he could multitask like no one else.

"What are you looking at?" he'd bark to the people in front of him, his subtle way of dismissing any sort of criticism of his lifestyle choices. Lucas chuckled a little at the memory, having watched him do it countless times before.

"They've got all kinds of medical personnel down there already, Moore," Stein said while handing him a printout of the location. Hadn't the man heard of Waze?

"I'll find it on my phone," Lucas said, promptly dropping the paper into the recycle bin.

"This is right up your alley and allows you to put that fancy medical degree to use for a change," Stein said before heading back to his office.

The so-called "fancy" degree was, in fact, a medical degree from the University of Nevada. While a perfectly suitable learning environment for him, it wasn't exactly the most prestigious of medical schools, according to his overbearing parents. They were able to look the other way, however, when it came down to the all-important two letters after his name: MD.

Lucas completed his residency at University of Washington where he discovered, much to his very traditional parents' dismay, that he didn't really like medicine all that much.

"You will finish medical school!" his mother scolded him at the table one evening on break. "You will disappoint the Gods, not to mention the break in your father's heart!"

"Mom, I don't want to be a slave to the machine that is American medicine today," he volleyed back. "I didn't go to medical school to serve the pharmaceutical industry. I want to help people, and that's becoming even more difficult in the age of socialized medicine."

"You will eat and get some clarity before making such rash decisions," she said, dumping another helping of curry onto his rice.

"But it isn't rash," he said. "I've had three years to think about this. I had more fulfillment working for the student medical review than anything else. Look at Sanjay Gupta! He's made a career out of journalism that was founded in medicine."

"Sanjay still practices medicine and makes his family proud," she said, getting up to retrieve the naan left by the stove.

"Why do you always uphold the most impossible standards for me?" he questioned as he stirred the food on his plate.

"Because your father and I did not come to this country to have you become like everyone else. You have a purpose. It is a dream that is important to this family. We left so many behind to do this, Lukesh. Don't forget that." His mother began to sob into her apron then, and it was his cue to leave the room.

Two weeks later, a simple interview about the cost of medical degrees would open the door to a new dream for Lucas and change his path in a way he never imagined. He was selected from a large group of residents, all strapped with six-figure debt and who hoped to recoup costs through a promising medical profession.

"It all sounds simple when you begin the process," he told the camera. "You are thinking about saving people and changing the world. But the loan amounts increase and, before you know it, you are wondering how you will ever repay the skyrocketing cost of medical school without becoming a surgeon or other specialist. Those slots are few and far between. Most of us will become family practice doctors in a vast medical practice somewhere, swimming in a sea of debt with no end in sight, not to mention the cost of malpractice insurance for this litigious world we now live in."

After the interview aired, Stein picked up the phone and left a message.

"Hey, kid, this is Joey Stein from Channel 9 News," he began. "Listen, I have this freelance opening, and I think you'd be perfect for it. The gig is a health reporter position, and you are very well-spoken and have the right look for television. Give me a call."

Lucas picked up the phone to return the call immediately and, two months later, was offered a full-time position. At first, he was given the health beat. He wasn't satisfied with the boring story assignments offered at first, the ones populating everyone's social feed. Instead, he worked his connections at the hospital, digging up interesting tidbits and survival stories that gave viewers a perspective they couldn't find anywhere else. Stein saw the potential immediately and encouraged him to broaden his reach. Lucas gave insight on crime-scene autopsy reports, motor vehicle accident injuries, and the latest virus taking the world by storm. It fit him perfectly, and he often found himself in the thick of it, asking the kinds of questions that first responders rarely, if ever, were asked at the scene.

"We're pairing you with Clark," Stein said, returning Lucas to the present. "He just wrapped up an interview at the Microsoft campus, and he'll meet you there in thirty minutes, traffic permitting," he said with a chuckle. "That means I need you to put your photographer hat on for this one until he gets there." The jargon of the newsroom didn't come easily to Lucas at first. While he picked up medical terms easily, he had to constantly educate himself on the language of news to figure out exactly what was going on. Photographers, who were often thought of as holding a digital camera to take still pictures, were actually cameramen and women who captured video and stills of any given scene to create stories for live television, as well as images for the digital platforms. He found that experience was the easiest way to learn, and after fumbling his way through meetings and assignments for the first year, it was finally starting to sink in.

"We need the usual: first responders, victims, public information officer comments. I want that emotional hook, Moore, not a bunch of statistics that nobody gives a shit about, you understand?"

Lucas nodded, shoving a notebook and pen into his messenger bag. Apparently, he was old-school too.

"The web desk is looking for first photos, Lucas," Stein continued. "That means you waste no time getting into people's faces. You need to be front and center at this thing and send back your images immediately, got it?"

"Got it."

Lucas climbed into his black Mazda 3, throwing the bag onto the passenger seat and plugging his phone into the jack. His practical vehicle, a proud purchase the year he graduated medical school, wasn't as flashy as his older brother's Mercedes. His brother could afford such luxuries as a top corporate attorney. Lucas, on the other hand, had to pick a more fitting model for a struggling student turned reporter with a mountain of debt and the meager salary he earned at the station.

He pulled into traffic on Mercer Street, considering the viaduct but then switching routes after checking traffic conditions. It seemed clear at the moment, but who knew how long it would last on a Wednesday afternoon? Why the middle of the week was always the worst for traffic was beyond him.

He took the stadium exit, hoping to bypass the mess that was constant through downtown. He weaved his way on the north side of the accident, taking familiar streets in his Capitol Hill neighborhood. It wasn't exactly a straight shot but far more effective than the usual routes, especially considering street closures that likely happened as a result of the accident.

When he arrived at the scene, it was surprisingly organized. He was expecting total carnage, but it was quite the opposite. Police were busy taking statements, while firefighters directed tow trucks toward the damage. Had it taken that long to get here? What had he missed? He checked his watch to be sure, quite pleased with his time. Clark was nowhere to be found.

The first three witnesses gave relatively the same account of what had happened. The bus was in the right lane, heading east on Yesler. A garbage truck came barreling up Boren. He heard witnesses telling police that the driver was erratic, swerving around vehicles and encountering at least a half dozen near misses. Lucas handed one credible witness a microphone, and she clipped it to her blouse. He pulled her into view on his phone and hit record.

"It just wasn't going to stop," one woman told him, eyes wide with the memory of the day's events. "It was literally like watching a train wreck! The bus driver yanked the wheel to avoid him, then bam! The bus was rolling and the truck flipped upside down."

"I can't believe those people walked out of here alive," said an old man who had been following the bus some distance away. "I mean, a few didn't make it, I hear. I think the driver is dead, obviously," he gestured to a gurney nearby before telling Lucas he had seen the driver slumped over the steering wheel earlier.

"It's weird, but, for the most part, almost all of them were OK," the old man continued. "If you had seen the wreck right after it happened, you'd be wondering how that is even possible."

"Did you notice anything unusual?" Lucas asked witness after witness.

"Well, I was afraid to get out of my car at first," said a woman in scrubs, an employee at Harborview, as noted on her badge. "I just finished a long shift at the hospital, and honestly, I could barely keep awake driving home. I got out and walked onto the sidewalk to get a better view."

"What did you see?"

"Oh, I don't know. This sounds crazy, but I could see a burst of light inside the bus. Kept fading in and out. I thought it was some sort of explosive device or fire at first." She snapped her gum, remembering the moment. "It was just so weird."

"What do you mean? The light or something else?" Lucas asked.

"Well, I got my phone out of the car and called into the pit. That's the—"

"I know what the pit is. Emergency room."

"Yes," she responded, clearly impressed. "Well, I told them to get ready. This is going to be a bad one. They wanted to know how many casualties, and I looked up to count. There was that glow again, sort of moving through the bus. A minute later, all those people started piling out the back. It was amazing. I ran up to check them out, and not one scratch. It's the craziest thing I've ever seen, and I've seen everything."

He studied her for a moment, trying to assess her credibility. The woman obviously wasn't some freak. She had a medical badge from the hospital and, aside from being overly tired, seemed pretty believable.

"And where are the survivors now? Can you point any out to me?"

"Sure. That lady over there with the little boy. She's one. And the old woman on the bench over there."

"Thanks, I really appreciate it."

He started to leave then remembered, "Oh, your name, and can you spell it out for me for the camera?"

After acquiring her info and offering his card, Lucas exchanged numbers with the woman, though he knew where to find her. Better safe than sorry. He made his way across Boren, careful to avoid the broken glass on the pavement. He saw the mother first and approached her cautiously, careful not to run her off before getting her on camera. He had to work fast if he was going to scoop the competition. None of the others had arrived yet, so there was likely just enough time to get the "emotional hook" and send it off to the station before five.

She was sitting on the edge of the sidewalk, knees pulled to her chest. A foil blanket was draped around her broad shoulders. Her son, no more than six or seven, played a sort of imaginary hopscotch just steps away.

"Hi, I'm Lucas Moore," he said, hand extended in greeting. "I'm a reporter from Channel 9 News. I understand you were on board the bus today?"

She took his hand firmly. "Yes, I know you. I think? Kind of a crazy day." She didn't hold the usual expressions of a victim. Her presence was calm and composed, as if she were just waiting for a friend to pick her up for an afternoon outing at the park. Strange.

"May I record our conversation? I would love to know what happened here today," Lucas said as he sat beside her, hand at the ready to whip out his phone the moment permission was granted. She didn't answer right away. She watched the clouds dance around the sun as a peaceful smile crossed her lips.

"Sure, why not?" she said turning her eyes toward her son. "Baby, watch the glass, OK? Mama's going to talk to this nice man." The boy just kept playing, counting.

"He's always playin'. And countin'," she said.

"Your name?"

"Anita Brown," she said, with an almost questioning tone. An alias? He truly was becoming as skeptical as Stein. The poor woman had clearly been through a great deal today. He quickly moved on.

"That's my son, Malcolm." He pointed toward the boy.

"What happened here today?"

"Well, I was just sitting here trying to figure that out myself," she began, staring down at her peeled and cracked fingernails. She had just about picked every hangnail and peeled every split nail and created some new ones that weren't there yet. It was a nasty habit.

"I was taking the bus from downtown. Malcolm had an appointment today," Anita said as she slowly turned her head toward her son, taking a moment to watch him play. "He's autistic, and we see a specialist on Tuesdays."

Lucas glanced at the boy, considering his condition. He seemed a little distracted but not unlike any other boy his age. Anita watched for a moment longer before turning back to Lucas.

"He's pretty low level or I guess 'high functioning' as they call it. He has some trouble with textures, sounds. He can get overly focused on things, especially his numbers. He's real smart though. I mean real smart." She smiled sweetly at her son and gave a small wave before continuing.

"We got on the bus, found our seat. Malcolm was playing with his Rubik's Cube. He loves that thing. I was just looking out the window. We were seated toward the back. We were coming up toward Boren. I know that because our stop is just past fourteenth," she said and pointed down the street. "Over there. Malcolm goes to school at Bailey Gatzert Elementary School."

She paused then to shift her weight to a more comfortable position. He was patient, allowing her to relax into the conversation. This was how he would get his "emotional hook."

"I saw this dump truck coming toward us, and that's honestly all I remember. Honest to God."

She shook her head and stared at her hands for a moment, examining each finger. He zoomed in slightly, capturing the moment before slowly tilting back up toward her face.

"I can't believe I'm still here."

"What do you mean?"

"I saw the light, Mr. Moore. I was a total goner. You know what I'm sayin'?" She glanced up toward his face, making sure he was prepared to hear the rest of the story. She continued, though cautiously.

"I didn't think about nothin'. I wasn't even worried about Malcolm because he was right there with me."

"On the bus, you mean," Lucas offered, feeling a bit anxious.

"No," she said quietly, then slowly raised her pointer finger toward the sky. "Up there."

"Oh, I see." Lucas wasn't sure how to answer her. He wondered about a head injury. Stein was going to think this is nuts. Lucas knew chances at any sort of raise would be out the window if he didn't make this stick. He continued on, hoping the woman was in her right mind.

"I could hear my own mama's voice," she began again. "She said, 'It's not your time yet.'"

"Was she on the bus with you?"

"No, sir. She's been dead now going on three years."

Lucas studied her face, considering the truth of her claim. Then he remembered the light the nurse had spoken about earlier. He pushed on.

"So, you were looking from above or somewhere else?"

"I was somewhere else entirely," she said, eyes wide with disbelief, recalling the moment at death's door. "It was like being in a thick fog or something but in the daytime 'cause there's lots of light."

"Like, a quick flash of light or a steady light?"

"No, like daytime or something, but in a fog," she said, choosing her words carefully. "It's hard to explain."

"So, then what happened? You're obviously here."

"I was watching Malcolm. He was laughing and playing and…talking. To me. Not numbers or sounds but real talk like, 'Can we go for an ice cream?' Or 'Can we go to the playground, Mommy?' I was so happy to hear him talk," she said, choking back tears.

"Were you scared?"

"No!" she blurted with excitement. "I felt so calm inside. I was…happy. Then my body became real warm. I felt something pulling on me. I shouted for Malcolm, but he was just skipping ahead. I opened my eyes and…"

She stopped then, digging in the pocket of her faded jeans. She retrieved a wadded-up tissue and began to dab the tears from the corners of her eyes, which were heavy with mascara.

"I opened my eyes, and a young woman was staring at me," she said cheerfully, remembering the moment. The tissue was becoming damp with tears and decorated with streaks of black mascara. The woman had to have at least five coats on if she could still produce the black serum on the tissue.

"I thought she was an angel from a TV show or somethin'. Like you."

"How do you mean?"

"I mean she looked like she could be on TV, very beautiful," she said, her face showing the struggle to remember. "She just smiled at me, and I was so relieved." She exhaled then, allowing the tension of the day to escape past her lips. It must have felt like the lift of a thousand-pound weight by her expression.

"Then, I remembered Malcolm, and it was as if she read my mind."

"Where was he?" Lucas asked.

"He was on the floor, not moving. I was so worried, but the same woman kneeled down and touched him." She inhaled sharply. "A light surrounded us. Not like the fog when I was up there," she pointed skyward. "But a real golden light. Real pretty glow. I felt so calm. I could feel him returning to me. My precious boy." She choked back a sob and blew into the tissue.

Lucas paused for a moment. This was the gold he was looking for. He watched her regain composure, not turning the camera away for a second.

"What did you do?"

"I was just watching. I wasn't scared or nothin'. I knew he would come back to me. He did! He woke, and he leaped into my arms." The tears began to flow again as she lifted the tattered remains of the tissue to her face. Lucas just stared for a moment, not quite sure what to ask next. He reached into his bag, digging around for a tissue. He found one in a small side pocket and handed it to her.

"You don't understand this, but, my son," she said, dabbing her cheeks, "he never hugs me." Her eyes met his, now as red as they were deep brown when they began the interview.

"I just held him," she said. She looked at Lucas for a moment, tears forming in her eyes before returning her gaze to the camera lens. "For me, it was like hugging my son for the very first time."

That was the money shot Stein always harped on about. He savored the feeling, hoping she would say a little more, but the moment just passed. He made a mental note to make it a pivotal part of the story. She looked for her boy then, a smile emerging from her lips as she watched him jumping and counting his way through boxes built entirely in his mind. Lucas followed her gaze, landing the shot on the little boy. He stopped abruptly, staring right at her.

"Mama, can we get some ice cream?"

"Yes!" she cried out, then scrambled to her feet and swept him into her arms. This time, happy tears. "Yes, baby," she said. "As soon as I finish with the nice man." He returned to his imaginary game, quietly humming as he hopped.

Lucas seized the moment of generosity. "May I talk with him for a moment?"

"Well, like I said before, he's not the best with talking, let alone to strangers."

"I can give it a go, with your permission of course," he coaxed. Anita slowly nodded her approval.

Lucas approached the boy, trying not to be overly cautious, while tempering his expectations of anything usable from the conversation.

"Hi, Malcolm. I'm Lucas. Can I speak to you about today?"

"Sure," the boy answered, still focused on his game.

"What do you think happened here today?"

"It was kind of strange," Malcolm said, counting the number of jumps under his breath.

"I'm sure it was," Lucas said. Malcolm seemed pretty alert so far.

"I wasn't scared though," Malcolm said, voice wobbly as he jumped from box to box. "It was actually pretty cool."

"Cool, huh?" Lucas asked, though he felt a little dense in his feeble effort to bring the communication down to the boy's level.

"Yes, and I'm not afraid to die anymore," the boy said with a smile. "I know I will be OK. But they told me I had to go back to help my mom."

Lucas kept the camera steady through the boy's game. He sure didn't appear autistic. In fact, he spoke better than most boys his age.

"It's just so much easier now," Malcolm said, eyes joining with the lens.

"Easier, how?"

"After the lady touched me and I came back, I can say what I think all the time. She really helped me."

"How did it feel when she touched you?"

"I really don't know," he said, abruptly stopping his game. "I just opened my eyes, and I was back here, but I can talk now. It's easy. Like my numbers. I didn't want to go at first because I was afraid. I didn't want to go back the way I was before, and I didn't. They said I wouldn't, and I didn't. Then, I thought about my mama, and I wanted to go back to help her. She needs me."

"Well, Malcolm, that's quite a story you have to tell."

"Yes, I told you it was strange. But that lady was very magical. Like a glowing angel."

"An angel?"

"Yes, the angels told me she was chosen."

"Chosen? How do you mean?"

"She's here to save people," he said rather matter-of-factly. "That's what they told me."

"Did they tell you the girl's name?"

"Woman. She's a woman. She's old enough to have children. She's not a girl."

"Oh, OK," Lucas said, chuckling. "Well, do you remember a name?"

"Una," he said, stopping the game.

"Una?" Lucas asked to confirm.

"Yep! Her birthday is January 1, 1997. That adds up to one. She's the one. Like her name!"

"Who told you her birthday?" Lucas asked.

"She did," he said. "With her mind."

Lucas thought it time to wrap the interview. He now had a new lead to go on—a first name and date of birth—though he wasn't confident it would check out. If what he was hearing was right, however, he was onto the story of a lifetime. He thanked Anita and Malcolm, exchanged information, and wrapped up the interview. He turned back toward the crash site, just as Clark was pulling up to the scene.

"Hey Clark!" Lucas shouted as the photographer jumped out of the van. He stepped onto the toes of his shoes, making his way through the glass mosaic on the pavement. He pointed out the obvious interviews before excusing himself to make a phone call back to the station's assignment desk.

"Janna. It's Lucas."

"Oh, hey, Lucas," Janna answered cheerfully.

"Hey, Janna, listen. Want you to do something for me. Could you do a search on a woman—mid-twenties, first name Una."

"Say that again. Una?"

"Yes. Date of birth, 1/1/97."

"Last name?"

"Don't have one."

"Oh," Janna said, a little annoyed. "Well, the first name should make it pretty easy."

"Dig up whatever you can find and, if you do, call me back. I mean, immediately."

"OK. Got it."

They taped the rest of the interviews, gathered some b-roll, and got to work on the story. The station's helicopter was hovering over the scene. Clark motioned Lucas to a position near the crash scene, handed him the mic, and cued him for the live broadcast.

As he wrapped up details of the scene, turning to take in the wreckage, his attention turned toward Malcolm. He could see the boy, arms outstretched as he rushed to his mother's arms. The two held each other tightly, smiling faces that could have been so easily replaced with a river of tears. It took everything in his power not to cry on camera.

CHAPTER THREE

Una sat quietly inside the ambulance. A foil blanket was draped over her aching shoulders. This was an odd day.

She considered how it all began, drifting deep into the crevasse of her memory yet retrieving very little on the other end. How could she not recall the most significant moment of her life?

"It's the trauma," the paramedic said, searching her face for clues, shining a bright penlight into her pupils.

"I'm having a hard time remembering...well, anything," she said, a look of concern washing over her face.

"Like I said, totally normal," the paramedic continued, as his eyes crisscrossed the list of standard procedures. He was obviously new to the job, Una thought, but didn't say a word for fear of eroding his confidence.

"For what it's worth," he continued, "everything should return to normal once your body emerges from the shock."

"Well, that's comforting," she responded. "But how long will that be?"

"Anywhere from a few hours to a few weeks. It varies person to person."

"So, can I go then?"

He looked her over again before responding.

"You seem just fine to me, which is nothing short of a miracle considering the condition of that bus over there."

His eyes motioned behind him to the crash scene. He turned his head with a look of bewilderment. With frown lines and a furrowed brow, he seemed older somehow. Una looked beyond his baby face to the mangled steel and assorted parts on the pavement. It was truly astonishing that she and the others had survived. A silence filled the small space between them, forcing each to the corner of their own minds.

As the tow truck pulled up, the paramedic's words broke through. She welcomed the return from her fragmented thoughts. It was not unlike reaching for a volume switch, his voice growing louder with each word he spoke.

"We should have you looked over at the hospital to be sure, but I'd hazard to guess you'll be sleeping in your own bed tonight," he said with a weak smile.

She watched the responders descend upon the scene like ants at a picnic. Across the intersection, she could see a line of TV crews, each one ready to offer the latest from the scene to hungry news viewers eager to know more about the accident that brought the city to a halt in the middle of rush hour. She guessed it was an important story, but she didn't consume much news these days. The place was buzzing with cameras and reporters scrambling to find some new angle to the story.

She recognized one of the reporters almost instantly. He was one of the few that made it into her social feed on a regular basis. She liked his aggressive style. Luckily, one of the other passengers caught his eye before he saw her. She needed to get out of there.

Una pulled the foil blanket from her shoulders, folding

it neatly before setting it on the gurney opposite her. She stood up slowly, allowing the blood to redistribute inside her body to be sure she wasn't going to faint. Everything seemed to be OK, even better than ever. She started to take the couple of steps down from the back of the ambulance before remembering her backpack.

She recalled seeing the pack lodged between a metal bar and the window. There was no way she'd leave that behind on the bus. Some of those recipe cards were part of her history. She looked back inside the ambulance to find her pack sitting on one of the stretchers. She was overcome with a sense of relief. She crawled inside to retrieve it and remembered the hooded sweatshirt at the bottom of her pack. She pulled it over her head and instinctively put the pack onto her shoulders, surprised with how good she felt physically in that moment. The walk home wouldn't be problem, as long as she could avoid the crowds and reporters hovering around the scene.

She looked around for a moment, considering her escape route. North Boren was packed with satellite trucks, adorned with various TV station logos and slogans. They all blurred together. West Yesler was dotted with emergency vehicles. The reporters had most of the victims in front of cameras on South Boren. She would have to weave her way through the crash scene and head east on Yesler if she had any hope of escaping the madness.

She watched closely as three of the reporters were called over by some official. She had to make a break for it in the midst of the distraction. It was now or never. She slipped through the crowd unnoticed, their attention fully focused on the scene. A little less than two miles, and she would be home. The walk would do her good.

Thirty minutes later, she saw the complex and her front door—not one news van in sight. She was eager to cover the last few yards unscathed and find her way safely inside. The bigger question she was not quite ready to answer was how long that feeling of safety would last?

As she climbed the few steps to the small covered porch, she caught a glimpse of the front window. Brit was sitting on the couch, the television flickering onto her face and the walls behind her. Her posture said everything. She was rigid, leaning forward, and completely engrossed in what she was watching.

She knew.

Brit was a budding attorney and well-versed in the science of argument and the art of a well-crafted question. Una gulped in anticipation of the line of questioning that awaited her once she opened the door.

She slowly reached for the knob to discover the front door was locked. Una dug to the bottom of her side pocket to retrieve the key. The key caught the lock, and she entered the small foyer, removing her shoes. She could feel her backpack sliding off her shoulders and falling to the floor with a thud. She was so exhausted. If her bed was here in the foyer, she would drop onto it and find sleep quickly.

"Una, what the hell happened to you?" Brit shouted from the next room, her voice bouncing off the walls of their modest townhouse. "You're all over the news!"

"Hold on, I'll be right there," Una said weakly. "Just give me a minute to put some stuff away and clean up."

The walk home—one that would have been an easy distance on a normal day—was enough to do her in. She finally noticed her feet throbbing as she climbed the flight of stairs to the second level. She heard footsteps behind her, but she wasn't exactly ready for the confrontation.

"Here," Brit said, and offered the backpack at the top of the stairs. "Girl, are you all right? I'm seriously worried about you."

Brit touched Una's shoulder and gave a slow pat. It was an unbelievable show of affection for the woman who considered a cactus the only living thing worth having in the house.

"I'm fine, I'm fine," Una reassured her. "I'm just a little shaken, that's all. More emotionally draining than anything else." She knew Brit's concern was just a warm up. Nothing got past her for long and, if it did, she would catch up quickly.

Brit was a fantastic roommate. Neat, tidy. She knew when to engage in conversation and when to retreat to her own space. She was sweet when it counted and fiercely loyal. Who would have thought such good things could come from a Craigslist ad? Una was grateful for such a devoted friend, but she wasn't in the mood to deal with the onslaught of questions. She stepped inside her bedroom and considered closing the door. Brit quickly read her mind and placed her palm directly center.

"Listen, woman. You have to tell me what happened," Brit pushed willfully, punctuating her comment with a gentle push to further open the door and get Una to start talking.

Una stepped inside the en suite bathroom, catching her reflection in the mirror. She looked so drained, as if her very life force had been rattled to the core. She splashed cold water on her face. The frigid temperature caused color to return to her cheeks. She reached for a hand towel and patted her skin dry. She stared for a moment, considering the change she felt inside and whether it was now showing on the outside. She looked exhausted but otherwise exactly the same. Maybe it was all in her mind.

She opened the door to find Brit on the edge of the bed, knees pulled to her chest. She slowly turned her head, watching her friend as she moved through her evening routine. She was on her feet in an instant and pulled Una around by the shoulders to face her.

"What happened on that bus, Una?" Brit began slowly. The interrogation was about to follow. "That was you in the video, right?" Her dark eyes danced, moving from side to side as if to study Una's eyes for truth.

"I…I, I don't really know exactly," Una said, eyes falling to the floor. "One minute I was riding along, and the next I'm pulling shards of glass from my back and the heels of my hands. There was this really large piece that was lodged right between my shoulder blades," she said, reaching around to point to the exact spot.

"What?" Brit asked, spinning her around and yanking up her shirt. She studied the spot for a moment and then let out a long sigh of relief. "I don't see anything."

"I know," Una said. "When I pulled out the glass, within moments the bleeding stopped, and I felt well again. It was as if nothing had happened."

"Weird," Brit added. "So, the marks and stuff just disappeared?"

"Yes, like it never happened," Una said. "Then, I was walking through the cabin of the bus, touching everyone I could see. I would watch them go from lifeless lumps to seemingly normal beings. Some even seemed healthier than when we boarded."

"What do you mean? How do you know what they were like before?" Brit asked.

"I mean, from what I remembered of those people from the bus stop," Una answered, almost confused. "One woman was so old she could barely walk."

"And when you touched her?"

"It was as if years melted from her face. She appeared younger. More vibrant somehow…but…"

"But what?"

"While I felt great for a while, I now feel so…drained," Una said. "Like a battery with no charge left. I just need to sleep now."

Her friend, recognizing the lack of energy, much less the lack of response, reached for the blankets, peeling them back and pouring her friend inside them. Una dropped onto the firm mattress. She snored softly. Whatever happened, it clearly had drained her, Brit thought. She would continue with the questions tomorrow.

Brit made her way down the stairs and plopped herself onto the couch. The TV was flashing before her, sound, thankfully, muted. She watched the video once more, hoping to retrieve some sort of understanding as to what happened to her friend.

Una woke to a feeling of wetness on her cheeks. Tears were pooled in the corner of her eyes. She turned her body toward the clock, taking the tattered comforter with her. 6:15 a.m. She had slept just over twelve hours, something she had not done since graduating from culinary school.

She knew Brit would be anxiously waiting at the breakfast table, a mind as full as the cereal bowl in front of her. Una was still grappling with the previous day's events. She remembered hearing on a podcast once that good news takes time, while bad news happens in an instant.

But was this bad news?

How could helping innocent people escape certain death be a bad thing under any circumstances? The media made heroes of people like that on a daily basis. She saw it every day in her feed. Perhaps it involved changing fates. She was now that fate. But what now?

It was a question she wasn't prepared to answer just yet. She longed for the clock to roll back twenty-four hours. For once, she was happy it was Saturday. She needed time to think. She had always considered her chosen profession a welcomed event and weekends more of a burden than anything else. But now, her feelings had changed. She had awakened to a new calling.

CHAPTER FOUR

"Who was driving the truck?" Pyrus asked, pouring scotch into a crystal glass. Neat. Ice was for wimps and women.

"Jaxson Washington, sir." Callahan's voice blared through the speaker, his fat face filling most of the screen. He let his eyes drop from the lens, a total sign of weakness.

Pyrus Payne was anything but weak. His reputation as a businessman and investor made even the most aggressive on the street shudder at the mention of him. He let the drink settle on his tongue, allowing the bitter and sweet to settle deep into the back of his throat before slowly swallowing.

"And for how long has this Jaxson been driving for us?" Pyrus asked in his best southern drawl.

"Fifteen years, sir. No other marks on his record."

"Well then, what happened? Did the accelerator get stuck?"

"No, sir. It appears Mr. Washington had some sort of… diabetic episode," Callahan answered, almost shuddering as he said it.

"Jesus, Callahan, you make it sound like a reality show or something. Diabetic 'episode.' Did the man not take his meds or what?"

"Doctors aren't sure yet. They are evaluating."

"Well, we're obviously going to be sued for this, so let's assemble the legal team and prepare for the worst. I want to escape this little mishap with as little damage as possible, you understand?"

"Yes, sir. We've contacted Bryce in legal and alerted the accounting team. We'll prepare the early settlement offer, and you should have it tomorrow at the latest."

"We've got to catch them early, Callahan. We're lucky most people escaped unharmed, and only one vehicle was compromised." Pyrus paused to take another sip. "Throw a little money their way, and they will take it. Can't imagine there are too many smart people riding a city bus these days."

"You'd be surprised, sir. I ride the—"

"Goodbye!" Pyrus ended the call, staring at the screen for a moment. "Fat fuck," he muttered under his breath before reaching for the bottle beside him.

As he watched the liquid gold pour into his glass, he tried to imagine the faces across the negotiating table. This was not going to be difficult. Even the smallest dollar amount would be a welcome change from their day-to-day struggles. He pictured immigrants, addicts, single mothers, and a host of other losers drifting through life on the daily route. He wasn't one to dwell in struggles. And empathy? That was simply out of the question. You created your own opportunity in life. And luck. Leave nothing to chance. That was the Pyrus Payne way.

He hit the remote's source button and returned to the news, downing the rest of his scotch in the process.

"What a fucking shit show," he whispered to himself as he poured another.

Pyrus took no prisoners. His ruthless reputation was legendary, mainly because he had planned his way to the top. The one percent of the one percent. That was always the goal. A titan of industry was an understatement. Money was the driving force, but it had always been about absolute and total power. Garbage man at nineteen. Garbage titan at twenty-five. Nothing in Payne's world was done without careful calculation. This accident was no exception.

You don't rise to the occasion; you sink to your level of preparation. He heard that from some football coach once. He decided to make it his own.

It was the Pyrus Payne brand he carefully crafted from the beginning to intimidate, overtake, and completely destroy anyone or anything that stood in his way of total domination. This day was nothing special. He certainly wasn't going to let a little accident with insignificant casualties ruin his day. It was a mere scratch on the perfection that was his conglomerate, which was more a work of art than a series of holding companies—each one earning a place in the overall portrait that was his legacy.

Pyrus took his earnings to the gambling floor, literally at first, and then more seriously in the backrooms and eventually boardrooms of Las Vegas. He thought it the most logical place in the world to invest in garbage. After all, he viewed the strip as nothing more than a giant cesspool of humanity walking aimlessly from hotel to hotel looking for a distraction from the reality of their lives. It was a match made in heaven.

He started with a series of small investments that mostly consisted of strip malls on the edge of the action. The return on investment wasn't too shabby either. Convenience stores had some of the highest markup, and it was very easy to capture customers when you were the only game for blocks. And nobody wanted to walk for blocks in the insufferable Vegas heat.

He proceeded to snatch up as many little stores as possible over the course of a year. In time, he had grown his investments to an unprecedented level, allowing him to move to the heart of the strip. Nothing pleased him more than to see the men who had once so easily rejected him now begging for a piece of the action. Success truly was the best revenge.

Palmetto was an aging property when he happened upon it in the 1990s. Once the glory hole of the strip, the now archaic structure was in desperate need of a face-lift, more like an extreme makeover. He gathered his team, and they assessed the property, noting the aging structure, the outdated rooms, and the smoke-filled casino floor.

It was an advance copy of a new film called *The Matrix* that catapulted Pyrus's standing on the strip. The blockbuster had captured his imagination, and he knew immediately he was on to something. All at once, he could see the shining structure before him. The Neo Hotel was born inside the media room of his palatial Vegas penthouse condominium. Upon a cocktail napkin, he drew the grand structure and named the towers, ballrooms, and casino games. He called the planners immediately to share the vision. Opportunity affords no man sleep, he would say, phoning his East Coast team at all hours, barking orders, and firing those who impeded progress.

How they would ever lift the fog and smell from the 160,000-square-foot room was beyond him, but that's what the team was for. They would figure it out or else. In true Pyrus fashion, not one detail was overlooked. From the flooring choice in the lobby entrance to the toilet paper holders in the rooms, his eyes scanned and his hand approved every single purchase on the property's then high eight-figure renovation, a significant sum at the time. When it was finally finished—in record time, of course—he learned that it might have been easier to just to blow it up and start over. But there was something comforting in those walls. He liked the history of it. Souls were still searching here, and the demons had never left the building. It was exactly what he wanted.

Now, many years later, he sat staring through the windows onto the same strip that afforded him enormous opportunity. Human garbage. Real garbage. The afterthoughts of the world, the weak and wasted, became opportunity in his hands, and he made the most of it. But even Pyrus Payne could see change on the horizon. The accident today would just expedite things. He wasn't sure where the inspiration would come from, but Pyrus was certain in its appearance. He would just…know.

He also knew that his new clientele—the ones frequenting the strip today—likely had little knowledge of the film that had inspired the first generation of Payne Properties. He wanted a younger generation running through his hotels, taking endless selfies, and posting and streaming their adventures live inside his vision of the property. That wasn't happening in its current form. *The Matrix* was something their parents watched. He had considered a *Hunger Games* theme years before, but the idea was just too outlandish and, honestly, was not long-standing. It was a fad, and he was more interested in concept. Something classic. Besides, what would he do? Starve the guests? Why not? Think of all the money he would save, or worse, lose to the other properties. He needed something new. An inspiration that was otherworldly.

He instinctively reached for the remote and turned up

the volume. A visual person, Pyrus was touched through the eyes, not the ears. He would know it when he saw it.

Another in a series of channel-flipping adventures began. He spent no more than a second going from one to the next. It seemed the only feasible way to consume television these days—images viewed in passing frames, just like a social feed.

There were the usual suspects: housewives, catty women, steroid-injected muscle men tackling one another. Ridiculous. He landed on FOX News first, but soon grew bored of the endless banter. It seemed obvious to him which side was right, so why even invite the argument? Now, every other news channel was doing the same. Why it was taking the media idiots so long to figure out that people just wanted news was beyond him. Maybe he'd buy the channel. It would be easier than watching this.

CNBC was reviewing the day's top market performers. He stopped for a moment, eyes scanning the screen for his ticker symbol. There it was. Still down, and the fucking lawsuit would take it down even further.

He flipped one channel up to CNN. An extremely attractive woman was set against the backdrop of the Seattle skyline. With full, pouty lips and seductive brown eyes, she had his full attention.

"Little is known about the driver's medical history, but early reports suggest a diabetic episode likely caused the horrific crash that left three dead in Seattle today."

"Horrific?" Payne shouted at the screen. "People lived, you fucking idiot. It wasn't horrific!"

"Fiona, any word on the driver's condition?" the anchor asked.

"We understand the driver is currently at Harborview Medical Center. He is stable but not yet responsive. We are told that authorities are standing by to speak with him as soon as he wakes."

Unresponsive? Why hadn't Callahan told him that? Pretty sad when you learn the latest about your business on CNN. Finally, the excuse he was looking for. He would fire him first thing tomorrow.

"This is not good news for Payne Industries, after the recycling fiasco last summer, in which Eagle Waste Management, a Payne Industries subsidiary, was reportedly going through trash of residents in an effort to improve recycling efforts. Citizens are now suing the city and have named Eagle Waste Management in a suit claiming a violation of privacy. Fiona, do you see a lawsuit in the future for this case?"

"There's no doubt that the bus driver's family, as well as the families of the two deceased passengers in this case, are devastated by today's events. While it was clearly an accident, I could see families pursuing legal action against Payne Industries for not regularly screening drivers with medical issues. Time will tell, Louisa. Back to you."

"Fiona Douglas, reporting live from Seattle where a terrible crash involving a city bus and an Eagle Waste Management garbage truck left three people dead and sent dozens more to the hospital. And now, just into the newsroom, we have new footage of the crash from a witness standing at a nearby bus shelter. Let's take a look at this shocking video that has now gone viral."

Pyrus looked toward the screen with interest. He swirled his scotch in his glass, watching closely as the video appeared. It was a low-resolution file in comparison to the sixty-inch set, coming through pixelated on the screen. The video began with a shot at the person's feet, then shakily moved upward to put the crash site in full view.

"Oh my God! Oh my God!" the man screamed as he moved toward the scene. The footage was moving back and forth with each step forward. He stopped about thirty-five feet from the site, capturing the aftermath of the event that had just happened moments before.

The bus, front tires deflated, sat still just east of the intersection. It was fully blocking access to very busy Yesler Way. Pyrus knew the location well. The garbage truck, his garbage truck, was upside down. He could barely make out the driver through the vehicle's window.

"They build 'em tough," Pyrus mumbled to himself, taking a long, slow drink in the process. Still no buzz. He poured another, hoping for the numbness to wash over him.

The camera then whipped back to the front of the bus.

"What is that?" the man whispered as a glow spilled through the windows, bathing the pavement with a golden light.

"What the…" his voice trailed off as he moved closer to the vehicle.

Another burst of light appeared, then another. The light seemed to follow the movement of someone inside, who appeared to be methodically moving row to row.

The sound of breaking glass caused the man holding the phone to jump. The screen took a spinning path toward the pavement. And then darkness. The lens was pointed directly at the pavement.

"Shit!" the photographer shouted as he picked up the case. The lens found a wobbly path back to the crash site. The man adjusted the focus and light and then zoomed in slowly. The scene came into clear view just then, as the first passengers made their way through the broken glass and debris. Witnesses began to approach.

"Are you OK?" a man in a suit asked a woman with a young son.

"I think so," she said, studying her hands. During this moment, the photographer had missed perhaps the most important part. He turned his phone to follow the commotion behind him and brought into view the driver of the garbage truck as a young woman approached. The footage was so shaky it was almost impossible to make out what was happening. As the video ended, the anchor returned to the screen.

"As you can see, a most emotional scene in Seattle this afternoon. Thirteen passengers emerged unharmed from this horrific crash that tied up traffic for hours. The driver and two passengers were pronounced dead at the scene."

Pyrus reached for the remote then, and with a single click, silence filled the room. It was so quiet he could actually hear the ice melting in his scotch, crackling and hissing its way into the perfectly aged nectar he now brought to his lips. There was no better medicine for this moment. Except for maybe one. Phone in hand, he made his way to the sprawling Vegas skyline before him.

She picked up after three rings. He knew she was making him sweat. He hated the powerful hold she had on him. It wasn't just a weakness; it was a sickness. He was obsessed with her.

"Pyrus, how are you?" she asked seductively. He was instantly soothed by her velvet vocal cords. Her accent still captivated him. Part British, part Somali. Jade was a vision in his mind not easily erased.

"Hey, you wanna join me on the terrace?" he asked with a smoky voice. Scotch always made his throat a bit scratchy.

"Absolutely," she purred, ending the call.

Within moments, she was slinking her way toward him, the chiffon of her fuchsia dress clinging to every curve. He patted his left leg, an affectionate gesture to let her know he was just relaxed enough to let her in. She gave him a knowing smile, a little uneasy about the scotch glass perspiring on the end table. He seemed to be consuming more and more these days. But he was still in control of it. Always in control.

He stopped her before she dropped onto his knee. He grabbed her right arm, pulling her directly in front of him. He beckoned her to twirl in front of him, his favorite move to examine what she had done to prepare herself for him. She twirled instinctively, giving an eye roll the moment her head was directly opposite his, wondering why he always commanded this move.

"Stop!" he ordered her, just as she turned in profile. "What happened here?" He gestured to her left wrist, a black and blue outline of a fingerprint had formed on the skin.

"You did that to me," she answered with a questioning tone. "Last night, remember?" Her answer made him doubt her even more.

He pulled her wrist to his eye, considering the size of his own thumb in comparison to the one on her wrist. It was definitely larger.

"Who exactly are you screwing without my knowledge?" he asked, giving the wrist an extremely tight squeeze, waiting for her to cry out in pain before releasing it downward.

"You are it, my love," she said with whimper, turning her soulful eyes to meet his, fighting back tears in the process.

He waited for her eyes to drop to the floor. The truth always emerged when she did.

"It was my trainer," she finally admitted, "but it's not what you think."

"And what makes you think your mind is on a level even remotely close to mine?" he asked condescendingly. "I know you have a thing for him."

"He was holding my wrists during a difficult bench press. He didn't want me dropping the weight on my chest."

"That would truly be a shame," Pyrus growled. "Considering how much I paid for those things."

He took her face into his hands, forcing her eyes to meet his. "Next time, consider covering up your imperfections before entering this room." His eyes were filled with disgust as he pinched her cheeks. "And wear a little more blush next time. You look ill." He dropped his hands from her face and reached for his scotch, watching her closely as he downed the contents in the glass.

"You always find a way to deceive me, don't you?" His lips broke into a serene smile.

She held his gaze for a moment before he gestured her to the liquor cabinet to recharge his glass. She was thankful the liquor had taken effect, otherwise she would have more than a small bruise on the wrist to nurse in the morning.

He watched her glide toward the cabinet, graceful and elegant. He could never allow her to know what he really thought about her. It would certainly go to her head. No, it was best to keep beautiful creatures in a constant state of insecurity. It was an easy way to ensure she wouldn't leave anytime soon.

"You know I'd love to throw you down on this floor right now, but I have to round up my entire legal team and come up with a new plan by the time the sun pops up over the Bellagio."

"Business," her eyes turned toward the wall of windows before them, taking in the night draped over the strip. Her wrist was throbbing almost as much as her head, but she had to keep up appearances if she hoped to get out of there quickly.

Pyrus knew her look. If he had any hope of getting laid tonight without blunt force, he'd better soften the blow and quick. No woman could hold his attention this long and there had been dozens. Hundreds even. Then, there was Jade.

She reached for the glass on the end table, taking a seductive sip before letting him off the hook. Such a sick game they played, she thought, but the lifestyle he afforded her made it well worth the temporary suffering she endured. He always came around in the end.

"Baby, I saw something on Instagram a minute ago, and I think you should see it," she said slowly, handing him her phone.

He opened the app and scrolled through her feed, landing on the video. The images immediately got his attention. Jade moved her head in closer, as he cranked the volume.

"There were initial reports claiming the first video was a hoax," she said over his shoulder. "This new video gives a much closer look at what happened today." She knew it was important to stay invested in his business dealings. He would lose interest quickly otherwise.

The video, like the last one, was shaky to start. The mumbling of the bystanders was inaudible in the background as the person holding the phone stepped toward the scene.

There, on a stretcher, , was the dump truck driver, Jaxson. His position was almost peaceful, as if he were laid to rest there by some fancy funeral home. A ravishing woman reached for him. It was the same woman from the earlier video, but the camera angle made it impossible to see who she was. The camera, focused on Jaxson almost exclusively, revealing the back of the woman's head, not her face. When the woman touched Jaxson, Pyrus could tell by her hand that she was young. Pyrus instinctively moved his own head around, as if commanding the camera to shift and bring her into view.

Within seconds, Jaxson's eyes began to flutter open. It was unclear if this was the result of the woman's touch or some other phenomenon that brought him back to life. The lens dropped to the photographer's feet and went to black. Pyrus began to search for other videos in earnest. He found a few live feeds in the process and listened to various experts weigh in on the different videos cropping up. They debated what they saw—not sure if it was some sort of coincidence, a hoax, or if the woman who touched him had some power over him, drawing him back to life.

"In the digital age, there are no secrets. I believe that woman has some sort of power. She has to be filling everyone's feed by now," Jade concluded.

Pyrus shook his head and closed the app, eyes settling on Jade.

"Well, if the woman is everything they say—or some sort of witch or mystic—then I would say the settlement payout presents a new opportunity," he said, raising an eyebrow.

"What do you mean?"

"Think of the possibilities, Jade," he said, eyes dancing. "We could have this woman set up in the theater downstairs, and she could put those so-called healing hands to work right here in the hotel."

He chuckled just then, thinking how deceptive the whole thing was. The sad thing was that people were so desperate out in the "real world" that they would believe almost anything that promised something better than the current situation.

"Interesting," Jade responded, meeting his eyes, masking her annoyance at the fact that she always seeded his good ideas. Jade was his muse, bringing forth the dance of opportunity in his head.

"Well, I better get to it," he said, snatching the glass from her hand and rising from the leather chair. Jade rose to her feet to meet him, giving him a peck on the cheek.

"Maybe tomorrow," he said casually, "I'll take you to our favorite steakhouse at Caesars."

"Fine," she said, rolling her soulful eyes, feigning disappointment.

She squeezed his hand and brushed past him, just close enough to arouse him. She needed to remind him what he would be missing. Oh, he felt it. She could see the rise in his slacks. Blood was flowing away from his brain. When the door clicked shut, he pondered the gravity of the situation. No pain, no gain: his personal motto. Perhaps this situation presented early labor pains of a new part of Payne Industries. He licked his lips, ready to pounce on the opportunity.

CHAPTER FIVE

A ray of sunlight streamed through the window and fell onto Jaxson's chest. The heart monitor beeped softly beside him. He was alive. It was the steady rhythm of his heart that welcomed him back into his surroundings. He was groggy but otherwise felt perfectly normal. He shifted positions in the hospital bed, stiff from the event that had happened only a few hours before. He remembered his heart, beating loudly inside his ears.

Fragments of his memory of the accident were pulling together like a thousand-piece puzzle.

He remembered the physical symptoms first. He could feel his blood sugar beginning to plummet and recalled wiping the beads of sweat from his forehead with a Starbucks napkin. His left hand was canvasing the vinyl seat, searching for a Clif bar in the door pocket. Another cliff of sorts had emerged, however, and he plummeted off the edge, arms spread wide, not knowing what he would meet below. He recalled the darkness closing in as he anticipated what would meet him on the other side. Light surrounded him, holding him softly as if he had leapt inside a cloud.

"You ready?" a voice said in the far off distance. He found himself back inside his childhood room.

Jamie J. Kemp

His brother, Jayden, stood beside him in the mirror. While the two did not share the same look, they were one and the same in heart and spirit. He remembered staring at their reflections for a moment, feeling the bond between them. Jaxson was just fourteen minutes older but the smaller of the two from the start. It was as if each of them had been created for their parents. Jaxson was slighter in frame, sensitive and caring, temperamentally much like his father. Jayden was a warrior from the beginning, the spitting image of their father physically. Leader, athlete, and knight in shining armor. He loved to rescue anyone and anything that came into his path, much like their mother. Jaxson didn't even raise an eyebrow when his brother came home from school one sunny afternoon to declare his future plans.

"Hey, whatcha doin'?" Jayden said, as he pushed open the door and flopped down on the twin bed, barely big enough to fit his now six-foot-five frame.

Jaxson, who was five inches shorter, was situated at the nearby desk, an area Jayden avoided in general. Jaxson preferred to sit when next to his taller, more masculine brother. His slender build seemed dwarfed by his brother's physique. Jayden didn't bother with the books, rather relying on his athletic prowess to carry him into the right college. It was no wonder every university in the country was eager to sign him.

"I'm working on this final application," Jaxson answered quietly, considering if his essay would be good enough to impress another elite college panel.

"That's nothin' for you," Jayden replied, reaching for the baseball on the nightstand. "Which one this time?"

"Howard," Jaxson said, allowing little enthusiasm to escape.

"You just need the mindset, brother," Jayden encouraged. "You're letting them win before you've even set foot on the field."

"Easy for you to say," Jaxson said with a laugh, as he populated his name in the application field.

It always perplexed them how they held such opposite names for who they were. Jaxson, the more masculine name. Jayden, the more sensitive one. His mother thought the name would help the smaller of her twins and make him more powerful. She knew the other wouldn't have the same struggle. Jayden entered the world nearly double the size of his twin. Yet, while his body was slower to grow, Jaxson's mind flourished. He absorbed everything so easily. It was one of the many things Jayden admired about his brother. That and his enormous heart.

"Listen, I know graduation is still a couple months away, but I finally made a decision about my future," Jayden began, noting his brother hadn't even looked up from the computer. "Are you even listening to me? This is important."

"Oh, yeah, of course," Jaxson said, closing the lid of the enormous old-school laptop, one of the first of its kind. It was a gift from the community fund set up to help the boys shortly after their parents died. The tragic event was still something the two rarely talked about.

"So, I thought about it and…" Jayden paused before answering.

"You're going to Florida," Jaxson finished the sentence. Jayden shook his head, considering if now was the time to tell Jax after all they had been through. It was extremely rare for Jaxson to not answer correctly. He started to worry.

"No, bro, I'm joining the Army," Jayden said, watching his brother's eyes closely as the news began to sink in.

"I did not see that coming," Jaxson said, looking from his brother to the window. Neither said a word for a few moments until Jayden finally continued.

"You know I love sports, but I just can't decide which one would be best," Jayden began. "They were all pressuring me to focus in on just one. I can't do that," Jayden said emphatically, reaching for the ball again. "Then, I was at that college fair two weeks ago and started talking to this recruiter, Matt Bryson. He was like me in school, good athlete, not so great student. After listening to him and how he's made a career of it, well, it sounded like the best option for me."

"So, you think going and getting your ass blown up in some desert is better than playing football?" Jaxson asked, anger building in his voice. "You've got to be kidding me!"

"Now wait a second. This isn't as bad as you think it is," Jayden said, placing the ball back on the nightstand as he sat up and squared off with his brother. "They will pay for my college, and I can even become an officer if I want to down the line."

"Wait, you are enlisting?" Jaxson asked. He didn't even allow his brother a chance to answer. "No, you need to go to college first! Mom and Dad would have wanted that," he said, before letting out a long, exasperated sigh. Jayden was careful not to answer.

"Jay, you need to think about this carefully," his brother said with a fatherly tone. He hated stepping into this role now that both of their parents were gone, but he had no choice in the moment. He had to get through his brother's thick skull before it was too late.

"You've got every college in this country wanting you to play football, basketball, baseball," Jaxson continued. "You have more options than I do! Why in the world would you throw that all away to be tortured by the government in the prime physical years of your life?"

"Listen, Jax, I'm joining, and that's final," Jayden said with a furrowed brow before bouncing up off the bed. "As much as you'd like to pretend you are Dad, you'll never replace him."

Jayden stormed out of the room, and that was the last they ever talked about it. He joined the Army that summer as an infantry man. His promotions were fast, and he earned the rank of sergeant in just under two years. Discipline was always easy for Jay, probably from all the coaches, workouts, and teammates he endured playing sports all those years.

Jaxson stayed behind that fall, opting to attend Pacific Lutheran University. Like his father, he studied theology, with hopes of standing in the pulpit one day. It never happened. The first semester, he took an elective course in African studies, and he was hooked.

Graduation day was upon him, along with a sense of dread. He knew Jayden wouldn't be there. His brother had just moved into Special Forces a few months before. Jaxson watched Gran through the mirror as he straightened his tie. With a generation lost between them, he felt a deep sense of melancholy. If only his parents were here to celebrate this moment. He imagined his father standing beside him, a broad smile spreading across his handsome face. Three generations considering the possibilities of his future.

"In spirit, Jaxson," Gran said, patting his shoulder for comfort. "Always here in spirit."

He concentrated on his own reflection, searching for his father's face in his own. His brother, Jayden, seemed to glean all of his dad's striking features, but he had his mother's heart. Jaxson, was the exact opposite.

He remembered the news filling his ears on that tragic day, still fresh in his mind seven years later. He could smell the smoke in the charred remains of his father's church. His memory took it further, welcoming in the Old Spice, pipe tobacco, and cinnamon breath mints that conjured up memories in his father's office inside Lake Hills Church. Jaxson had spent hours there in his youth, memorizing the periodic table of elements, state capitals, apostles, and anything else his father put in front of him. The scent traveled through his brain and rested heavily on his heart. He wanted to cry and, at the same time, let forth a primal scream so deep he was sure it would shake the foundation of the house if he let it go. He suppressed it, out of respect for his Gran, and turned his memory toward his doting mother.

He could see her now so vividly in his mind, passionately playing the organ in the back while his father practiced his weekly sermon at the altar up front. They were an incredible team, cosmically joined in a shared purpose of community and unity. The pews were always full on Sundays. People were drawn to the place, some traveling as far as fifty miles to attend Sunday service. The fire on a Thursday morning in December was ruled a hate crime. Hate filled Jaxson's heart for the first two years. But Jayden faired far worse from the circumstances, turning to petty crimes at first, but sports saved him before the system could claim him. He would have certainly ended up in jail had Gran and a cadre of coaches not intervened.

"Your great-grandmother Minnie would have loved this moment," Gran whispered into his ear, brushing wrinkles from his graduation gown.

"They're here, Gran," he said, as he took her busy hand in his and led it toward his heart.

"You're a good boy, Jaxson," she said, looking down to avoid a stream of tears. "Always responsible while your brother goes off and plays G.I. Joe somewhere. Nothin' but a game of roulette that boy is playing."

Red and black. Appropriate colors for the life he had shared with his brother. Red, for all the blood, sweat, and tears to bring them both to this moment. And black, well, because. It was Jaxson's chosen power color. Not only because of his heritage, but it was also a strong source of identity and pride. College had helped him embrace that even more. His degree in African studies was a symbolic gesture to those before him, particularly his father.

He stared at himself again, his Gran now firmly fixed beside him. There was so much sacrifice to get him to this moment.

He wished his parents had been there that day, even Jayden, the prodigal brother who returned time and again to dim Jaxson's light since joining the Army. If he was really honest with himself, he would admit he had lived in the shadow of his sibling his entire life. And now? Well, no matter how hard he had worked, Jaxson was always the second choice in Gran's eyes, even though she seemed less than enthusiastic about Jayden's choice to make the military his career. She always preferred Jayden, probably because he looked so much like their father, her only son.

In the beginning of his grad school search, Jaxson was so sure of a future far from Seattle's skyline. He wanted to dip his toes in the Atlantic. He wanted Morehouse, Howard— anywhere east of here. He soon lowered his expectations to a state university. Then it became any college that offered something more than a part-time job and an urban atmosphere beyond a few fast-food places and senior center that doubled as a concert hall.

Jaxson would steady his heart at the sight of a postman, knowing that showing any sign of elation over what was left at the door would just make his Gran feel more devastated at the words "We regret to inform you…."

"That's fine! Didn't want to go there anyway!" Jaxson would shout confidently each time he opened the bin to receive yet another graduate program rejection. His grades at university were, admittedly, not the best. But his words, his passion for history, ran deep in his veins, pumping possibility into his now very humble heart. Bare branches appeared through the kitchen window by the time he finally accepted temporary defeat.

"They've won the battle, Gran, but not the war," Jaxson said, as he straightened his tie at the breakfast table. He kissed her cheek before filling his mug with coffee. "It is time to get a job, and everyone's hiring for the holidays," he offered as he reached for his laptop, logging in to various job sites. "Just a temporary bump."

"It's time to pray, Jaxson," she said, never removing her eyes from the front page of the paper.

"You know how I feel about that, Gran," he answered firmly, taking a sip from a very strong cup of wake-up. "Dad's up there just laughing, like he does. He knows it's a test. I'm gonna pass the test, Gran. You'll see. I'll retake the GRE in the spring. Better score means better opportunity."

"I just think it's a good idea to show a little gratitude, son," Gran said. "Let the Father know you acknowledge it."

"I told you, Gran. I know he's up there looking out for me."

"I mean THE Father, son," Gran replied sternly, grabbing her Bible off the end table and shaking it for effect. She was clearly not suggesting; rather she was demanding. He quickly gripped the book, mumbled something under his breath, and finished with a solid "Amen" before finishing his coffee and kissing her on the forehead. He was out the door before she had time to comment about it.

He quickly landed a retail gig downtown, selling cheaply made clothing to parents of spoiled children. Why anyone would choose the flimsy styles he so neatly folded each day was beyond him. Any touch of an iron would clearly ruin the threadbare material manufactured in some distant part of the world, likely by children younger than the ones the shirts and pants were intended for. He finished organizing the table, but within minutes, his work was quickly rummaged through. He waited a few minutes before starting again. He considered the task a sort of meditation. It was better than having to ring up the ridiculous totals at the register.

The holidays passed without incident, and as the New Year came and went, he was soon pounding the pavement for a more permanent position. He didn't feel quite ready for the GRE exam again, so he studied to acquire a commercial driver's license as a backup. Just a temporary speed bump, he reminded himself, as he pulled into the parking lot of Eagle Waste Management in Bothell. This could give him a chance to know his rejection letters in the bin more intimately, he reasoned, as he waited for his name to be called in the rather sterile reception area.

An hour later, he walked out with the job and an opportunity to learn. Yes, he would be learning about garbage, but he thought it might make him more appreciative. He told Gran all about it that evening over a steaming bowl of ham hock and bean soup.

"It will be fine, Gran," he said reaching for her hand. "I start at 4:00 a.m., and I'm off at 2:00 p.m. That will give me a chance to work on my GRE score and prepare packets."

For once, his decision seemed to brighten his Gran's spirits. She was actually smiling as she reached for the rolls, spreading butter and honey to the point he couldn't see the bread anymore.

"You deserve this, son," she finally said. "But it had better be temporary. I've watched you work so hard for everything. Picking up someone else's trash? That's for other people, not you. Academics? Now that's your calling!"

"What?" he said, with a drop of his spoon. "You think that it's stupid to start at thirty-eight dollars an hour—more than double, mind you, what I would make at some damn retail job—to help us survive?"

She met his stare and made a pointed gesture to shift her eyes to the cross on the wall.

"Language, baby. You know I don't like those words in this house!"

Jaxson took a deep breath knowing what he said next would be crucial to ending what could be a full evening of silence between them.

"It's just a little detour," he began. "Maybe…maybe I needed some…humility to better understand our ancestors and struggles."

"They already struggled a million lifetimes for you, Jaxson," she hissed.

"But it will help me be a more compassionate teacher, maybe even a professor," said Jaxson cautiously. He knew he misspoke, turning a mere campground blaze into a forest fire with a few simple words. "I'll be the one who actually understands because I haven't been living inside a book like all those other people they accepted. They'll say, this guy has lived it! No shame in that, Gran, no shame. YOU taught me that one."

She glared at him then, honey now dripping onto her hands. Jaxson picked up his spoon and shoved the remaining contents in the bowl into his mouth, rather his big, fat mouth that always seemed to say the wrong things these days. He got up to wash the dishes and dried and returned them to the cupboards. It was still early, but he went straight to bed. The mattress welcomed his tired body. He felt a sense of peace fall upon him as he closed his eyes on the picture of his parents on the nightstand.

Jaxson would see that picture again in the tunnel of light. It seemed like they were waving a welcome. Upon further reflection, it was more like they were waving him away.

Fifteen years of sanitation services now behind him in the blink of an eye. It was an endless route that allowed him afternoons at the side of his ailing Gran. He saw her then, standing beside his parents.

"Go back, Jaxson!" she screamed to him across the light.

"Go back to what?" he yelled back. "You're here!"

He took a step toward them as two angelic figures stepped in his path. "You have an important purpose," he heard them all say in unison. He was sure of one thing in that moment. He was not going back if it meant driving a garbage truck. His heartbeat filled his ears once more. A magnetic force pulled him toward his body. A new beginning. His eyes fluttered open. Eyes as brown as his own stared back at him.

"Wha…" he tried to speak. He felt confused, yet surprisingly stable, almost grounded to the earth below him like never before. No more discomfort. No feeling of highs and lows. It was how he felt before his Type I diabetes diagnosis at age twenty-five. He remembered walking out of the doctor's office after the diagnosis. He stopped for a moment and stared up at the clouds and toward a future he could never quite see.

But now he could see.

The light filled his room and his soul. His heartbeat strong and steady. He didn't know the woman who saved him, but he was sure she was a giver of life and purpose. In an instant, he knew his purpose in the short term. He would follow her and retrieve his life from the bin. He was confident the rest would work itself out.

"I am not the garbage I am collecting," he whispered to himself. It was a revelation.

He knew it with every beat of his heart.

CHAPTER SIX

P etra turned the key in the rusty lock, swearing under her breath as she struggled to open the door. The hallway of the halfway house just off Union Square was full of people who talked to themselves all the time, so why should she be any different? She quickly closed her eyes as the door creaked open. She wanted to be surprised, or perhaps less disappointed. At this point, anything would be better than where she had been.

"Home sweet home," she whispered as she slowly opened her eyes.

The room was basic but not too terrible by halfway house standards. She scanned the room, all 150 square feet of it, taking in her humble surroundings. A small window with bars on the outside evenly divided the cramped space. Sunlight made a weak attempt to burst through the bars but somehow only enjoyed a brief escape. The peek-a-boo game with the burning orb of the sun left the tiny room with a dull, gray light. Curtains that would now likely classify as rags, framed a view of the old, battered brick building next door. No view of Elliott Bay from this space.

The rest of the room consisted of an old desk, upon which sat a copy of the King James Bible. Petra wondered if the particle board could hold the hardback's weight. A small, wooden chair with a metal back, reminiscent of her elementary school days in Ukraine, was tucked neatly into the opening below. Across the room was an equally wobbly chest of drawers. Beside it, a twin bed was wrapped tightly with worn white—now yellowing—sheets and a musty army blanket. That concluded the tour.

Petra dropped her black, leather duffel bag to the floor, took two small steps to the edge of the bed, and promptly fell backside first toward the mattress. That was a mistake. The springs offered no support to her slight frame, with just enough give to feel the metal box frame below. She lay quietly for a moment, taking in her freedom for the first time in five years. As a sort of peace began to wash over her, the sound of sirens and rushing vehicles rattled the window and frame, threatening to shatter the glass. At least they aren't coming for me, she thought, as she breathed in the dust-filled air. Between the dust and musty odor, it was clear no one had occupied the space in some time.

After a quick catnap, she woke with a renewed sense of purpose. This time, she vowed, things would change. Petra stepped toward the worn leather duffel and opened the sticky zipper. Inside was everything she owned: a tattered pair of jeans, black ballet flats, and a Ramones T-shirt she picked up in a thrift shop near the Canadian border before she was busted for what she hoped would be the last time.

Her slender fingers grazed the bottom of the bag, locating a travel-sized toothpaste, a worn-out toothbrush, "savage red" lipstick, and a memo pad. Her pen had lodged tightly into the corner of the bag, almost tempting her to give up on setting yet another list of goals, or rather, failures.

Pulling the pad and pen from the duffel, Petra made her way to the rickety desk. She opened the pad to the first page, reading her thoughts from a few days before.

The word "GOALS" stretched boldly across the top. After five years in a women's prison, she had plenty of time to consider them carefully.

No more shortcuts in this life.

No more bad men.

No more excuses.

No more time behind bars.

That last one, on second thought, should be at the very top of the list.

Looking back, life seemed so simple when she wrote the goals the day before her release. But now, on the outside, she knew it would not be so easy to attain the goals before her. Choice, Petra surmised, was a Western notion.

In Ukraine, the choices had always been made for her, or at least that was her experience. Choices—around clothing, which cut of meat would be best to serve for dinner on Tuesday, the way to go to work today—were all made for her. Lines at stores were occupied by the lucky few with tokens in hand. Meat, for the most part, was imagined in a typical meal of lukewarm root vegetables and watery broth that made up a sickening stew.

Choice was a luxury few could afford in her homeland. In fact, it could be that the very idea of choice was what so quickly caused her demise since arriving in the United States. Was she so conditioned to simply follow that she really had no thought before action? As she thought about it further, she realized that she chose action over thought in every bad decision she had made so far. It was time to change that.

Petra stood to stretch at the thought and reached for a bottle of water left on top of the dresser. She examined the seal. It had been broken, but the liquid filled to the top of the bottle. Good enough, she thought. She sat down in the desk chair and looked through the bars to her past, considering her choices since arriving in the states seven years ago. She tried to remember if she had broken a mirror because it truly had been seven years of very bad luck.

1. *Choosing America over Canada.* This had been a good choice in that there were actually warm states she could settle in and finally shake the cold of Ukraine. She was done with the two seasons in Ukraine—miserable winter and insufferable summer. Still, in retrospect, Canada probably would have been a better choice.

2. *Meeting Razor.* The name alone should have been a dead giveaway, but his tall, muscular physique and shiny bald head had her hypnotized from the moment she met him while waiting tables in Arlington, Virginia. She fell for his looks but was lured by the money he offered her to join what would be an elaborate crime ring.

3. *Following Razor West.* It seemed like the most logical move at the time, considering that the DC-area winter and summer she experienced seemed nearly as bad as any in Ukraine, not to mention the rising rent on a basement studio that flooded in spring and housed hordes of rodents and snakes in the summer. Razor's piercing green eyes almost hypnotized her into making the leap. It was a move that would send her entire life into

a downward spiral. If only she had stayed in DC. Life may be much simpler, maybe even warmer than it was now.

4. *Taking up an offer to "entertain" gentlemen on the road.* It was Razor's idea at the time—yet another decision made for her. At first, the choice offered her more money than she had ever seen. But it soon became an exchange for pharmaceuticals that were absolutely necessary to numb and even block each "experience" from her mind. As Petra's clientele grew, Razor added in a "housing fee" for whatever cheap motel they would occupy in the early morning hours. She had just enough time to nap, shower, and prep herself for another day working through men's wallets by way of some seedy hotel bed.

5. *Leaving town at the dead of night with Wally.* True, he was a chubby, rapidly aging software salesman, but upon completing his regularly requested blow job and conversation afterward, he would describe a place called the Pacific Northwest that left her ears hanging on his every word. There was a taste of freedom in his fluid that made her do the impossible one day. Petra told Razor she would be working "The Center," known as convention row, and would not return until she had made at least four grand. Petra still had her model looks and charm then, so the goal wasn't out of reach, especially with wealthy businessmen swarming the place. Motivated by the prospect of decent money, he allowed her to pack a bag to change if necessary, no questions asked.

6. *Running off and marrying Wally at the Little Chapel in Vegas.* The ceremony was as short as the time left on her green card. They honeymooned in a little condo Wally owned several miles off the strip. It wasn't the most romantic of nuptials, but at least she was free from Razor. She knew the cops were on to Razor, and she would be a casualty of the fallout if she didn't get away from him. Besides, Wally seemed kind and caring, offering her a glimpse of the future she had always dreamed of. It was better than rotting in jail with Razor or murdered in some seedy hotel room.

7. *Meeting Waldo.* Wally would go from sweet and loving one moment, to dark and moody the next. Petra had named Wally's dark side "Waldo" because with the slightest word or touch, he would flip the switch. It felt at times like the children's book where you search for the hidden man in the striped shirt, but eventually he always appeared rather suddenly before her eyes. She put up with his moods and harsh words in the beginning, but as Waldo emerged more and more, the emotional abuse became physical. Slaps. Fists pounding into her flesh. Sunglasses became her favorite accessory, even though the sun never shined in Seattle, not in the sky and certainly not in her heart.

8. *Buying arsenic online.* In Ukraine, a dial tone accompanied any internet connection. Computers in a home were for the chosen few. Most,

like Petra, found themselves surfing in a café or corner shop that had made a business of the remote connection. Your search in a café was as anonymous as the many users before or after you. How could anyone know she had made such a simple purchase? It wasn't even on her radar when she hit "purchase."

9. *Lacing Waldo's food and coffee.* It was not a quick death to be sure, but it kept his fists off her face and his focus elsewhere. It took a few months, but Waldo eventually began to disappear along with the number on the scale. His rapid weight loss from a mystery virus had doctors perplexed and Petra hopeful.

10. *Calling the cops when Waldo/Wally passed.* In Ukraine, the body is viewed by authorities and then disposed of without many remarks. She had witnessed it many times in her home country intimately with the passing of her immediate family. First, Petra's little brother, Sergei, was taken from her by influenza at the age of eight. Petra by that time was twelve and forced to care for her brother day and night for the better part of two weeks. Two years later, her father, growing increasingly tired since the passing of Sergei, died from heart failure. She thought at first it was more from a broken heart but later came to realize the backbreaking factory work, seven days a week for two-and-a-half long, hopeless decades, tends to rob a man of life itself. Then, not even a month after her father's death, her mom passed

on. Her symptoms suggested cancer, but this time she knew a broken heart was to blame.

Petra pushed the list aside for a moment but thought back on her arrest. When the authorities arrived at the door, the experience was worlds away from her home in Ukraine. A trio of workers examined the body briefly, even snapping a few photos for good measure. She would later learn about something called DNA, as the woman in charge informed Petra that they would be conducting an autopsy to determine cause of death. Petra had not known this strange word. It certainly wasn't something you find in the *Guide to Conversational English*.

She watched the workers carry Waldo/Wally's body away in a black bag. For Petra, there was no mourning Waldo's demise, but Wally was another matter. She felt a sense of dread and remorse as they carried his now almost slender, cold body from the townhouse. She watched them open the van door and, with one synchronized movement, place Wally inside. A single tear trickled down her cheek as the van pulled out of the complex.

She gave herself a good slap on the face. "No time for sadness," she muttered, and with the click of the door latch, raced to the computer to type the newly learned English word into the search engine.

Ah-Top-See.

No results.

A-topsie.

Nope.

A-topsy.

"Do you mean *autopsy*?" the search engine suggested.

She clicked on the first link and felt her heart leap into her throat.

"Also known as post-mortem examination."

She quickly entered "post-mortem."

The search engine returned: "To determine cause of death."

She knew in an instant that she was screwed.

Of course, in Ukraine, you wouldn't think to clear your computer history, remove cookies, or simply wipe your entire hard drive clean. No, Petra didn't do those things because she had only known computers at school, a café, or other public location. She left the glowing box sitting right where it was. The recent search still open.

Petra leapt to her feet and made a mad dash for the bedroom closet. She grabbed Wally's black leather duffel and, in it, dropped a pair of faded jeans, underwear, old socks and sneakers, and her favorite "red savage" lipstick for luck. As she made her way out of the townhouse, she caught a glimpse of herself in the mirror. Her bright blue eyes were now beet red from the stress of the day, her baby fine, blonde hair framed her perfectly proportioned face. She dug into the bag to retrieve her red lipstick and applied it liberally. Giving herself a wink, she left the two-story townhome in Shoreline confident she had evaded the authorities.

Three to five days for results, they had said. That was enough time to make her way north to Canada and what should have been the first of a series of good decisions, not terrible ones. But the morgue was quite empty the day Wally was wheeled in, and the coroner welcomed the work coming off of a rather long weekend of the usual suspects. Wally's cause of death was clear before the first slide was stained.

Petra was picked up at the border gate, just three steps from what should have been her first choice of Canada. The press picked up the story in a matter of hours and called it the Mail Order Murder. Clearly, they had not checked the facts of her past and that was either comforting or terrifying depending on how she looked at it. Petra's pathetic excuse for an attorney did one thing right, though. He proved Petra's abuse thanks to a handful of witnesses in the complex. She was locked up for five years.

Now, pen back in hand, she stared at the blank page before her. She had a whole new set of choices to make. Where would she go? What would she do for work? The best decision seemed to be the outskirts of Las Vegas. She vaguely remembered now, but the little condo where she and Wally sipped two-dollar champagne from Elvis cups seemed her best hope. She had to leave this place, no matter what her parole officer had said. Her planning was interrupted by the blare of sirens rattling the window. She didn't bother unpacking. She told the woman at the desk she was doing some laundry but instead made her way to the nearest bus depot.

She arrived to find the line of dirty transporters. She immediately longed for the feeling of freedom that driving her own car could provide. She wanted to drive down a twisting, turning road and feel the wind between her fingers as her hand draped hopefully out the window. What she got instead was a nauseating ride on a bus filled to capacity.

Petra turned her head toward the window, staring at the fingerprints and slime that coated the glass. She struggled to hold back the vomit that was bubbling up from her stomach. She was thankful she hadn't eaten earlier; otherwise she would have puked all over the passenger beside her. Not that he would have noticed. The man was stinking drunk on cheap liquor. It reminded her of home. Of course, for Petra, home was not a place that brought forth images of warmth and comfort. Home was a constant struggle to survive. She would often try to conjure up images of her family, but most of the time she only recalled their long, sorrowful faces. Her memory was clear on the fact that the place was utter misery.

Now, here she was, traveling down I-5 in the cover of darkness with drunken strangers, most of whom were heading to Las Vegas to fuel the vices that kept them far from their thoughts and even further from themselves. She knew leaving the state was a risk, and her parole officer would be pounding down her door in that dump heap of a halfway house in about six days. It would be enough time to make some decisions about what to do next, even if it meant sitting for hours on end on the bus to nowhere.

Petra closed her eyes for a moment, imagining the tiny condo that she shared with her late husband for a few days after their drive-thru wedding. She remembered him shuffling through the one bedroom in his tighty-whities, shoving Twinkies in his mouth while making promises of a new life in Seattle. A better life, he said. How wrong he had been. At the time, she was so desperate for something positive to happen that she stupidly believed him, grasping at some hope of a future that offered her the kind of life she always wanted but wasn't quite sure she deserved.

Her mind turned to a Motown song playing on the boom box in the living room. She remembered drunkenly embracing Wally in the sparse living room, spilling box wine from plastic cups while angling their bodies in a movement that didn't quite resemble dancing. She could recall his round face, a five o'clock shadow turning rapidly into a gray jungle that gave her glimpses of a demented Santa she had seen in a movie once.

It was the first time she allowed her subconscious mind to seep through. As she looked around at the dirty condo, she began to see that she had made a terrible mistake. She didn't allow the realization to linger long. Anything was better than where she had been.

She wandered drunkenly into the kitchen, pulling the plastic tap from the dented box of wine that probably should have been front and center in the vinegar aisle. She allowed the Chablis to pour generously into her Elvis cup. It tasted like shit, but she was fine with the end result. A complete numbness that resembled a sort of bliss. As the battle between heart and gut began to subside, she fell into the dizzy feeling that contorted her body around the living room in what looked like a haphazard striptease. She remembered undressing, Wally's eyes becoming more glued to her with each item falling to the floor. She felt loved. She felt desired. It still remained one of the happiest times in her life.

She inhaled deeply then, allowing the sickening smells of liquor to wander through her nostrils. How she hated the smell of alcohol. Years in prison had turned her craving for booze into a distant memory. She was glad for that experience. She would often watch her fellow inmates from the corner of her eye, making deals in the most casual of circumstances for the chance of a momentary high. The passing of a hair brush or toothpaste. The often poorly acted attempt of a greeting by handshake or fist bump. They would bump casually into each other, touching palms and passing the day's promised escape. She had been pressured to try, but she knew her addictive personality would lead her down a rabbit hole with no return.

She hoped that the condo was as she remembered. While its flea market furnishings weren't at all luxurious, it was the closest thing to home she had ever known. The place in Seattle only reminded her of Waldo, outbursts of anger and his slow demise. If she found the condo in Vegas to be in working order and free of the occasional tenant, she may just take a leap of faith and put down some roots. Sin City seemed an appropriate place to start over, given her track record to date.

She closed her eyes, returning to the conscious act of mouth breathing, hoping to grab a few minutes of shut eye before the bus pulled into Portland to offload passengers and picked up more lost souls for the long trip ahead.

Please let this be a new beginning, she thought to herself.

She considered a prayer, but who would listen? It was clear that whomever was in charge beyond this world had long given up on her. It was a pointless pursuit. She adjusted her head into a more comfortable position, braving the slime on the window. As the lines blurred before her, they seemed to offer a small sliver of hope in what was otherwise a nearly unbearable situation. At least she was moving, rather than rotting away in a place bathed in bad memories.

She had fallen asleep at some point on the ride, but she awoke to find the bus wasn't moving, and her surroundings were bathed in orange neon. She decided to stretch her legs, relieve herself, and browse the contents of the nameless mini-mart while the bus was refueled. If not for the air freshener she found at the counter of the truck stop in Reno, Petra wasn't sure how she would stomach the remaining hours of road ahead. The pine smell, while nauseating at first, offered a sort of clarity as the miles rolled on.

As the miles to Vegas counted down on the passing signs, it became clear in her mind that she would have to reinvent herself. She was on the run now and had to put forth an image that was respectable and at the very least presentable. Petra wasn't sure how she would accomplish such a task without money. By the time the bus reached the next stop, she had devised a plan.

As the last of the conscious passengers exited the bus, she began scanning the rows around her with an eagle eye. The remaining group before her was mostly unconscious. If she timed it right, she could quickly rummage through bags and scrounge for loose change and dollar bills in their wallets and purses. It wouldn't be her proudest moment, but what do you expect from a woman who just got out of prison and left the state while on parole?

She lowered herself onto all fours, quickly moving through the rows, looking for easy targets. A purse stored haphazardly under a seat was her first find, and she rummaged seamlessly for its contents. She emerged with twenty bucks. Not much, but a start.

She quickly dug through other purses, coat pockets, wallets, and zipper pockets on the sides of bags. She was careful not to place her hands in the sticky and wet spots that covered places on the filthy floor.

By the time she made her way to the back of the bus, she was $483 dollars richer. She could have walked away with a much larger amount, but she was careful not to take too many big bills. Anything larger than twenty bucks was sure to get noticed by the more sober passengers, and the last thing she wanted was an inspection from the large and rather gruesome driver. She made do with the ones, fives, tens, and twenty dollar bills. It took her all of seven minutes to sweep through the seats, a trick she learned from her sordid past working the streets.

The click of the pump was her cue to stop. She moved back to her seat in a flash, her take tucked safely in her underwear. She settled in as the first of the returning passengers boarded the bus. She felt a little ill as she considered her transformation. She had enough now to purchase some hair dye, modest makeup, and tinted contacts. That would be enough to fool the distracted police force in Vegas if they were to ever come for her.

What she really needed was a job to sustain herself. She didn't have many skills that didn't involve illegal activity, but she was willing to try. She knew a little about serving others, so to speak, while working for Razor, and she did hold down a waitressing job for a few months in DC. There was no reason why she couldn't call herself a customer service representative on a resume. Perhaps she could fake her way into a job as a hostess or even a cocktail waitress at one of the fancy casinos. Maybe she could even manage people. She had worked in the prison's kitchen for a brief time, peeling potatoes and putting up with insults. After a time, she was even put in charge of the sorry crew serving breakfast and lunch. That had to count for something. She might as well put those miserable years in prison to use.

The driver boarded the bus, giving the passengers a less than pleasing pout before dropping his fat ass into the seat. She felt sorry for him in that moment, wondering just how far they would have to travel before they could all relieve themselves of the urine smell that seemed to permanently linger in the stale air. The engine purred to life, and they soon were pulling out onto the highway again.

Jamie J. Kemp

She turned toward the window, eager to breathe in the fresh air. Before long, she fell into a deep slumber, dreaming of bussing tables and flopping down on the couch at the end of the day. As her environment came into view, she saw she was in Ukraine. While her location may change, her dreams of a stable, comfortable life wouldn't. She longed to return to a home she was yet to discover.

CHAPTER SEVEN

One taste, and it will all be better.

Matt was just three cars back from ordering, his stomach stalled by yet another meeting that forced him to skip his usual noon lunch hour, or rather, the five-minute shoveling he called lunch these days. The drive-thru line was enough to do him in. Another week of the complete and utter bullshit that was his job. As if being an accountant for a law firm wasn't enough boredom, now this.

One taste, and it will all be better.

He had at least nine transactions to get through by 5:00 p.m. He couldn't remember the last time he had actually left work on time, not that he had much to go home to. There was a nearly empty apartment in Lower Queen Anne he shared with his goldfish named Cat, a leave-behind from his neighbor who moved out abruptly last fall. He saw the bowl and a simple note in front of his door one morning. All it said was "Sorry, I didn't know who else to give him to." Matt noted the long "whiskers" drooping from the creature's face and thought it looked like a cat. From there, it just kind of stuck. Accountants weren't the most creative when it came to stuff like names, but they sure were creative when it came to the numbers. He was so pleased that Cat had outlived the modest houseplants he bought at Christmas time. Maybe he could keep something alive, beyond himself.

The long wait only made him stew more about what was waiting for him at the office of Breeland and Associates. Breeland could shove it because today he was leaving on time. Was it not enough that he arrived every morning at 6:30 a.m. like clockwork, pulling into the Smith Tower, ready to do battle with endless spreadsheets and invoices? Actually, the numbers were more like allies in a never-ending war that was billable hours. While he thought about it, all the lawyers in the office could get lost too. The latest rate increases were enough to drive all the clients to madness, and he was the one to take every phone call and explain after the bills arrived. Come to think of it, there was really only one client who was enemy number one today, along with the damn lawyers who supported him. Pyrus Payne this particular day would require him to wear an invisible armor worthy of the greatest battles in history.

The firm had an entire division devoted to tax law, and it was the only one willing to take Matt when he requested the transfer from practicing law to accounting for it. It was right in the middle of the recession, when he joined the firm as a junior associate. He was the last guy in before the markets collapsed and, without billable hours, he was facing the unemployment line. When the opening came up in the accounting department, he jumped at the chance to move out of the law and practice the skills acquired from his other degree in accounting.

The mini-van in front of him inched its way toward the intercom. He could just catch a glimpse of the menu and considered his choices. He couldn't seem to choose between the number nine and the number four. His mouth watered at the possibilities.

One taste, and it will all be better.

He was thinking of the double-double when an alarm sounded through his car's audio system. He had to change that ring, but it was the most appropriate one for the constant line of emergencies that interrupted his phone day and night as more and more cases were settled out of court. He touched the button on the steering wheel, reluctantly accepting the call.

"This is Matt," he said, filled with dread.

"Where the fuck are you, Fat Matt?" It was Ransick, more like Rancid, as Matt liked to call him. He was a brown-nosing twit of a man who got high on other people's misery by day and vodka by night. While he had been at the firm just a month longer than Matt, he was absolutely convinced he was superior in every way because he held a law degree from some big-name university back East. What Matt didn't disclose often was that he held a law degree from Stanford, still considered lowly by his East Coast colleagues. It was one of the big reasons the firm hired him over the 408 other applicants at the time. He had finished law school in two years but was always bothered by the idea of practicing the law for a living. While it was true many of the corporate attorneys found themselves buried in paperwork most of the time, Matt preferred numbers to words. He was more than happy to sink into a spreadsheet for hours on end, rather than tackling thousands of documents searching for key words on any given case.

"Payne's people are going to be here in twenty minutes!" Ransick shouted, vibrating the rearview mirror.

For once, Matt was thankful for the mini-van full of kids in front of him. It would take them at least two minutes to place the order and another four to five at the window. That would be enough to possibly avoid Payne's people and force Ransick to actually do his job for a change.

"Dude, I'm just on my way back from the post office," Matt lied through the speaker. "I'm totally fine on time. I'll be there in a minute."

"Who the fuck goes to the post office today?" Ransick said, as if viewing Matt on some secret surveillance. "Just own up, man. You're in some fucking drive-thru, about to order the fries I'll want as payment for you being fucking late to this meeting."

Matt's face grew warm with anger. He was actually growing sick from Ransick's read of the situation. How the hell did Ransick always know? Was he that predictable?

As if he heard the question, Ransick returned with a quip: "I'll take the biggie fries, if you can keep them in the bag long enough to drive the thirty seconds back to the office."

"I'm not…" Matt stammered. "I, I wasn't—"

"Save it, Matt!" Ransick shot back. "Just don't be late! Payne's people are gonna shit when they see you missing from this settlement meeting, and I am NOT managing this alone."

Matt had worked on the Payne account before. Payne's people were genius at working around tax code and the law in general. That's how he first became acquainted with the firm's biggest client. The settlements were numerous and kept him busy. In general, Payne's hired guns at the firm were far too buttoned-up to ever set foot inside a courtroom. They were focused on getting to the lowest figures possible on whatever case was before the courts and get it settled. Fast. But this settlement was different. He noticed a lot of closed-door meetings in the last couple of days. The most senior partners at the firm were involved, including Dick Breeland, the firm's namesake and managing partner. Something else was up. He glanced at the time again and looked up to see the mini-van had pulled forward to the first window. The driver behind him began to tap the horn.

"See!" Ransick returned. "I knew it!"

One taste, and it will all be better.

"Fine, I'll be there—"

The connection abruptly ended. Great. He wanted to stall as long as possible and slowly pulled forward to the intercom.

"Hello?" The voice of what sounded like a child chirped on the box.

"Sorry, uh, ma'am, uh, miss," Matt said, sweat began to drip as his hands slipped on the wheel.

"What's your order?"

"I'll have the number five, the number seven, the number three," Matt began. "Oh, and make those a Big Kahuna. And I'll also take an order of the Big Kahuna fries."

"What do you want to drink with those combos?"

"Um…diet…Coke?" he asked, realizing how ridiculous it was to order diet when the meal that he would wash it down with was anything but. "In a super Sumo cup, please?"

"Sure…is that…it?"

Now he felt embarrassed.

"Um yes…big office order," he offered.

"Your total is $27.97 at the first window."

Matt put the car into drive, realizing he forgot to say "thank you." Why did he feel guilty about things like that?

As he inched toward the window, Matt quickly calculated the total in his head. If he had ordered the number nine, instead of the number three, he could have upgraded and saved at least $1.65. Oh well. Ransick would give him all kinds of shit if he just dumped a smaller-sized fry as part of the meal on his desk. It wasn't worth the humiliation he would face for the rest of the week, let alone the day.

A pretty young woman, no more than eighteen, greeted him with the total. As he handed over the fifty-dollar bill, the aromas of the fryers began to awaken his taste buds. His mouth was watering at the thought of the Big Kahuna double-double. It was likely the only pleasure he would experience today, and he wasn't about to waste it.

One taste, and it will all be better.

Matt waited for the mini-van to grab what seemed like an endless assembly line of bags. He could see grubby little hands pawing through the contents, eager to find the Kahuna Kids prize at the bottom of the bag. As the driver slowly pulled away from the window, Matt followed close behind. Another woman, even prettier than the last, waited at the sliding window. He gave her his best smile.

"Ketchup or salt?" she asked, as she passed the bags through the window.

"Nope, I'm good. Uh, big meeting."

"Uh-huh," she sighed, as she passed through the Sumo cup of diet disaster.

She gave him a pity-party smile, a real "poor you" of an expression that made Matt fume. He took small comfort in the fact that this woman probably sees this scenario more often than not.

"OK then, have a great day," Matt chimed in as he placed the Sumo cup in the holder, bags covering the passenger seat.

He practically peeled out of the parking lot, not so much out of embarrassment but hunger pangs. He pulled the first bag into his lap and began to shovel the fries in. Ahhh. That was so much better. Kahuna was like crack to him. No other fries and burgers came close to the greasy goodness now populating his taste buds.

He finished the fries in mere seconds, considering Payne's people as he ripped the wrapper off the double-double, all while crossing three lanes of traffic to make the left on 3rd. Why do pricks always seem to have the money? The answer was simple but not particularly satisfying. Because they're pricks.

He wanted to be late, just to show them who really had the power. He sunk his teeth into the long-awaited first bite. Orgasmic. If women could be as satisfying as this burger, he'd make a point to have a date every night of the week. The moment of satisfaction burned through his brain. It was a high as potent as any drug on earth. He downed the second, stopping only briefly to consider the greasy goodness, then mowed through the third, placing the last bite in his mouth as he pulled into the parking garage.

Matt grabbed the Big Kahuna fries for Ransick and sucked down the remaining contents in the Sumo cup. A large belch was brewing in his gut, but it would have to wait for the elevator. If he released it now, it would echo through the garage like a distress call. He adjusted his belt buckle down as he waited for the elevator. 12:58 p.m. Where is the damn elevator? So much for the power play he had planned in the car.

The elevator doors popped open, and he pressed the number five multiple times, hoping that pressing it more often would cause the metal box to rise faster. The machine rattled its way upward, finally settling and opening as the digital reading on his watch read 1:00 p.m.

"Hi Matt…" Claire chirped from behind the reception desk. "Ransick is waiting for you in C-3."

"Thanks, Claire."

He waddled his way along the long corridor toward C-3 at the other end of the office. With windows on all sides, it was a perfect spot to deliver what is often bad news. Matt picked up the pace, craning his head over cubicles, trying to catch a glimpse of the room's mood through the modern glass doors. Ransick had already fogged them. He dropped the fries on Ransick's desk, grabbed his tablet, and prepared for battle. He opened the large glass door to find Ransick waiting with Payne's people at the far end of the table.

"Matt," said one of the Payne people, an elegantly dressed woman who looked like she just stepped out of a magazine. "Nice of you to join us."

Her eyes scanned over Matt's appearance, landing directly on his rather expensive, red striped tie. Matt looked down to find a glob of mayo that must have dripped from his burger. Great.

"Let's hope you keep the books cleaner than your appearance," she said, as the others offered chuckles of approval. "Just try not to get any grease on the paperwork."

Payne's people outlined the tragedy that happened nearly a week before. Matt remembered the headlines in his social feed but didn't think much of it at the time, other than that it was a terrible accident not far from where he worked. He recalled traffic was still pretty backed up when he left the office that evening.

"If you're not familiar with what we are talking about, Matt, it may serve you well to catch up on the accident and subsequent media buzz," the woman said directly to Matt after going over the situation. "I know you have an eye for detail, and we need your eagle eye to catch anything that could affect the settlement. Mr. Payne wants this taken care of quickly. We'd like settlement checks prepared and distributed by the end of next week."

When the meeting ended, Matt headed directly to his desk. He opened his email to find a message from the woman in the meeting already in his inbox, including links to a number of videos related to the crash. He clicked on the first link and watched the video, then proceeded to review it an additional nineteen times. Why couldn't he stop watching this? Apparently, he wasn't alone. The clip had been viewed over 15,961,234 times, and growing by the second. Maybe because it was…weird. And unbelievable.

He spent the rest of the day watching the links, reviewing every frame and memorizing details about the crash itself, how it was reported, the people involved, and the murky images of the young woman at the center of the controversy. He preferred the word *miracle* but knew Payne's people would never see it that way.

Definitely some crazy shit, he surmised, as he leaned back into the rather uncomfortable office chair. The metal frame released a loud squeak under his weight. His thoughts turned to the offer before him. Why in the world would they make this kind of offer? The numbers were almost too embarrassing to type. The list of names sat before him on the screen. He pondered each person's circumstance. Ten thousand dollars per passenger. That was it. He had prepared fender bender settlements larger than this.

Matt had prepared countless settlement checks at the firm over the years. Never had he seen such a pathetic total figure at the bottom of a spreadsheet. And the dump truck driver? Not even on the list. He was told the man would receive seven-and-a-half weeks of severance. One week for each year of service times 0.5. It was utterly disgusting.

Later that night, he typed the final figures into the spreadsheet. "Are you fucking kidding me?" he uttered to himself. He thought maybe his tired eyes had read the email wrong. He double-checked to be sure. Breeland, his boss, had sent the email just after midnight and about three beers too late. The email's chime had roused Matt from a deep sleep. He had read an earlier email that the spreadsheet was due by 9:00 a.m. He figured he had plenty of time if he went in before 6:00 a.m.

The following morning, his desk phone was already ringing when he opened the door, a light flashing indicating he had messages. Three annoying flashes every morning it seemed that reminded him of just what a grind his job had become. He grabbed the call just before it went to voicemail.

"Matt, come down here a sec," Breeland barked into his ear. "I have a question about the Payne numbers." More like, he's in pain over the numbers, thought Matt. But what was the point in expressing it.

"Sure thing," Matt answered, returning the receiver to its cradle.

He tapped his mouse, bringing the spreadsheet to the foreground. Methodically hitting print, he rose from his chair, stretching a little before padding down the hall to Breeland's office.

He passed Sheri, Dick Breeland's obnoxious, beady-eyed assistant. God, he hated that woman, though he couldn't exactly pinpoint why. Perhaps because she had organized the collection of shitty meetings that led to this unfortunate settlement.

"Is he expecting you, Matt?" she asked in a rather condescending way, giving him a body check with her eyes in the process.

Like that. As if he didn't know his own schedule.

"Yes, Sheri. He called me, and that's why I'm here," he said, giving her a knowing glance. She stared at him blankly.

"Because he called, Sheri. I'm here because he…called."

"Matt! Get in here!" Breeland shouted from the corner of his spacious office.

He entered through the double doors. As usual, Breeland was sitting on the pale blue sofa tucked away in the far corner. The view of the Seattle skyline never got old, and Matt wondered what it would be like to walk in and see a breathtaking view of Elliot Bay every morning instead of his view of random homeless people pissing in the middle of Pioneer Square.

The décor of the room looked like it had been pulled directly from the set of *Mad Men*. Well, more *Mod Men*, to be exact with the addition of the steel-frame bookshelves and sort of hunting lodge accents. Breeland obviously had other people design the space before he arrived because what he layered on top of the modern chic décor—antlers, cigar boxes, and Carnegie hardcovers—just didn't seem to belong there. Now that he was really taking it all in, Matt thought the actual description would be *cave man* if it were ever featured on one of the bazillions of HGTV shows that would flash by his remote now and then. Not that he ever stopped to actually watch or anything.

"Come in. Have a seat," Breeland signaled, not bothering to look up from his phone.

Matt watched Breeland clumsily type in a text. The early morning sunlight splashed onto the desk, shooting the light almost directly into Breeland's eyes. It highlighted his gray hair and wrinkles around his eyes, making him look much older than he actually was. In ordinary office light, Breeland's face remained relatively smooth for a man his age. Matt guessed mid-fifties, but Breeland's stature and manly good looks made him appear almost timeless. It was probably all that time in the "great outdoors" that he was always bragging about. The guy was in love with his masculine side. Matt watched him with envy. He handed a copy of the report over to Breeland. He flipped to the spreadsheet, and reached for his reading glasses before speaking.

"So, Matt, I was looking over the figures and thought there must be some sort of mistake," Breeland began.

"How so?" Matt questioned.

"Well, it seems pathetically low for one, not to mention no check for the driver. I saw that he is receiving the standard severance. I thought we were missing some zeros or something."

"No, Dick," Matt said, making sure to accentuate the man's name. He always had a feeling of satisfaction saying it. His own private joke. "Those were the numbers provided by Payne himself. Would you like me to resend the email? I believe you were copied on it."

Breeland paused for a moment as if to consider a response, glanced at his phone nervously, and then cleared his throat. "No, no," he said waving his hand dismissively. "Well, maybe. When you have a moment."

Matt had worked with Breeland long enough to know that "a moment" meant "this moment." He dug into his pocket to retrieve his phone, entered his code, and proceeded to find the email.

"Mr. Payne was adamant that the numbers remained fixed as a first, last, and final," Matt added as he hit the send button on the email. "He instructed that we are to pull from Payne Industries, Inc., not Eagle Waste Management, the subsidiary."

"But why?" Breeland asked, as he waited for the email to come through. It arrived with an alert sound, and he opened it, quickly reviewing the information.

"I think he is trying to avoid a class action against the parent company, not just Eagle. Thus, he's going right to the top to end it. That's my two cents, anyway."

"I don't like the accounting on this one," Breeland said, as his eyes lifted from the spreadsheet. "Did you advise him that this could get messy?"

"You know Mr. Payne and his people, Dick," Matt said. "It's a one-way communication style."

"I suppose," said Breeland. "Well, I'll call him later this morning to verify. In the meantime, please be on-call for any changes necessary. They want this wrapped up as quickly as possible. The less time that passes, the faster we can close our part in this entire matter."

He looked at Matt then, as if to convince himself. He drew a long breath in before continuing.

"For most of these folks, ten thousand will be a life changer," he said. "I watched the news last night and, I mean, considering these people walked away unharmed, even healed—their words!—I would think it's a generous offer. Don't you think so?"

Matt looked down at the document in his hands, not sure how to answer. Generous? *Generous?* That was a word he would never use in this situation. Ever. He was used to cutting at least six figure checks in any settlement Payne proceeded with. This was truly unprecedented.

"If I may speak freely, sir?" Matt asked. Breeland studied him for a moment, before giving him the nod.

"Those poor people, in some cases literally, boarded a bus likely because they couldn't afford any other way around town. They sit back to endure what is probably a long, tedious ride made longer by countless stops from here to there. They wake up to find themselves under heaps of mangled metal and, miraculously, retrieved from the claws of death. This had to be a situation, rather, a life-altering event both terrifying and, from everything I've seen on video, mind-blowing. Now, they are about to be told that they will be given ten grand for their unfortunate luck and burden of boarding the bus that day. Even the most bargain basement auto insurance policy would pay more than what Payne offered this unlucky group of individuals."

Breeland stared at him blankly, as if Matt were speaking a foreign language. In the case of Breeland, it was probably true. The man was born with a silver spoon in his mouth and had inherited the firm from his father. He wouldn't know poor if it hit him in the face, much less the language of it all.

"So, we're supposed to walk in there and say, 'Gee, sorry that happened to you. We hope you'll accept our *generous* offer.' It all just seems a little naïve of Payne to not expect a fight from these people. That's all I'm saying here."

Breeland began to drum his fingers nervously.

"Matt, I'll handle Mr. Payne, and you keep your thoughts on this to yourself. I don't want anyone outside this case knowing a thing about this, got it?"

Matt fumed at the response. After years of service and working on settlements far bigger than this, the least he deserved was to be heard sincerely by the man who ran the place. Why he thought Breeland was any different was his mistake.

"That's all for now, you may go," he said as he made his way to the wall of windows overlooking the bay. "Oh, and Matt?"

"Yes, Dick?" Matt answered, peeling himself off the vinyl chair. He glanced toward the wet bar, fully expecting to see a butler pouring a drink. God knows he would need one after the settlement meeting.

"Stay away from the fast-food places for lunch today. Payne's people will be here at one, and your appearance yesterday was noticed. Keep extra ties in your office and try a salad for a change? We have a reputation to protect here. I'll have Sheri prep the proposals. We'll go through it all then."

Matt nodded and walked through the double doors, not even giving Sheri a second thought. His rage was growing with each step back to his office. How dare Breeland question his numbers! And his appearance? He had saved their asses so many times, yet they pick this moment to question the numbers and his lunch choices? Fuck all of them! He'd drive to Kahuna the second they opened, and this time, he may ask for extra ketchup to decorate his blue striped tie ahead of their little meeting, a little symbolic blood for the fight that was about to take place between him and Payne.

CHAPTER EIGHT

Jaxson flipped mindlessly through the channels. He looked for a report on the crash but landed on breaking news in Switzerland. Even though the news was tragic, he stayed on it for a while. It was a welcome change from the continuing coverage about the accident.

"Hmm," he pondered out loud, considering the bombing that had happened just eight hours before in the Swiss capital. Blasts of this nature were turning into a daily occurrence.

Every time he saw an incident like this one on the news, his thoughts would turn to Jayden. He wondered what part of the world his brother was occupying, and more importantly, what business he was performing. He pictured his brother under some sinister disguise, blending in among nations. A secret archangel waiting in the wings for the moment to pounce. Jayden had twenty years of service under his belt, enough to retire, but Special Forces had a powerful hold on his brother. He was certain that the decorated soldier would not separate easily from the life he created in service. It wasn't just a career for Jayden; it was his full-blown identity. The conversation they had all those years ago in their bedroom made him chuckle now, considering how well his brother had done in the Army. He couldn't imagine him doing anything else.

Jaxson continued to watch the images unfold on the news for a while. What a mess. He wasn't even sure if that thought was directed toward the state of worldwide terrorism or his own situation. Jaxson was beginning to feel like a prisoner, spending the better part of a week bedridden in a hospital bed and nearly another two at home under close observation. The hospital staff seemed completely perplexed by recent events. His once debilitating Type I diabetes was now completely absent, and they wanted to understand why.

"Doc, I think you need to just chalk this one up to a good old-fashioned miracle," Jaxson remembered saying as he packed up his meager belongings for his release from the hospital. The endocrinologist Jaxson had been seeing since his diagnosis was beginning to show signs of age. He considered what Jaxson had said and then, judging from his change in facial expression, quickly dismissed it altogether.

"Jaxson, what we are seeing in these labs is nothing short of extraordinary," Dr. Frain said as he located the pen in his pocket, scanned the paperwork and, after a careful pause, signed the release forms. He gave Jaxson a pensive look as he passed the papers to the nurse. He waited for her to leave the room before speaking.

"We both know this disease has had a firm grip on you for years, Jaxson," the doctor began. "You know as well as I that your symptoms were only getting worse, especially related to your diabetic neuropathy. Not even a month before the accident, we were beginning discussions about clinical trials because your symptoms were worse. That was before I had any idea that your vision was so adversely affected."

"Doc, I would have told you if I had known it was going to be a problem," Jaxson said. "I thought I could manage it." His eyes fell to the floor.

It was the first time he even considered his doctor in all of this. This one omission of fact could cost the doctor big time, especially had he been allowing his diabetic patient to drive with worsening symptoms. He scanned his memory in that moment, trying to locate the conversation and exactly what he had said about his symptoms. The doctor's voice broke up the frantic search.

"While I am cautiously optimistic about your progress since the accident, and the fact that your lab results show that you are no longer symptomatic, I'm not at all certain it won't return." He gave Jaxson a thoughtful stare, as if willing his words to sink in fully before proceeding.

"We are going to keep a close eye on you while you rest at home," the doctor continued. "We will have a nurse assigned to you so that we can monitor symptoms and offer a plan for moving forward. If we see that you show no signs of the disease, then we are going to want to study you further to understand exactly why this happened. You could be the key to reversing this debilitating disease."

"I'll do whatever you need, Doc," Jaxson said, excited about the thought of returning home and sleeping in his own bed. "But know that, right now, in this moment, I'm simply grateful," Jaxson said, tossing his hospital toothbrush into a plastic bag. "My legs and feet don't hurt. My vision? Never better. I feel like I've been given a second chance here, and I'm just going to try and enjoy my life without any thought of insulin shots and managing blood sugar."

He sat down on the bed to pull his shoes on and then looked up at his doctor. He was genuinely worried that something he said or didn't say would cost this man his livelihood. Dr. Frain was the captain who navigated the murky waters of his disease. When he considered a life free of symptoms and medication, it was a tremendous relief.

"I'm sorry I didn't tell you," Jaxson said as he looked the doctor square in the eyes. "I really didn't think my vision was a thing. I remember things getting blurry, but I just thought it was a spike or something. The next thing I know, the truck is upside down and everything was dark. I had never been so scared. Then, light. Peace. Like the hymn, was blind but now I see."

Dr. Frain pushed the hymn from his mind as he put a hand on his patient's shoulder. "I'm all for miracles, Jaxson. But I'd feel a lot better if it were confirmed by science."

"Fine, fine," Jaxson said, nodding his head in agreement. "Whatever you need me to do."

Jaxson had followed the orders at home, welcoming in the nurse each day to check his vitals and engage in small talk. It was a moment of light in his otherwise dark and boring day. He took a long sip of strong coffee, staring at the dark liquid in his favorite mug. His eyes returned to the images on the screen. So much darkness in this world, he thought.

After several minutes of staring mindlessly at the images of the bombing, he was relieved when Keisha walked in. Finally, a return to the light. She was incredibly self-assured for such a young professional, and her bedside manner seemed to imply more therapist than day nurse.

"Hey, Jaxson, how are you feeling today?" Keisha asked just a hair above the din of the noise coming from the screen. He could hear her removing her coat and gathering her things before pouring a glass of water. He insisted she make herself at home, but she remained a total professional, always offering a glass before starting the blood draw.

"Hey, Keisha," he spoke up, clicking the off button on the remote in the process.

He decided to leave the darkness inside the box today. Keisha walked into the room, eyes crinkling in the corners, a big smile spreading across her full lips upon seeing his face.

"See? I'm feeling fine as wine, girl," Jaxson added and returned her smile. Same as yesterday, he wanted to add, but decided against it.

"You do look well today," she said, pulling up a chair and handing him the glass of water before dropping her medical bag by her feet. She checked his blood pressure, pulse, and blood sugar, then drew his blood for further testing. The standard routine.

"Remarkable," she said after a moment, staring at the numbers she had jotted down. "It's as if you were never diabetic." She threw in another one of her award-winning smiles. He volleyed another her way.

"How can that be?" Her eyes met him with deep intention, as if to will the truth from the body before her.

"I honestly have no idea, but I feel better than I have in years. No tingling in my feet, pain in my legs. My vision is just perfect, and my blood sugar ups and downs seem to be a thing of the past," Jaxson said as he rose from the chair. "I nearly died in a crash caused by diabetes only to emerge free from it entirely. Go figure."

She watched him stroll out of the room. He really was fine, and she didn't just mean his state of being. His six-foot frame was a vision. His dimples made it hard to keep it professional. Gorgeous, she thought. So, why wasn't he married? She was dying to ask him that question but thought the better of it as she glanced at the stethoscope in her lap.

He emerged from the kitchen with two cups of hot tea in hand.

"So, am I good to go or what?" Jaxson asked as he handed over the steaming mug. She picked up on a hint of orange and allowed it to linger before answering. She knew he wanted out of the house, but he was going to have to wait out the week as the doctor ordered.

"Jaxson, you know the answer to this one. You ask me every single day, and my answer hasn't changed. You only have one more week. Everyone wants to make sure you're all right before you resume your normal life."

"You mean, Mr. Payne wants to make sure you keep my ass out of his truck and my face off the TV," Jaxson said with a smirk. "I am not sick, Keisha. You've checked in on me every day for a few weeks now, not to mention the couple I spent in the hospital before that. I am ready to move past this."

"I know, I know. But I have a job to do, Jaxson," she said sympathetically. "The fact you have not only recovered from the accident but also are seemingly cured from Type I diabetes is nothing short of a miracle. You could—"

"—be the key to curing this insidious disease. I know, I know, I know. But I also know this is about money and lawsuits. I don't want to work for him anymore! I told you that!"

He paused for a moment before continuing.

"And don't think I don't know you're documenting every conversation that goes on here. Well, let me say for the record that I consider this set of circumstances a wake-up call for the ages. I've been given a second chance and want to live my life to the fullest, not spend my days driving mindlessly from route to route. By God or the universe or whatever you call it, I am here and nearly all of those people are OK. For those who aren't, I'm eternally sorry. OK? I'm sorry. Is that what I need to say to get the hell out of here?"

He turned to the window, watching the hummingbirds hover around the feeder. The only bird to fly backward, he thought. How appropriate for this moment. All the momentum in the world, yet he felt like his was stalled. Wings frantically flapping but no movement forward. Only backward. He was so sick of this house. He was certain he would leave and never return upon his release from these walls.

Keisha studied him for a long moment before responding.

"Jaxson, nobody is out to get you here, I promise," she began. "I will talk to Dr. Frain and submit my report tonight. I hear you. I just want to be sure, that's all. This is my livelihood we're talking about here. My reputation. I don't want to get this wrong. My daughter depends on it."

Jaxson turned from the window to face her. God he was selfish, he thought, as he crossed the room and placed a hand on her shoulder, giving her a gentle nudge of encouragement.

"Don't worry about it," he said. "Just submit it on the deadline. It's only a week. I can manage."

"You just want to get my ass out of here so you can go back to your video games and game shows," she teased.

"I do love me some *Family Feud*," he said, dimples emerging. Her heart leapt at the sight.

He plopped down into the recliner and stretched his legs before reaching for the remote. Keisha reached for her medical bag and returned her mug to the kitchen.

"They have a new *Star Wars* opening this weekend," he said while she washed out her cup. "Didn't you say your girl loves those movies?"

Keisha emerged from the kitchen, bag over her shoulder. "She does, but we're probably gonna wait. Too many lines."

"But that's part of the fun," he said as he flipped the remote from channel to channel. "All those weirdos and their costumes."

"Hey now, my girl is one of those weirdos," she said with a laugh. She could see his image laughing in the mirror that hung across the living room. He looked happy, content. She considered him more than a patient for a brief moment.

"Maybe next week," she added, pulling keys from the corner pocket of her bag. "Take care of yourself, Jaxson, and I'll see you on Monday. Hopefully, with the final checklist before your release." She gave him a smile before heading out the door, sun spilling into the room, just missing the edge of his chair.

"Leave it open, would you?" he asked as she stepped through the door. She nodded before heading down the steps.

Damn. Another weekend alone. Before the accident, he couldn't even count the number of weekends he spent solo without a second thought. But now, things were different. He wanted the connection and inclusion that only human contact could offer. Well, it's only a little while longer, he thought. He survived the accident, he would survive this too.

His mind wandered to a thought of Keisha and her little girl in line. He imagined the two, surrounded by Wookies and light sabers. While he never met his nurse's daughter, he imagined her as a little mini-me—a more beautiful, darker throwback to Leia, with fake buns in place of ears. He smiled at the thought.

When he really thought about it, he realized a couple of weeks were nothing in the span of a lifetime. A mere blip.

He closed his eyes to take in fully the spring weather that crept into the room. His favorite season. For fifteen years, he had waited for a second chance in life. Perhaps this time he'd actually get out of the starting blocks. On your mark. Get set. He was waiting for the gun to fire.

As if on cue, his phone ring spewed the sound of bullets into the air. It was Jayden's ring. He jumped to his feet and raced to the phone plugged into the charger.

"Hey, Brotha!" Jaxson greeted him enthusiastically. "I thought you were overseas!"

"Hey, Jax. The commander told me about the accident," Jayden said solemnly into the phone. He sounded a bit distant, but that wasn't uncommon after coming off of an assignment.

"Hey, I'm just fine, better than fine actually," Jaxson said, easing his brother's fears.

"Well, it's a good thing then because this incident and a few others this past month were the final push I needed," Jayden said.

"Are you finally taking that Pentagon gig?" Jaxson asked.

"No, Jax. I'm coming home. For good."

CHAPTER NINE

As the plane descended, the bright sun moved comfortably into its warm gray blanket, ready for a long nap. Pyrus sighed as he watched the rays fade away. This is why he hated the Northwest. Gloomy was the only way to describe the weather and the short trip in general. He couldn't wait to get it over with.

The pilot spoke just as Pyrus put his tablet back in the briefcase.

"Sir, we'll be landing in a few minutes, so time to buckle up and throw that whiskey back."

Pyrus chuckled, as he set the glass down. The pilot, Sam, knew him so well. Gabrielle, the flight attendant and Sam's rather shapely wife, came to retrieve the glass and bring him a hot cloth for his face. He wiped away the stress and tension, if only for a brief moment. He wished Jade had decided to join him, but then he thought the better of it. She would have complained the entire time, something about not being able to wear her favorite suede pumps. The woman was high maintenance, but it was a small price to pay for her beauty and company.

"Anything else I can get you, sir?" Gabrielle asked, as she passed by his seat. The dress today was particularly clingy.

"No, darlin'. I'm fine. Just need to take a moment before

this rather long, boring day. He winked at her then, and she smiled rather coyly.

He could see the outline of her hips and the mold of her ample breasts. Sam was a lucky man. Was it wrong that he coveted the man's wife? Not really. Power definitely had its privileges. It was this knowledge, rather feeling, that made him aroused. Not to mention the woman was unbelievably gorgeous.

"Have that whiskey ready for me when I board this afternoon."

"Of course, sir," she said, her lips perfectly pouting the reply. Her long, auburn hair draped elegantly past her shoulders. Was there ever a time when she didn't look perfect? Pyrus couldn't recall. She had always reminded him of Jessica Rabbit—a cartoon that had beautifully come to life.

He watched her walk to her seat and buckle in, the strap barely able to cover her bustline. Sam was seriously lucky. It would take a minute for the bulge in his pants to subside. He thought of the settlement then, and his arousal faded. Problem solved.

The plane touched down as the rain pelted the windows. Seattle was particularly blue today, like a beautiful woman who is sick all the time. Sam said that once, and Pyrus couldn't agree more. He longed for the Vegas weather or the sunny skies of his youth in the Deep South.

He had made a point to avoid this remote part of the country since college. He still loved his Huskies for sure, but the rest he could leave behind in a second. He worked as a garbage man while attending the University of Washington. All through school, he invested smartly, and by graduation, he had plans to buy the company. That's how the world worked for Pyrus—working hard while others weren't. Sacrificing, saving. Some luck and timing. But it all came down to seizing the opportunity when it appeared, and when it did, Pyrus never hesitated.

He could hear his mama's southern drawl so clearly in his head.

"Are you out of your ever lovin' mind, son?"

His parents were the bane of his existence, or at least that's how he remembered it. Mom loved her liquor and gardeners. Father had a penchant for gambling and mouths from the South. Funny thing was it didn't matter if they were framed in lipstick or cigar smoke. His father tried desperately to hide his bisexuality, but everyone knew—perhaps, everyone but the man himself. He never admitted to it, even on his death bed at the age of forty-seven. The death certificate stated pneumonia as the cause, but everyone knew it was AIDS. Southern folks don't like to admit the truth publicly, at least not where Pyrus grew up. It was much easier to bury heads in the Gulf Coast sands.

While his parents didn't set the best example, one thing Pyrus did know is that they were cunning. It was a trait he would carry with him well into adulthood. After all, it took careful planning to keep up a perfect appearance all those years while fucking the gardener in the guest house or giving some guy a blow job in a swamp. How the two weren't swallowed by gators in all those years of indiscretion was beyond Pyrus.

He didn't care that his childhood was all a smokescreen. He had money, prestige, and all-American good looks. That last one served him well when it all came crashing down after his father's funeral. Years of back taxes and gambling debts left the plantation in the hands of the government. His mother moved on rather quickly to an overweight, loudmouthed oil baron. Pyrus was tainted seed in the new man's eyes. It turned out his father had fucked the man's sister and her husband. Many suspected it had gone on for years. Mother didn't care. She was happy to resume her lifestyle, with or without her son.

Pyrus made his way west to the most remote location he could find. He considered the wilds of Alaska for a minute, but Seattle was about as far as he could get with his money at the time. It was fun for the first summer before he started school. Then, the rain arrived and the suffering began. He spent his early mornings running garbage routes, long afternoons in classes, and endless evenings studying at the library. Except for the occasional co-ed, his fun in college was limited, but his funds were ample. Pyrus was determined to be the all-around success his parents had not been.

Two days before graduation, he decided to reward himself with a night out with the boys. He hadn't made many friends in college, but the two he did have were usually found at the local bar, cheering on this or that on the screen. Sports never really interested Pyrus, except for college football. There was a passion there that the pros just seemed to lack. It was as if signing a big contract was at the expense of the reasons why they played in the first place. That evening would lead him down a different path the moment Candace walked through the door.

Candace was beautiful, smart, and charming. She impressed him with her extensive knowledge of whiskey and her father's ample fortune. Their night together was passionate, almost tantric. Their carefree, whirlwind romance was interrupted a month later by a double line on a pregnancy test. Within two months, the couple were wed at her father's mansion, just about the time Candace was beginning to show. They welcomed their son the following winter.

Their small, mewling son had Candace's soulful brown eyes and, except for the shape of his eyes and outline of his mouth, had little resemblance to his father. A tear in her uterine wall during delivery meant the boy would be their only child. Pyrus was fine with that. Children were never part of the plan anyway. This just meant he kept up appearances a little faster than he intended.

Candace chose to stay home with the boy, and the two were inseparable. While Pyrus thought her choice was lazy, he did like the appearance that a family brought to the boardroom. It made him more successful to investors: a better risk. Over time, Candace and her happy housewife act began to drive him nuts. He wanted the kind of woman on his arm that his counterparts had: models, actresses, the gorgeous and instafamous. His wife paled in comparison to the others at the countless functions they attended and it was becoming painfully obvious she was older. His counterparts preferred to trade in first wives for a younger, flashier second. He couldn't wait to be rid of her when their son was grown. In the meantime, he filled his time and share of vaginas on the various trips he took in the name of "business."

When Candace became ill, Pyrus decided it was time to separate. He really didn't care how she went about treatment and recovery. She no longer served him, and that was a problem. He knew his behavior would force her to make decisions about him, their son, and the future.

After a year of insufferable acts of mistreatment, she finally conceded and hired a divorce attorney. The boy, now a teen, fully supported his mother in every way. Pyrus

Jamie J. Kemp

wondered for a while if the breakup would affect his image. It actually was quite the opposite. Because it had been Candace's decision, he looked like the victim. Women of all ages and backgrounds immediately flocked to his side in support. They threw themselves at him for the better part of three years before he finally settled on Jade. She was just as conniving and difficult as he was, and that only made him want her more. He couldn't wait to get home to her, listen to her soft purrs in his ear, and then seduce her in the kitchen before he would carry her slender, perfect body off to bed.

The chopper was waiting on the tarmac, the blades creating a monsoon effect of the weather, whipping up rain and wind as he struggled toward the open door. It would be a short flight to downtown—just enough time to review the settlement. He didn't bother to look on the flight up. He was too busy eyeing his next venture, a resort in Dubai. Jade loved the Middle East. It would make a nice birthday gift, if she could behave herself until then. He knew something was up with the trainer. Ordinarily, he would aggressively confront her for lying to him like she did, but he was too busy with the settlement to care. For now. The cameras he had installed in the gym would eventually reveal the truth.

Ordinarily, Pyrus wouldn't bother with a meeting like this. But the videos surrounding the crash were intriguing, and he could sense an opportunity in the making. If this woman could do what he believed she could do, there was no telling how far he could take it. Unless it was all an elaborate hoax. He hoped his people weren't wrong on this one. The video was certainly promising evidence. The views were in the hundreds of millions in a matter of days. If nothing else, it was a good marketing opportunity for the resort, a sort of last hurrah before he blew it to smithereens and started over.

The chopper touched down on the roof minutes later, and he found himself back in the rain briefly. Why the woman who greeted him was walking so slowly was beyond him. Keeping his eyes low to avoid the spray of rain on his face, he noticed the high heels that adorned her feet. The impossibly high platforms made her look like she belonged wrapped around a pole rather than in a settlement meeting, not that he minded the idea.

"We're in the main conference room, sir—down the hall and to the left," she said, gesturing like she was on *Wheel of Fortune*. Pathetic, he thought, as he walked past her, allowing Peter, his lead counsel, to take the lead.

"How long is this going to take, Peter?" he asked, glancing at the Tag Hauer watch on his wrist, a gift from Jade. Rolex would have been better.

"For your part, about an hour, sir, if they all agree," Peter answered.

Peter rolled his eyes, giving the signal that it could take considerably longer if the parties didn't agree. They had better agree, Pyrus thought. He didn't have time for this bullshit. Peter knew the look Pyrus was giving him. He wanted it over with as much as the boss did.

He walked into the conference room to find the group waiting. He looked at the faces around the table, searching for the young woman from the video. They all looked eager, maybe even a little irritated. How could these people not be grateful for what he could provide? Poor people, he thought, grateful for the smallest gesture and greedy when it came to the largest. It was as if the entitlement increased with every decimal.

"Let's get this show on the road, shall we?" Pyrus said, confidently seating himself at the head of the table.

As he took his seat, his fingers immediately began drumming on the table's surface. The doors flew open then; a young woman entered looking flustered and disorganized. Late, he thought. Pyrus hated when people were late. It was disrespectful of his time.

"Sorry about that," she said breathlessly, scanning the room for a place to sit. "My Uber took forever and I'm not inclined to ride the bus these days." She said hello to her fellow passengers, offering hugs to a few as she made her way around the enormous conference room table.

The chubby man sitting to his left bolted from his chair quickly, offering his seat. Pyrus was less than pleased as he observed the man's disheveled appearance. Why in the world would the firm employ such a slob? He made a mental note to have Breeland fire him once the settlement paperwork concluded.

"Thank you," she said, her gaze leaving the fat man's face and turning to Pyrus.

Even though she quietly took her seat, Pyrus noted that the entire room was captivated by her. This woman had presence, yet lacked confidence. Every eye was on her, awaiting her next move with bated breath. He was annoyed, considering they should all have eyes on the man who was about to change their futures.

He observed her carefully, allowing his first impression to sink in. He watched the room as well, considering the reactions of the survivors. He was usually right about these things, but considering his plan, it was important to confirm what he felt in is gut. She appeared warm, inviting. She put people at ease. She wasn't aware of this, and that was to his advantage. That's what made it so strange. She was likely impressionable, gullible. It would be easy to mold her and shape her to fit his plan. Opportunity in the making, Pyrus thought, his lips curving to form an evil smile. This could be his biggest money maker yet.

He sat quietly, wondering who would begin. It wouldn't be himself. He knew that for a fact. Peter opened the meeting with a brief overview of the accident and presented the facts of the case, carefully choosing his words.

"Mr. Washington was driving at approximately fifty miles an hour, fifteen miles over the speed limit. This was due to the fact he suffered a diabetic episode. The medical situation caused him to experience symptoms of nausea, sweating, and general malaise. As a result, Mr. Washington did run the red light, resulting in the crash. The company stands by Mr. Washington in these findings and is prepared to offer each person here a lump-sum payment of ten thousand dollars."

The room was silent, as if waiting for Peter to continue.

Pyrus watched their faces as each one carefully considered the offer on the table. Ungrateful idiots, the lot of them, he thought. Peter swallowed hard before proceeding.

"Payne Industries understands that the accident caused undo stress on many of you, but the facts show that it actually improved the lives of most of you. A young boy who is now cured of his autism. One of you noted a disappearance of hives after the accident. And a third was confirmed by her doctor to be free of cancer. These are extraordinary outcomes. We hope this money will give you a fresh start and allow you to put it toward a new future that this accident has offered. This is a chance to pursue your dreams."

"What are dreams, anyway?" Pyrus asked, gaze drifting toward the window. "Are they nothing more than fragments of our shattered bliss?" He lingered on the last word, careful to ask the question with a certain uptick in his voice.

"I had dreams once," he spoke again, turning toward the room this time.

"What a lot of people don't know about me is that I was the victim of a hit-and-run crash when I was at University of Washington," Pyrus said, scanning the room for reaction. A few raised their eyebrows. A couple more crossed their arms in a defensive gesture. Pyrus pushed forward.

"A man nearly ran me over with his car while I was biking to school. He didn't have insurance, so I didn't receive a settlement. But I didn't whine or snivel. I picked myself up by the bootstraps. I worked hard during my rehab at Harborview. I built something from nothing. I worked for two years to earn the money to pay back the hospital for my stay. I lived on tuna in a can."

He caught himself then, careful not to jar his audience. He wanted to make sure they heard him, but he didn't want to scare them. Yet. It was his job to hook them, convince them that this was the best deal they would ever get in their lives. Peter clearly wasn't capable of it.

Pyrus turned to one of the fortunate in the room, first gazing, then piercing into the man's soul with his eyes. He paused before speaking, rubbing his lips together as if to hold back the thought from escaping his throat.

"This is the best deal you're ever going to get."

Most in the room were engaged with what he was saying. The series of sentences he was stringing together to make it sound like he cared about their lives and well-being was making him nauseous. The truth was he didn't give a shit about these people. He wanted this meeting to be over as quickly as possible.

He was just about to glance at the last pair of eyes in the room when he saw her. Her face was serene. She didn't seem bothered by the conversation at all. She was taking in every word. That was clear. Her gaze never broke once. In fact, he didn't recall seeing her blink once. He dared her into a sort of staring contest as he laid out the forthcoming figures in the settlement, hoping it would rattle her somehow. It didn't. She was completely unphased. Almost disinterested. This was the woman who emerged from the wreckage unscathed. She was the one who supposedly brought the others back to life. He was intrigued then, watching for changes in her expression as he laid the offer on the table.

"So, ten thousand dollars in total for each of you right now," he paused for effect. "Another ten thousand this time next year," he paused again.

The mood remained for the most part, unchanged. "I'm sure for many of you this is more than generous, given you emerged from the wreckage injury free and well."

"You've said that a few times," a young man said with a cross of his arms.

He left the numbers to linger in the air with the others, not bothering to respond to the young man, who wouldn't know a future if it hit him in the face. These were life-changing sums, he thought, glancing around the room to see if any of them were on board with his inner monologue. The fat accountant to his left shifted, making a farting noise in the process. What a fucking slob.

"That was the chair," he said out loud. What an idiot. No one said a word.

"And you think this is enough, for each of us?" the young woman asked, rather coolly. "Life changing, as you put it?"

"Well, I think it's a very generous offer. I could just have insurance claims pay out the settlement, but I wanted to be, well, decent," he answered arrogantly.

"Life changing?" she asked again.

"Yes, I would say for the people in this room, that is a life-changing amount."

The young woman stared at him, watching as he rocked back and forth in his chair. She was close enough to strangle, he thought, but he needed her if there was going to be any sort of profit out of this pathetic situation.

Why don't you leave now?

He heard the voice so clearly in his head. What the fuck did she think she was doing? Using her voodoo magic to trick him into a new offer? Never!

He glanced around to see if others had heard it too. She had the audacity to ask him to leave his own meeting? Who the fuck did she think he was? Clearly, she didn't know who she was dealing with.

If you want the show and this situation to go away, leave now.

He glared at her openly, bolting out of the chair and stopping in front of the windows. The rain outside was relentless, water streaming down the glass. He wasn't about to leave his own meeting. This would be settled today or no deal.

I'll make sure the others agree.

A sense of calm fell over him, it was an uncomfortable feeling. He couldn't remember a time when he felt so out of control yet so completely content with the decision. It was off-putting and unsettling. He tried to shake it off, but it only intensified. He turned around to face the woman, a mere girl in his eyes, with no power whatsoever. Why had she intimidated him so?

Because you need me.

"No!" he shouted, slamming down his fist in front of her.

She merely smiled at his overreaction. The others tensed in the moment; a few started to gather their things to leave.

Then stay. Better yet, offer more.

The group looked at one another before returning their eyes to her. Each settled back into position, ready to receive a new offer from the head of the legal team.

"One hundred fifty thousand dollars each," he said. "Final offer."

She nodded to each of them before returning her gaze to Pyrus.

"We accept," she said calmly, extending her hand to formalize the agreement. He spat in his palm before clasping hers, a bolt of energy escaping into his body as she stared into his cold and crazy stare.

He wasn't intimidated by anyone, certainly not some spit of a girl from God knows where. He cleared his throat and broke from the unspoken contest between them. His anger was bubbling under the surface. He had to keep it at bay for the moment.

"Fuck you!" he shouted. He didn't care if she took the show or not. With that, he spun on his heel to leave the conference room, a cold, swift-moving breeze following him out.

I'll be there.

He stopped abruptly before exiting, slowly turning to face her. He returned her inner response with a glare before disappearing through the double doors.

How could these people not see what was before them? If he had that kind of money at a time when he really needed it, there is no telling what he would have done. What he could have become that much quicker! This little accident would set Eagle Waste Management back two years between the legal costs, settlement, and spiraling stock price. Two years! His pacing had become a sort of military march. It was intentional. He didn't want his emotions on display. He had to gain control. And the girl? A fucking shit show! Well, at least there would be a show, the only good thing to come out of this miserable trip. Her healing power, or whatever bullshit she was passing off as healing, wouldn't have any effect on him. She would make him money, nothing more.

He headed down an empty hallway and found a darkened office. He slipped in without anyone noticing. He didn't bother to turn on the light. He located the office chair and sat for a moment as a strange feeling overcame him. Was it worry? A foreign concept for sure. Perhaps... doubt? He couldn't put his finger on it. His gut was out of sorts. His feelings...were nonexistent. This was a negotiation, not a marriage proposal.

He thought of Jade then, her slight frame draped over him. Her full lips pressing gently on his cheek. He could taste the whiskey on his lips. A bulge was rising in his pants at the thought. He had to stop. He wanted nothing more than to escape the room, rather the building. Another ten minutes and he would slide into the town car, grab lunch at the bar of his favorite old haunt, board his private jet, and leave this whole situation behind him. For good.

He glanced at his watch. If he left now, he'd be home in time to get dinner with Jade. He lingered for a few minutes more before slipping back into the hallway. He marched right past the conference room and headed for the lobby. He wasn't going to loosen his grip by leaving now. It was this deal, or nothing. His presence, or lack thereof, was enough of a message. He walked right past the conference room and toward the elevators. He'd text Peter and have him offer the Vegas show to the young woman. No need to talk through the details face to face with her. She appeared to be real enough. He could fool the public for six weeks or so and make a profit. He may lose a little more than he intended here today, but if she took the show, he'd make far more than imagined, turning some very sour lemons into a lemon drop.

CHAPTER TEN

Una looked at the screen in wonder, considering her options. She could delete it and the endless trolls that were calling her video a sham, pointless, altered, and a host of other descriptive words she didn't care to consider. But what of the countless more who were enraptured by the images, wondering if they too could be saved by this miraculous woman? She felt helpless just watching the video take on a life of its own as others watched, commented on, and shared it in their own feeds. It didn't matter how it had come to life. All she knew was that her fate was in their hands, for better or worse. What mattered was what she was going to do with her gifts now that the show was upon her.

She knew that the crash and all that was to follow would be a true miracle in the making, laying out the possibility of what life could be without the limitations of the mind and circumstance. She just wanted to share her newly acquired experience and let others bathe in the possibilities. The comments were polarizing. Some were on the side of what they saw. Others were vehemently against all that it showed. Why would people not want others to be healed? It was so confusing to her.

"Knock, knock," Brit chimed at the bedroom door with only a crack of the door providing a view.

"Hey you, come on in," Una offered with a pat on the bedspread beside her.

"Whatcha doin'?" Brit asked lightly, watching the computer screen as she landed on the bedspread in a heap.

"I was looking at the comments from the videos that were posted," Una answered, wondering how much she should tell her friend about the show.

"You know I know," Brit said emphatically.

"I figured," Una said in an eyeroll.

"Good, because I want to talk about what's really going on…in you," she said, gesturing to her friend who was so different now that the crash was behind her.

"I'm honestly fine," Una began quietly. "I just, I just…"

She let a pause land between them, both searching each other's eyes for the answers, filling in the gaps they couldn't read. Una could read Brit's mind. She knew Brit doubted the whole thing at first, even going so far as to wonder if her friend was a fraud. But now, she seemed to be embracing this new reality or at least the fame that all the videos provided. She could sense Brit wanted to know more in that moment, and it was time to tell her the truth.

"It felt weird at first," Una said.

"Weird how?" Brit asked in usual lawyer fashion.

With a deep breath, Una unraveled the events of the crash. She walked her through the long day baking cupcakes in honor of Monet, the homeless man in the alley, the strange knowing before impact. Not a detail was left out as she watched Brit's face change with each vision in her memory. As she described the moments following the crash, her friend's face fell. She then walked her through the settlement, details she knew Brit would absorb given her current studies. Una unburdened herself and lay all her thoughts on the bed, the room, the house that stood around them. No detail, no feeling was missed.

"So, a hundred and fifty thousand dollars?" Brit asked. "That's better than ten, that's for sure."

"What happened to me, on that bus, it was the most peaceful feeling. It must have been what it was like when my mother first held me after emerging from the womb or something," she said. "I know that sounds crazy, but I'm totally serious. It changed me somehow… profoundly."

"I believe you. Go on," Brit encouraged.

"Well, Pyrus Payne, the one who owns the garbage company, he offered me a job, sort of."

"A job?" Brit asked, her eyes bulging from her head.

"Yes, and I said…yes."

The silence hung in the air; only the hum of the computer remained.

"You said 'yes' to what, exactly?" Brit said in her best future lawyer voice.

"I said 'yes' to healing others," Una answered calmly.

"I'm sorry, what?" Brit asked, incredulously.

"I have a show now. In a Vegas casino. I'm going to be healing people on a stage."

Brit looked at Una carefully before responding. "But how do you know you can still heal people?" she asked. "What if it was a one-time-only scenario?"

Una could almost see her friend's blood pressure rise as she responded.

"I thought about that at first, but then the settlement happened, and I changed the entire outcome of that meeting, Brit. With my mind."

She could see her friend was skeptical, but Una went on to explain how it worked: the energy in her field, the ability to move it toward another being, the influence and power she held inside her that she was just starting to discover.

"So, I am going to Vegas, and I am going to help people in a show. I really have no idea what it's about, but I'm all in. Isn't that what they say in Vegas? All in?"

"Oh my God, Una, do you hear yourself right now? This is crazy!" Brit rose from the bed in frustration, almost taking the bedspread with her. "You can't just leave your life because of what happened in a moment on a bus," she said in a scolding tone. "You have no idea if you can actually heal others. I don't care what you say happened in that settlement. That could have been a fluke! What if your ability was just an isolated incident? What if it was just brain chemistry or whatever as a result of the crash? You know, how mothers lift cars off their babies and stuff? Then, what? You stand on a stage and look like a complete fool. Or worse! This Payne guy sues you and takes you for everything you have!"

"And what exactly do I have, Brit?" Una asked. "I have a so-so job at a start-up bakery. I have one good friend in a city I have never been able to call home. What do I have that's holding me here?"

Brit stared at her friend, struggling to find a strong rebuttal.

"You need to think this through a little before blindly following some corporate trash to the desert," Brit said without blinking. "That man is known for exploiting anything and anyone in his path. I've looked into him. I'm just trying to look out for my friend here. You get why I'm concerned, right?"

Una took a deep breath before answering. "I just know this is my future."

The two friends stared at each other, as if closing the gap between two different worlds.

"You're fucking crazy, you know that?" Brit reached for her friend, knowing only physical contact could end this moment. The two embraced, and Brit could feel the confidence in her friend's grip, a sense of calm overcoming them both at the prospect of a future in the desert. Una urged her silently to support the move.

"I believe you," she finally said. She crossed the room and gently closed the door.

Una knew Brit wouldn't leave to follow her to Vegas. She had her own studies and future to consider, and while she believed Una's words, she was still skeptical of her power. Una needed people who believed in it if she were to make the show a success, much less survive Pyrus Payne. She knew they would come—a team of misfits banded together for the sole purpose of changing lives on that stage. She would start with Jaxson. Given the news of the settlement, she knew he would rise to the challenge. She pushed the computer to the side and closed her eyes to meditate. If she was going to make a go of this new life, she would need a far greater power behind her. She welcomed in the colors in her view, breathing in the comforting presence. She wouldn't just walk into her future blindly. She would co-create it.

CHAPTER ELEVEN

He recognized the number immediately. Weeks and weeks of worry had built up to this moment. He picked up on the third ring, holding back for a moment before hearing his fate.

"Hello?"

"Jaxson, it's Zach."

Jaxson gripped the phone, his knuckles turning white in the process. Zachariah Slade, his attorney, filled the phone with his thick New York accent.

"So, the settlement happened today. I wish you could have been there because I don't like to relay this kind of information over the phone."

"You know I wasn't cleared to leave the house," Jaxson said pensively. "And Pyrus? That guy would have eaten me for lunch. Total shark. You know that."

Zach sighed deeply then. Jaxson didn't take the bait. He let the moment breathe.

"Well, it's a case of good news, bad news," Zach proceeded. "The good news is that the final offer is on the table, and Mr. Payne will not be negotiating. He made that clear."

He paused for another moment. This time, Jaxson interjected.

"And?"

"Well, they offered each survivor a cash payout of one hundred fifty thousand dollars each."

The air felt heavy as Jaxson considered if this was the good or bad news.

"As for you," Zach said, pausing again before continuing, "they will offer you ten thousand dollars toward medical expenses, and they will pay you a week of pay for every year of service."

"Ten thousand dollars for medical?" Jaxson screeched into the phone. "The bill is ten times that amount! You've got to be kidding me!"

"There's more," Zach said, taking another deep breath into the receiver. "This obviously means you are out of a job, but I think you already know that."

"I do."

"And the company may..." Zach seemed hesitant to continue.

"The company..." Jaxson encouraged.

"The company plans to counter sue you, Jaxson," Zach said slowly. "For one million in damages."

"What?"

"I don't think they'll have a leg to stand on, Jaxson. It was—"

"An accident!" Jaxson screamed. He spun around quickly, catching his reflection in the mirror. The blood had drained from his face. It felt like one of his low blood sugar moments. His head began to spin, vomit building in his throat.

"Yes, I know," Zach continued. "Between the medical evaluation and the witnesses, I would say that you are going to be just fine."

"But they could tie me up in court for years," Jaxson sputtered. "I don't have the money to pay for you or any of this!"

He sat down, swallowing hard as he placed his head between his knees. Deep breaths. *This is just a moment. It was a bullshit moment for sure but just a moment. No, it wasn't. This was life changing.* He picked up the pace between breaths, slowing the on-set of a major panic attack.

"Jaxson?" Zach persisted. "You still there?"

"Yes," Jaxson answered after a moment. Air passed through his nostrils and the dizziness subsided.

"Look, I know these last few weeks have been a hell of a wild ride, but I'm going to get you through this. Legally speaking, that is."

"Zach, I really appreciate that, but you know and I know that this is not your specialty."

Jaxson remembered the first moment he saw Zach's face. It was plastered onto the back of a bus stop bench. Slicked-back hair. Wide grin. *Fight back. Call Zach.* He was nothing more than a personal injury lawyer—a rich one, but an ambulance chaser nonetheless. The advertising must have worked because Jaxson recalled the image after the first phone call about the settlement. He knew he couldn't go into the negotiations in his present state. Zach was his only hope.

"I'll get more information this week and call you on Friday, OK?" Zach wasn't a bad guy, really. He was just in over his head, and his less than confident tone wasn't exactly reassuring.

"All right," Jaxson answered. "I'll see you then. Thanks, Zach."

He could barely get the man's name out before the call ended. This was not the outcome he had hoped for. Then again, what did he expect? He had a diabetic episode and crashed a dump truck into a city bus. Lives were lost, and that was on him. The guilt began to bubble up again; tears began to flow from the corners of his eyes.

"Fuck," he muttered. Instinctively, he glanced up at his Gran's picture on the end table. He could almost hear her scolding him from the other room.

"Don't you say that devil's word around me!" He pictured her standing in front of him.

"That's no way to deal with your problems, boy," the old woman would continue, wagging her finger in the process. "An educated man has no room for curse words in his vocabulary."

That education hadn't done much good, he surmised, as he sunk back into the chair.

"I'm done," he said to the ghost in front of him. He wasn't sure if the one he was speaking to was Gran, himself, or Jayden. He often spoke to his brother about his problems, even though they hadn't been in the same room in years. He remembered that his brother would be showing up anytime. The pain seeped into his heart at the thought. The two were inseparable at one time. What happened to them? He knew the answer, of course, but it seemed easier to question it rather than accept the reality that the two drifted apart some time ago.

He thought of his parents and that fateful day. Jayden insisted on going with them to church, but Jaxson held him up to help with a school project that was due the next day.

"Why do you have to do this right now?" Jayden asked, flopping down on the bed next to the desk.

"Because I covered your shift at the market yesterday so you could go see Lorraine. You owe me one."

Despite their differences, Jaxson and Jayden were inseparable as children. They looked nothing like each other, but that didn't stop his mother from getting their names confused in a moment of anger. He remembered her scolding them for coloring on the walls or shoving random objects into the toilet to see if they would disappear in one flush or two.

She would grab each of their wrists, yelling one brother's name to the other, as they snickered in response. That only made her angrier and generally led to the lame punishment of the chair stare, in which the two sat in chairs facing each other until they could come to the realization of what they had done. It never really worked. They would end up making faces at each other until one would burst out laughing, usually Jayden.

"You two stop this at once!" she would shout, bursting into the room and air spanking them with a wooden spoon before sending them upstairs as further punishment.

Of course, what she didn't know is that it wasn't punishment at all for the boys. They would sit quietly on the floor, playing with toy soldiers or Legos, waiting for her anger to pass. What they didn't know about their mother was those moments of silence without the boys were a welcome reprieve from the constant activity.

The two secured jobs at Pike's Place in their teen years, first sorting fish and cleaning them at the market. Eventually, Jayden was promoted to tossing fish for tourists, a job that Jaxson never quite got the hang of. He didn't like going home smelling of the day's catch. Jayden would just laugh it off. He couldn't care less. Jaxson secretly admired his brother for his ability to shrug off any trouble that came his way. It is probably what made him an excellent soldier. Nothing seemed to phase Jayden.

Jaxson sat for a long while, considering his options.

"What options?" he asked out loud.

He would have to turn over the measly settlement to his attorney to fend off the wolves at the door. He'd have to find another job. He had some savings but only enough to last a couple of months. He had the house, of course, left to him and Jayden in the will. He spent years rising before dawn to do a thankless job only to have it amount to this.

Jaxson pulled himself out of the chair and shuffled his way to the kitchen. He started to make tea but remembered the whiskey in the cabinet. As chaste as she was, Gran did enjoy a glass or two in the evenings from time to time. He was thankful for her habit in that moment.

He opened the cupboard to find the bottle and two crystal glasses before him. He poured one for him and one for Gran, pausing briefly before holding his toward the ceiling.

"To you, Gran," he toasted, putting the brown liquor to his lips.

It burned down his throat, causing him to cough for a moment before proceeding. He wasn't much of a liquor guy, but today seemed the exception. He finished the glass in a matter of minutes, then proceeded to pour another. And another.

The liquid medicine hit his head after a while. The numbness was a welcome feeling in what appeared to be an impossible situation. The doorbell buzzed, causing him to bring focus back to the room. He walked toward the door, feeling a little unsteady as he crossed the room. Three small glasses, and he was already done for. What kind of man was he anyway? A boring man with no life, he thought, as he turned the lock and opened the door.

The package was on the mat; a small Post-it note was attached. He bent down to pick it up, almost losing his balance. He would need his glasses to read it.

After about ten minutes of searching, he found the bifocals crammed between the cushions of the couch. He had always been farsighted, needing readers as a teen. Too many years siting inches from a computer screen was likely the cause of further eye strain and vision decline. His other vision problems had disappeared after the crash, but it appeared this one was here to stay. He pulled the Post-it from the package. It was a phone number. The area code wasn't recognizable.

He opened the envelope, pulling the paperwork from inside. Much of it was the formal settlement paperwork, but the last sheet was a letter. His heart raced at the sight of the handwriting. It was perfect, almost like Gran had written it herself.

Jaxson,

I was on the bus. I know this all must be overwhelming. I've left my number in the hope you will call. Until then, don't lose hope.

The number was scribbled in place of where a name should be. He stared at the letter for a moment, then wished he hadn't pulled the whiskey from the cabinet. He could see Gran shaking her head. He passed out in the chair, awakening to a darkened room.

He made his way to the bathroom, then the kitchen to make some tea. As he poured his first cup, he remembered the number. Glancing at the clock, he was worried it would be too late to call, and he certainly didn't want to after having been drinking. He retrieved the package and pulled out his phone. The battery was almost dead. He would have to talk fast.

Silence greeted him as he called the number. The phone wasn't ringing through, and he was about to hang up. He was expecting voicemail when a familiar voice filled the line. "I'm glad you called, Jaxson." He recognized her tone and cadence immediately. It was the woman who saved him at the crash site. He felt relief for the first time in weeks.

"Hello," he said brightly. "I've been wondering what happened to you. I wanted to thank you for everything."

"Jaxson," she replied. "I'm sorry you've had to go through this, but we all have struggles to overcome in this life."

He was too enraptured by her voice and the memory it evoked to respond.

"How did you know where to find me?" he asked.

"A man at the settlement meeting agreed to pass on my note," she said. "I wanted to see how you were doing."

"I've been better," Jaxson said, sighing afterward.

"I have something to run by you," she said. "I wanted to know if we could meet in person to discuss it. Are you able to leave the house yet?"

"Not exactly, but my nurse is supposed to be here tomorrow morning for a final check. I'm hoping for good news for once."

"I have a feeling it will be. Why don't you meet me tomorrow at Mojo's coffee? 3 p.m.?"

How could he refuse?

"Sure," he said. "If I get the all clear, I'll be there."

"See you then," she said, ending the call.

He kept the phone to his ear for a moment before plugging it into the charger. Tomorrow is going to be an interesting day, he thought.

As he drifted off to sleep that night, Jaxson felt a peace like never before. His head wasn't spinning from drink as the darkness took over; rather, a calming reassurance filled his weary mind.

He woke to the sound of birds at the window. Early morning sunlight flooded the room. He was in the same position he fell asleep in. He sat up, worried he would feel the pounding of a hangover headache or stiffness from the lack of movement, but he felt surprisingly refreshed.

He was invigorated as he moved through his morning routine. He looked around his cluttered living space and began to pick up the mess from the day before. After breakfast, he showered and waited for Keisha. She was always a bright spot in his day.

"Hey, Jaxson," Keisha said, as she made her way through the back door. "I brought you some—"

Keisha stood at the entry of the living room, stunned by what she saw. The place was cleaned up, dishes put away, and Jaxson stood tall at the picture window, clothes pressed, face shaven.

"You look…well," she finally said. He looked better than well. He was gorgeous.

"Thank you," Jaxson said, inviting her to set her stuff down. "I thought it was time to join the living."

"Well, I would say you have succeeded," Keisha said, averting her eyes. She had to remain professional, but she felt flushed, butterflies flying in her stomach.

"Well, let's do this." Jaxson clapped his hands as he made his way to the chair.

Keisha pulled her instruments from the bag and began the usual diagnostic tests. His numbers were incredible. The very picture of health. He smiled as she pulled her stethoscope away.

"Good?" he asked.

"Better than good, Jaxson," Keisha replied. "Incredible. In fact, you're cleared. What happened? Why the sudden change of appearance?"

"Well, I learned I'm going to get next to nothing for the settlement, and my company is going to add further insult to injury with a countersuit. But you know what? Today is a new day!" He stood up then, stretching his arms and walking toward the window. "I'm ready to start living again, Keisha. What do I have to lose?"

"Nothing," Keisha answered dreamily. She couldn't believe what she saw. This man in front of her was unrecognizable from the one she had been treating for the last weeks. Sure, his stats were normal, but he had seemed defeated and his appearance was disheveled. Now, he was the picture of perfect health, both inside and out. She would be sad to leave him.

She noticed the photograph on the mantle. Why hadn't she seen it before? The two boys were clearly related, each one flanking his parents. Perhaps that was what was going on here: he had a twin, and the imposter had taken Jaxson's place.

"I like this picture," she said, running her finger along the edge.

"Oh, that's me on the right, my brother, Jayden, on the left, and our parents of course," he said. His smile quickly faded as he stared at the image.

"My parents died in an accident many years ago," he finally said after a few minutes.

"I'm sorry," said Keisha, looking back at him. "You haven't mentioned a brother before."

"Oh, that's my brother, Jayden. He's in the Army. Special Forces. He's actually coming home, I thought, yesterday?

That's the Army, though. Never quite know when he's going to drop on my doorstep. It's been a long time since he's been home. He was my best friend."

Keisha stared thoughtfully at the picture, wondering what his brother would be like now. "I'd like to meet him sometime. Glad you two are still close."

"Well, as close as the Army allows, anyway," he added, walking up beside her. "You know that stuff they say about twins? How connected they are? It's all true. We could practically read each other's minds as kids."

She looked closely at the picture, looking at all the differences between them. "For a moment, I thought maybe your twin had taken your place, but obviously that's not the case with the two of you," she chuckled.

"I wish," he said, taking the picture from the mantle. He smiled for a moment, then began to tear up. "You think he looks good here, you should see him now. He's built like a truck. Every school wanted him to play ball. He had a different path." He returned the picture to the mantle and made his way to the kitchen. Keisha instinctively followed.

"You know, when my parents died, I didn't leave my room for two weeks, except to attend the funeral. Jayden kept me alive, running food up and down the stairs."

He handed her a cup of tea he had poured before her arrival. She took it gratefully.

"I didn't know how I would go on after that," Jaxson continued. "I was just so worried he would leave me forever and that I'd never see him again. But then the Army and, well, I had to let him go, I guess. Best thing he ever did. I'm just so glad he didn't go with them that day."

"How did they die?" Keisha asked.

"They died in a fire at the church," he answered. "It was

my father's church. They ruled it a hate crime."

"Oh, that's terrible. I'm so sorry," she said, looking thoughtfully at him.

"I know I should have faith, and my Gran is rolling in her grave right now with me just saying this, but I struggled to believe after that," he said, then paused for a moment. "It was a really difficult time. Makes this stuff happening right now seem pretty insignificant."

"You just look so different today. I mean, I didn't know you before, but you seem happier. Normal," Keisha offered with a coy smile. Her gaze dropped down to her nurse's shoes.

"Was I not normal before?" he asked with a laugh.

"No, no," she said. "I just mean that you look good. Really good."

"Well, thank you."

He looked intently into her caramel eyes then, considering the possibility of a future beyond her medical visits. She matched his gaze, moving slightly toward him.

"Oh wait," he stopped her. "What time is it?"

She looked down at her watch. "Almost three?"

"Oh shit, I gotta go. I mean, I can go, right?"

"Yes," she said, feeling a deep sadness at the thought of him leaving.

"Hey," he said, taking her hand. "Thank you for nursing me back to health and…being a good friend."

"You're welcome," she said slowly.

He kissed her on the cheek and reached for his jacket on the hook.

"You can lock up before you go?"

Keisha nodded.

He turned back from the door before stepping out into freedom.

"Thanks, Keisha," he said, truly heartfelt. "We should catch that movie sometime with your daughter."

Hope soared in her heart as he smiled over his shoulder, closing the door behind him. She welcomed the feeling that overcame her, breathing in his scent as he left the room. She would see that film with him, and have the ending between them play out just as it always does in the most romantic movies.

CHAPTER TWELVE

The bus stopped abruptly at the entrance of the depot, settling down with a hiss as the driver opened the doors. He reached for the receiver and barked, "Las Vegas! Final stop. Everybody off!" Petra hoped it was final. She didn't want to live her life on the run. She would be no better off than the day she left Razor.

She had the duffle clutched in her arms for the second half of the journey, so no need to rise and shove her way to the door. She watched the weary travelers gather their meager belongings. Where were they going with possessions packed in paper bags, ratty old luggage, or tattered purses? To a casino, perhaps? The chance of dropping a few coins in the hope of hitting a fortune? She felt badly then, considering what she had taken from those same bags and what had fallen between the seat cushions and beside the crumbs of food on the bus floor. The last passenger took his time to rise and watched her curiously as he gathered his things.

"I know what you were doing when we stopped," he said.

Petra's heart sank. He was between her and the exit, so there was no possibility to escape unnoticed.

"I…I…," she stammered, hoping he didn't know the full scope of her crime. His T-shirt was torn, and she could glimpse a tattoo of a bird wing on his chest. He definitely had the look of someone who understood indiscretions. The man wasn't unfortunate looking, though the artwork that covered his muscular arms had the look of a hard life. A broken heart. A classic pinup girl with perky tits. Serial numbers across each of his thick fingers.

"I know what you did, but the question for me was 'why'?" he asked, taking a small step in her direction.

She remained still, hoping the silence and her sullen expression would be enough to erase his memory.

"Look, I'm in no place to accuse you of nothing," he said. "I'm a criminal myself. I'm a guy with a rap sheet a mile long and a mom down the road. I noticed how nice your ass looked while you were searching under those seats."

He followed up his assessment of her with a wink and flashed a gold grill that could easily be worth more than every ticket purchased on the bus trip. It was pretty obvious he was a hardened criminal capable of squeezing the last breath out of her with the clutch of his claw-like hands. She had to play this right, or there was no way she was getting off this bus alive, much less without being crippled and in seething pain. She couldn't afford a hospital stay right now; that is, if she even survived it.

She smiled coyly at him, considering her next move. There was no way around it. She would have to meet his demands, and she knew it likely involved having sex with him or risk getting raped before the cleaning crew arrived. She really studied him then, trying to find the redeeming qualities underneath the scars on his face, dirty appearance, and a lifelong collection of tattoos. For one, the guy spent time in the weight room. His arms were massive. His eyes were a steely blue, and his head was completely shaved, probably as much for a receding hairline as the lice. He was tall, and his shoes were enormous.

She was intentional with her next move. She started toward him, slinking her way down the aisle, lightly touching the tops of the seats with her fingers. She held his gaze, knowing from her previous life that eye contact was a big part of the seduction. His eyes moved down to her breasts, and he licked his lips in anticipation. Done deal.

"What is it that I need to do to get off this bus?" she asked, dropping her voice into a sultry purr.

"Me," he said, and in a flash was in front of her, grabbing her breast with one massive hand, squeezing her ass with the other. He shoved his tongue down her throat, practically swallowing her whole in the process.

"Fuck me now, and you can leave," he whispered into her ear. It was almost erotic, if not for the fact he was a criminal, the bus smelled like ass, and the moment wasn't anywhere near what she had seen in countless movies in the prison media room. Knowing he likely had been locked up for some time, she took comfort in the fact it wouldn't last longer than a few minutes, if that. He stopped abruptly, grabbing her face between his rough fingers. She could feel the callouses like sandpaper against her cheek.

"I ain't had a woman in a few years now," he said, "and I don't want to rape one to get what I need." He looked at her with an intensity she hadn't seen before. In that moment, she honestly believed him.

"There's a hotel," he said. "I got some cash. I'll pay you to do it." Perhaps he did know her better than she thought. He looked like a little boy, desperate for mom to give in to his demand. She needed the money and, with a prayer in her head, gave him a brisk nod.

He grabbed her hand, slung her sorry bag over his shoulder, and grabbed his own in his open hand. They stepped off the bus into an oven. The stifling heat nearly took her breath away. Sweat quickly beaded on her forehead as they made their way onto the boulevard.

Within minutes, they were standing in front of a hotel, not at all what she expected to see. The place was relatively new and not nearly as seedy as she expected. They stepped through the automatic doors to the lobby. Petra went straight for the watercooler while her brut of a soon-to-be lover checked them in. She poured him a glass and walked it over. He looked shocked by the gesture, quickly gulping down the contents before handing her the cup. She filled them again and turned to find him in front of her.

"Let's go," he said, taking her hand and guiding her toward the elevator. The hotel wasn't exactly top of the line, but it wasn't terrible either. It was the kind of place that business travelers passed through, not that Petra was in a place to judge. This was the nicest place she had seen in years.

"My mom used to work here," he offered as the doors closed and the gears guided them upward. "She was hired to clean the place when it opened. Not just clean but actually manage the cleaners and stuff. It was pretty cool."

"What happened to your mom?" Petra asked, looking up at him. He was well over six feet and, as she studied his physique, in incredible shape. She felt a sensation between her legs at the thought of him on top of her. She hadn't been with a man in years. She was actually warming up to the idea.

"She retired a couple years ago," he said. "I've been such a disappointment, I know, but she never gave up on me. I'm gonna be staying with her for a while and help her around the house with projects and stuff. She's real happy I'm out and coming home."

The doors dinged, opening onto a hallway of blue carpet covered in gaudy white diamonds. The room was at the end of the hall, and he quickly opened the door, holding it for her as she entered the room. She panicked for a second, considering her past experiences and all that could happen next. But none of it did.

"I'm Steve, by the way," he said offering her his hand as the door clicked behind them.

"Petra," she said, taking his hand and then unexpectedly throwing her arms around his neck.

She kissed him slowly then, taking in the feel of his gold teeth with her tongue. He picked her up and walked slowly toward the bed, continually kissing her as he gently lay her down. This is not at all what she expected to happen. She planned on seeing old candy wrappers and spilled soda contents on the floor of the dirty, old bus as he raped her into submission and numbness. This was something else entirely.

The sex lasted far longer than she expected it to, their bodies melding into one position after the other, lips and tongues intertwined with each move. While he released her orgasm within minutes of penetrating her, he was eager to outlast her, encouraging her to let go again and again before finally releasing his seed deep inside her, staring deeply into her eyes as he caught his breath between spasms. He held her gaze for a moment, before slowly withdrawing from her and flopping down on the bed beside her.

"My God," he said, and paused before finishing his sentence. "You are by far the hottest chick I've ever seen."

"You're just saying that because I'm the first chick you've been with since your release," she added with a laugh.

"No," he said, running his fingers across her breasts. "You are seriously hot."

"Well you were completely a surprise to me," she said with a knowing smile.

They both laughed then, a sweet release in a place of mutual beginnings. They were both starting over, and this was the perfect reset button. After another round of passionate, intense sex, they napped for a while, holding each other as if they had done so for years. Afterward, his whispers of desire slowly faded into a soft snore. It was something that would have annoyed her before, but this time she somehow found it to be comforting and almost welcome.

After a few hours of rest, her eyes opened and focused on the clock. It was just after five in the morning. She didn't want to leave this place and face the realities beyond the door. She wanted to lie here, content in the arms of a stranger, anticipating what would emerge between them.

"Stay with me for a while," he whispered into her ear. It was exactly what she wanted to hear.

CHAPTER THIRTEEN

D ad wouldn't be home for another few hours. There was just enough time to shoot up and feel the numbness for a while before another unbearable dinner together. Wasn't this a sight to see: his father's only son, sitting in the back of a closet, searching through an old shoebox for his stash of smack. He prepped for a moment before slowly dispensing the liquid in between his toes. The rush was intense, an immediate calm. He needed it today. No, he needed it every damn day, multiple times a day, if he were honest with himself. He preferred not to be so honest. Best let the secret fall to the floor with the weight of his limbs. The substance was about to take over.

His head hit the carpet, and he began to examine the fibers. For a moment, he felt only an immense sense of relief. He was free of his mind and the constant stream of thoughts. The pain he felt inside was so overwhelming at times that only the drug could suffice. It felt so good to be free of his grief.

Mom had been dead two years now. He hadn't thought about it that much until writing down the date in a blue book before a big exam that afternoon. What pained him most was that his father didn't even acknowledge her death until a few days afterward. It was all he could think about, not even bothering to write down the answers to the essay questions in front of him. The exam could wait. Did it even matter? Not really. He had all the money in the world. He never understood why college was so important. What purpose did he really serve, other than to not screw up the legacy his father had achieved before him? The college had sent a letter a few days before, telling him they had reevaluated his "scholarship." He was no longer a member of the archery team, and his chance of Olympic glory was gone with a few pointed words on a page. Privileges had been revoked. He had totally missed the target, literally and figuratively.

Archery was the one thing Marco had embraced in his restless youth. It may have been a gorgeous movie star with the same passion that sparked his interest in the first place, but it was his dedication to the sport that led to an incredible mastery in a matter of months. Marco was that kind of kid. Once he put his mind to something, it would happen. He didn't allow questions or doubts to enter his mind.

Grades were always a problem, and it took a number of phone calls from his father to various board members to secure his entrance into the Ivy League college of Marco's dreams. But as the time to depart drew near, he settled on a different plan to attend a local university. He wanted to stay close to his mom's memory. It wasn't easy at first, tackling subjects that he mostly ignored in high school in favor of staying by his mother's side. But archery was something else entirely. He would hold the bow squarely in his arms, drawing the string to his shoulder, breathing steadily, and releasing at the perfect moment. One. Two. Three. He started at the outer rings, not so much out of choice as necessity. His left arm was stronger than his right. Once he corrected the stance and positioning, it was on. He would spend hours in front of a target, setting his position, breathing steady and...thump. Perfect nearly every time.

His mom was the most encouraging of his passion, sending him video clips and lessons from various YouTube channels, and later when she knew the hobby had turned into an obsession, books about performance mastery and camps with masters of the sport. Books were not something Marco ever embraced, but he would spend hours clicking through the endless e-books his mom would send, reading her comments in an email after. Within months, he had won every competition available on the West Coast. Within a year, he had risen to the top in nationals.

A shoulder injury was fuel to the fire that was addiction. The painkillers timed with the diagnosis of his mom's cancer. He had snuck one or two of her pills before, hoping it would help him sleep a little better at first. Then, the injury and several refills later, he was addicted to the feeling and serenity the pills would provide. He wondered if his mother knew. He would walk into the converted study just off the foyer, now her bedroom, peaking coyly around the corner, before smiling brightly at her in the doorway.

"How did it go today, baby?" she would ask weakly.

"I hit thirty-five of thirty-six," he would say, bounding into the room and plopping down on the bed beside her.

"And what happened to Mr. Thirty-Six?" she would ask, a look of longing in her eyes. He knew how much she wanted to be there. What she didn't understand is that she always was. She was there, inside his heart, and steadying his breath.

"Well, my breath was a little off," he said nonchalantly, looking out the window to avoid her stern look. She knew he was on something. He couldn't hide the glassy look in his eyes from the woman who knew him best. He hoped she would change the subject.

"Who is she?" she asked rather annoyed, not bothering to address the elephant in the room.

"Mom, she was the most gorgeous girl I've ever seen!"

"I'm sure she was a sight to see, but she cannot capture your focus. Any woman who would do that is not supportive of you. I don't care what level of competitor she is."

"She was, well, she was—"

"A distraction, Marco!"

"Yes, there's that. She was a distraction, but a good one. Besides, my shoulder is still bothering me after last week's competition. I don't know what it is, but coach says it has something to do with my rotator cuff or deltoid?"

"Marco, you should know this stuff more than just a rattling off of terms you looked up on the internet," she said with a knowing look.

Mom could always do that, know exactly what his actions were at all questionable times. The real question was, how did she know? It was as if a secret camera had been installed inside his mind at birth that she alone could view.

"You're right," he said, looking away from the window and landing his face squarely in front of hers. Their facial features were so similar. She looked lovingly at him, patting his arm for good measure.

"Well, go upstairs and get my perfume. All these chemicals are making my sense of smell go away. I want to take in my Dior for a moment and remember dancing the night away in a French night club."

God, he loved her. As he thought this, his brain flooded with memories of school functions and endless parties on the patio. His mom was so stylish and elegant before the illness—a remarkable figure that looked rather out of place in the school halls, backyard barbecues, and playdate pickups in his elementary years, long before his dad had hit it really big. She always looked more expensive than him, any of them really. His father never deserved a woman as wonderful as his mother. He was glad when they divorced.

His eyes fluttered open to the sound of an alarm. His phone was going off just steps away. Marco always set reminders when it came to his dad. Being late didn't just cost him time in the form of lectures but money for every minute late taken from his trust fund account. With everything that had happened over the last two years, one wrong move could mean the end of his lifestyle. It was a risk he wasn't willing to take. Not right now anyway. He would have to keep up the charade for a few more years. At twenty five, the account would be his to manage alone.

He felt pathetic. That's what drug addiction was, really. Just a giant loop of waking and committing to quit, only to find himself shooting up before noon. He was a slave to the feeling the drug provided him. The pills were too expensive and traceable. He preferred a more affordable high he could get anywhere and anytime. He would linger down the hallway of a nearby apartment complex, landing in front of door 311. It was the dealer's inside joke for the band from the nineties. He felt awkward knocking to the lyrics, "Amber is the color of your energy," but it also brought a small comfort before the door opened.

Sometimes, he would hum along with the knock if he was lucky enough to remember to resupply before the last of his dregs entered his system. Sometimes, not as much. He would slide down the wall, then wait, and shake and sweat until the door opened eventually. As long as the money was there, it would always open for him. He could count on that at least.

He didn't intend for the prescription drugs to take hold the way they did. He thought a few months of painkillers while he waited for his shoulder to heal would be enough. But the doctor hadn't told him about the growing need inside his brain. Now, heroin had him in a death grip. The drug wasn't just powerful, it was part of him. The molecules had seeped into his bloodstream at first, but over time had bonded to his organs, the very strands of his DNA. He had no idea how he would rid himself of the substance that had kept him alive the last few years. But at some point, he would have to stop, or life itself would be stopped for him.

He found himself getting more and more agitated in class, waiting eagerly for the bell to ring, only to rush home and shoot up to shake off the day. He knew it was insidious, but there wasn't much help. When he finally admitted out loud that he had a problem, his doctor just told him to stop by the next appointment. When Marco attempted to tell him he was addicted, the man only made him feel guilt and shame for not managing his grief properly.

It was a difficult time for Marco. His parents had divorced at the height of his mother's illness. He always wondered if she was far sicker than she let on when the divorce was at its ugliest moments. She never disclosed that, always the class act, never saying a word about what a monster he really was.

A tear trickled down his nose at the memory. How his mother had lived as long as she did was amazing. She always said she was hanging on for him. He was glad for her presence but felt so ashamed toward the end. He was high most of the time, fading in and out of reality much like his mother did on the morphine. They endured the pain together, hers from the cancer and his from the thought of living a life without her. Marco suspected that she knew, but she never said a word, rather taking his hand, patting it softly, and falling back into a deep delta sleep.

He had thought many times about joining her in whatever was beyond this world. Overdose would be easy enough. It just required a slightly larger syringe, or enough to snort, and that would be it. He considered it a few times, even loading the liquid to the very top, only to dispose of it later. Not yet, he would think. He heard her voice so clearly in his head in his most desperate moments. *There's something out there for you, Marco.*

While his family had all the privileges money could buy, he wasn't at all happy with his life. The estate attorney encouraged him to sell the house right way, a total mistake when in the throes of grief. He followed the advice anyway, banking the money in the trust and opting to rent a beautiful modern home on the other side of town. He wanted to feel close to his mother and keep living in the house, but the pain was far too intense. The less he was reminded, the better.

Over time, his mother's memory, her voice, never faded. Nothing had changed as far as his love and devotion to her, not even with the move miles away. He would often hear her guidance, telling him to do this or that. Sometimes it was as simple as what to buy online; other times it was more encouraging. *It will all work out, or this is only a bump in the road.* Those were two of her more frequent phases. But how would it all work out when he had no direction? He felt like a lost cause.

The phone rang, bringing him back to the present. "Sperm Donor" appeared on the screen. He pulled himself off the floor and answered.

"Hello, Dad."

"Marco, don't forget about dinner tonight. The staff is making steaks," his dad spoke into the phone, his speech a bit slurred. "I trust your interview with Ace went well, right?"

Dammit. He completely forgot about the interview with Uncle Ace. The man owned half of the city, albeit the not so great part.

"Oh yeah, man," Marco attempted to answer soberly. "It was great, great."

"OK, well get your ass moving. I will be home in about an hour and should just meet you if you leave now from that goddamn place you're living at now. Why you have to be so remote, Marco, is beyond me. Join the living for fuck's sake!"

He dreaded the dinner in his current state but hoped the Lyft there and a venti Americano would be enough to sober him up.

"You need to get a job, asshole. You're an embarrassment," his father said before the three beeps silenced their conversation.

A long night, followed by an even longer lecture. He had better things to do. Perhaps, this time, he would just skip it. He would leap into the great beyond and find his mother waiting for him on the other side. Until then, he could conjure up a cloudless dream and fall under the influence of a burdened future.

CHAPTER FOURTEEN

I t was unseasonably warm as Jaxson strolled down the street toward the coffee shop. He had considered taking the bus but thought the better of it given the recent turn of events. Before, he would have struggled to make it the eight blocks, given the circulation issues in his legs. He would likely contemplate if he should stop and check his blood sugar in route. But not today. He wasn't tired at all. In fact, he couldn't recall a time when he felt like this. Maybe as a teenager. Even then, he was in terrible shape from always sitting at a desk and hiding in the back of every gym class. He did eventually develop a tolerance for working out, but it took strong words from his doctor for the click to finally happen.

He wondered if Jayden had already landed on his doorstep. He felt a twinge of guilt that he wasn't there to greet his brother but knew deep in his heart that his twin likely needed a moment or two or three to himself. War took a lot out of a solider, but Special Forces? That was another matter entirely. He saw Jayden change slowly over the years—more pensive, less revealing. It often resulted in an awkward silence between them, one he never understood or quite got over. They had always been so close in their youth, telling every misadventure, triumph, even how far they made it with various girls at school. It was innocent and endearing. It was nothing like that now.

Jaxson happened upon the coffee shop unconsciously. He had crossed the street without even knowing. It made him uncomfortable when the subconscious mind took over. How did he even get from here to there? It didn't matter. He was the happiest he had been in years and wasn't worried in the slightest about the uneasy feeling that was attempting to take him over. He spotted her almost instantly.

"Jaxson." She stood to greet him, extending her arms to offer an embrace. "How are you feeling?"

He welcomed the contact, holding her for several seconds before finally releasing and looking her in the eye.

"I feel amazing, and something tells me I have you to thank exclusively for that." He was studying her face, taking in every feature before settling in the seat across from her. He was in a terrible state when he first saw her at the crash site. Now, he was overcome with her beauty and grace. She was another person entirely from the one in his memory.

"I'm sorry to hear about the settlement," she said, without even once breaking her gaze. "What did you decide to do?"

"Decide. Decide?" he repeated in the form of a question. "I don't think it was much of a decision," he responded after a moment. "More like a desperate move that anyone in my shoes would take."

He stared at her for a moment, awaiting her response. She didn't oblige.

"OK, OK," he finally said, repeating himself once more. "Keeping it real for a moment?"

"Of course," she replied.

"I am a washed up, useless man, who managed to fool the establishment of this company to keep me around for so many years," he started. "I mean, it's not like I didn't get a raise along the way. Four percent is very respectable in most circles."

She didn't say a word, but her eyes encouraged him to continue.

"Before, I had big—no, huge—goals," he proceeded, staring off into the distance as if to recall them to memory. "It's just that the universe or God or whatever didn't have that in the cards for me, so, here I am," he said with a shrug of his shoulders. "Are we going to order coffee or something? I feel kind of guilty sitting here and all without paying my way."

She smiled at him, kind of like the look his mother had given him all those years ago. She was wise beyond her years, he thought, considering the years of age between them.

"That's what I love about you, Jaxson," she said with a knowing smile. "Your world just collapsed, and you're wondering if the coffee shop will get its due in the process."

"I guess I do that," he said with a humbled look.

She smiled, circling her eyes around his features and taking in his face.

"So, what's up?" he asked after the coffee arrived at the table. He didn't even recall ordering anything, but what was presented was exactly what he was wanting: a nice cup of coffee, no cream, no frills. Just straight-up black. He loved his order that way. He took a sip and found it to be the perfect temperature. Never did he recall a more perfect cup of coffee.

"Man, this is really, really good."

She watched him take a few sips before finally getting to the point of their meeting.

"My name is Una," she began. "I don't think we were ever formally introduced; moreover, I'm not sure if you would have remembered my name in that terrible moment."

His warm expression began to fade, trying to recall if an introduction ever happened. She wasn't exactly how he remembered, but her presence was the same. She was warm, inviting, her skin a warm brown. As each second passed, her amber eyes seemed to draw him in further. He didn't feel like she was going to scam him, but his gut told him she wanted him to do something.

"Jaxson, don't worry. I don't want your money or anything. We both know that wouldn't be in your best interest," she continued. He looked at her peculiarly, as if she had read his mind. "I want your time."

"My time?" he asked incredulously.

"Your time, and your guidance, if you'd be so kind as to offer them to me."

"Of course, I owe you my life," he said looking intensely into her eyes.

She continued. "It isn't about debt, or repayment, or anything involving money or material possessions. This is about helping people. I believe you are the best person to help with that, Jaxson. You are such a generous soul. You showed me that even in our conversation a moment ago— always concerned about the well-being of others. I truly love that about you."

He stirred uncomfortably in his chair. "Love that about me? You don't even know me, Uma."

"Una," she corrected, without as much as a twinge of annoyance.

"I'm sorry. I'm not that good with names," he said, as his cheeks turned a bright crimson.

"I'm quite good with them," she added. "So, we should make a great team." She reached for his hand, patting it lightly before releasing it again.

"How do you know so much about me? We have barely met."

"I really have no idea," she said after a moment. "A feeling deep inside me. I was a pretty regular person before all of this. That crash changed me as much as it did you."

He looked at her then, really studying her face. How did this woman know so much about his soul? Perhaps it was the accident, he surmised. Or she gained access to the records?

"I didn't gain access to any records, I promise," she said. He was officially creeped out by this conversation, but at the same time, basked in its warmth.

It was as if this woman knew him at his core. He had many reasons to deny the possibility of a connection, but he didn't want to. He wanted to go with the feeling. It was the kind of connection you felt with an old friend. That feeling of knowing someone forever, even though you only had a conversation on a plane for an hour. It wasn't a romantic connection, but a sibling vibe. He and Jayden always wanted a little sister. Perhaps now they had one.

"Now that you're ready," she began again, "I want you to consider the possibility of joining me in Las Vegas."

"Las Vegas?"

"Yes. I've been offered a show, of sorts. A chance to heal others in the way I have healed you."

Jaxson laughed nervously at the proposal. It was the only emotion he could think to release in that moment. She waited for him to consider the offer fully before responding. She watched his face go through an array of emotions—

happy to sad, excited to confused. Eventually, she watched a feeling of knowing wash over his face.

"This is the right thing, Jaxson," she finally said. "You can help people. You know what it's like to be healed. You can relate to them in a way that no one else can."

"What about the others on the bus?" he asked. "Are they joining the show as well?"

"No," she answered. "I thought about the others, but they have their own lives to consider. Besides, I just don't trust them in the way that I trust you."

He stared at her for a second, wondering exactly why she had chosen him over the others. She instinctively answered his question.

"When I was healing you, it was like reaching deep inside to the very core of you. I saw things and felt it all so deeply. Your parents. The church fire. The bond you have with your brother. Your grandmother's embrace at graduation. The disappointment after. It was like your whole life played out on a movie screen in front of me. It was strange and all-consuming. It was almost as if I needed to know you before I could heal you. I'm not sure if that is a requirement of the process or what, but as I was reading you, I was able to go deeper. It rebuilt your human code, so to speak. It was what I needed to repair you physically."

She stopped then, putting her face in her hands. She could feel the doubt inside him.

"I know. This is all too much. I hedged my bets on whether you would believe me," she said, with a shake of her head.

He reached for her shoulders, embracing both sides and pulling her toward him. Without hesitation, his mouth opened and blurted out, "I'll do it."

She looked up at him with confusion at first, almost surprised that he would say yes to her unusual proposal. "Really?" she asked, just to be sure.

"Yes," he said emphatically. "I have no idea how much help a garbage man will be in a Vegas show, but if you're sure, I'm game to try it."

She smiled broadly, trying to emit a confidence she was still building inside herself. Una wasn't sure what would happen next, but she knew he would run home to tell his waiting brother everything that had transpired. Their relationship was pivotal to this opportunity. She knew she couldn't do it without them.

"Is it all right if I ask my brother to join me? He's just home from the Army."

"Of course," she said. "He's waiting for you now."

Jaxson glanced at his watch and bolted upright from his seat.

"Oh man, I better go," he said, throwing down a few bills for the coffee before bolting out the door. "Call me!"

Jaxson stepped onto the sidewalk, almost bewildered by the exchange that just happened. Did he actually accept an offer to go to Vegas with this stranger? But she didn't feel like a stranger. She was a mystery, for sure, but not foreign at all. She felt like a sense of home, a knowing of what should be. He didn't fight the feeling as he closed in on his front door. He reached for the key as he took the steps in twos. His brother opened the door before Jaxson could put the key in the lock.

"Brotha!" Jaxson yelled, throwing his arms around Jayden's larger frame.

"Hey man," Jayden said, eventually releasing into the embrace. The two hugged for a moment.

"I need to talk to you," Jayden finally said, and the two let go and made their way toward the living room.

"Your trip OK? I was thinking about those C-5s and other pieces of shit you have to fly home," Jaxson said, as they plopped into their chosen seats.

"Yes, it was fine," Jayden said, looking pensive.

It was not an uncommon look for his brother when he was first home from a tour of duty. Jaxson eased back into his seat, ready for whatever his brother had to throw at him.

"I want you to listen to me without judgment right now," Jayden finally said, looking his brother squarely in the eyes. "I had an experience."

"An experience. You've had a lot of experiences, Jayden."

His brother rubbed his temples in frustration.

"I mean it, Jax," he said after a moment. "This is important."

Jaxson said nothing, allowing the space between them to shrink. He hoped the breathing room would draw them closer. His brother began to speak.

"I was working in a remote part of Africa recently, in disguise, as I often do. My mission was to free this woman who had been taken against her will in a market. She wasn't just any woman. She was a diplomat's daughter. My role was to gather the intel and figure out where she was being held." Jayden paused for a moment, considering his next words before continuing.

"I was talking to a boy, a local," his brother continued. "He was a contact I groomed over time, very friendly. I formed a bond with him, almost like a son. One day, we were talking in the street, more like an alley. His back was toward the cross street, and he was telling me about a woman, someone who appeared to him in a dream."

Jayden stopped then, working hard to fight back the tears. Jaxson had never seen his brother so upset. He was usually so composed, not the man he was slowing revealing. "It all happened so fast," he continued. "Two men on a moped, swiping of a blade. The boy fell to the ground. I was trying to find the injuries. When a doctor took him away, I was sure he was dead, but that night, I dreamed of a woman. The culture over there, they are very superstitious. They believe this stuff transfers, like I picked up on the boy's energy or something; you know what I'm saying?"

"Not really," Jaxson said, shifting in his chair.

Jayden dropped his head for a moment, clearly struggling to find the words before looking his brother dead in the eye.

"The woman from the video. The woman who healed you. She was the one in my dream, Jaxson. She said if she saved him, then I had to get out and come home."

Jaxson furrowed his brow in response, wondering if his brother was confused or blurring the course of events.

"Jay," Jaxson said, reaching for his brother's shoulder. "It's all right. You've had a lot to deal with. It may just all be coming out now. When did this happen? After you saw the video? It's probably something that was in your mind. You know, you were worried about me, right? That's probably what it was."

"No, this happened before I saw the video of you, maybe a few days after your accident, but before I saw it," Jayden said. "Anyway, let me finish. I went to the hospital the next day and that boy was healed. His gut was slashed, Jaxson. There's no way he could survive something like that. That woman healed him, Jax. She did something to him, and to me."

The two brothers looked at each other: so different in appearance, but so close in heart and soul.

"I'm coming with you to Vegas," Jayden said after a moment. Then he disappeared into the other room.

"How do you even know about that?" Jaxson asked.

Silence was Jayden's only response.

CHAPTER FIFTEEN

P yrus was about to step out on the terrace when the phone rang. He really didn't want to have to deal with this today. He wanted only Jade for an afternoon. He would often watch her slide into the pool, sun gleaming on her skin. Except for the occasional drone, the area around the pool was well protected, private. He loved to follow her frame as she strolled around nude, gracefully lowering her body onto the edge of the pool. At times, she would allow her fingers to skim the top of the water as if testing for the perfect temperature. Rarely did he find her in the water. It was foreign to a woman whose ancestors wandered the African deserts for centuries. It made sense how she could tolerate the suffocating heat of Vegas. It was home to a woman like Jade.

Like everyone in Pyrus's life, Jade had a purpose. He wouldn't allow her to rent space in his head if he didn't see value in what she had to offer, even beyond the bedroom. Fifteen years ago, his indiscretions during his marriage never bothered him. He saw the various women as stress relief. It helped to vent the pressure of business with vigorous sex, sometimes so twisted that it even turned off the most experienced escorts.

It was through the escort service that he was introduced

to Jade. He could see immediately that she was different. Jade had no agenda, other than making enough money to afford her a lifestyle she had only seen in television shows as a child visiting her wealthy grandparents in Mogadishu. Because Jade was beautiful and not much a burden, her tyrant grandfather would allow her to stay for a month each summer. When the time ended, he would cast her out into the street with no expectation of her return. He believed he was making her tough, fortifying her spirit by sending her away to fend for herself as she made her way back to her family in one of the various camps outside of town. It was a rite of passage. She was expected to find her way back to her family, just as he had done during countless conflicts in his own youth. Only this kind of perseverance would ensure she had the ability to survive in a world that would swallow the average person whole. But Jade was anything but average.

She was the oldest of eight and had watched her mother's looks fade with each birth and the regular struggle that went far beyond the camps they inevitably found themselves in for short periods of time. Jade knew birth control and wealthy men were the keys to a new life. She would not be a burden to her parents any longer than she had to and she was desperate to find a way out. She did not want to be left wandering the desert with children in tow, searching for a permanence that would never be found.

One afternoon, after being tossed out from her month-long stay with her impossible elders, she didn't make the usual trek back to the camps where her parents had stayed during her absence. Instead, she traveled deep into the city, searching for a way out. Her statuesque figure made her appear much older than her fifteen years. Eyes from every direction always found their way to Jade and her confident, if not slinky, walk. She talked her way into a job at a local travel agency, easily passing for the eighteen years required to obtain the position.

Within a few months, she was delivering travel itineraries throughout the city. After a year, she was working for the agency's top clients. One afternoon, she knocked on the door of a powerful diplomat with business connections in Europe and a wife far away in Hong Kong. After a few months of regular encounters with him, Jade found herself on the streets of Paris, capturing the eyes of designers and agents. Modeling came easy for the tall beauty, but she found the work to be tedious. Standing for fittings for hours on end, she soon learned that her body was no more valuable than a bit of flesh in the window at the butcher shop down the street.

It was another model who first introduced her to the escort world. Many of the young women she roomed with, most of whom were not nearly as pretty as Jade and far less successful, picked up extra income entertaining wealthy men while on the road. Jade, who was often booked by top designers, knew it was her way into a world of privilege her upbringing could never provide. She also knew that her busy schedule would never allow her the time to mingle with the kind of men she needed to achieve the status she craved.

It wasn't long before Jade found herself in the middle of the world's most powerful men. She was devastatingly gorgeous, but her approach, her tenderness, were so captivating it seemed no man could resist her. When Pyrus first set eyes on her, he knew he was in deep trouble. Soulful, alluring Jade soon captured him completely, and the two had been inseparable ever since.

"Darlin', I just have to take this quick call, and then I'm all yours," he said. It was the kind of thing he would never say to any other woman. But Jade wasn't anyone. She was as brilliant as she was beautiful.

"I'll be here waiting," she purred, kissing him on the cheek for good measure.

Pyrus made his way to the living room, pouring a scotch to prep himself for the work ahead. He grabbed the remote and spoke into the speaker, commanding the connection to appear on the screen before him.

"Callahan here," one of his top advisors said nervously.

"So, where are we at with the Vegas deal?"

"We have the venue secured in the Neo. The magician show has been moved off-strip. A payout was required."

"Why a payout?" Pyrus asked. "I thought we had it in the contract we could do whatever we wanted with the show?"

"Not quite that simple," Callahan said with a guttural cough that followed. The man didn't look well, but Pyrus pressed on, only seeking the information he needed before returning to his more important reunion with Jade.

"What, you have a cold or something?"

"Something," Callahan answered, before continuing.

"Well take some medicine or something. It's annoying! What did we have to pay?" Pyrus asked, taking another sip in the process.

"Fifty-four thousand dollars," the man said with another cough. "But it's a small price to pay for what the woman is going to bring you."

"OK, so when will the new stage and show be ready?"

"Well, we looked into the immersion theater that you asked about, but it was cost prohibitive. We can have the show as outlined in the original proposal up and running in the next two weeks."

"Two fucking weeks? Why not two days? What the fuck am I paying these bastards for?"

Callahan shifted in his chair uncomfortably, coughing again in the process. The man clearly had a cold or something, but Pyrus didn't care enough at the moment to ask.

"I'll take it up with management on Monday," Callahan finally added.

"No, you will take it up this weekend. There's no rest for the wicked here, Callahan. Get it done, and let me be crystal clear that we are launching one week from tonight. Fridays are always the best nights to launch," Pyrus said with a pour of another drink. "I'm not waiting two fucking weeks."

"Fine," Callahan said defeatedly, suppressing another cough. "As long as the woman is here and ready to go, we'll make it happen."

"Oh, she'll be ready," Pyrus said confidently.

"Yes, sir," Callahan answered with a cough. "The rooms are confirmed."

"So, what's up with that cough of yours?" Pyrus finally asked.

"Well, that's what I was hoping to talk to you about. I have lung cancer, and I'm going to be out for a time to get treatment," Callahan said, his head dropping in defeat.

"Take all the time you need," said Pyrus, mouth forming a slight grin. "You're fired."

"What?" Callahan said with a gasp, before launching into a series of coughs.

"You're. Fired." Pyrus said again, taking a sip of his drink. "One week of severance for every year served."

"But that's only seventeen weeks," Callahan shouted into the screen. "What about medical?"

Pyrus clicked the system off then, not bothering with the details. Weed out the weak. That was the only way. His other men, healthier men, would handle it behind the scenes. He took the bottle with him as he made his way to the terrace.

"What's going on out here?" he asked in surprise, watching Jade wade her way down the stairs into the shallow end of the infinity pool.

"Just waiting for you," she said, looking back.

After leading all day, all he could do was follow her into the deep end of the pool.

CHAPTER SIXTEEN

I t was his first weekend off in as many weeks. Lucas had worked two twenty-hour shifts back to back following the accident, only stopping to nap in an edit bay and dive into some fast-food provided by the editor who usually occupied it. He knew this was the story of his career.

He set the alarm well before dawn, hoping to avoid the Saturday slog to Portland, which usually involved a large number of weekend warriors looking for adventure, or the regular city traffic that had seemingly grown overnight to encompass even the most southern parts of the metropolitan area. If he left after 9:00 a.m., he knew he would be crawling in a line down to Tacoma and the military base nearly forty miles south of downtown for hours. He preferred darkness and copious amounts of coffee to sunlight and swear words. There were enough of those in the newsroom.

He flew through the city, past Boeing field and I-405, then swerved his way through the Tacoma curves, and settled into the hypnotic I-5 drive beyond the base before the sun made a fleeting appearance over the top of Rainier. He always loved that mountain, nestled firmly along the Cascade range, sunbeams bursting at its peak like a bright star on a perfectly shaped Christmas tree. It reminded him that he needed to get outdoors more often, and more importantly, to call his mother.

He saw the "Welcome to Oregon" sign and instinctively checked the time. Just under three hours. That had to be a record on I-5 these days, he mused, as his tires met the grate along the Interstate Bridge. He couldn't believe her mother had agreed to the interview. It had taken him nearly two weeks to convince her, but one idle conversation last Wednesday seemed to do the trick.

He noticed how the trolls had finally taken control of the conversation online. If there was one thing he had learned in the brief conversations with Marisol, he knew that she was fiercely protective of her daughter.

Three rings and a click. At first he thought she had hung up again, but then he heard her breathing.

"Hal-lo," she said, a thick accent filling the line.

"Hi, Marisol?" Lucas asked rather timidly.

"Yes," she said, trying to pretend she didn't recognize his voice. "Who's this?" And there was the confirmation.

"This is Lucas Moore calling from Channel 9 in Seattle," he began confidently, before his mind overwhelmed him with panic. His timid side took over. "Is this a good time to chat?"

"I don't think so," she said, pausing for a beat before continuing. "I told you that I do not like the press."

"I know, I know," he said, tapping into the cub reporter he had left behind a little over two years before. "I just thought you might want to comment about all the trolls online doubting your daughter and her incredible healing abilities." The journalist inside of him cringed at those words, but he continued in earnest.

"What are these trolls?" she asked.

"Oh, those are people on the internet who post cruel, insensitive, and rash comments in an effort to upset others and get an emotional, often negative response. Given you are Una's mother, you have to be her biggest fan and most staunch supporter. I'm looking for that angle of the story to give it a more positive spin."

"Yes…" she said, allowing him to continue. He almost dropped the phone in shock.

"Well, I wanted to know if you have something to say to all these doubters?"

She paused for a long moment. Lucas almost broke the silence by reframing the question but stopped himself just as she opened her mouth once more.

"Are they doubting her?" she asked.

The woman had to be living under a rock, Lucas thought, but chose wisely to keep that one to himself.

"Yes, Marisol," Lucas said with a disgusted tone. "They are doubting your daughter and her healing abilities. Have you seen any of the videos online?"

"Online? No," she said. "My friend showed me the video, but I was too busy wiping away my tears of joy to finish. But my daughter called me and told me about it. She is good."

"Why don't you share that story, Marisol," Lucas said, a genuine concern overtaking his tone. "Tell your daughter's story now that she's not able to."

"What do you mean, not able to?" Marisol asked.

"Well, as I understand it, your daughter signed a non-disclosure agreement with Payne Industries, which means she is not allowed to grant any interviews to the press. People like me," he said, more simply. "I want to tell your story, Marisol. Will you do me the honor of telling your daughter's remarkable story?"

And that's all it took. Marisol dropped her guard, and Lucas didn't hesitate to set it all up before she had a chance to change her mind. This had to be his biggest interview to date, but he didn't let that show. The two were laughing by the end of the phone conversation, as he promised to show her all he was seeing online.

He pulled up to the small house on the east side of town; a chain-link fence framed a beautiful English garden. He stopped himself before heading inside, checking his reflection in the rearview and closing his eyes to repeat a mantra before opening the car door.

"My subjects open up to me in ways beyond my imagination."

He hoped that would be true today.

The door opened to reveal a beautiful woman. She had a classic look reminiscent of screen sirens from the early years of cinema. She was humble in her greeting, despite her breathtaking beauty.

"Hi, Marisol. I'm Lucas Moore from Channel 9 News," he said, extending his hand in greeting.

She awkwardly took his hand, weakly shaking it. It clearly wasn't her usual style of greeting.

"Come in," she said, motioning him through the threshold.

The inside of her home surprised him at first. Every wall was washed in bright, vibrant hues that seemed to pull him into a setting far away from Portland. It was so different from the woman he had conversed with on the phone and the one who stood before him now.

"Your home is beautiful," he offered, taking in the comfortable furnishings in the sitting room off the foyer.

"Here," she said, guiding him into the living room. She sat in the chair, leaving him the spacious couch.

"I'm just going to take a moment to set up my gear," he said, nodding to the bag he had just dropped rather loudly on the floor.

"No problem," Marisol said. "Would you like a coffee, tea, or water?"

"I would love a coffee, thank you," Lucas said, considering if consuming more caffeine would turn him into a jittery mess. He had already downed a venti from Starbucks on the drive.

"On second thought, how about tea and some water?"

She nodded and smiled sweetly before leaving the room. He went to work setting up the camera equipment, wondering if he had packed the new lavalier microphone, before discovering it in a side pocket. He was nervous. He closed his eyes and took a few deep breaths before setting up a light and checking his audio levels.

Marisol returned with a tray, placing an elegant cup of tea on the coffee table and a tall glass of water into his hand. He thanked her before gulping it down, almost embarrassed when he stopped at the bottom of the glass.

"Sorry," he said, setting it down on the wooden surface. "It was a long drive."

She settled into the chair and helped him place the microphone on the edge of her colorful blouse. He stepped back to start recording and then sat down on the couch adjacent to her.

"Marisol, I'm going to start by having you state your full name," Lucas began.

"Marisol Conchita Alvarez," she said.

"Marisol, thank you for granting me this interview," Lucas said, clearing his throat before continuing. "The accident must have come as a great shock to you."

"Yes," she said. Rookie mistake. He realized he hadn't even asked a real question, never one with a simple yes/no response. He was grateful he had chosen water over coffee.

"How did you find out about the accident?" he asked.

"I work for a hotel downtown. The security boys were watching the television when I passed by, and I saw it on the screen."

"What did you see?"

"I saw my daughter," she said, tears forming in the corners of her eyes.

Lucas paused for a moment, giving her the room to continue. It was something that Stein had beat into his head over the last year or so, scolding him every time he interjected before getting "the goods." He waited another moment, hoping she would continue. He handed her a tissue, and she did.

"She was standing over a man. I think, What is happening? Is she…hurt?" She started to cry, dabbing the corners of her eyes with the tissue and holding up her hand for a moment before regaining her composure and continuing.

"Were the images of the crash shocking?" Lucas continued. Dammit, he thought. Another obvious, yes/no question.

"Yes," she said. "I could not believe my eyes! She stood over the man, holding her hands over his dead body. Then, he was awake. He was OK, and I was so relieved. I was confused."

"I'm sure any mother would have been. What did you see next?" he asked. Better, he thought, waiting for her response.

"I saw the bus she was riding in," Marisol said, choking back a sob. Lucas waited another long moment, praying she would continue before he would have to say something. No such luck.

"I know. I saw the bus myself, with my own eyes," he said, with a hand gesture toward his own sockets. He felt almost foolish doing it in the moment, but it seemed to connect with her.

"That's right," she said with a sense of awe. "What was it like?"

"It was awful," he recalled. "It is a miracle anyone emerged from that bus, let alone your daughter."

Marisol smiled, as if remembering her daughter was still alive. Lucas searched her eyes, almost willing her to continue, but she didn't.

"Yes, it is a miracle," she finally said after several seconds of silence.

"Did you know your daughter was a healer?" he asked.

"No," she said. "But she is a miracle."

"What do you mean?" Lucas asked, carefully framing the question with a sensitive tone. It was something he had heard in a consultant meeting once. He was grateful for the recall in that moment.

"She was born, and I have no idea why," Marisol said. Lucas was perplexed, his curiosity now moving to the front burner.

"There's a story there, Mrs. Alvarez," he said, almost cheerily prompting her memory. "Take us back to that moment."

"I tried to have her at home," she said. "But I had been in labor for many hours. My cousin, who was a roommate at the time, borrowed a car from someone in our building and drove me to the hospital. I was there for three days, in and out of labor. Una was born at midnight. She was a perfect baby. I didn't think I could have a baby, so I was so happy. I cried out when I heard her cry," she said, now starting to cry herself.

"Do you have other children?" he finally asked, hoping the answer was yes to lift her mood.

"No, no," she said, dabbing her tears with the tissue. "Actually, the doctor told me it was a miracle I was pregnant in the first place."

"What do you mean?" Lucas asked.

"Well, I had to have the surgery after the birth. They took my uterus."

"Yes, I understand that." Lucas reassured. "But that was after."

"No, they look around when I was in the operation," Marisol said. "I have no tubes to make the baby."

"You don't have fallopian tubes?" he asked, eyes widening.

"Yes, that's right," she said with a nod. "I have no tubes to make the baby."

"But how did you get pregnant without fallopian tubes?" Lucas said with a shake of the head. "That's impossible."

"I don't know, but it's true."

Lucas studied her face a little longer before proceeding. He asked her the usual questions, like her response to troll culture and all that online videos invited these days. She answered honestly and graciously. He really did enjoy her company. And the tea was better than his own mother's tea. That was an admission he would keep to himself.

But he never let the medical discovery go. Perhaps he really was a doctor at heart. He was fascinated with the idea of a woman conceiving without tubes, though his scientific mind deduced that they were likely functioning before but were part of a total hysterectomy. It wasn't something Western doctors would embrace, but overseas? It was a total crap shoot.

She walked him to the car, offering to carry his backpack. It was a polite gesture and one he was happy to oblige. As he closed the hatch, she wrapped him in her arms.

"You don't know how good it felt to finally tell someone that," Marisol said, tears starting to flow again.

"I'm not sure what you mean," he said rather shyly. His interview was decent, maybe even one of his best. But he wasn't sure if it exceeded his expectations of what it would be on his drive down.

"I haven't told anyone about the birth," she said, looking at him rather nervously. "It is the first time I shared the story about…" her eyes lowered below her waist. "My anatomy, I mean."

"Do you remember the name of the hospital?" he offered. "I'd be happy to try and track down the record."

"San Mateo," she said, and proceeded to tell him the town she was living in at the time and offered up directions like a local would. He nodded politely, unable to keep up with her elaborate description of the locale and its physical features.

"I'll look into it," he said. Lucas was proud of himself. It was the first time he had conducted an interview where medical knowledge was revealed, and he didn't once offer up the fact he was a doctor by training. He hugged her once more before sliding into the driver's seat. He would do his best to hold off Stein until he got to the truth. If all of it were true, he wasn't about to be scooped on the story of a lifetime.

CHAPTER SEVENTEEN

Una swiped the card on the reader. With a faint click, she opened the door slowly to reveal the penthouse suite. It was unbelievable. Her humble upbringing made her feel as if she didn't deserve any of it. She pushed the same feeling aside a few hours before, as she settled into the lamb's skin seat onboard the private jet. She wasn't ready to wake from the dream just yet. She stood in the foyer for a moment, wondering when Jaxson and his brother would arrive. She knew there would be others, but for now, the brothers would be enough to help get the show off the ground and keep Pyrus and his team at bay.

It was the most opulent space she had ever seen. Ultra-modern décor filled every inch of the space. How they managed to keep it so perfectly balanced between lavish and clean was beyond her. Minimally lavish. That was the best way to describe it. She never had an eye for these things. The most extravagant thing she had ever done with decorating was buy a new bedspread from the clearance section of a T.J. Maxx. The color was a little strange, but the feel of it made the purchase worth it. This space made the bedspread feel like a distant memory.

The suite took up the entire floor: eight bedrooms and nine bathrooms in total. She walked through the living area, lightly touching the back of the white leather sectional that anchored the space. It was as soft as the seat she had chosen on the flight. A massive kitchen was just off to the side, complete with every appliance and luxury kitchen gadget that money could buy, as if they would need it. An entire staff downstairs was waiting to bring them food from two of the top restaurants in Vegas that were housed on the lower level. She had understood from the woman who checked her in that presidents, foreign heads of state, even royalty had graced the rooms within.

She looked around for a moment before choosing her bedroom. Massive floor to ceiling windows stunned her as she opened the door to the first room at the other end of the hall. She could make out every major hotel on the strip below. She had only been to Vegas once before for a friend's twenty-first birthday party. Suffice to say, the accommodations at the time were far less than this, so much so they weren't even on the strip.

She wandered through a few more rooms before settling on the first one. It wasn't the biggest, but it was welcoming, and the expansive views were a beautiful distraction from all that was waiting downstairs in the theater. The king-sized bed and its crisp, white bedding beckoned her to drop her things and sink in for a quick nap, but she had work to do.

A small desk sat in the corner by the window. She pulled out her laptop and plugged in all of her chargers. She was perplexed as to how to begin. There was so much to share with the newly formed fan base. After the details of the show were presented, she had met with the hotel's public relations team, a move designed to excite her about the show. She explained all the reasons behind posting the original video, apologizing for the comments and trolls that it had attracted. The team of three just smiled knowingly, hiding the fact they were more than impressed by the millions of views. Their eyes sparkled upon her every word, not even a flinch of concern. With a few reassuring words, her stress level had lifted and the dust of the crash and its aftermath had seemed to settle for the moment.

"Una, I'm sure your job would allow a leave of absence given everything that happened to you this past month. They love your work. Besides, at your age, taking risks is an important part of life, at any stage of life, really," the lead woman said with a toothpaste ad smile. "Sometimes, we need to shake things up a bit in order to know where we are needed. It's a way to make your path known, and with the response to the videos posted so far, I'd say the path is remarkably clear."

Una didn't know what to say. She hadn't thought about leaving Seattle or the bakery before the accident. She had been there a little over two years and had already taken on some of the most challenging orders. She didn't want to lose ground but knew this was far more important.

"It is important," the PR woman offered. "You should know that what happened, what will happen, is going to transform many lives, including yours."

"How so?" Una asked.

"Hasn't it already? Have you been back to the bakery since it happened?"

Una hadn't been back. The first few weeks after the accident were consumed with the settlement. She spent the time in between monitoring the videos posted online and wrapping her head around this extraordinary power she now possessed. It was all so surreal. The other videos recorded by witnesses were now on YouTube, garnering upward of a billion views in total.

"It's just that I didn't expect all of this," Una finally said. "I do know it's important, but it's also overwhelming."

"It's only forty days of shows, a little less than six weeks in total," the woman said, offering her hand to Una across the conference room table. "You can do anything for six weeks," she said confidently. "My father once told me that when I made the decision to move across the country and go to school in Washington, DC. And, look at it this way, if you want to go back to your life before all of this, at the bakery I mean, then do it when it's all over. At least you won't have any regrets."

Una extended her hand to the woman, feeling a tingling sensation ripple through her body. It was like an energy boost and anxiety reliever all in one shot. She felt the relief pour over her as the answer became clear.

"Let's do it," Una said, a smile forming on her lips.

She didn't recall many bystanders around the day of the crash, but she now realized that the shock obviously clouded her of the countless phones that were capturing the event from every angle. What really fascinated her was how negative people were, particularly over the video she posted.

…Photoshop!

…Fake news!

…What a bunch of bullshit.

…Someone has a lot of time on their hands and really poor effects.

…I wish those people had just died that day, then we wouldn't have to see their stupid faces all day every day since!

It seemed so odd to Una that a true miracle was such a bad thing in the eyes of so many. It was as if they didn't want to believe in anything that was remotely good in the world, or as if vile reactions to blessings in life were a source of power and control over their own situations.

After the meeting with the public relations team, and subsequently agreeing to the show in Vegas, Una's fears about the thoughts and comments of others slowly dissipated. Not all who liked and followed were friends, of course, but that didn't seem to bother Una at all now that she had guidance.

The voice she had heard in the minutes following the accident was proving to be a powerful guide in her daily life, and Una found herself tapping into the source through meditation a few times a day. The connection to the beyond brought her a sense of calm and peace, even revealing powerful visions of what was to come, preparing her for the shows and the powerful reaction they would cause.

She asked the team to help her monitor the reactions and comments. They set her up with a laptop and simple software program and watched remotely as Una kept fans abreast of what was happening since the crash.

She went right to work after the meeting, setting up a new profile and considering what exactly to share each day. She wasn't sure how granular the posts could be or how much was too much. She had her own pages to think about but nothing like this new persona she had evolved into.

Dear friends and followers, I am heading to
Las Vegas—forty days of shows where you can
experience miracles for yourself. More to come.

The comments began to pour in.

Another freak show coming to Vegas!
#fakeittilyoumakeit

Tragic to capitalize on people's misery!

Wut iz the world comin 2!

Hope is here! Booking now!

This shit has got to be better than some of the acts
that have been there for a million years.

As she watched the comments populate the thread, it was like a slow crucifixion of all the crash had represented. Una believed that what she experienced was in fact her own resurrection, a sort of rebirth, only into a time that she never anticipated, let alone knew how to navigate. But she had to trust what was happening now. After all, her life had changed dramatically since the crash, and it seemed like so far, it was all for the better.

The decision to leave was an easy one. Her employer didn't allow a leave and made no promise she would have a job if she returned. She decided to burn the remaining vacation days she had banked and walk away. It's not like she had rent or even food to worry about in Vegas, and the settlement money would be enough to help her start a new life when the shows were over. Pyrus had made promises of payment after the shows were over but wouldn't commit to any payment until it was a proven success. She considered what she would do if payment came through at the end. She could afford to pay off her mother's house. She didn't want to think about that now; instead, she was consumed by the idea of healing others on a public stage. She wasn't sure she would know what to do. She had to have blind faith it would all work out.

She was overcome with sleep then, wondering if a short cat nap would revive her enough to explore what was next. She needed to see the theater at some point and share pictures and teasers about the show with her followers. It was unreal how quickly the whole thing had exploded. Over four million followers so far, and she had only been actively posting for about a week. Night began to fall over the room, and her eyelids grew heavy. Watching the neon reflections on the wall, she wondered what the experience would bring.

Notifications were blowing up her phone nonstop. She decided to check in one last time before calling it a night. Tomorrow would be a busy day of meetings and details about the show. She considered the crowds that were about to descend upon them. Una wouldn't care about their circumstances. Even the most downtrodden would have a place in her heart. She wondered what it would be like to heal dozens, if not hundreds of people a day. The possibility filled her heart in a way she didn't expect. It wasn't seeded in fear but rather an intense joy for what was to come.

CHAPTER EIGHTEEN

The electronic beat pulsed loudly within her skull, driving her to the surface. Petra was conscious but definitely out of sorts. It was almost like she had a terrible case of the bends. Her limbs, even her lips, felt heavy, and her mind was foggy. What had happened the night before was not accessible in the confines of her mind.

She felt a stickiness under her fingers as she attempted to pull herself into a sitting position. The small pool of blood had formed where her head had been. Her temple was throbbing; her cheek was hot to the touch. Petra grabbed onto the toilet tank and attempted to hoist herself up, but the effort only drained her more. She reached for the last square of toilet paper, dabbing the side of her face. The square immediately turned crimson. She had to get out of here. She was in trouble.

A surge of energy coursed through her veins. She reached for the handicap railing and pulled herself to her feet. She nearly stumbled as she reached for the door handle, grabbing the top of the stall door to steady herself. She released the latch and pushed the door open, stumbling forward like a newborn calf.

She reached for the sink and began running the water, searching for paper towels in the process. She caught her reflection and stared for a long moment. Her left eye was nearly swollen shut, the side of her head was badly bleeding. Her lower lip was split open, and both cheeks were covered in angry bruises. Someone had done this to her, but her mind couldn't recall a face.

She remembered the bus ride in flickers and flashes, a golden grill revealed through a sinister smile. It was the guy from the bus. Slowly, the memory formed like a jigsaw puzzle before her. Bits of this and that coming together to form a small recollection of the previous night's events. It was all becoming clear.

The two had left the hotel just after 9:00 p.m. They were both ravenous after endless hours of sex. She seemed to remember spending more than a full day in the small room, twisting, turning, and contorting into various incarnations of sexual being. Desperate, hungry, sated. She remembered him running his calloused fingers along her spine, pulling the weight of his muscular body onto her, thrusting himself deep inside and staying there quietly for a moment or two. It was certainly not the kind of experience expected between a hardened criminal and former sex worker. They were two people used to using others; perhaps that is why it had been so good. They used each other up over the course of as many hours or days, she wasn't quite certain.

She blotted her face with the towel, wincing as she attempted to close the gaping wound at her temple. From the looks of her face, she was lucky to even be alive, let alone upright. She needed a doctor but had no way to pay for it. She noticed a small handbag tethered from her shoulder from a tarnished gold chain. Inside, she found a few pills and a wad of cash, a couple grand from the looks of it. She had on what appeared to be a very expensive pink sequined dress. Leopard print pumps adorned her feet. She couldn't recall how she acquired the clothes she was wearing, much less what she had been doing in them during the last as many hours.

Petra did her best to dress her wounds, wishing she had a paper bag to put over her head when she made her way out of what was obviously some casino bathroom. She could hear the slot machines outside, the bells and tones beckoning the less fortunate to claim some far off fortune. When she bent down to take a sip of water, blood drops followed, staining the porcelain bowl below. She drank from the faucet, not realizing until now just how thirsty she was. How long she had been on the bathroom floor was beyond her, but she had guessed for quite some time. Rarely in Vegas would another person stop to help someone slumped on the floor of some random restroom.

She didn't bother to clean the blood off the floor of the corner stall, opting instead to form cold bricks out of the towels available, one for now and one for later. She held one to her head, stopping to examine herself once more. Her reflection was a pathetic sight. Tears began to form as she looked away in disgust, repositioning her bag before walking rather unsteadily toward the door.

Electronic sounds filled her ears as the door opened onto the casino floor. Few people were walking around, even fewer were sitting in front of the thousands of screens. It had to be morning. But how could one really tell inside of a casino?

She looked left and then right, considering her options before heading straight toward the slot machines, meandering her way through a maze of bling and zing. She dodged the occasional gambler, clinging to the button that would bring forth fortunes untold. That was one thing about Vegas. The city had a way of keeping people trapped on the floor for hours and, by the looks of some of these people, days.

She must have circled the casino floor at least three times before realizing she had returned to the same bathroom from which she emerged. She was desperately looking for signs of an exit. In the distance, she could see the word "theater" in neon. She wandered in the direction the arrow had pointed, figuring that it was the most logical place to find a way out.

Petra saw the guards gathered in a corner. The two seemed to be comparing notes. She didn't want them to see her in this state. The encounter would only evoke questions she wasn't prepared to answer right now. She disappeared back into the forest of machines, keeping the theater sign in range of her good eye. After several more minutes of meandering, she landed upon it. She saw a lone bench tucked out of the way. She sat down for a moment, head throbbing, but a bit better than it was when she woke on the bathroom floor.

She was about to get on her feet again when an entourage came around the corner. She watched the group form quietly in front of the theater doors. As the group came to a stop, an image appeared before her. The woman was dressed in a flowing white dress. Her skin was glowing. She was a vision, obviously some kind of starlet preparing to captivate audiences with an upcoming showcase at the casino. The stranger was nothing short of breathtaking. Petra found herself holding her own breath as she watched the others around her. They seemed focused on what the young woman was telling them. One of them caught her eye and shuddered at the sight before her; then a look of sympathy washed over her face. She tapped the starlet on the shoulder and motioned her Petra's way. Her eyes appeared like diamonds shining upon Petra. Within moments the young woman was standing before her, kneeling down to examine her face and wounds, those seen and those hidden deeply within.

"What happened to you?" she asked. "I can sense that you have come a long way to get here, but you're not home yet," the woman said finally, looking deep into Petra's eyes.

"I have come far," Petra said in return. "You have no idea."

"I have some idea," said the angel before her, taking Petra's hands into her own. "Why don't you join us inside the theater," she said. Not waiting for a response, she pulled Petra to her feet.

The group shuffled into the theater, keeping a careful collective eye on Petra. She continued to hold the paper brick to her head, which was now crimson brown from all the blood collected. A worker rushed ahead of them, disappearing backstage for a moment. Lights flooded the stage. The lights shining from above were a combination of blues and reds. It wasn't much larger than a typical auditorium. The space seated maybe five thousand at maximum capacity.

"It looks like we may have our very first customer," a worker said enthusiastically, motioning the group to the front of the stage. Petra couldn't understand what was happening, a feeling of fear rushing from her gut to her throat.

"I don't know what this is, but I think I should be going," she said, turning to thank the woman in the white dress.

"Please don't go, Petra," the woman said.

"How do you know—"

"You have been badly hurt," she continued. "I would like for you to come onto the stage with me." The woman motioned the rest of the group to take the seats in the front row. "I guess we're doing this right now."

Petra considered her surroundings for a moment, too confused to refuse the proposal. She was mesmerized by the glow of the woman's skin.

"All right," she finally relented.

Una took Petra's open hand, guiding her carefully up the five steps to the stage floor. They walked toward the center of the stage, the woman squaring her off to face her. The two looked at each other for a moment before Una reached for the makeshift brick at Petra's temple. She took it out of her hand, looking around for a place to toss it. Another woman walked up to the front of the stage to retrieve it.

"This will only take a minute," she said, reassuring Petra. "Please, give me your hands."

Una closed her eyes, repositioning her feet at the same time. Petra became nervous, perspiration forming on her forehead.

"No need to worry now; just let it all go," Una said. "Please breathe in light with me, and exhale the darkness."

As if on command, Petra took a deep breath in. Light, almost appearing as smoke, moved from Una's lips and into Petra's nostrils. The exchange lasted for thirty seconds or so, but to Petra it felt like several minutes.

"I don't know where to begin," Petra began, tears forming in her eyes. "I've done so much wrong, made many, many bad decisions."

"Choice is a gift," Una said quietly. "The end result is neither bad nor good. It is merely a learning that all in human form must endure."

"But what if I didn't learn? What if I keep repeating my mistakes?"

"You must learn to trust yourself and to find your footing."

Petra choked back a sob, her head dropping toward the stage floor in shame. She remembered what happened in an instant. Steve invited her to dinner that first night, then lavished her with gifts from a few stores on the way back. They shacked up in the hotel for a few more days before he presented the idea. She could return to her roots, if only for a little while, offering her body for money in exchange for the room with Steve. She refused at first, but he threatened her physically, leaving her little choice but to walk the strip. She sat alone at the bar, waiting for the moment to strike.

It was her first one, she was pretty sure. He seemed normal enough, claimed to be an investor in town for a meeting. He offered his room key and two thousand for the entire night. She agreed but stepped into the restroom first to freshen up, promising to join him a few minutes later. She couldn't believe her luck as she made her way down the hall toward his room. Upon opening the door, she was immediately attacked. The man had three friends waiting inside, each taking a turn raping and beating her until they fell to the floor exhausted and drunk.

She remembered waking up to the sound of snoring, at first thinking she was back in the room with Steve. She pulled down her dress and stumbled toward the door, barely remembering her bag and shoes. She heard one of the men stir as she quietly closed it behind her, weaving her way down the hallway to the elevator, frantically pushing the button. She woke later in a pool of blood on the bathroom floor. Tears poured from her eyes, as much out of relief for the memory as the shame that followed her there.

"Forgive yourself, Petra," Una said. "It is the only way through. And whatever has happened to you, has also happened through you. It is done now."

Her eyes flew open then, a rush going through her body. She no longer felt the agony of loss, resentment, reluctance. She felt retrieved from the abandoned chambers of her heart. She realized in that moment she had made her home in those abandoned chambers for the better part of two decades. She felt herself rushing through them, breaking through the very structure of the muscle within. Breath burst forth as if for the first time.

"I forgive myself," she finally said, air released from her lungs.

The gash on her head began to close, bruises fading, leaving only a rosy trail in their wake upon her cheeks. Within the span of a minute, she was fully healed, not just outside but within. She stared at her hands, observing the glittery glow on her delicate fingers. It was a sort of mystical stardust that only the touched would know, as if providing physical proof of what had happened in the moments before. Petra reached for the woman before her, wrapping her in a warm embrace as laughter released from her throat.

"How did you do that?" she said drawing away. "You're amazing!"

"I am happy to see this woman before me," Una said with a smile. "I am Una, and this is my home for a short while. Where is your home, Petra?"

"Looks like with you," Petra said without any hesitation. She didn't care about all that came before her. She had finally arrived at her front door. She was home.

CHAPTER NINETEEN

The world looked so different to Matt as the Vegas skyline came into view. He wasn't sure if it was because of what had happened last night or perhaps the moment he met Una in the office. Either way, the world was different and Matt was more than okay with that.

He thought of Una, sitting quietly confident in the conference room and then later in the breakroom. He watched her fill a water glass before interrupting with a cough. She was serenity itself, bright eyes with just a hint of a smile, like the Mona Lisa. He knew that the others would laugh at that assertion, but he didn't care.

Their brief conversation and the offer that followed touched Matt to his very core. How someone so mysterious could be so open and see so much was beyond him. It was as if she reached inside of him and plucked at his heartstrings to play a concerto that only he could hear. It was the song in his heart that seemed to reveal all the potential inside himself.

"I know this day was hard for you, Matt," Una said. "You take things so personally, don't you?"

Matt nodded in agreement, dropping his head in shame.

"Don't be ashamed of caring," she said after a moment. "Indifference? Apathy? Those things should always give you pause in a place like this. I'm guessing that working here would be very exhausting at times, especially when you know the other side deserves more."

"You have no idea," Matt said, raising his eyes to meet hers.

They stood there for a moment in the hallway, just looking at one another knowingly. It wasn't awkward. It was exhilarating. Almost as if they continued the conversation inside his head. The knowledge of this, of course, was too much for him to imagine, so he went with the feeling, rather than the words she whispered that day.

He recalled the words inside his head like puzzle pieces of a masterpiece that was about to become his life. Destiny. Fate. Hope. Healing. And above all, purpose. Matt had craved a sense of purpose since graduating college early at the age of twenty. Law school seemed like an easy way to delay the inevitable, so he took the LSAT and was accepted immediately. It was his first job out of university. Not one to drink in college, he found himself lost at after-work functions in the nearby bar, yet he was far more mature than most of the men-children he worked with. The fraternity culture was nauseating on its best days, a leech on his spirit at worst. He was happy to be putting it behind him, particularly for a woman like Una.

She was fearless; he knew that. Anyone who could stand up to Pyrus Payne and not bat an eyelash had to have balls the size of the sun or more money than God. She didn't strike him as particularly rich, and she certainly was female, so perhaps she possessed a power that stretched past his comprehension. That wouldn't be hard to do, he thought to himself. Aside from his boring routine and work, Matt really didn't put much thought into anything else. He just accepted whatever life threw at him.

Not anymore.

After Una left him that afternoon, he found himself sitting in front of his computer screen. The work before him seemed so meaningless now. He knew what he had to do and, oddly, it didn't scare him at all.

He was contemplating what to say before settling on a simple "I quit." He clicked print, and barreled his way down the hall to the printer and retrieved the paper. Luckily, Claire was on break, and horse-faced Lorna was at the desk filling in. The woman didn't even look up from the beauty magazine she was obviously reading, not so inconspicuously buried inside what looked to be an important file. What a joke this place was. He couldn't wait to put it all behind him.

He stopped at the supply room to grab a small box. He didn't keep many personal effects in the office. The less his merciless coworkers knew, the better. Besides, what would he put in a picture frame anyway? A picture of his goldfish, Cat? Cue the months of teasing that would follow if he did.

He went back to retrieve an envelope from his desk, gently licking the sticky substance before sealing his fate. He spent the next full minute packing up his belongings: a small umbrella, his favorite calculator, and a notepad with the words "hang in there" across the top and a clinging cat paw at the bottom. Well, he wouldn't have to hang in anymore. He considered leaving it for the next poor sucker who took the chair after him but thought better of it. It was the first and only gift he received from Claire at last year's Secret Santa party.

But that was in the past now. He was on his way to a new life with Una in Vegas. She had told him he would be handling the business aspects of the show, including contracts, charitable donations, and payroll. He would file for the business license on her behalf as soon as he got home. He couldn't wait to get started. It would be a fresh start and get him out of the boy's club. He was beginning to realize he had gone to work at a place that embodied everything he had hated about his past, yet it gave him all the necessary skills to use on his new path. Bullying, jocks, endless teasing, tasteless jokes, inequality, unfairness, and sadness accompanied every case that was settled. He loathed coming to work each day, except for Claire. He would miss her. He was starting to regret the fact he had never asked her out when she suddenly appeared in his doorway.

"Hey you," Claire said. He jumped upon seeing her, then settled into his typical nervous response.

"Not much," he said, licking his lips, realizing in the moment that she hadn't asked what he was doing. He was searching for some balm to make it less obvious it was her who triggered the response.

"What are you up to this weekend?" he asked shyly, hoping she wouldn't notice the box. She was looking particularly gorgeous, makeup just applied, obviously ready to meet up with her fabulous friends somewhere downtown.

"I'm meeting up with some friends," Claire said coyly, looking down at her designer shoes. "You wanna join us? We'll be over in Belltown at this new place called The Gate."

Claire paused, waiting a moment for his response, but then continued. "I have no idea if it's good or not, but it's Friday, and we should at least celebrate that, right?"

"Um...sure...maybe?" Matt replied almost in the form of a question. He was considering what he was about to do and the kind of mood he would be in after. Of course, he would be happy. He just wasn't sure if it was the kind of happy that needed to be cherished alone or served up in the form of shots in front of strangers. It was likely somewhere in between.

"OK, yes, I'll join you," he said shyly. She giggled, and his heart melted. "I just have to meet with Breeland, and then I'll be right behind you." The words made him blush. Matt wasn't a lady's man by any stretch but dated a few girls in college. It was enough to make him a little experienced, well, enough to not completely embarrass himself with a woman like Claire.

He could tell she was reading his mind because she started to blush too, a dusty rose that filled in her perfectly chiseled cheekbones.

"I'll see you then. Text me when you're on your way?" Claire asked, reaching for her phone.

"I don't have your—"

"What's yours?" she asked with a smile.

She captured the number and sent him a quick text to verify before turning to leave the room. He craned his neck to watch her walk down the hallway. She was so gorgeous. Sometimes he couldn't believe a woman like her would be interested in a guy like him. Claire was in his phone!

He watched Claire leave and then sat for a moment, working up the nerve to walk into Breeland's office and tell him to shove it. But it just wasn't like him to do something so crass, and that's the very thing he was struggling with. He was still intent on leaving on good terms, even if it meant swallowing his pride in the process.

He set the box below his desk and reached for the envelope. The opening was still wet from licking it a while before. Breeland would be leaving any moment now. He had better make a move now if he hoped to catch him before the weekend. Funny how the executives always left early on

Fridays. In a law firm, early was always around 8:00 p.m. He wondered if that was the normal course of business everywhere else or just here.

Breeland was reaching for his jacket as Matt knocked on the door.

"Matthew, did you need something? I'm about to leave for the day."

"Well, sir, just a moment, if you have one," Matt said nervously, stepping into Breeland's office without the usual protocol of an invite in. He took the seat in front of Breeland's desk. Better to do this across from one another, rather than at the sitting area.

"Is it about the settlement?" Breeland asked, raising an eyebrow at his employee. He could tell things were out of sorts.

"No, not exactly, but I will say the settlement is the reason for my visit," Matt said nervously, perspiration forming at his temples. "I have decided to leave the company, sir."

"Why in the world would you leave now, Matt? You have years under your belt. You're well on your way to moving up."

"Well, Mr. Breeland, I think if that were the case, I would have likely received at least one bonus check in the time I've been here," Matt said, inhaling deeply.

"If it's a bonus you want, then we could make that happen right now. I know living in this city isn't easy, and there are people struggling to keep up with the rising cost of housing. You rent in the city?"

"I do, sir."

"Well, how about a bonus of ten thousand right now. Would that keep you engaged for a while?"

"It's not about the money," Matt said, shaking his head, even more pissed off at the fact he didn't ask for this years ago.

"Then why in the world would you leave a great job at the top firm in the city, let alone the West Coast? I know this settlement has been a real bitch, but we worked it out, and the others coming up aren't nearly as difficult as this one," Breeland said, tipping back into his seat.

"I don't want to work here anymore!" Matt shouted, rocking back into his seat, head in hands.

"Son, you need to—"

"I'm not your son! I am the whipping boy in this place! People don't respect me here! They make fun of me!"

Breeland looked around nervously, checking for someone nearby to help. He considered calling security but stopped himself as Matt continued.

"I purposely avoid people in the hallways. Avoid! Not dodge, or nod politely—I fucking avoid them! I haven't had one intelligent conversation with anyone who works here! It sucks! It's soulless! I fucking hate it! I quit!"

Matt slammed the letter down with his fist on the desk, as sweat and tears dripped down his face. Breeland offered him the handkerchief from his breast pocket. Matt always wondered if it was real. He wiped his face before offering it back. Breeland quietly refused.

"Matt, listen to me. You don't want to do this. I…hell, even Mr. Payne. We love your work. Aside from your unsightly appearance at times and your bumbling ways, you have really proven yourself a loyal worker."

"Mr. Payne doesn't even know I'm alive." Matt said, anger bubbling in his throat.

He wanted desperately to cough the feeling away but thought the better of it. His confidence was building and he didn't want to stop the momentum.

"You're referencing the same guy who tried to fire me

multiple times for reasons like food on my tie. Or I said 'um' too often. Or I didn't present the checks with confidence. How the hell does a person deliver palpable checks—pathetic checks!—with confidence?" Tears were starting to form in his eyes, but he was too angry to let them flow.

"Look, Matt, I know Mr. Payne seems unreasonable at times," Breeland said. "But he is the reason we are employed! You must remember that he's the client. We must do what he wants if we hope to continue drawing checks every two weeks! Clients like Payne are very hard to come by, and they're reliable!"

"Life is more than drawing a check, Mr. Breeland," Matt said, looking his boss dead in the eye. "I just can't. And I don't even care anymore if you understand."

The two sat there for a moment, staring the other down in the hope one would flinch. It never happened. Matt stood and pushed the letter toward his boss. The game of chicken was over.

"I resign effective immediately, Dick," Matt finally said.

Breeland sputtered a response as Matt marched out the door. He didn't even bother to grab the box. He felt for his phone, keys, and wallet and walked boldly out the door. It was the bravest thing he had ever done.

He didn't bother to head for the parking garage, instead opting to walk freely toward Belltown. The gray sky broke open then, revealing the sun in all its glory. It was a sign: the sun and its light guiding him toward a new and bold future with Una. He couldn't believe what he had done just moments before. He rejoiced in replaying the moment during the mile-long walk to The Gate.

The place was packed like most on a Friday in Belltown, welcoming the sea of overworked programmers and executives, all looking for a moment of bliss at the end of a very long week. He spotted Claire immediately, approaching the table with a newfound confidence.

"I quit!" he said proudly as he approached the table.

"You what?" Claire gasped, looking bewildered at this new man in front of her.

"I fucking quit! Those piece of shit bastards! Let's drink!"

Matt had never had this kind of confidence before. He charmed Claire's friends with his story, inciting all the reasons why he walked out the door, all the while wondering why he hadn't done it years ago. Things he shouldn't have ever said, things that he always wanted to tell Claire, were blurted out between shots of top-shelf liquor. It wasn't a night for the cheap stuff. Matt was going out. And he was going out big. It was the highlight of his life so far. And he didn't think of food. Not even once.

CHAPTER TWENTY ────────────

As dawn broke over the strip, Jayden's eyes fluttered open. The stale, cold air circulated through the room. It was the coolest air he had felt in months. His last assignment had been brutal—hours on end wrapped in layers of linens. The turban nearly did him in, working neck muscles he never knew existed. His dreams and nightmares took him back to the alley each night. The plan, the confusion, and the woman most of all. The woman he now knew as Una, standing before him in a flowing white dress, her neck adorned in golden layers and sparkling jewels. It reminded him of a piece he saw at the Metropolitan Museum of Art in the Egyptian wing: beautiful and fragile, but she was anything but.

He felt much calmer now that he had seen her in the flesh, a reassurance of his plan to follow. As much as he had grown into a powerful leader through the years, Jayden was used to following. It was part of his military DNA. On his countless assignments in his career, he learned very quickly that questioning and doubting often got you killed. He had learned to trust his superiors to guide him through some of the most dangerous situations imaginable. Why was this any different? After seeing his brother free of a disease that had disadvantaged him since early adulthood, it was only further confirmation that the path they had chosen to take together now was the right one.

He checked his watch on the charger. 4:44 a.m. It had become more than habit now to rise at such an early hour. In reality, this was more like sleeping in for Jayden. He liked the quiet in the moments before dawn. It was his time to check in with the forces that guided him and often saved him on a daily, if not hourly, basis. He sat up and adjusted the pillows behind him, closing his eyes and taking in a deep breath.

"Spirit, protect me today. Work with and through me. Help me to see that my work is for the greater good. Help me to remove the darkness that follows. Help me to see the light and covet the shadow."

Jayden never got comfortable with starting a day or an assignment without checking inside first. It was often the only thing that got him through, particularly if the order involved death and destruction. It helped him justify his actions in some small way, even if he knew deep down that what he was doing was wrong.

"It's for God and country," one of his superiors would say. He believed that for a very long time. But living around the world has a way of opening the heart and the mind to other pathways, other ways to connect with something greater than ourselves. God was more a universal spirit to Jayden now, rather than the labels he had grown up with.

"With and through me," he would say to himself, slowing his breath before pulling the trigger. His skills as a sniper were unmatched in the field. He had started with a kill count, but when the numbers grew into the middle triple digits, he finally gave up. He didn't want to forget, but at the same time, it seemed the only way to continue. He had to compartmentalize. What he was doing wasn't what Jayden would do; it was what a warrior would do.

Toward the end of his career, his doubts and fears began to grow. He found himself checking in more often, listening for guidance, searching for a sign that would help him understand what he was doing and his true purpose. The children were the hardest part. He would see them slip into explosive vests through his scope; he would swallow hard at the prospect of ending a young life before it even began.

"One life or many?" he would whisper to himself over and over as he watched the children, or their mothers, make the ultimate sacrifice. He would end his day in deep contemplation, rarely talking to the others in the unit. If they were making the same sacrifices, then how were they any different? Their struggles were the same. He didn't need another burden. Jayden also knew that if he revealed his true feelings about it—rather, revealed any feelings whatsoever—it would be the end of his career.

What else could he really do in the civilian world? It wasn't long before the contemplation became depression. It washed over him in waves, taking hold of his mind, body, and soul. When he would head back to headquarters, he found solace in the weight room, pounding out set after set, even after coming off of physically exhausting missions in the field. He didn't care. He would just plug in his headphones and forget about the world for a while. Lifting allowed him to be in the moment safely without the constant danger in the field. It was a healthy outlet, until he started taking the pills.

He remembered it starting with tranquilizers. He'd take a few to keep to his hand steady and his heart rate low. He found that the medicine helped him stay focused in chaotic environments. After a while, the pills weren't working as well anymore. He'd find himself between missions, drinking into the late hours, waking with a splitting headache, berating himself and punishing his body by sweating it all out in the gym. By then, Jayden wasn't drinking to just take the edge of anymore. He found himself hiding it from others, separating himself from the group, and downing whatever he had stashed away before returning blurry-eyed and docile. It hadn't gone unnoticed.

He remembered the day before he saw Una for the first time. He was sitting inside a blind, fully camouflaged in the burning desert landscape. He was watching for his targets through binoculars, wiping away the sweat from the eyecups every few minutes. He had spent nearly a month moving in and out of a nearby village, posing as an African nomad, searching for intel on the pirate operation that was crippling the shipping channels in the nearby Red Sea.

The flies were the worst, sitting happily on his skin, drinking in the salty liquid that poured from his body. He'd quench his thirst from a CamelBak every half hour or so, just enough to keep him hydrated, but not enough to make him puke. The targets entered his view as the sun reached its peak in the sky. The camels moved slowly through the barren landscape. Two children followed behind in chains, their faces covered in dust and defeat. He studied them for a moment, but neither fit the description of the diplomat's daughter. He knew that taking out the targets would mean the slow demise of the children in the desert sun. For the first time, he was truly conflicted. He watched them move closer, almost within range. Instead of placing his finger in position, he reached for his side piece. Tears began to flow as he muttered obscenities. He rolled onto his back, putting the weapon to his temple, heart racing, and sweat dripping.

"Forgive me," he whispered before slowly pulling the trigger. Click. And nothing.

He had forgotten to load the piece, something he hadn't done in his entire career.

He began to sob uncontrollably, letting years of emotions rip through his body. He sank into the feeling, as it swallowed him whole for the better part of an hour, maybe more. He watched the flies land on his hands, considering how their small, insignificant existence was worth more in this moment than his own. His targets at that point were long gone, and he would have to report back what had happened. Weapon malfunction? Nobody at headquarters would buy it. He was done.

He waited for the sun to set before packing up. He checked his water supply, drinking the few drops that remained before changing out the bag just in case he didn't get a chance to stop again. He took a few sips of the new liquid, allowing himself to drink to the point of retching. His gag reflex kicked in almost immediately when the vodka started pouring down his throat. He had forgotten he snuck a fifth into one of the pouches.

"Whatever," he muttered. He was so furious. He couldn't even kill himself correctly today. He sat up as much as the blind would allow and took several long sips before changing the bag out for water. He used the felt tip pen in his breast pocket to mark a small "v" at the top. As good as the liquor tasted on his lips, he didn't want to make the same mistake again. True, he wanted to die an hour ago, but a slow, dehydrating death in the desert was not what he had in mind.

He returned to post later that evening. He was certain the commanders had drones overhead, but nothing was mentioned. He slipped into the makeshift barracks, dropped his bags, and immediately hit the shower. He stood under the water, contemplating what he would say if his superiors cornered him. He was nearly sick with anxiety, running every possible scenario in his mind. He let the cold water pour over his skin, drinking in the refreshing feeling. He drained the bag and toweled off. His mind was just about settled when he emerged to find Colonel Briggs waiting at his bunk.

"What happened out there, Washington?" the colonel asked, part anger, part concern in his deep voice.

"Equipment malfunction, sir," he said, quickly falling on his sword. No use lying about it now.

"We were wondering what was going on, but we lost signal just as we saw the caravan approach," he said. "Did they spot you out there?"

"No, sir," he said, furrowing his brow at the notion.

"I know you're the best we've got, Washington," the colonel said, placing a sturdy hand on his shoulder. "The sand can grind your gear. Get over to supply and have them swap it out."

Jayden gave the colonel a knowing nod, as the brut of a man ambled toward the door. He was surprisingly light on his feet for a man of his stature. His face wore the years of war like a badge of honor, wrinkles appearing like strategic maps on his forehead and around his eyes.

"You want a drink, son?" the colonel asked, turning back to Jayden. "I've got a twenty-year scotch in my desk. Said I wouldn't open it until we are done."

"Are we done, sir?" Jayden asked.

"You are, Washington," he said matter-of-factly. "Your orders are in. You have some decisions to make. You'll have to follow up with the contact in a few days, but that's the end of the line for you. Consider this my thanks to you for all you've done for us out here."

Jayden gave the man a weak smile. "Sure, I'll join you in a minute."

The next day, Jayden found himself in the alley with the boy, and later the dream of Una. He was no longer filled with despair, craving liquor and isolation. His direction became instantly clear the moment he saw the boy sitting up in the hospital bed. The decision was made for him.

Now, he found himself looking down onto the strip. The sun had yet to make its appearance. He was thankful for the magic hour, knowing that something far more significant was about to transpire, something that would erase all he had done. He wouldn't let the darkness eat him up again.

He emerged from his room, fully expecting to be the first one up. But Una was sitting on the couch in the center of the room, staring dreamily at a painting on the wall in front of her.

"Isn't that a beautiful work of art?" she asked, tilting her head slightly to capture a different view.

"It most certainly is," Jayden answered, sitting down beside her. He marveled at how flawless her skin appeared in the early morning light. It was as if the sun was purposely highlighting her best features, dancing down the ends of her hair, highlighting her crown with a beautiful halo.

"Jayden, I want you to know that you are forgiven," she said after a moment, turning to look him in the eye.

"How do you mean?" he asked.

"Your missions, your…kills."

"What would you know of that?"

"Plenty."

She looked at him intently, as images of the countless faces flashed suddenly through his brain. He grabbed his head, willing the visuals to stop.

"I want you to know that things are as they should be," she said quietly. "Sometimes death is the only way to be released from a life of pain and misery."

"Are you saying all those people were miserable? Because I tracked some of them for days, even weeks, and I can tell you that they were anything but, hugging their loved ones and kissing their children." A small tear formed in his left eye, bulging in the corner before slowly falling down along the outline of his nose.

"It is OK, Jayden," she said, taking his hands in hers, and lifting them to her lips. She kissed his knuckles lightly, much like a mother kissing a child's injury.

"Well, it's not so easy to forgive myself," he said after a moment, attempting to loosen his hands from her grip, softly sighing when she wouldn't relinquish them.

"I thought I was healed back there," he said after a moment. "I'm finding that I was free of many of my habits, but the pain I feel remains."

"That is normal, Jayden," she said purposely. "The only way to heal from our pain is through it."

"But why can't you make it all just go away?" he asked. "I'm so damn tired of punishing myself. I've asked the Spirit to heal me countless times, yet I still feel so empty inside, so guilt ridden."

"What do you think the lesson is from your experience in the Army?" she asked.

"To carry out the mission. To be a brave soldier. To save my country and the world from harm."

"No," she said simply, searching his eyes, waiting for the answer.

"To forgive myself?"

"No," she said again, almost willing him to come to the conclusion.

"To know I have saved more lives than I killed," he said finally.

"Yes." She was smiling then, taking his hands once more. "Jayden, if not for your actions on countless occasions, the world would not be what it is today. True, you disguise your actions in the name of God and country, but in reality, you probably saved ten maybe even twenty times the lives in the process, lives that are here for a purpose. Lives that are here for good."

"But what is good? Killing some dude in the desert sun? Watching him fall to the ground in a heap?"

"Killing is wrong, Jayden, but some people are destined to be soldiers, to save the lives of many in the name of the few. Throughout history, we have seen this play out. Many souls have been lost in battles that seemed meaningless, yet in the bigger picture, in the scope of humanity, may have been some of the most important work that was ever done. I'm not talking about the killing of leaders like Hitler. I'm referencing the men and women who brave the elements, spend hours in war centers searching for targets that are driven by forces that cannot be understood. Their motives clouded. And this is on both sides. All sides, really."

"So, you're saying that all souls in the fight have an agenda, some good and some bad."

"At its most simplistic form, yes," she said. "Good and bad are very simplistic in their own right, but there are people who are here for their own agendas, there are those who cannot break free of the darkness that clouds this planet, and there are those who are here to fulfill sacred contracts."

"Sacred contracts," Jayden said back, wondering if he had fulfilled one.

"You have," Una said. "You performed your role on earth purposely. For that, you are forgiven."

"I just don't understand any of this," Jayden said with a sigh.

"You're not entirely meant to, and if you did, it would blow your mind," she said with a laugh. "Believe me, this kind of understanding is very new to me as well."

"So, you're saying it's all connected. It's all for a reason. And if I saw the entire chessboard, I'd surrender."

"Or, you would win," she said. "At least that's what I'm hoping for now that we have joined forces, so to speak."

The two sat together in silence for a moment, before Jayden rose to make some coffee for the group and tea for his new friend. He didn't understand it all just yet, but he knew that in the end it was for the greater good. It was fulfilling a sacred contract he was bound to, whether he believed in his ability to fulfill it or not.

CHAPTER TWENTY-ONE ──────

P etra woke to sunlight flooding the room. She pulled her arms from underneath the sheets and examined them fully. No evidence of the encounter was left behind, not one bruise or mark.

She leapt from her bed and made a line for the bathroom, closing examining her face, looking for any scars or marks to remind her of the events over the last few days. Nothing remained. She smiled at her reflection, marveling in the fact that she seemed even better than before. Her eyes sparkled and skin glowed like polished porcelain.

Today was the start of the shows. She had agreed to help out with the crowds, welcoming strangers and their problems with an open heart and mind. Forty days didn't seem like such a long time in the scheme of things. After all, she had just endured years in prison, and this was far more interesting, if not empowering. Una herself had made a call to the parole officer, explaining all that Petra would be doing at the show. If she agreed to check in and could successfully complete the time, the state would release her from the terms of her parole. Petra was dumbfounded when Una told her, wondering how she convinced them to do it.

"Mr. Payne may have had something to do with it," she said with a shrug.

Then again, this was the same woman who had healed her body and soul in a matter of minutes. Anything is possible. That was her new motto.

She showered and dressed quickly, meeting the others in the living room to go over the plans for the first appearance. She was briefly introduced to Una after the events on stage. The others she met in the suite afterward. They were each welcoming, sharing a few experiences that led up to a meeting with the woman before them. Yet, they all seemed to get along so well, communicating easily as their roles were defined.

Petra would be helping to identify the neediest in the crowds at the shows, gathering personal information and leading each backstage for the experience. That is what the group had decided to call it, an "experience" they could either embrace or reject. No judgment in between.

Matt would be running all aspects of the business, along with Jaxson who primarily would focus on Una's schedule and press requests. Jayden was in charge of security, given his military training. Una was in charge of social media with Petra handling things once the show began—no small job considering that she had now amassed over ten million followers without performing a single show.

There were many holes still left to fill, but Una assured the group that those would take care of themselves in time. A few had wondered if those healed at the shows would join their growing brigade, but none of them bothered to ask. Una seemed incredibly relaxed, sharing social responses from time to time, stepping away into a corner to quiet herself before the first show. The group seemed to join her in the mood, quietly asking one another questions and dressing before heading down to the theater about an hour ahead of schedule.

"Everyone," Una said to the group backstage, gathered in the confines of a modest dressing room. "I would like us to gather and set our intentions for the evening."

The group surrounded her, eyes focused on their healer, wondering what to expect in the next few hours. Petra was eager to race to the lobby, seeking out strangers in need of a transformation.

"Petra, you may go. Trust your instincts."

Petra nodded at Una and closed the door behind her. She winded her way through the maze backstage, exiting the side door the casino worker had shown her earlier that day. It was the same door she entered to be healed herself. The door opened upon a large crowd forming two long lines in front of the theater. She was astounded by the people before her. They seemed to be in all forms, from "why in the world would that woman be in line here in her designer shoes and handbag?" to "desperately seeking anything to heal the trouble you see before you." She didn't know where to begin.

Petra made her way to the front of the line, closing her eyes for a moment before proceeding through the center of the two, searching for eyes that would speak a truth she would only know once she saw them. She started with the most obvious choice.

"Sir, what is your name?" she asked to the man with the crutches.

"John," he said, giving a glance to his mother next to him.

"He has multiple sclerosis," she said. "We aren't even sure if this is going to work, but we have to try, right?" Her eyes began to fill with tears.

"You two make your way to the side door, and we'll see you inside," Petra said, motioning security to help.

"Pick me!" one cried from a distance. Petra continued with the guiding force inside her.

"You, with the red jacket," she said pointing to a tall, elegant woman who almost seemed to be hiding from her.

"Oh, I don't want to—"

Petra approached her, bringing a finger to her lips to silence her.

"Go to the door over there," she whispered in her ear.

The woman nodded and made her way through the crowd to the door; others groaning as she passed.

"She doesn't need to be healed!" shouted someone down the line.

"She's obviously rich!" another shouted. "She doesn't need healing!"

Petra didn't let their comments detour her from her task. She went with her gut. She pulled several others out of the crowd, never questioning inside if they were the ones to be healed. On and on, she proceeded through the line, reaching the number Una had given her earlier. She turned back to the crowd stretched out before her, the theater no longer in view. She made her way to the doors, where she directed the others. A couple of stragglers tried to make their way into the group, but Petra quickly spotted the imposters.

"Next time," she told them sweetly, gripping each on the arm as she directed them back to the line. The few seemed to smile in return, welcoming her embrace as a healing they wouldn't get from the mystery woman they so desperately came to see.

"Hey, wait!" someone screamed toward the front. "That's where we go to get healed!"

The crowd erupted and started to stampede toward the door in earnest. Petra searched the crowd wildly for security. A group of menacing figures appeared in a matter of moments, along with Jayden, to break up the commotion and get the lines back in order. Petra's heart raced as she led the group through the side door.

Whatever the result of the first performance, it was of no consequence to those attending. They were there to see a one-of-a-kind show. It wasn't the usual hypnotists, magicians, and trapeze acts that dominated the strip these days. This show had captured the eyes of the nation long before the marquee had lit up.

Most in attendance were hoping to make it to the stage, but what they didn't know is that everyone who entered would be healed. Una wasn't sure she had the ability to do it, but a voice inside pinged her with the idea as the show plans came together. It was a surprise Una never planned to disclose to her guests. She wanted them to discover it on their own, if they ever would at all.

As the doors opened, the crowd excitedly made their way to assigned seats in the theater. The rumble had turned into an impressive roar when the lights were dimmed. A single spotlight shined down on the woman they had clamored to see.

Applause ripped its way through the room, fully surrounding her on stage. Una was draped in a long white dress, ornate jewelry dripping from her elegant neck. She was as still as a statue, her head bowing down to the floor. The applause was being replaced by audible voices, questioning what was happening. She did nothing for the first two minutes but was listening closely to what the audience was saying, drinking in every word of surprise, anticipation, and anger. A meditative music began to play quietly in the background, just enough to hear, but not so much as to draw attention from what was happening.

As the music began to build, Una waited patiently for the talking, questioning, and swearing to stop. It took the full two minutes for the crowd to finally grow quiet. She smiled as the last voice dropped off in the distance. She allowed the nothingness, as the one-note song continued to hold court over the crowd's collective mood for another full minute before she finally spoke.

"In the silence," she began, "you will find all the answers in the universe."

Every eye was instantly trained on the woman, watching closely to see what she would do next.

"If you are not silent, still, and completely quiet for periods in your day, your week, your life, you will find yourself weary, drained, and dissatisfied with everyone and everything around you."

She looked up at the crowd, some gasping at the sight of her glowing face.

"And you will never clearly hear the voice that guides you from beyond."

A few in the audience whistled, but not enough to break the feeling.

"You mean God!" a man shouted near the front.

"However you choose to define it," Una answered. She paused to collect herself before continuing.

"This is about you and your sacred contract. The very reason you are here. The purpose you have vowed to fulfill."

She waited a long moment, scanning the crowd for reaction. Every person was watching her closely, some with pensive looks, others more serene, still others with tears running down their cheeks. She was beginning to touch them with her words. She could feel it. She couldn't wait until she could touch them with her power. It was growing inside her now. She tapped in further before proceeding.

"Love, like life, ebbs and flows within us. There are moments when we believe in all the possibility and promise that seemingly guide us toward a nirvana on earth. We look for it in the eyes of another: a man, a woman, a puppy, a stranger. We look for others to evoke the promise and the purpose that we so desperately crave."

"I feel you, sister!" Someone shouted from the first three rows. A few whoops and hollers followed.

"But it is only within ourselves that we shall ever be free of the chains that bind us here to the earthly experience. We are the ones that make us sad, miserable, unhappy, unfulfilled, unloved, and every other 'un' word you could possibly live in your life. The world is not meant to be lived in the 'un'. The world is meant to be lived 'in'. In contact, in connection, in relationship, in person, in love, infinitely."

She waited a moment before continuing. "But we seem to forget this. Why do we forget this?"

Una could see the confusion emerging on the faces in the crowd.

"That is not a rhetorical question," she said and laughed; a few in the crowd joined in.

"We forget because of the others we walk this planet with who are also living by their own sacred contracts to live, to love, to find their own purpose—and that often means that we are swallowed up in someone else's agenda. We forget who we are. Well, that ends tonight."

The house lights came up in the auditorium, shining a light on the first few rows.

"Tabitha Jefferies, you are the first I welcome to the stage."

People began to applaud, though lightly, as the statuesque woman rose out of her seat and made her way to the stage. A stagehand placed a small microphone that extended from her ear to her cheek. Una held out her arms in welcome. The two embraced as the music swelled, ethereal and serene. Una then guided the woman directly in front of her, placing her hands on her shoulders and positioning her just right. She ran her hands down the woman's long arms and reached for her hands. It was obvious the woman was nervous, but Una closed her eyes for a moment, and within seconds, she began to relax. The music moved from minor chord to major, volume reducing as the lighting dropped to a single spotlight on the stage.

"What has been troubling you, Tabitha?" Una asked.

"What hasn't been troubling me," the woman began with a giggle that quickly turned to a sniffle and then tears.

"My husband died last year, very suddenly."

"I'm so sorry to hear that. How long were you together?" Una asked.

"Twenty years in total. We were married for sixteen years."

"That's quite a long time. Did you have children?"

"Yes, we did. We have two boys. Trey, after my husband, and Tristen."

"The four T's."

"Yes, how did you know?" Tabitha asked incredulously. Una simply smiled.

"What happened to your husband?"

"He was running. He was an avid runner and athlete. He played pro football for a few years and he loved working out. Running was his stress relief. He had a big meeting that day. He ran an advertising agency downtown." She sniffed again. Una offered the woman a tissue and waited for her to dab her eyes before continuing. "He never came home. They thought he maybe disappeared or something at first, but I knew he would never do that. It took them a few days, but they eventually found him. He had fallen into an arroyo. There was a rope draped across the trail. He must have run into it or something because he fell and hit his head on a rock." She began to sob, unable to continue talking. Una folded her into her arms for a moment; the audience sat in total silence, watching the exchange unfold.

"How can I help you?"

"Since the accident, I just can't seem to find my way through this grief. I feel so overwhelmed, so lonely. I find myself drinking way too much. First, it was a few glasses of wine, and then a full bottle. Sometimes more. I don't know how to stop. My boys are struggling in school. Some days, I can't seem to get off the couch. We had a nanny before. I spent most of my time volunteering for the school board and a couple of nonprofits in town. It was important for Trey's 's image at the time, but I just don't see the point anymore."

"Why did you start drinking, Tabitha?" Una asked quietly.

"I wanted to go to sleep. I needed to calm down. A friend brought over a bottle. Then other friends too. Probably fifty in total after everyone made the rounds." She dabbed her cheeks and blew her nose. "We had always enjoyed our wine in good times. We used to call it mommy juice. I'm not going to lie. I probably had a problem before Trey died. I just chalked it up to stress and all the functions I had to attend. There is always wine available. It is sort of part of the job. I usually just eat salad and stuff. I need to stay trim and keep up the appearances, you know? Wine can put weight on you if you don't watch yourself."

Una reached up and brushed the hair away from the woman's eye and looked at her. It wasn't a look of judgment or punishment, but the most understanding, forgiving look Tabitha had ever seen; it also beckoned her to open up in a way she couldn't believe.

"I had an affair right before it happened. It was a man I met on the various boards I'm on. He was successful and interesting, not to mention handsome. We connected after one of the meetings and decided to get coffee. That turned into making out in the car, which turned into four months of secret meetups in various hotels, not to mention his car in a random park. I feel so ashamed. He had a family too: three kids and a wife. We both seemed so happily married on the outside, but the more we talked, the more we both realized that we were living a lie. It wasn't what we really wanted. We wanted adventure, romance, shared interests, and conversations after dark. We were each other's confidant. I don't know if we were in love, but it felt like it was something close to that. It was certainly passionate. It offered me a key to the chains that were my life."

"Were you going to tell Trey about this man?" Una asked.

"No, I had no plans to. But I screwed up one day. I left my phone on the counter while I was in the shower. I know he saw the texts coming through or at least heard them coming through. Trey never said a word about it, but when it happened, I ended the affair immediately."

"And what about your boys? How are they doing?" Una asked.

"My boys? They sit like crumpled paper on the floor of their rooms. They are lost in their devices. I do my best to help them, but they often storm off and answer me with slammed doors."

"How old are your sons?"

"Fifteen and thirteen. They were so fragile. They are still."

"Tabitha, you cannot mask your pain with liquid in a bottle. You must allow yourself the clarity to truly feel your sadness and grief. Drinking away Trey, the boys, and the life you created with your husband is not sustainable. You will lose everything if you continue this way."

"I know that, but I cannot stop. I tried the meetings. I only go back to what I know."

"Find your purpose. That is what you will crave—more so than what is in the glass in front of you."

"But what is my purpose?" Tabitha asked desperately.

"What did you know or love before Trey?"

"I…I don't know," she considered. "Cheerleading?"

Una let go of Tabitha's hands and turned toward the audience.

"Purpose is often revealed to us when we are young. But for some of us, it is clouded. That could be because of parents who are not capable of loving us fully due to their own circumstances. It could be because we are too distracted by the needs of others, a sibling who is ill or parent who cannot keep a job. Whatever the case, it is up to all of us to search within ourselves to find what it is we are meant to be in this world."

She searched the audience for reaction, trying to read if they could understand what she was saying.

"You must become quiet. You must listen to that voice inside you. You must put down your phone and turn off your computer and television. You must sit and listen to the world humming around you; its perfect rhythm becomes a heartbeat and your connection to the divine. You must reach inside. And that doesn't mean a job or a career choice always. Sure, some of us are meant to heal others, and we are instinctively drawn to medicine. Others are meant to construct or create. Some of us are here to teach, others to learn. Some of us are meant to guide others through life and by our simple daily actions—cleaning a hotel room, changing a tire, weeding a garden—we are there in service."

She turned to Tabitha then, reaching for the woman's hands once more.

"You have served others, though not from your core, Tabitha. You have served under the guise of a successful image—an illusion—not from the heart. This is why you did what you did. You wanted to connect with your heart. You reached out to this man because it was the closest thing to that, but I assure you that you hurt more hearts than you helped with your actions. You were not true to yourself. That must change now."

She reached for Tabitha's hands and placed them gently on her heart.

"When you go through your life heart first, you will find your purpose. You will be guided to your truth. You will learn to not do this selfishly. You have sons who need you. You have organizations that need you. You are too wrapped up in your own heart and head that you cannot even see what is right in front of you. Your purpose is here. You just need to reach for it."

Una placed her hand on the woman's forehead. "Heal this woman and release her from the darkness inside. Let her emerge from her shadow and embrace her flaws so she can build toward a new truth. Let her shine authentically for others to see."

Tabitha's skin began to glow as Una spoke the words, the audience gasped and watched closely as the luminescence began to fade.

"You have much to do, Tabitha. You will find love again but in a way you will never expect. Go forth in truth."

Tabitha embraced Una, waved to the crowd, and walked down the stairs to her seat. The crowd returned a lackluster applause, some crying out for the "real people" to be healed, not the rich. Others shouted that she must have paid her way to be first in line. Anger was rippling through the rows as Una turned back to the crowd. She raised her hands up, as if to command them to quiet down. The crowd responded within a minute.

"It may seem that Tabitha is not worthy of healing. But know that we are all worthy. Sometimes those with the most physical abundance are the most broken. They sit in their large houses and drive their luxury cars to jobs that they don't find meaning in. They return to families they have neglected or empty rooms with no one in sight at the end of the day. They are as lonely and wounded as any one walking the streets with no possessions. They have created much abundance but not in the areas of their lives where it counts the most: love, connection, companionship, service. Those are the true riches in this world. We cannot walk this life alone. Often, for reasons of jealousy or envy, the richest in the world float aimlessly on rafts of isolation. They are adrift on a sea of illusions. It's a life they want the world to see, but it is not their truth. We must all find our truth. We must all find our meaning. We are all here for a reason. We all have purpose. Please bring John Adelman to the stage."

John reached for his mother seated next to him in the front row. He struggled to stand, gathering his crutches as he made his way toward the steps. Two stagehands stepped down to help him onto the stage. Una walked forward to greet him and escorted him to the spotlight in the center. He leaned forward onto his crutches, smiling at her as the crowd quieted its applause.

"Hi, John. What brings you here today?" Una asked, placing her hands upon his shoulders in the process.

"I…am…John Adelman. I struggle with multiple…sclerosis."

"I see," said Una, washing her eyes over his body, taking in his illness with her breath.

"How long have you struggled with this, John?"

"Four years…this…summer."

"How old are you?"

"Thirty-nine," he answered slowly.

"What did you do before this happened?"

"I was…a…lawyer. And…an…athlete."

"What sport did you play?"

"I was…a…runner. A marathon runner."

"This is a different kind of marathon you are running now," Una offered.

"Most…definitely."

"How would you say this illness has helped you?" she asked. "What gifts have you received from it?"

John stood thoughtfully for a moment, considering his words before answering. "I…would…say that it…brought me…closer…"

Una paused a moment longer, making sure he had finished his thought.

"Closer?" she finally said.

"To my…family…to myself…to…my God. I was not… religious before. I am…not now. But…I learned who…is there…for me. And…that's not…to…say…it's not…my work. Like, all…lawyers…are bad."

The crowd laughed, and John looked out to the audience. "They aren't!" he shouted. A quietness swept through the auditorium.

"I…think…you all…expected me…to say…they are… or…they fired…me. They did not. I still…work…on some cases. Though much…more…slowly than before."

"What kind of law do you practice, John?"

"Immigration," he slurred.

"What made you choose immigration law?"

"I had…a girlfriend…in college…who…was deported. It…was…devastating. I read…everything I…could to try… and help…her."

"What happened to her?"

"She…went…back to…Jordan. It…was right…after 9/11."

"Have you seen or heard from her since then?"

"No…I tried…and…I came…close to…finding her. But then," John shook the crutches then, as the audience let out their audible disappointment.

"What will you do after you are healed today, John?"

"I will keep…working," he said thoughtfully. "Faster, like…before. And…I would…love…to run…a marathon… again."

"John, you have helped so many people with your work," Una said, reaching for his hands. "But you never forgot Mena, is that right?"

"How did…you know her name? That's…true. I was… so…busy with…law school," he said slowly. "Then, working…at…the firm. Then, this…" tears began to flow from his eyes. He looked back at Una and said bravely, "I am

Jamie J. Kemp

OK…but…I could…be…better." He chuckled at his own response, and the crowd joined in, all eager to see what would come next.

"Well, John, we were talking about purpose before. I'm sure you heard all of that from the front row."

"I…did. I…would tell…the lady…before…me…that… it will just…find you…if you are…open and…stop trying… to control…everything. I…have no…control now, but…I am always…open."

"Let's do this, John," Una said brightly. "Close your eyes."

John did as commanded, swaying slightly as Una gripped his hands.

Even though the auditorium had a strict no phone policy, everyone in the audience reached for a device and began recording what was about to happen. Una didn't bother to tell them to put the phones down.

"Heal this man of all his ailments. Make him whole. Bring him joy. Continue to fill his heart and soul with love." The glow appeared on his skin, pulling him into a perfect posture. He was no longer leaning onto his crutches, but rather rising with the pull of each particle of light. Within moments, the crutches fell to the floor. He looked at Una with disbelief and joy, tears pouring from his eyes as he pulled her into a long embrace.

"You're the real deal!" he shouted as the audience erupted in applause. Every person there had tears flowing, feet fixed to the floor in a standing ovation.

"Oh my…" he said, holding out his arms in front of him and shaking his legs before breaking into a little jig on the stage.

"I can't believe this!" he said, laughing with utter joy. The audience continued to applaud and cheer, many shouting "Hallelujah!"

Una raised her hands toward the audience, and the room began to quiet down.

"How are you feeling, John?" she asked.

"Are you kidding me? Fantastic!" he said, as more cheers followed.

"I'll be honest," he continued. "I wasn't entirely sure this was going to be real today. I told my mom that it would be entertaining if nothing else. Right, Mom?" He looked down to see his mother crying and nodding her head in agreement.

"John, there is one more thing I'd like to do for you, given all you have done to help people navigate through the immigration system, reunite families and loved ones, and help so many businesses and your community. YOU are the real deal, John," she said, gesturing for the audience to join her in appreciation. They showered the man with applause.

"You said you haven't seen Mena since college when she was deported back to Jordan."

"Yes, that's correct," John said, his new body shimmering and alive. He was the embodiment of health and as handsome as ever. It was probably the saddest day of my life, next to my diagnosis."

"Well, John, we live in a new world. What is Mena's last name?"

"Ibsies," John said. Una signaled toward the back of the stage.

"Let's call her right now? Can we get her on the screen?" She nodded, as Petra talked to her through the headset. It would take a few moments to look her up.

"It's going to take a minute to look her up, but we will find her for you, John," Una said.

The audience members screamed out in delight and

applause at the thought of Mena appearing on the screen. Una continued to interview John, asking him about his early years, college, and a few of the cases before Petra interrupted the conversation on Una's headset.

"John, it appears we've found her," Una said. The crowd erupted in anticipation.

"Are you ready to give her a call?"

John looked away for a moment, wondering if this was a dream, before nodding excitedly. Petra came onto the stage with an iPad in hand. Mena sat on the screen as Una spoke with her for a moment, briefing her on what was about to happen.

Within seconds, Mena appeared on the large screen behind them, with beautiful almond-shaped eyes staring through and raven hair cascading from her shoulders. It looked to be early morning where she was sitting, the sunlight spilling onto her head, forming a halo around her.

"Hello," Mena said through the screen, waving excitedly. The audience went wild with appreciation, leaping to their feet.

"Mena," Una said, prompting the audience to quiet down. "Thank you for taking this call today."

"This is about John?" she asked.

"Yes, it is," Una responded. "You are talking to me and about five thousand friends at the Trinity Theater in Las Vegas."

"Wow!" she said excitedly. "Where's John?"

"Did you look for John after that day you were deported?"

"Of course, I loved him so much. I…still love him," she said shyly. "That was before social media, so it wasn't so easy to find someone, and when it was finally available, it wasn't always accessible where I live."

Several audience members yelped in delight, a few blowing a whistle of approval. As Una handed the device to John, he took one glimpse and immediately burst into tears. After a few moments, he said hello to her, cheeks flushed as he instinctively put his hand up to the screen, then kissed it.

"Where are you living now?" he asked after a few moments.

"I work for a clean water project. Right now, I'm working in a very remote part of Africa trying to bring water to a small village there."

"Wow, smart and beautiful, but we would expect nothing less if you won John's heart," Una said with appreciation.

Several said "aww" at the comment, now causing Mena to blush.

"We were so lucky to find you!" Una said happily. Mena had responded to the message online immediately once she saw it was about John.

"John, what would you like to say to Mena?" Una asked.

"First, are you single?" he asked with a laugh. The entire audience joined in.

"Yes, yes, I haven't thought of anyone really since you," Mena said. A collective "aww" broke out once more.

"Will you be in Africa for long?" he asked next.

"No, I finish up this week, and I will be on a plane, straight to see you."

John turned to Una first and then the crowd, as if asking for permission to continue.

"If there's anything life has taught me over the last few years it's that you should appreciate your health, the people who really love you, and enjoy every moment you can. Don't waste your life. Live it!" he shouted.

The crowd responded with applause, cheering John on

as he hugged Una once more and turned to Mena on the screen.

"Mena," John said, putting his hand on the iPad. "I know you haven't seen me for some time and, in many ways, I'm glad you didn't, but I'm also sad that you weren't there to experience life with. I have missed you so much. I can't imagine another minute of my life without you by my side."

He dropped to one knee as Mena smiled brightly.

"Will you marry me?" he asked.

The theater went wild as Mena said "yes," the two smiling, laughing, and touching their hands to the screen before motioning Una toward them to join in the virtual group hug.

After much applause and tears, Una motioned to the crowd before speaking once more.

"John and Mena, I wish you both long lives filled with love, light, and many children. But maybe not exactly in the way you expect," she said, dropping a small hint of what was to come.

She smiled sweetly at them, the two blowing kisses to each other before ending the call. John hugged Una once more and turned to wave enthusiastically toward the crowd before making his way off the stage. The crowd cheered him on with every step.

Una proceeded to heal five others that night: a child with cancer, a veteran with crippling post-traumatic stress disorder, a drug-addicted pharmacist, and a couple on the brink of divorce after losing their home in a devastating fire. With each healing and story, the crowd grew more convinced that what they were seeing wasn't just a magic show. It was a life-changing experience that everyone should see. The posts and shares from inside the auditorium were extraordinary.

As Una disappeared backstage, the crowd praised the performance to one another out the door and to their many followers online. What they didn't realize was that Una had also healed each one of them of their most engrossing habits, addictions, and time wasters. Their desires to see the rest of the Vegas sites seemed to wane after leaving the theater. Many just wanted to go home and get back to their newfound belief in themselves and their lives. Una couldn't have been happier with the first performance, graciously thanking every person involved after the show that night.

"Thirty-nine shows to go, everyone," she said as her team gathered just off the stage. "This one was great, but there are many others yet to be healed. Let's fortify ourselves in the good work we have done here today and order some room service!"

They all gave each other a look of relief and started toward the exit. Just ahead of opening the door, Una turned to the group.

"Thank you all for the hard work," she said. "But more importantly, thank you for joining me on this journey."

As the group disbanded beyond the door, Petra tapped Una on the shoulder.

"Una, I was wondering who on the team helped find Mena for John? Was it Jaxson? He didn't mention it. If it was, that's impressive given how quickly we have assembled here."

Una smiled at her new friend. "Let's just say that help comes in many ways and in many forms, and I can use all the help I can get."

Una reached for Petra's arm, steadying herself before stepping into the elevator. Petra considered how draining the evening must have been for Una and noted the woman's weak physical state.

"Thank you for joining me, Petra," Una said, as the shining box made a beeline for the sky. "Good work picking the people out in the crowd. Even though we couldn't get to everyone, they will find in time that they too are healed; it just may take a little longer."

Petra knew in that moment that she had found her place in Vegas. The road here may have been bumpy, both literally and figuratively, but she knew her purpose. There was no going back now.

CHAPTER TWENTY-TWO ———

att sat back in the chair and marveled at the numbers in front of him. Between the performances and the various donation sites in the first week, Una's take for the show was hovering near eight figures. She was so gracious about it, never really asking for anything, other than suggesting the group find some worthy charities in need of funding. Matt made a note to look into a few of them that afternoon.

With more than two weeks of shows behind them, Matt noticed that Una was looking run-down after the most recent performance. She didn't conduct the usual debrief back at the suite, instead opting for some herbal tea and a hot shower. It had to be exhausting, pulling out whatever demons lie within the souls of others. On stage she seemed so unphased, but they all knew the performances were taking a toll. He wondered if she would make it through the forty-day run.

Matt glanced at the calendar. Twenty-three shows to go. An alert popped up on his phone. The managers at the theater had left another message. He forgot to turn his phone off silent mode. It was probably for the best he missed it—likely another "suggestion" to get Una a makeup artist. Considering how ill she often appeared toward the end of each night, he understood why. He was going to allow her to rest this morning, no interruptions. Several people had contacted the group, offering thousands of dollars for private sessions with Una. She seemed open to the idea, but Matt didn't give it a second thought. He was there to look after her well-being. Right now, it seemed to be a risk.

A soft knock fell on the door. He turned to find Una behind him, looking rested and alert. It was a welcome relief.

"Hi," Matt said, rising from his chair to greet her. "I was just going through the numbers from last night's show."

"How are we doing so far?"

"It would appear the show is a record-breaker for the hotel, if not the strip in general. You see the lines every night. You're a sensation!"

"Thank you, Matt," she said, taking the seat next to the small desk.

"Oh, and the theater managers keep calling me. I think they want to talk to you about makeup for the show."

"Makeup? Why?"

"Because—their words, not mine—you're looking washed out under the new lights. They think it's affecting the audience's ability to connect with you."

"What does makeup have to do with connection to the audience?"

"It makes you feel more alive and, uh, vibrant. Maybe even brave? Again, their words."

"Does performing miracles night after night not seem 'alive' enough for them?" Una asked.

"I guess not," Matt said, shifting uncomfortably in his chair. "I can tell them no, if you want."

"No, Matt, it's fine," Una said after some consideration. "I'll put on some lipstick and eye shadow if they think it's better for the show. So strange what they deem to be important. I would think touching as many lives as possible would be the big draw, but if it's lipstick they want, lipstick they shall get."

"Yeah, kind of lame, but I can find someone if you'd like. I can ask around."

"Sure," Una said, patting him on the shoulder before leaving the room.

He glanced at his phone and reached for his tablet. He didn't know the first thing about makeup, but he was sure the internet would have a thing or two to say about it. He was about to dive into a handful of reviews when his phone buzzed.

"Hi, this is Matt."

"Hey, Matt, this is Trina from Mr. Payne's office. He would like you and Una to meet with his team to discuss the show and some tweaks that need to happen immediately."

"Tweaks? What kind of tweaks? Is this about the makeup?" he asked, trying not to sound too annoyed.

"No, not exactly, though we still strongly suggest she apply something to help her stand out more during the performance."

"It's not really a 'performance,' but we talked about it and she's willing to do whatever."

"Great, I can send someone by this afternoon. As for the meeting, can the team come by the suite tonight after the performance?"

"Again, not exactly a performance, but yes, feel free. We usually get back up here around 11:00 p.m."

"We will be up at 11:00."

Matt stared into the distance as three beeps blared through his phone, signaling the hang up. He wondered what Mr. Payne would want to change about the show. It was a success. People were attending in droves. What could possibly be so wrong that it would need tweaking? He caught himself before spiraling into an analytical tornado that would keep the options whirling in his mind for hours. At least he didn't have to research makeup artists.

The door chimed at exactly 4:30 p.m. Matt leapt from the center couch and made his way to the entrance. The Amazonian woman on the other side looked annoyed, glancing over his head to take in the space.

"Is this where that show lady stays?" the woman asked, looking around some more. "This is nice!"

"Yes, it is," Matt said. "Hi, I'm Matt, and I run the show's business affairs."

"Hi, Matt. Or is it Matthew?" Tia asked. "I prefer formal names."

"Usually, it's just Matt, but if you like Matthew, go right ahead. You can set up in the first room on your right," he said, pointing her to the direction of Una's main bedroom suite.

"Well, Matthew, I'm Tia," she said, extending her perfectly manicured hand. She squeezed firmly, then made her way effortlessly toward the bedroom suite, exuding glamour with each step.

Una emerged from the kitchen area, watching the makeup artist roll elegantly down the hall. She gave Matt a knowing smile. The leopard print dress Tia wore hugged every inch of her slender, athletic frame. Not only was there no doubt the woman had a gym membership, but it was also very clear from the muscles on her arms and legs that she used it. Often.

"I would say I'm in good hands if she can make me look anything like herself," Una said. Matt nodded in agreement.

"Hey, I talked to one of the theater managers earlier," Matt said as Una joined him on the couch. "They want to come by the suite tonight after the show to talk about tweaks."

Una raised her eyebrow. "Then it must be happening," she said mysteriously.

"What's happening?" Matt asked.

"It's nothing to be concerned about, Matthew," she said with a raised eyebrow. "It's what we came here to do. They will just want us to do some things that, well, you'll see when they come by tonight. It's nothing to concern yourself with right now. In fact, it's working."

"What's working? The show?" Matt asked, a confused look falling on his face.

"Yes, Matt, the show is working brilliantly. We are doing exactly what we set out to do."

"And what's that?"

"Change the world, one soul at a time."

CHAPTER TWENTY-THREE

T ia stepped inside the room, removed her size twelve
purple velvet pumps, and rolled her bag to a corner
near the window for some natural light. She took in
the glorious view before setting up.

"You heal people from cancer, then you deserve to be
rollin' in this suite, honey," she said to herself out loud with
a chuckle.

She unpacked her case carefully and considered the
palette to use for such a beautiful face. She had only seen the
woman on video, but she was sure she could come up with
something fantastic. She was impressed the woman would
appear on a Vegas stage—more like a world stage—with a
completely naked face. Tia couldn't wait to put her paint
on such a flawless canvas.

That's how Tia saw every face she worked on: a canvas.
Some were worn, with cracks and crevasses waiting for the
perfect primer. Others were as smooth as silk. She pulled
forth colors she would choose for herself, the perfect high-
lighter to bring out the rich tones in the woman's skin.

Una rapped gently on the door.

"Come on in, girl! If you dare," Tia said with a laugh.

Una was more beautiful than Tia had imagined. Her
skin was flawless, save for the tiniest of wrinkles around

the eyes. Typical sun exposure stuff, but Tia had the perfect solution for that mess. Could she even call it a mess? This woman, with her complexion and natural curls was everything in that moment. She almost wanted to pack up her case and go for fear she would mess it up big time.

"Don't worry, you'll do a great job," Una said, extending her hand in greeting.

"I suppose I will. Girl! You. Are. Perfection!" Tia screeched, folding the woman in her muscular arms and moving her seamlessly to the chair beside her. The two made a more formal introduction before Tia got to work.

"Let me look at you for a minute."

Una smiled sweetly, watching as the tall figure before her took in her every feature. Tia kept gasping as she looked from her case to Una's face, rummaging happily to find the perfect colors to paint her masterpiece.

"This is going to be so fun," Tia said, setting her palettes on a small table and reaching for her brushes.

She went to work on her base, moisturizing and priming the skin before expertly applying foundation and concealer.

"You need to wear this stuff every evening. It's the only way your eyes are gonna pop with the terrible lighting in the theater down there. It's one of the worst on the strip."

Tia opened up easily to people in her chair, but Una was a whole different level of comfort. Before long, she was vomiting her entire life story into the poor woman's lap. She was careful not to drip words like "loss," "struggle," and "misfortune," even though they were the very ones she wanted to share the most.

Tia started at the beginning, or as far back as she was willing to remember. She was born in Fort Hood, Texas, the only child of a lesbian mother who was raped by an instructor in the Army during her advanced training. Tia's mother was an excellent soldier, following the rules to the letter. She was a tall woman with a larger frame and flawless ebony skin that seemed to glow even more as her pregnancy progressed. She hid her growing bump from her peers at first, blaming the weight gain on all the "delicious" food in the chow hall. But they all knew. It was a terrible event to endure, much less talk about, and her closest friends surrounded her and her son in a protective circle against a system that didn't value difference of any kind.

Tia was called Tommy back then. He knew he wasn't a male from a very young age. The feminine side of him naturally blossomed, an extreme contrast for many to his very masculine appearance. He would choose tetherball over football, dress-up with the girls over video games with the boys, and conversation over annihilation in one of the regular schoolyard brawls. He was unconventional and authentic in ways that others only dreamed of, a combination that made him a constant target for bullies. Tommy didn't care. The constant moves through the years always reminded him that everything was temporary.

After 9/11, his mother was deployed overseas and sent Tommy to live with his grandmother in Long Beach, California. The transition was difficult to say the least. He was a bright-eyed boy, used to the communities of progressive women his mother had surrounded them with. Despite the traditional values that so many military communities seemed to embrace, the circles his mother had formed in those early years always accepted Tommy fully. The move to Long Beach presented challenges he wasn't prepared for, particularly from his conservative grandmother, who would raise an eyebrow at his clothing choices and circle of friends. She would only take the sex talk as far as the surprise a breakfast egg revealed when an extra bright-yellow yolk appeared in the morning.

"Look there, Tommy," she would say, pointing to the double yokes frying up in the scalding pan in front of her. "There's twins on our plate this morning! That's how babies are made!"

He battled his way through his teen years in Long Beach, the longest he had ever lived in one house. The situations he found himself in were no longer as temporary. His mother would dip in and out of his life during that difficult time, showing up to surprise him in school halls or for a quick weekend away. He wondered what the conversation would be like if he actually said what he felt inside. He would stare into her eyes, considering the moment to spring forth his truth. The day of graduation, it finally happened.

His mother was home for three weeks, a forced leave of sorts after a long year in the desert. By that time, Tommy had already revealed himself as "Tia" to his handful of friends, an intention that he was more than ready to release into the world.

"I am not this," Tommy would say all through his high school years, referencing a masculine frame. He saw a more shapely, feminine vision each time he would look past himself in the mirror. He eventually blurted out the words just moments before leaving for graduation.

"Mama, I'm a woman."

His mother took him into his arms, and in that moment, he became she in her eyes.

She told Tia how she knew all along, but she had just waited for the moment Tommy would finally set himself free in the world, and she was patiently waiting to see the she inside her son emerge, not unlike the complicated birth she endured the first time around.

"So, how did you find yourself as a makeup artist on the Vegas strip?" Una asked, wondering what version of the truth Tia would reveal. Una could see the challenges the woman had faced in the last as many years. It was no wonder she would bend the truth to fit the circumstances at hand.

"I came to Vegas by way of Dallas," Tia said, applying highlights around Una's eyes. "You can only imagine how all of this went over with the cowboy culture down there."

How Tia was able to work and talk at the same time marveled Una. She watched her carefully, absorbing everything the woman told her in order to prepare her own face for the next show. Tia immediately dismissed the notion, informing her the hotel had already paid for services through the end of the show. She didn't bother to address Una's rebuttal and returned to the original conversation.

"That's where I got my operation, in Dallas," Tia continued. "And, well, many injections and pills later, I became the vision that is before you today." She stepped back and added a curtsy for effect.

"I have a feeling there is far more to this story," Una said, opening her eyes while Tia was applying the final touches. It was something that ordinarily would annoy Tia to no end, but this time Una could sense Tia was not irritated in the least by the subject ruining the masterpiece.

"Girl, there is way more to this story, but you think I'm gonna dump this shit on you when I barely know you?" Tia asked.

"Why not?" Una volleyed back. Tia sighed as she reached for more product in the case.

She proceeded to tell Una about all the months of prep and the pain that followed the operation and all the work to mold her into a working version of her final self, "a woman in waiting," as she liked to call it. The process had taken more than four years to fully achieve. Nips and tucks, shots, pills, therapy, all while she watched herself transform before her eyes in the mirror each day.

"I was like a butterfly emerging from a cocoon, honey," Tia said. "And this transformation is not for the timid, let me tell you. All those looks, stares, insults. You wouldn't believe the shit I've heard over the years. You have to have the strength of a thousand Goddesses to put up with it. And I do, believe me, I do."

If it wasn't for her transgender roommate, Gloria, Tia would have given up a few months into the process. She had found Gloria through a support group. The woman guided her through a difficult journey, a sort of shepherd across the valley of death. The death of Tommy.

"I remember the exact day I said goodbye to Tommy," Tia said, adding the final touches before putting the last of her items back into the case. "I was leaving Dallas and making my way to the city of neon lights, Las Vegas," she said with a chuckle.

"There I was, packing up my things, making phone calls about utilities—you know, all the shit you do when you move," Tia said remembering. "I found this baseball cap from the L.A. Dodgers. I couldn't believe I had kept it through my moves, but there it was," she said, holding back tears.

"I put that hat on, walked right up to the bathroom mirror, and gave myself the longest, boldest stare," she said, lip quivering. "I was done with him," she said convincingly.

"I was DONE. I took that hat, marched it out to the garbage bin in the back of the building, and I threw it away. Never looked back."

"Tommy is still a part of you," Una said. "He is your strength and courage. He is the one who takes the shots—literally and figuratively—and never flinches."

The tears began to flow from Tia's eyes. "I suppose he is," she finally said, reaching for a tissue in the case. Tia stopped to grab Una's face and place it in front of her own.

"Listen, I don't say this very often, and I'm completely fucking sober," she said with a smile. "I love you, and you look great. I have no idea why I said all that today, but you made me feel so comfortable, and it just kind of spilled out of me or something." Tia was dabbing back tears when a knock came at the door.

"It's time to head down," Matt said, watching for Una's acknowledgment before closing the door.

"Great job," he said to Tia before closing the door.

"I'm coming for you next," Tia shouted through the door.

"So, are you are really doing my makeup through all the remaining shows?" Una asked Tia, taking her hands.

"Girl, I would do your makeup for life," Tia said, and the two folded into a warm embrace. Tia welcomed the feeling into her body—the uneasiness, the insecurities melting away. This was her time to walk completely in Tia's shoes.

She told herself years ago that Tommy was the past. It didn't affect her anymore. That was a lie. She could see that very clearly now. But this time, she was finally ready to let go of all the bad feelings around that tall, sad, silly, and glorious little boy. She would welcome him into her chair and add a little blush for effect.

CHAPTER TWENTY-FOUR ———

The theater lights dimmed as the slow, melodic music began to play. Images of nature danced playfully on a screen at the back of the stage. It truly was a show now, very different from the earlier performances so many had viewed online. Every night presented something a little different. Payne's people wanted to keep things interesting and give them a reason to attend in person, rather than just watching it online. Not that it mattered now. Every performance had sold out within hours of the first show appearing before the masses on the internet.

Una walked up from the back of the stage, taking several slow steps forward before finding the spotlight. Tia had worked her magic, bringing out the woman's best features. She looked like any Hollywood starlet under the lights. The crowd roared its approval.

"Beauty. In everyone and everything," Una began. The images of nature transformed into collages of people's faces behind them. "That's what tonight's show is all about."

"We believe that beauty is only found in the physical world. A chiseled form. A perfectly proportioned face. Tall. Petite. Thick. Thin. The images you see every day in countless places, the ones you probably never even thought to consider, bombard you and tell you what you ought to believe beauty really is."

Hundreds of images began to fill the screen behind her. Models on magazine covers, women in a salon, influencers in swim apparel, a gorgeous man shaving, sexy playmates frolicking in front of the camera, and a video of a man working tirelessly at the gym.

"But beauty begins inside the soul. It radiates from us a light that touches everyone and everything we come in contact with. Kindness, love, inspiration, truth."

More images appeared, this time of young children singing in a chorus, an old man picking a flower, a maid making a luxurious bed, a teenager running his hand along the side of a car, a young girl performing a cartwheel while her friends clapped vigorously, and a hand wiping away a tear from a boy's eye.

"To see something with heart forward is to see the beauty in everything."

The screen slowly faded to black.

"So how did we come to define ugliness in our world? Fear. Pain. A darkness that consumes us into thinking and believing if we are not alike, if we show difference, we will be ostracized, forgotten and insignificant. We fear becoming unlike everyone else. That fear grows into a belief. And we begin to live in the 'un', viewing anything different from us as unpopular, unimportant, unworthy, and unwelcome."

A small light, like a sun, filled the center of the screen behind her.

"There is a saying that beauty lies within. That is absolutely true. Beauty does not live in the world of 'un'. It lives 'in' all of us. Beauty is intelligence. Interchangeable. Interpretive. Incomparable. And above all, inclusive."

"What if I were to show you two dogs, side by side?"

An image of two dogs appeared on the screen. On the left was a beautiful golden retriever with deep brown eyes and silky fur. On the right was a scraggly mutt, part terrier, part wiener dog, oddly shaped with patches of fur missing.

"Upon first glance, I'm sure most of you preferred the dog on the left."

She looked back toward the screen, studying the two images along with the audience.

"The other dog looks rather unfortunate by our modern standards. Not the type you would proudly walk down the street, right? But what if I were to show you this…"

Video began to play of the first dog: the retriever barked excessively into the camera. The dog began growling while the person behind the camera worked to coax the creature with a treat. The dog snapped several times, eventually going after the man. The camera dropped to the floor as the man cried out. The video abruptly ended.

"That dog, it turns out, was born that way. He was overly aggressive from the start. The owner was so reluctant to put the pet down, despite the fact he hurt everyone and everything in his path for over two years. The man who owned this dog was sued by a neighbor, who claimed it had attacked her dog, shown here…"

The video played once more, this one obviously taken from a phone. It started out shaky, showing the second dog seen previously. The oddly shaped pup pranced happily toward an elderly woman. She reached out to pet the creature's head, dousing him with praises.

"Get my pills!" she commanded, and the dog disappeared behind the door, returning a few moments later with a small pink bag he had retrieved from a bathroom on a low shelf. He dropped it in front of her, barking happily at his good deed. She showered him with love and devotion, before turning to the camera.

"See! I told you he could do it. So smart! Good boy!" The video ended, and the side-by-side images appeared on the screen once more.

Chatter began among the patrons; many started to argue which dog was better or worse, more beautiful or less. Una allowed the chatter to continue for upward of a minute before continuing.

"How do you feel about these creatures now? Do we embrace beauty on the surface? Or do we reach for it deep within the shell we call flesh and bone? Do we love something more because we can see it? Do we love something less because it is wounded?"

The audience fell silent.

"We judge things. We believe what our minds tell us, even if actions are to the contrary. We all want to believe desperately in today's instant gratification world that beauty is innately good and that ugly is bad. But that is rarely the case. We believe if we put forth an image that is generally accepted as beautiful, even if it is not how we were born or intended, then we will have a better life. An easier go of it, so to speak. But if we are not right within, how can we ever be truly beautiful? How can our light possibly radiate through an exterior that is crafted in an image of something other than ourselves? How can we possibly shine when it is anything but our truth? Well, we are all here to find our light in the darkness tonight. We are here to find the beauty in ourselves, in each other, and in our world as a whole."

"Make me beautiful!" someone shouted from a middle row.

"If you radiate your most authentic self from the inside out, you already are."

The crowd applauded as Una raised her hands up, reading the energy radiating from the rows before her.

"Bring the soul called Pippa Davos to the stage."

Pippa rose from her seat with some difficulty. At nearly 485 pounds, getting around was difficult, but trying to fit into a tiny theater seat was another matter. She rose with some difficulty but made her way to the front of the stage. She steadied herself in front of the stairway, not sure how she was going to get up there. Two assistants walked down to greet her, each offering an arm to escort her up.

"Way to start with an ugly sow!" a man yelled from the side as she walked her way up, attempting to start an insulting chant from the crowd in the process.

"I will not have that here," Una said, gesturing to the security guard below. "May you go forth in love and light."

The audience gasped at the abrupt action that followed. The guard pulled the man from the chair and walked him briskly to the side door.

"Fuck you," he yelled, as the guard pushed him through the door.

"Let's hope that's all the ugliness we will see here tonight," Una said as she reached toward Pippa and folded her into her arms.

"Hello, Pippa. Why did you come here tonight?"

"My friend made me go," she said with a chuckle. The audience joined in.

"Did you not want to attend tonight?"

"Not really," Pippa said, dropping her head down.

"Why not?" Una asked, bring Pippa's face back up toward the light.

"I think I'm just fine the way I am. I don't think I need to be healed or whatever."

"Why don't you tell us about yourself?"

Pippa proceeded to tell Una and the audience about her high school sweetheart, Ed. The two met in geometry class junior year and fell in love in fall semester of senior year. Pippa had offered to help him with math, and Ed was smart enough to take her up on it. A kiss over some random theorem had sealed the deal, and the two were inseparable for the rest of the year.

Caps and gowns were being ordered when she broke the news to him after school. She was pregnant, and there was no way she was giving up the baby. Ed was such a beautiful person, inside and out. Pippa knew the road would be tough, for sure, but the challenge only made her race toward her new life with a sense of hope.

To her surprise, Ed wanted to keep the baby too. They waited until after graduation to break the news to their families. The usual comments ensued, with a few biting and downright mean insertions that almost made them rethink their post-graduation plan. Instead of heading off to their dream back East, they would attend community college together in the fall. With the baby due at the first of the year, they both agreed that she would take off winter term. He would take off spring term when the baby was big enough to handle bottle feedings. Pippa attended classes right up to the winter break, never once complaining about the growing baby inside of her.

They decided not to get married right away, rather opting for the unwedded bliss that so many were choosing today. A marriage seemed to offer little more than a piece of paper in a lockbox somewhere, and the two were determined not to be bound by a government institution. Instead, they decided they would take it one day at a time, waking up each morning to recommit to the blissful relationship they found themselves in. Crossing the threshold to adulthood seemed enough at the moment. A commitment ceremony would feel perhaps more appropriate when they could make heartfelt toasts and invite grownups beyond their parents and their parents' friends.

Their son was right on time, entering just a few minutes after midnight to mark a new year. News teams gathered to welcome the New Year's baby, a tradition that made them both uncomfortable. But they were in love, with each other and the baby. Baby Jordan was everything Pippa could have dreamed of; they named him after her younger brother who died of leukemia at the age of two.

Unfortunately, leukemia tends to run in families, and Pippa's genes could not be escaped. The family of three had a blissful first year, juggling schedules, feedings, diaper changes, and all the other stuff that parenting presents, both known and unknown. Shortly after Jordan turned one, symptoms started to appear. The horror of having to endure another loss in the family was too much for Pippa's parents, and they soon abandoned them, even though they had grown to love and accept the young family in every way possible.

Jordan reached his terrible twos, an age which couldn't be more aptly named. Pippa began to put on weight rapidly, between the doctor's appointments and hospital visits, all while juggling school. It felt as if the world was collapsing upon her, and food became her only solace.

Even Ed, her sweet, loving, and devoted partner, began to fold into himself. They watched their relationship wash away with every beep of the hospital monitor. Pippa would take the first shift, Ed the second. Before long they had become strangers in a nightmare of a routine that seemed to pass so slowly, as Jordan's decline accelerated. Jordan just wasn't getting any better, and as his heartbeat faded with each passing day, they knew their relationship would go with it.

Jordan died on a Thursday.

Since that time, Pippa found comfort in the countless food delivery apps that populated her phone.

"I don't usually leave my apartment because I don't need to," she said to the audience—perhaps the first time she had admitted it out loud. "There are a million delivery services now. Who needs to?" Many in the audience nodded in agreement.

"But do you have any connections in your life?"

"Not really," Pippa said with some consideration. "I mean, my roommate, Birdie, is probably my only true friend at the moment. I talk to some clients on the phone about this and that, but they aren't really my friends."

"Do you think your lack of connection has anything to do with the state of your health today?"

"The state of my health?" Pippa asked defensively. "I don't eat that much, and I feel healthy."

"Do you use food as a means of comforting yourself?" Una asked.

"No," she snapped. But as she thought about it, the truth began to emerge. "I don't think so…I mean, I do eat salads and healthy stuff sometimes when the group makes me. I belong to one of those support groups for eating disorders and stuff. That's how I met my roommate."

"Pippa, what if I were to tell you that your issue has little to do with food itself but rather with how you cope with stress and a lack of connection and purpose in your life."

"I have a purpose," Pippa responded quickly. "I'm a digital designer."

"I understand you have a job, but what are you doing to share your light with the world?"

"Well, I…" Pippa paused to consider the question. "I, I design pages, and I'm really good at it."

"But are you helping people beyond your job? Are you growing? Are you living in the world?"

"I don't know," Pippa said defeatedly.

Una took Pippa's hands into her own.

"Your story is so powerful," Una said. "You have to realize that there are many others going through what you have, overcoming grief and sadness and fighting against the forces that want to keep us in that state. When I look inside, I see disease, Pippa. Diabetes, the beginnings of heart disease, joint damage, sleep apnea, just to name a few."

Pippa looked concerned. "I thought I only had diabetes," she said fearfully.

Una looked at her thoughtfully. "Pippa, it's not even about the size of your clothes or the weight on the scale. It's about your health, physical and mental. I know you're battling depression. I know your body is fighting disease. This weight you're carrying around is a slow suicide for you. It would be such a tremendous loss if you allowed it to happen. Why wouldn't you want to be as healthy as possible to share your gifts with the world?"

"Because I can't," Pippa said, tears beginning to flow.

"Because why?" Una prodded.

"Because if I do, I am going to lose again. I can't lose anymore!"

That was the moment Pippa realized she was holding on to her weight. To see the numbers go down on the scale was like losing a part of herself she simply wasn't ready to let go of.

"I'm worried I'm going to lose my memories of my little boy and a time in my life when I was really happy," she said, tears streaming down her face. "I can't be happy! That would mean I didn't care about them. I do care! I won't lose that!"

Pippa bowed her head, choking back the sobs she had buried so deeply inside of her.

"You won't lose that, or you won't lose the weight?"

"Both," Pippa finally said with a sigh.

"Have you ever thought that by losing the weight you will actually gain your life back?" Una asked.

The crowd began to applaud. Una raised her hand to silence them.

"Each pound could represent a new experience you could have, an opportunity to touch the lives of others with your story?"

"No!" Pippa said defiantly.

"No?" Una asked. "Is it change you are afraid of? We all change, Pippa. It's a fact of life. I was riding a bus home, and my life changed in an instant. I think I understand what you are going through to some degree."

Pippa raised her head and looked Una straight in the eye.

"Change…is scary," she said.

"Then, let's start that journey together," Una said with encouragement. "Right now!"

The crowd unleashed approving applause, then, before Una had a chance to raise her hand, fell silent.

"You're already beautiful inside, Pippa," Una said after a moment. "You're beautiful on the outside too. But it's your overall health that's of concern here. You have shown so much caring and giving of yourself to the point of neglect.

Would your family want that for you?"

"No," Pippa said.

"Then what do you say? Let's do this!"

The crowd erupted in applause, encouraging the woman on stage to take the leap into the unknown.

"Let's transform every organ, every cell in your body so that your light may shine through to touch others in need of your story. Can we do that now?"

Pippa thought about the question before her. She feared being a sellout to all the women out there claiming their bodies and owning their truth within them. But she also knew the weight on the scale today and the physical ailments she battled were keeping her from the outside world. She wanted it that way, truthfully. But she was afraid she would be transformed into some supermodel's frame. She wanted to define her best body on her own terms. She wanted her authenticity to shine through, no matter what the scale and her clothing size revealed.

"Pippa, when I suggest to you losing the weight, I'm not suggesting you be anything other than who you truly are. That may mean you are somewhat lighter than you are now. It may mean you are significantly smaller over time. In truth, it's not even about the number on the scale. It's about your ability to move freely. To be free of disease. To be the healthiest version of you."

"I haven't walked 'freely' in years," she said with air quotes and a laugh.

"Wouldn't it be nice to do so?" Una turned toward the audience then. They rewarded her question with thunderous applause.

"This is not about turning this lovely person into the vision our culture has accepted as a standard of beauty. It's about removing the barriers that keep us from connection, that protect us from the outside world. Some of you here know exactly what I'm talking about. You too have grown to a size that insulates you from the hurt and pain. Others use their size as a means to get attention from others, good or bad. It's a reminder that you are still here among the living, a way to further punish you for deeds you've done in your past, or to continue the abuse you endured at one point. You don't deserve that. You deserve to shine."

Una raised her hands up toward the audience. "I don't want you to think about losing, my friends. I want you to think about gaining: gaining back your health, your presence in the world, your strength, your commitment to others. I want you to gain back respect and confidence in yourself. I want you to release yourself from the loss. Let go of it now. Gain back your life!"

With that, she turned back to Pippa, bringing forth a smile from the woman's lips. Her eyes closed as Una reached for her shoulders.

"Please send love and enlightenment to this woman. Break through her insulated walls. Let her know that it is her brokenness, with all its cracks and flaws, that allows the light to shine through. Let her know that by losing, she is gaining far more in her life."

The glow appeared on Pippa's skin, and she shuddered with the sensation. A light tingling rippled through her limbs as she took a deep breath in. She felt she could stay in the light forever, allowing it to envelop her with its enormous force. This was something far more magical than she ever anticipated. As the light began to fade, she didn't appear to be any different physically, but inside she was glowing, filled with the effects of a power far greater than she had ever known.

CHAPTER TWENTY-FIVE ————

Pyrus stepped out from behind the curtain to the side of the stage. Whatever this woman was doing was nothing short of hypnotism. She had somehow convinced everyone watching her that her actions were authentic. He was sure the people had been planted. There was just no way a person could possibly be healed of diseases and traumas. Either way, it was convincing to the people watching, and as long as they had money to spend, he couldn't care less if they were healed or not.

To Pyrus, most people were nothing but helpless sheep being led to slaughter from a pathetic life lived to half of its potential, if at all. All that talk of service and gratitude was something you say to people when you're trying to placate them into believing they matter when they truly don't.

He would have to wait until morning to see the preliminary figures, but he was certain that the result of Una's charade would be a vast improvement over what the last few years had yielded. Even A-list singers in the hotels along the strip couldn't draw the crowds that Una had in just one night. It started with a line of ticket holders flocking together like wounded birds in the designated waiting area before the show. Now, people from all over the world would hang out for hours inside the casino, hoping to catch a glimpse and be magically healed just by being in her presence. Of course, he knew that was bullshit. As long as they were dropping money in machines, drinking, or grabbing a bite to eat in that time, it was fine. If they loitered for longer than thirty minutes without spending a dime, security would tap them on the shoulder and usher them toward the underground mall.

He had heard grumblings among the staff that Una appeared weak and even disoriented after recent performances. She had better continue her antics through the entire run, he thought. Otherwise, he would have to get to work on the demolition project immediately. He'd have to pull some strings with the city to get started so quickly but knew a bribe went a long way in Vegas. He never understood why they delayed construction projects. It was just more material coming into the city, more jobs, more people, more votes, and ultimately, more power.

The city and bribes reminded him of his dinner with the governor the night before. Pyrus had every ambition to become far more than a mogul. The ultimate power was in Washington. There had been concerns about his personal life, given that he was divorced and only supported his child monetarily. Nobody would want to vote for a man with a broken background, the consultants once told him, but Pyrus didn't question it for a second.

"Most of the people in this country are far more broken than me, and they will more easily relate to what I have to say about their meager lives," he told one of the empty suits.

"It's just that, on paper, you're not as wholesome as other potentials in the field," said the consultant. "Besides, you don't want it to look like you're hiding something."

"I have nothing to hide!" Pyrus shouted, fist pounding on the table in exclamation. "From my southern roots, to a long-suffering wife, and a child who wouldn't know discipline if it hit him in the head! I think there are far more in this country who can relate to that reality, rather than some fabricated family that only exists on television."

He took a sip of scotch and walked toward the window of the large dining room. All eyes were fixed on him, hanging on his every word.

"I have proven that a broken road can lead to the most majestic places. Just look at what I've created!" he screamed, causing some in the room to cringe.

"That's exactly what this country needs right now. Discipline! Hard work! Grit! Enough with the soft talk and hand-holding that seems to be on every available broadcast and newsfeed. All we see are people whining because of their circumstances. They can get their asses out of bed and get after it or just give up and let the other guy have the job. Survival of the fittest!"

The men shifted uncomfortably in their chairs before him. A few glanced at each other for reassurance. Pyrus was having none of it.

"You!" Pyrus pointed at a weary man he didn't recognize at the end of the table.

"Me?" the man asked.

"Why, yes," Pyrus said. "Nice of you to join us." The group chuckled with approval.

"You don't agree with me," Pyrus said in a low growl, zeroing in on the so-called advisor flanking the governor. Pathetic. "What do you have to say about it?"

"I would say that you should focus on the financials. That's what people want to hear. You're the guy who is going to grease their pockets. You're the one who is going to help them achieve their dreams."

"And what are their dreams exactly?" Pyrus asked, motioning for the waiter to recharge his glass. "I mean, given all the data you must look at on a regular basis."

"I would say that the people want to know that they can put food on the table, for one. That their jobs aren't going overseas, putting food in the mouths of foreigners who will ultimately take us to war. I would say that greed is the motivator in these difficult financial times. I would say that you should focus on the wallets and not get too personal."

"Too personal? Money is personal. Money changes lives! My base understands that. It's these other idiots without money that we have to worry about. They think they know better thanks to all this new media out there. They have a place to go and vent and create movements and protests and everything else that makes them feel the power they never had. They think that this is about human rights, and women's rights, and children's rights, and dogs' rights. When we start talking about laws for pets, gentlemen, well, it has truly gone to the dogs then. We might as well elect Fido for president because the new American idiot wouldn't know the difference!"

"Here, here!" the governor said, and the men raised their glasses in support. A knock fell at the door, and after a moment it opened.

"Reginald." A tall, slender woman appeared at the door. "We must be going. Our guests are here, and you cannot be late. I am not making excuses for you again." She gave a scolding look before closing the door behind her.

"Women," the governor said as he turned back to the group. They chuckled collectively at the response.

"I better go, gentlemen, but feel free to stay and talk through whatever you need to," he said.

The governor set down his drink and crossed the room to shake Pyrus's hand.

"I have an idea to give your show gal some credibility and help you with the voters," he said. Pyrus raised an eyebrow at the comment, wondering what he was holding in his feeble mind.

"I have some friends high in the church, if you know what I mean," the governor said, sensing that Pyrus needed a bit more information. "The Catholics, in particular, are on speed dial. And the Mormons and Baptists, of course. Give me a call, and let me walk you through what I'm thinking."

"Sure thing," Pyrus said, slapping the man's shoulder in support. "I'll have my girl schedule something later this week."

The remaining group discussed options for a while, considering potential donors and making plans for when would be best to announce the candidacy. Pyrus was excited at the prospect of running for office. It was the one thing that would give him the ultimate power he craved. No amount of money would ever top that feeling.

The roaring crowd brought Pyrus back to the present. He left the theater through the side door, walking confidently into the crowds on the casino floor. He stepped up to the roulette table and gave the dealer a nod.

"Mr. Payne, great to see you this evening," the gorgeous woman said. Pyrus placed a thousand-dollar chip on the table.

"What is your bet, Mr. Payne?" the woman asked with a smile. He glanced at her name tag and gave her a wink.

"Black, Zelda. Always, black."

Zelda set the wheel in motion, as a waitress placed a scotch in front on him. The ball bounced violently for a moment before settling into place. Pyrus took a sip, confident in his choice, making a silent bet of his own in his head. If it lands on black, the show would be extended, and he would announce his candidacy after it ended. If red, he would destroy the hotel after the forty-day run. As the wheel slowed, his eyes searched for the ball; numbers whirled into a blur as he focused in to see it cradled in a black slot.

She gave him a knowing smile, placing his winnings and her personal business card on the table before him. A double hit, so to speak. He raised an eyebrow before smiling wickedly at her, placing his chips on the snake eyes.

"Good luck," Zelda said seductively, before spinning the wheel again.

Pyrus never needed luck. It was all about planning and preparation. He knew that the forces that guided him were firmly in his corner. And this time, it was winner take all.

CHAPTER TWENTY-SIX

The previous night's show created a waterfall of comments on all platforms. Una struggled to keep up, following the chatter and reactions as they built on the livestream. The idea of streaming the show came from Una directly, who wanted to share her message with a greater audience.

Television networks had approached, offering to air the broadcast live in prime time, but Una was reluctant. She didn't want to limit the show to a passive screen that many would have to watch later to experience. Besides, it was only when others were watching live that Una had the full power to heal them. They had to feel it as she was performing. It was the only way she could break through.

How far they had come from the original video of the accident! It was a little unnerving in the beginning, having to follow every comment and ensuring the video didn't drop out. The first few livestreams were rough, but they got better with time. Last night's had reached over forty million at its peak, and there had not been one single drop in the entire two-hour performance.

The audience didn't know, of course, about the healing that was taking place with each view. Some were resistant and took much longer to penetrate. The experience often left her weak and exhausted at the end of the night. To cover, Una had told the group she was concerned about the state of the world, particularly in the United States, where the country seemed to have lost its way. The positive energy—the force that spread love and light from person to person—seemed permanently blocked. It was concerning and draining.

"Why is it after some of the shows you seem so energized?" Jaxson asked one evening on their way back to the penthouse suite. "Yet, others seem to leave you so depleted at the end?"

"It depends on the energy from those watching. If people generally believe, if they are embracing what they are seeing and not fighting it, the experience is fulfilling for all, including me," Una said.

"But there are many skeptics," she continued. "It's like a pool of energy forms from those who don't believe in the power of healing. Some just don't want to be healed at all. Sometimes, it's as if sitting in the pool of pain becomes a crutch for people. They are afraid to face the darkness inside of them. But what they don't know is that it keeps them from living with purpose."

Jaxson opened the door to the suite, and the two headed toward the kitchen as Una began her nightly ritual of making them a cup of herbal tea.

"But what if those people believe their purpose is pain?" Jaxson asked, reaching into the cabinet for a pair of mugs. "Isn't that what we've been told? The human experience is supposed to have pain. You know, the whole idea that from the rain comes the rainbow."

"Pain is certainly a part of life," Una said thoughtfully. "But not to the extent that it consumes us. We can sit with pain for a while, but we cannot make it our constant companion. Pain is meant to move through us, not stick to us permanently."

The two sat together at the island, each dipping tea bags into the water, willing the essence of chamomile to seep into the steaming water.

"There are many people who visit the show who are in terrible pain," she said. "You've seen it. I am there to help them release it. It can only happen when the participant is willing to kick the pain to the curb, as if to say, 'That happened to me, but it doesn't define me.' Does that make sense to you?"

"It does," Jaxson said, blowing gently at the contents before taking a sip.

"You look troubled. What are thinking about?" Una asked, even though she knew the answer.

"I was wondering what pain I am making permanent," he said.

"Perhaps the loss of your parents?" she asked. "I know how important they were to you. Did you ever really have time to process that loss? You were so young at the time."

"I don't know if I ever allowed myself to fully grieve that loss," Jaxson said, remembering the chaos that followed in the days, weeks, and months following the fire. "I jumped into my studies full force. Jayden threw his energy onto the field. I focused on what was ahead of me, rather than remembering. It was easier that way, I guess."

"If you could say something to them now, what would it be?"

"I would tell them I love them both very much," he said. "I would hope they are proud of me, even though I didn't turn out the way they imagined. I would ask them to heal my brother. I can see he's still tortured by what he experienced in the Army."

"They want you to be happy, Jaxson," she said. "They want you and your brother to move forward, to live, and to love."

"I know, but..." Tears began to flow from Jaxson's eyes. He found it impossible to stop them. "It would be one thing if we knew they were going to die, if they had died from illnesses or something, like Gran did. But when it happens so unexpectedly, there are so many unanswered questions. There are so many things left unsaid."

"Did you tell them you loved them?" Una asked.

"Every day, almost. It's just that we had a fight earlier that morning before the accident. I wanted to join some club or something. I don't even really remember what it was. They said it would be too expensive. I was so pissed at them. Now, I feel so guilty about that. I didn't leave things the way I should have."

"That's just normal life stuff, Jaxson," Una said reassuringly. "We all do that. You're human."

"I know. But I feel like I am such a disappointment to the legacy they created in that church. I should have followed a path into ministry. I should have fulfilled their wishes."

"Don't you think you are part of something now, though?" she asked. "Isn't that a ministry in a way? I realize that we aren't affiliated with any sort of religion, but we are performing miracles every night, Jaxson," Una said.

"You mean, you are performing miracles," he said.

"But I couldn't do it without your help and support," she said. "Why do you think you're all here? This is not a solo gig."

The comment made him laugh. She was happy to see his dazzling smile make an appearance.

"Now that I think of it, if that accident hadn't happened, I would have never done this. I'd still be driving a truck in the early morning, moving through my daily routine hypnotically. I wouldn't have met you."

"You are right about that, Jaxson," she said. "Here, take my hand and close your eyes."

Jaxson did as Una asked. At first, it happened in a series of flashes. Memories of his parents. His mother laughing in the kitchen, spaghetti sauce all over the floor. The impromptu food fight that followed. A warm embrace after school. His father clapping with joy as Jaxson brought home his first report card. A wink from across the pulpit.

"I'm so proud of you, son," they whispered in unison in his ear. Then he saw them standing before him.

"We love you, Jaxson," his mother said, embracing him tightly.

"You're doing just fine, son," his father said, folding his arms around him. He felt a jolt of electricity shoot through his veins, a warmth like he had never known.

"Don't regret anything," his father said. "We are always with you."

"Everything is as it should be," his mother said, eyes sparkling as she bore into his soul.

"One more thing," his father said.

"Call Kiesha," his mother said.

A single tear rolled down his cheek and dropped onto Una's hand, waking him from the experience.

"You see," Una said, wiping tears from her own cheek. "They are in their beautiful heaven now. They are with you, able to transcend space and time to be with you and Jayden. Believe it."

He folded her into his arms, giving her the most genuine hug of his life. He stayed there, drinking in her essence, so grateful to know her and to be a key member in her growing tribe.

"And call Keisha," Una said, pushing the phone toward him. Jaxson reached for it without hesitation. It was time to start loving, not just living.

CHAPTER TWENTY-SEVEN ———

The noise of the television pierced his ears, but thanks to the scotch the night before, the fog left lingering in his head was still thick. After a few moments, Pyrus remembered why he had set the channel to wake the night before. Whispers of a recession were rippling through the trading floor, and he wanted to be up on the topic before talking to the team in New York later that morning. He didn't want to hear it from them. They would only tell him what he wanted to hear. They couldn't be trusted. No, he wanted to see what the media had to say about it. He needed leverage. Those pukes wouldn't know what hit them after he covered them in facts and figures. He would bury them so deep, there wouldn't be anything left to do but fire them. What a bunch of pathetic half-wits. It was a wonder why they lasted this long managing his investments. He'd take care of it immediately after the call later that morning.

Pyrus left nothing to chance when it came to his money. After all, he alone had earned it, with little help or influence from the outside world. It made total sense that he should be the one to call the shots from day one. Sure, a few of the fund managers had decent suggestions from time to time, but he would never let them know that. Praise made people weak. Better to keep them on their toes by challenging their

Jamie J. Kemp

thinking and keeping their jobs in jeopardy. Otherwise, what was the incentive to work hard?

He watched the coverage before the bell, hoping to gain some insight into what exactly was happening on the strip. He figured it would be a topic, considering how many investors dumped money into the countless resorts the masses visited every year.

A fool and his money are soon parted.

He had made an absolute fortune off of that one quote. He considered how many drunken fools had lost their wages, nest eggs, even homes and businesses at his tables. The notion made him chuckle on his way to the bathroom.

He flipped the TV on above the sinks, listening closely as he examined himself in the mirror. He flexed his biceps and triceps, looking for marked signs of improvement. That trainer he hired hadn't done shit to improve his definition. He'd said the supplements would counter the negative effects of drinking. What a bullshit suggestion.

Right now, it appeared his workouts achieved marginal results at best. Marginal was not an acceptable result for Pyrus. He would fire the trainer this afternoon and hire the hot chick one of his hedge fund buddies suggested.

The commentator dispensed another lecture about expectations and results. He was sick of pathetic people who were simply incapable of delivering on promises. He entered the water closet to empty his tank before stepping into a cold shower. He cranked the volume of the built-in speaker in the process. As he was rinsing the shampoo from his dirty blonde hair, he heard the announcer mention Vegas. He shut off the valve and listened as a commercial filled the air, water dripping from his chiseled frame. He stepped out of the shower, drying himself off in preparation for the story ahead. He cranked the volume on the monitor above the vanity.

"Turning our attention now to the West, as news of the Vegas economy has investors worried about the future of Sin City."

"Oh, please," Pyrus moaned as he ran the razor over his angular face. "Always making mountains out of molehills."

"A precipitous drop in business has investors and hoteliers worried. Tourists seemingly want nothing to do with the behaviors and activities that give Sin City its infamous name. Business on the casino floor was down more than 21 percent in the last month, with bar service also down double digits at just under 20 percent. The striking percentages have investors worried that the appeal of so-called adult Disneyland is no longer in favor with younger consumers, who are turning away from alcohol in favor of other recreational activities."

"Bullshit," Pyrus said under his breath, glaring at the screen in the process.

He quickly brushed his teeth, checked his hairline, and slapped on aftershave before stepping into the enormous closet to dress in his usual uniform: Armani suit; crisp, white shirt; no tie; no socks. He waltzed into the kitchen to whip up his power breakfast—a protein shake with flaxseed and super greens. It was a nice counter to all the alcohol he ordinarily consumed in the evenings. He sucked the shake down quickly, chasing it with a cup of strong black coffee.

The routine reminded him of Jade. He remembered their plans for the steakhouse and barked a reminder into his phone before scooping up his keys and slipping on his favorite designer shoes.

Everything was perfectly coordinated in Pyrus's world.

He settled for nothing less than perfection in those around him. Why should he default to the look of some tech head or ordinary office slob? Ray-Bans completed the look as he headed for the elevator, breathing deeply as it plummeted to the first floor at rapid speed. He glanced at his Rolex before chirping the Tesla to life. He sped out of the parking garage like a raging teenage boy, determined to rip the team a new one for not anticipating the Vegas numbers and subsequent press.

He wasn't surprised to find the office empty when he arrived at a quarter to six. It really was time for turnover. The gung-ho frat boys he had hired less than a year ago had been seemingly seduced by the strip and all the temptations that sucked up so much energy and focus.

He wondered if it was even worth talking to the new crop of minions; perhaps he could coach them in a way a big brother would to get them back on track? Why bother? There was a fresh crop waiting in the wings. He never took his finger off the trigger. Managing with fear, he found, was always the most effective method.

He rounded the corner to the wall of windows that made up his corner office to find his assistant typing away at her computer.

"Good morning, Mr. Payne," she said automatically, eyes never leaving the screen, fingers still flying across the keyboard.

"Good morning, Catelyn," he answered back. "Surprised to see you in this early."

"I'm always at my desk by 5:30 a.m. East and West Coast hours for me."

"As expected," he said, turning the knob and placing his bag in the corner cabinet. Lights and the television sprang to life as he moved around in his usual routine, eyes scanning to make sure nothing was out of place, and glancing in the mirror to check himself before turning on the computer and settling into the massive executive chair. Catelyn placed a file folder on the corner of the desk and delivered a cup of coffee, a freshly brewed Americano. He was a little shocked to see the steam rising.

"Did you expect me this early, or was this for you?" he asked, giving her a body check in the process.

"Does it matter, Mr. Payne? The East Coast is expecting your call at six. Anything else?"

He stared at her for a moment, contemplating her mood before answering. Catelyn wasn't an unfortunate looking woman: early thirties, pert tits, athletic figure, cold, steely blue eyes. He hired her immediately two months before after fucking his last assistant and demanding an abortion when he impregnated her after three brief encounters. She left with an appointment at the clinic, a sizable final check, and eyes full of tears.

He decided right then and there to never hire pretty young things out of college. He wanted sharks at the gate, preferably pretty, jaded women with nothing to lose. Catelyn fit the bill perfectly. Sure, he still wanted to bend her over the desk every time she waltzed in, but something made him resist her. She kept the frat boys in line, and her military background and undeniable work ethic were worth far more than a brief dip in her pool. She raised an eyebrow then, lips pursed. She was reading his mind and letting him know with one look that it was never going to happen.

"I prefer women, Mr. Payne," she said coolly before turning on her heel and walking back to her desk, closing the door in the process. He shook his head in disgust before pulling up his agenda for the day.

At precisely six, the call from New York came through. Callahan's pale face filled the screen. Hadn't he been fired already?

"Well, well, I see you're back from the dead Callahan," Pyrus said with a chuckle, taking a long sip of his Americano as he waited for a response.

"Sir, we need to talk about the show and getting people back on the casino floor if we have any hope of securing the funding for the next phase of construction," Callahan said, suppressing a cough as he turned to his colleagues. The table was full of suits: all middle-aged. He needed young blood in New York. He made a mental note to transfer the idiots he had hired from down the hall. The city and its women would eat them alive. Problem solved.

"I thought the shows were performing well. Why in the world would we end the run now?"

"Because the people attending aren't hitting the casino floor, bars, or any other venues inside the property when it's finished. Something is causing them to leave right after the show ends, and it's no longer worth our time to keep it going."

"Hold on, hold on," Pyrus said, wishing he had something a little stronger to put into the coffee in front of him. "Why the fuck are you idiots throwing this back at me? Why aren't you coming up with solutions to this so-called problem instead of dropping it into my lap to fix?"

"And there's the issue with Figaro, sir," a blob of a man from the back of the room spoke up.

"Who's talking?" Pyrus asked, knowing full well it was Kennedy.

"Kennedy, sir," he said, clearing his throat.

"What does Figaro have to do with this conversation?" Pyrus asked. Figaro was the casino's notorious pit boss, brought over from a competing property a few months after the Neo opened. Figaro was probably the only man Pyrus sort of respected on his payroll. He was known for his mob connections and brutal tactics to keep the high rollers in line and the trash talkers off the floor. Pyrus depended on Figaro to run things when he was away, not even trusting his own operations people to interfere in the most challenging of circumstances. Pyrus was never interested in the gritty details of Figaro's work. It was an unspoken rule between the two of them. He just knew the man would take care of business, and he was paid handsomely for it.

"He was healed on stage during last night's performance, sir," Kennedy answered, drawing in a large breath before continuing. "The video has gone viral. It's all over social."

"Figaro?" Pyrus asked. "THE Figaro who snaps off people's fingers for fun. The one who parts the seas of crowds when he walks my floor. You guys have the wrong guy. Why the fuck would he want to be healed? He runs this fucking town!"

"Sir, it's him, and Una's group confirmed it," Kennedy said nervously. "We're doing what we can to monitor the situation but thought it was important for you to know."

"And what exactly did she do to 'heal' him?" he asked with air quotes for emphasis. "There's no way that woman could heal him from the depths of hell he's gone to with the addicts, con men, and morons he deals with on a daily basis. Where is he? I want to talk to him. NOW!"

The group appeared stunned by the request, each man looking for the most confident among them to answer.

"He's… gone, sir," Kennedy finally said.

"Gone? Where the fuck did he go?" Pyrus asked. "Church?" he laughed.

"Actually, yes, sir," Callahan said. "He said something about a lifelong dream of joining the priesthood."

Pyrus let out a raucous laugh at the thought. With all the corruption Figaro had seen and taken part in over the years, the Catholic Church seemed the most logical place of all.

"Whatever, man, doesn't matter. Get Jimbo to fill in. Let's get back to business here," he said, rising from his chair and starting his usual pacing route. He wanted to know how the hell that piece of shit landed on the stage but decided to blast that question at the fuckups running the show at the casino.

"We understand that two of the managers will be visiting the healer's suite to address these issues with her directly," Callahan said, turning the discussion back to business. "As instructed, I told them to withhold payment if necessary, to get the message across that promotion and vouchers had to be part of the shows moving forward."

"Well, we have a week to lift the numbers, or the healer and her crew will be making Vegas their permanent home to pay us back for this mess," Pyrus said. "I expect that the message about the promotions will also be given to the casino floor and bar managers?"

"Yes, it will," Callahan said, the team nodding in agreement beside him.

"Good. We need to keep track of this woman and make sure that she doesn't leave until we are back on track with the numbers. Understood?"

"Yes," the group said in unison.

"In fact, tell Don and Steven we need to get that contract extended TONIGHT. She'll do it. Where the fuck else is she gonna go?"

The men stared blankly ahead at the screen, further confirmation it was time to clean house. No more empty suits. He'd address it after that clown of a healer was signed. It was time to call Jade and enact another phase of the plan. Now that Figaro was off the floor, he needed to put his most trusted assets in play. It was mission critical.

"Make sure that the woman is locked in until those promotions work. The only loss I'm taking on this is your jobs." Pyrus hit the end button on the remote before the group had a chance to respond. He pressed the button for Catelyn. She picked up immediately.

"Yes, Mr. Payne?"

"Get Jade on the phone," he said and waited for the call to appear on the screen. She picked up on the third ring, still sleepy but looking as gorgeous as ever.

"What the hell are you still doing in bed? Don't you have a training session to get to?"

"Hi, darling," she said, rubbing the sleep from her eyes.

"You look like shit. I'd better not see a hair out of place when we meet up tonight at Shay's for dinner," he growled. He had to keep the feeling of insecurity alive. Otherwise, as beautiful as she was, some other man on the strip would pick her up in a second.

"I know, I'm sorry," she said, knowing full well that if she hadn't picked up, he would accuse of her fornicating with the trainer again. It was the lesser of two evils.

"Hey, I'm going to need you to do something for me," he said, turning the discussion to the point of his call. She listened carefully, considering his orders before responding. She sat up, taking in the information soberly.

"Can you do that?" he asked. "Then fill me in tonight at dinner?"

"Yes, I think I can do that."

"I didn't ask you to think, Jade," he said cruelly. "I am telling you to do it." His eyes clouded over as he stared back at her through the screen.

She smiled weakly and repeated back to him what she was to do.

"We'll go over the rest of the plan when I see you tonight," he said, an evil smile forming on his thin lips. "And Jade?"

"Yes, my love?"

"Try not to look like the two-bit whore that you are," he said before ending the call abruptly. She rolled over and cried into her pillow. If nothing else, she thought, his plan may allow her an opportunity to escape.

CHAPTER TWENTY-EIGHT ————

From the moment he saw her, Jayden was captivated. A lightning bolt ripped through his body as he caught his breath. He had never seen a creature so beautiful. She was ravishing.

He was adjusting the curtains offstage, when a large bang filled the room. The backstage tech had pulled the ladder down too quickly, barely missing a stagehand as it fell with a crash onto the stage.

"You didn't damage the surface did you, Joe?" The director yelled from below.

Joe moved the ladder out of the way, apologizing to the guy who nearly met his fate in the process. "Sorry, kid. I released the latch a little too quickly. I thought it would catch!"

"No worries, man," the stagehand said, heart still pounding in his chest. "Looks like I used up another life today."

The ladder, surprisingly, had left no visible marks upon landing, much to Joe's relief. "That floor has to be indestructible because I don't see any marks."

Jayden was glad he wasn't on the stage. He didn't know anything about theater, other than the military definition of working in an area of the world.

And there she was, a vision before him. She was sitting

elegantly in the last seat of the front row, legs crossed like a member of the royal family. She was focused on the phone in the palm of her hand. Jayden's intense stare caused her to look up. Their eyes locked for what felt like hours, a knowing urge pulsating between them. Joe pulled the ladder up with a loud rattle, causing Jayden to break the stare. He glanced back at her, giving her a nervous smile before lowering his gaze. She didn't look away for a second, willing him to walk toward her and introduce himself. Without hesitation, he did just that, taking the seat beside her and locking eyes once more.

"Hello," he said, feeling more like a school-aged version of himself, shifting his brawny frame nervously. She smiled at him, flashing him a perfect set of teeth. He was done right there. This had to be the most beautiful woman he had ever seen.

"A woman like you belongs on the stage. You must be an actress."

"No, I am working for the hotel," Jade said with quiet confidence. Her Somali accent only captivated him more.

"I detect an accent," Jayden said, leaning in to close the gap between them.

"I am from Somalia," she said with a nod. He smiled at her, flashing his own set of pearly perfection.

"I've been there, though many years ago," he said, keeping his dark thoughts buried deep inside his head.

"You are a soldier then?" she asked.

"Yes, I was a solider for twenty years. United States Army."

"Thank you for serving," she said, a nervousness overcoming her as she let her eyes take in his muscular frame.

"What brings you to the theater?" he asked, cheeks now glowing bright crimson.

"I am here to make sure the technical changes are completed. We have the final shows coming up, and Mr. Payne wants everything to be perfect."

"Like you," Jayden said involuntarily.

"Well, that's very nice of you to say, Mister…?"

"Washington," Jayden said, extending his hand. "Jayden Washington."

"Very nice to meet you, Jayden Washington."

The lightning struck again as he took her hand. She was a delicate creature on the outside, but he knew a tiger lived within.

"I work with Una, the healer in the show," he offered. She nodded knowingly.

"Yes, I figured as much," she said. Her eyes did not break from his even once. "How are you feeling about the shows so far?"

"I think they are going pretty well," he said. "I mean the audience just goes nuts when she does her thing up there. I would say it's a pretty big success."

"But you understand the problems going on after the show, yes?" she asked.

"I've heard something about that from our business manager," he said rather coyly. He knew full well what was going on but thought it better to play dumb than reveal too much. This is where military training had its advantages. People were not to be trusted at first, no matter how beautiful and alluring they may be.

"I want to make sure that the plans to boost the audience are carried out tonight without incident." Her face transformed in an instant. She was still striking but a darkness filled her eyes. "Are you the one to talk to about this?"

"No, that would be my brother—"

"Jayden!" Jaxson yelled from the back of the theater. "Come on, man, we have a meeting upstairs. Let's go!"

"Jaxson, come down here a sec," Jayden gestured toward his brother coming down the aisle.

"Oh!" Jaxson said once his eyes found Jade. He, too, took on a schoolboy demeanor as he made the introduction. "Hi, I'm Jaxson."

"I'm Jade," she said, extending her hand elegantly. He took it enthusiastically, more like an anxious handshake in an interview. He smiled and shook her hand nervously, holding onto it far longer than he should have. She graciously pulled it away, moving her fingers to release the feeling of his grip.

"You are brothers?" Jade asked incredulously, noticing the drastic difference in looks. Jaxson was a much smaller, slimmer version of his brother's massive stature. "Adopted?"

"No," Jaxson said with a small laugh. "We're twins actually."

"He's the oldest," Jayden said. "I'm the baby."

"You look nothing like a baby to me," Jade said, giving him a seductive look and drinking in his bulging biceps.

Jaxson could see what was going on between them. A familiar jealously started to build deep in his gut. It was a feeling he knew well through the years. Women were always drawn to Jayden. Jaxson rarely captured a woman's attention, especially one as beautiful as Jade.

"Well, Jay, we better get up there," Jaxson said anxiously. "Jade, nice to meet you. Will you be at the show tonight?"

"Yes, I am the one handling the vouchers tonight," she said.

"Oh, well you can work with me on that. I should be up in the booth ninety minutes before the show. You can find me there."

"I will," she said, turning her attention back to Jayden. "Hope to see you later then, Jayden?"

"Yes, definitely," he said, extending his hand once more. "Very nice to meet you."

She took his hand, careful to apply the right amount of pressure. He picked up on the feeling immediately, giving her a warm smile.

She watched the two brothers walking up the aisle—so different, yet the mannerisms were oddly alike. She felt the heat from Jayden immediately. This was going to be easier than she thought.

Jayden focused on his phone while the brothers waited for the elevator.

"OK, what was that about?" Jaxson asked, the jealously and anger reaching a boiling point as the elevator doors opened to them. Jayden waited for the doors to close before opening his mouth to speak.

"Nothing," he said.

"Jay, what the hell are you doing?" Jaxson asked. The level of annoyance in his voice was something Jayden knew well.

"I was talking to her about the show, Jax," Jayden offered.

"You are trying to get her in bed!" Jaxson yelled, the volume amplified by the small space.

"I was not! It was a conversation."

"Brother, please. I've known you since the womb. We can't have distractions like this, Jayden. Besides, she works for the hotel. We can't have you fraternizing with the enemy right now. This is the last week of the shows, and we need to finish this clean, you got it?"

"Yes," Jayden said. "Why you always gotta do that?"

"Do what?" Jaxson asked, his testosterone reaching peak

levels. It was everything to not throw a punch his brother's way, not that it would have much effect. If only it could land squarely on his perfectly chiseled face. Come to think of it, a crooked nose might just do the trick.

"I was just talking to the woman," Jayden said with exasperation. "She was telling me about her role with the hotel. That is all."

"Well, as I understand it, that woman is Mr. Payne's girlfriend, and that makes her absolutely off-limits to you!"

The doors dinged open, and the brothers poured their anger right into the middle of the group meeting.

"Everything OK?" Matt asked. The group looked at one other and then back to the men in front of them.

"Yes," Jaxson said. "Just details about those vouchers tonight. The woman from the hotel was there. I need to meet her before the show." Jaxson looked squarely at his brother then. "Me!" he shouted to him. "I am meeting her before the show, not you!"

"Let's leave the sibling rivalry behind for a moment and discuss our plans for Saturday," Petra said, centering the group on the discussion at hand.

Jayden wasn't about to let the details of Jade's situation interfere with his feelings for her. He had only just met her moments before, but he knew the woman was his destiny. He hadn't felt anything like it. He wasn't about to let it pass him up. He would meet Jade after the show, even if it was in secret.

Una watched Jayden closely, wondering if she should clear the energy around him. She felt intense feelings of love and anger, a powerful and intoxicating cocktail that almost made her lose her breath. She would let it slide for now. But she knew, deep in her heart, that Jayden and Jade's affair was inevitable.

Jaxson arrived at the director's box early to find the gift cards and vouchers had already been delivered. He called Petra over and quickly devised a plan to distribute as many as possible at the end of the show.

"I don't understand why we have to do this," Petra said, arms crossed defiantly. "I'm so sick of them commercializing everything in this place. It's disgusting."

"Well, it's not like we have that many shows left anyway," Jaxson said, gathering the materials. "Let's just get it done and hope that they get results and stay off our backs."

As showtime approached, Jayden realized that he couldn't stop thinking about Jade. Her skin, her eyes, her lips. He was obsessed with the idea of her, let alone the words that were spoken and unspoken between them. He reached for his phone to send her a text.

"You may be the most attractive woman I've ever seen in my life," he gushed. Her response pinged through in a matter of seconds.

"I have to say that I found you captivating, Jayden. When can we meet again?"

"IDK. Maybe at the show tonight?"

"I have dinner plans but could meet you after. What time?"

"How about 11:30? Outside the stage door? You know where that is?"

"Of course. See you then."

His heart leapt inside his chest. He hadn't had these feelings since…ever. It wasn't just the way she looked; it was how she moved. She was thoughtful, considerate. That was something he loved about foreign women. They seemed to operate on another level of understanding. Perhaps it was growing up in a society where you don't know where your next meal is coming from, instead of what you're going to put on Instagram later. It was alluring. He was smitten. It was a new feeling. He wanted to bathe in it for hours. Days. Weeks. The rest of his life. The clock moved slowly through the afternoon. He walked nearly twenty-five thousand steps, pacing the length of the stage—back and forth, back and forth—wondering how he would contain himself until he saw her again.

He didn't wait for the clock to hit 11:30; besides, if you're early, you're late he surmised. He excused himself from the post-show meeting, claiming he wasn't feeling well. The rest of the group showed concern, but he brushed it off, saying it was something he had eaten earlier. He was there at 11:20, pacing a hole in the floor, wondering if she would even show up. At exactly 11:30, she opened the stage door. The two fell into a long embrace.

"Where have you been?" she asked.

"What do you mean? I was early."

"I mean, where have you been all my life?"

It was corny as hell, but it worked its magic. He took her face into his hands and stared longingly into her eyes. Without hesitation, he brushed his lips against hers, the familiar lightning sweeping through his body. Their tongues danced playfully at first; then the two sank into a kiss to stop time.

From the penthouse suite several stories above, Pyrus watched the video images closely. The cameras had caught everything perfectly. A smile broke through as he watched Jade work her magic over the Neanderthal before her. The plan was in motion.

CHAPTER TWENTY-NINE ────────

P etra walked in, laptop under her arm, phone firmly fixed in the palm of her hand.

"Hey, guys," she said, not even bothering to look up.

"Everything OK?" Una asked, joining her in the living room of the suite. The sectional nearly swallowed up the room with its enormity. Even Petra's five-foot-ten frame was dwarfed in the center of it.

"How are people responding to the show?" Una asked.

"Mostly good, but there are always trolls," Petra said. "You know, the usual haters. People who want to discredit everything they are seeing. You wouldn't believe the number of people who spew venom after seeing a child healed from disease. It just doesn't make sense to me."

"They are broken," Una said, in the way only a light-worker could. "That is why I wanted to start streaming the shows. I was hoping I could maybe reach these people, but not everyone can be healed, or wants to be for that matter."

"Idiots," Petra said, feeling angry at the prospect of people whose very existence depended on the suffering of others.

"Free will," Una countered, shrugging her shoulders in the process.

Petra spent most of the show in the booth at the back

of the auditorium, scrolling through comments that made fun of everything happening on stage, including what they were wearing, how they walked up the stairs, facial expressions, dress sizes, the way they talked, even the moments of realization. Petra found those moments the most moving of the "Una Experience" or "UE" for short as it was called by the online community. But the comments that disturbed her the most were about Una directly—the ones that were accusing her of being a fraud, a fake, a piece of shit. The complaints about the people chosen were also disheartening. The trolls seemed to be spreading rumors that each one on stage was planted and part of an elaborate hoax. Petra, of course, knew that wasn't the case.

In the beginning, it was easier to dismiss the negativity. Sure, there were accusations of Una being a fraud, or that the video had somehow been altered. But once average people stepped forward onto the stage, everything started to change. With every share, the negative energy seemed to multiply. There was something insidious about it. Now, she wasn't sure how to stop it.

"There has always been darkness, Petra," Una said reassuringly. "We must remember that anger, fear, and sadness only fuel the underworld. You must stay in alignment with me."

"But why is there darkness around something so good?" Petra asked Una, tossing her phone aside. "Why would people hate on the work you're doing up there? I just don't understand it!"

"Because they thrive on the suffering of others," Una said. "If it isn't happening to them directly, it's not worth considering, let alone believing. My hope is that over time, the light will break through. This place is in deep trouble."

"What do you mean, the hotel or this city in general?" Petra asked with a chuckle. "Outside of this suite, it's pretty obvious this place hasn't been remodeled in years."

"No, I mean the planet in general," she said. "I've asked for guidance on this, you know, when I meditate. There is a heaviness. People are more siloed than ever before. They connect through screens. Social sites have become a place where people can surround themselves only with people, things, and beliefs that are aligned with their current thinking. Because of this, they begin to accept whatever is put in front of them as absolute. They don't question it. People today can log into the ether and experience nearly anything they want, as long as there is a camera pointed in the right direction. There is no growth, no conversation, and no understanding. Power and popularity exceed service and authenticity. People are afraid to be themselves, to speak their truth. Only those with power and popularity are heard and believed, even if they don't represent morality. People are broken, divided, and covered in dark energy like never before. That is why this has all happened to me... to us. We need to help humanity break through."

Petra studied her for a moment before responding. She saw a love, an authenticity in the woman's eyes like never before. She seemed to have a plan that extended far beyond the shows. Petra was almost afraid to ask about it.

"How do you know?" Petra asked. "I don't think I've ever really asked you that before."

"How do I know that this place is in trouble? Or how do I know what to do when I'm up there?"

"Both, I guess," Petra said, eyes narrowing. It was the first time she really questioned Una's gifts and their origins.

"I think I've always known," Una said. "When I was a child, I could hear a voice deep inside telling me what to do or say around people, especially those who were broken or hurting. People were just drawn to me from the beginning. I always questioned why my mother and I suffered so much. But now I understand that whole experience was preparing me for this. It gave me a deep understanding of humanity, particularly the fractures, breaks, and crushing of the human spirit. I just knew what to say or do to mend them, even if it was just with my words at the time. But the accident changed everything. I believe I died on that bus. And when I did, I was shown all the secrets to our existence—the ones that we all know the answers to, but we are too distracted or scared to reveal them. It was as if I were handed the keys to unlock everyone and everything. And if I could trust in it, if I could truly believe in my power to open the doorway to any human soul's experience, I could heal the whole of the world."

Petra's eyes widened with surprise. She had suspected Una was a gifted healer. She had read about them and had even known one in Ukraine. Her mother had visited her many times, until she wasn't able to help her anymore. That was the moment Petra stopped believing in magic. It was also the beginning of her series of bad decisions.

Una could see that Petra was uncomfortable with what little she had revealed. That was the trouble with her position at times: knowing the power within but not sharing it to a level that others would be overwhelmed or scared off altogether.

"I realize now that was too much to share right now," she said. "In fact, I also just realized that was the first time I've ever told anyone what really happened. I mean, I shared a little with my roommate in Seattle immediately following the crash, but not like this. I trust you, Petra. I did from the moment I saw your bruised and battered face. I knew you would hold my power in your steady hands. You and the others are collectively doing that for me. It's a lot to process at times, but I assure you that what we are doing and how we are doing it is the best way right now. It allows us to have greater impact. I couldn't have done this alone."

"Well, I am glad that you chose this felon to take part in the adventure of a lifetime," Petra said, taking Una's hand. "If you had told me three months ago, when I was living in a box no bigger than that hallway closet, that I would be sitting in this place with someone like you, I would have never believed it. But life works in mysterious ways. I just hope that I'm up for the challenges we face in the process."

"People are going to believe eventually," Una said. "They have to."

"They don't have to do anything," Petra said. "And that's the problem. Free will and all, like you said. They are more content to be anxious and at the same time passive. I see it in the comments all day, every day. It's as if they are afraid to make any move at all, afraid to stand in their truth."

"But it is only through truth that we achieve total freedom," Una said. "Freedom from the underworld."

If power, celebrity, and popularity were the drivers of the underworld now, Petra could finally see that she and the others would have no choice but to make Una the absolute pinnacle of both if people were to ever believe her. The light would prevail if she had anything to do with it. Haters be damned.

"Not damned," said Una. "Transformed."

CHAPTER THIRTY

Jayden watched from the wings as Una healed another soul. He felt the weight of one thousand lifetimes ascend from the person before her, trapped in a cycle of abuse, addiction, and self-loathing. It was one of Una's most powerful efforts yet, as she talked the broken woman through lifetimes of behaviors that she just never seemed to shake.

Jayden watched the crowd's reaction, wondering what they were thinking when their expressions changed so abruptly from judgment to curious wonderment to full-on acceptance. It was beautiful to watch it unfold. Their faces were always so different when they entered the theater than when they left it.

"You've been cursed for thirteen generations, Carla," Una said. "The souls you've touched follow you like wanderers in a vast desert, desperately searching for water. Only in this lifetime, the water is truth."

It was as if a force far more powerful than her was taking charge of the vocal cords deep in her throat. It was something Jayden noticed more as of late. Una was changing before their eyes, becoming more confident in her abilities and gifts. Her physical state after the shows, however, was worrisome. He watched her carefully, studying her for signs of exhaustion and fatigue that she had exhibited more frequently after challenging individuals such as the one before her.

"I think of my children," Carla said sadly. "What have I done to them? How can they ever forgive me?"

She fell into a heap on the stage floor, sobbing uncontrollably. Una struggled to bring the woman to her feet, literally pulling her from the depths of despair. She folded the broken woman into her arms and strongly embraced her as she released years of unyielding pain.

"Why do you think your children don't love you, Carla?" Una finally asked as Carla's sobbing abated.

"Because I'm a lying piece of shit!" Carla spat into the microphone.

The audience gasped, watching her closely as she shuffled her feet on the stage floor.

"There ain't no way I would trust me!" she screamed.

Jayden inched his way toward the curtain, watching Carla and the audience for any signs of unusual distress. He was looking for patterns, scanning the auditorium for anything out of the ordinary. People with hats were always an issue. He had ordered security to set forth a "no hat" rule shortly after the first performance. It was too easy to hide under the bill of a cap, and Jayden wanted to physically see the eyes of each and every person in the place. It was nonnegotiable.

Carla seemed to settle down as Una stroked her shoulder. It was clear the woman was a tweaker. Jayden knew the signs well. He watched a friend fall into that trap shortly after separating from the Army with little money in the bank and without his right arm. He watched him wade into a sea of despair, his only lifeline a pill-pushing doctor from a pain management center. As he watched the woman on the stage, Jayden wasn't sure how long it had been since her last high, but he could physically see she was coming down hard from whatever she was on. He hoped Una could reach her in time.

"I am what most people hate," Carla said. "Hell, I hate me! I have robbed my mother; cheated on my husband with not one, not two, but five other men; I broke into my kids' piggy bank to buy drugs. Meth mostly because it was cheapest at the time. That's about as low as a person can go. I chose getting high over my kids!"

It was a comment that someone like Carla would usually follow with a smile or nervous laugh. Not this time. It was clear Una was breaking through. Jayden could almost see the original Carla, the one before the first hit, clawing her way from the depths of the dark tunnel that was addiction. He had traveled through the tunnel himself over the years. He even left a few sliding footprints and claw marks on the slow journey to the light at the other end. He was thankful to put it behind him and never look back.

Jayden shuddered at the thought of Carla's children, probably left alone to fend for themselves for hours, if not days, on end. He considered how his own father would advise a parishioner about something like this. It happened on more than one occasion.

Jayden recalled the countless lost souls inside his father's church, begging for some redemption for whatever they had done before. His father called them "part-timers," but it didn't mean that he treated them any differently from the most loyal parishioners who visited regularly on Sundays. His father embodied everything a minister should be: kind; caring; stern when needed; and, above all, an excellent listener. The man would listen for hours on end to sins big and small, rendering advice when asked. Most of the time, all people wanted from him was a good ear and a soft shoulder to cry on. They didn't want to be fixed or to have their problem solved. They want the dignity to work it out for themselves. That's what his father had always hoped to provide, a sounding board that reflected back the answer that was already inside of them.

His thoughts turned to Una. He saw so many of his father's traits in her—loving, listening, and always in the present—maybe even more so. It was so hard for people to live in the present, Jayden thought. That was probably because the present in these times was more overwhelming than ever: screens vying for attention, and eyes doing all they could to not engage, if only subconsciously.

Jayden watched the show come to an end. People rose to their feet, showering Una in applause he hadn't seen until now. Her work was far reaching, with ticketholders coming from every corner of the globe. She left the stage and went straight toward him, opening her arms in such a way he couldn't avoid the embrace. Not that he wanted to.

"Jayden, could you please get me some water?" she asked.

He retrieved a water bottle from his pocket and handed it to her.

"I believe we are reaching next level now," Una said smiling broadly. "Don't forget we have a meeting upstairs right after the show. Where are the others?"

"They are around," Jayden responded, moving his eyes in an effort to gather the group or at least pull in the memory of where they each said they would be during this performance.

"Jaxson is in the suite looking over the paperwork with

Matt; Petra is in the back of the theater with Tia, monitoring social media. And I have my eye on the place," Jayden said with a smile, which Una returned in earnest.

"Of course, you do." She patted his cheek before draining the bottle of its contents.

"Did it remind you of your father?" she asked as they made their way to the side door.

"Yes, actually, it did," Jayden said, not in the least surprised by her comment.

"I was so happy to see Carla break the curse," Una said happily. "You have no idea how much damage it does over lifetimes. It took me a couple times to access it all, but I got there and so did she. Another miracle in the books."

"How does it happen for you...I mean, the healing?" Jayden asked as they waited for the elevator.

Una paused for a long moment, pondering her response. "It's a guide of sorts. Or God," she finally said. "Or universe, or source, or light. Whatever you are most comfortable with. It moves through me. I make a request, and it answers. It works with and through me. It's that simple."

"That simple?" Jaxson asked with a laugh. "If it were that simple, then we would all be doing it."

"Everyone has the power to do what I do," she said with a straight face. "Very few have the trust that I have to allow it to move through them—to let the force, well, take over. You have the power right now, Jayden. As your father would say from the pulpit, just ask and you shall receive."

Jayden seemed uncomfortable with the concept at first, then allowed his mind to wander toward what kind of wishes he would fulfill. What would he do with such a power? End wars. Feed the hungry. Help the sick. It was all so overwhelming.

"You think your healing was by my hand alone?" Una asked as if reading his mind.

He thought about it but finally shook his head as the doors opened.

"We have the power within us. We set an intention, and then it is done. You set forth an intention to heal, and it was done. Once the intention is set, the universe goes to work to make it happen for you. That is what's happening with everyone walking the earth. They are happy? It is so. They are constantly sad, addicted, conflicted? It is so."

"So, you're saying we all have the powers that you do?" Jayden asked. "I don't believe that exactly. You heal people instantly. It's supernatural what you are doing. It is beyond comprehension. It is…magic."

"Is God not magic, Jayden?"

"Well, I believe God or the Spirit is always there, setting our minds aflame with ideas and thoughts. Not the bad ones, necessarily, but the good stuff that we think of, the stuff that helps us or other people."

"Yes, that is most certainly God in action. Or a higher self. Or your angels."

"Are you an angel?" Jayden asked, searching for the answer deep in her eyes.

"What is an angel to you?" Una asked in return.

"A being that has a positive influence over our lives," he said. "Dad would scold me for not saying a being from heaven, but I'm not so certain I conform to that view anymore. My mind was opened out there in the world. I've seen plenty of angels wearing human clothes, even on a battlefield."

She smiled at him as he retrieved the keycard from his pocket. She reached for his hand before he opened it.

"Jayden, by your answer, anyone walking the earth can be an angel, yes?"

"Yes."

"Then, I am an angel," Una answered. He could almost see the halo appear above her head.

CHAPTER THIRTY-ONE —————

M att paced in front of the door like a tiger in a cage. The managers had arrived several minutes early, forcing him into a vapid conversation. He loathed small talk. Tonight's show had been particularly challenging. They were down to the final performances, and the crowds were growing more tense. The casino floor outside the theater was filled with people desperate for help. He knew what Payne's people wanted: more performances. But he was certain Una wouldn't agree, or at least he hoped she wouldn't.

Jaxson noticed Matt's unease and quickly jumped in to occupy the sharks long enough for Una and Jayden to return from the show. Matt excused himself, pretending to text someone, but, in reality, he was running several scenarios through his worried mind of what this could all mean. Payne wasn't going to let go of her or the show easily.

From the foyer, he could hear Jaxson now making small talk with Payne's minions in the living area. Their niceties were limited to something about how hot the weather was in Vegas this week and this and that about high winds and canceled flights that caused complications for the desk employees. He really didn't care what they had to say right now. He wanted to leave the conversation to Una, Jax, and Jayden. They seemed the most capable of dealing with assholes from Pyrus's pack. He was about to walk back to the seating area when the door clicked open.

"Thank God," Matt said with utter relief. "I was wondering if you were going to leave me with these guys forever."

"Bro, we were gone like five extra minutes," Jayden said with an eye roll.

Una broke into a smile and greeted Matt with a warm hug.

"I'm sorry, Matt," she said, immediately filling him with calm. He didn't want to let go.

"We can't—"

"Let me handle it, Matt," she said reassuringly. "I'm sorry I was late, but I had some things to talk to Jayden about, and I know you understand."

Jayden gave Matt a knowing look as they made their way to the living room.

"Hello," Una said, extending her hand in greeting. "I'm sorry to keep you waiting."

Jaxson was seated with the managers and gave Jayden a nod when he walked into the room. It was twin speak for where to sit. Una smiled sweetly at them both before everyone took a seat, the brothers seated near enough for conversation but far enough to send a signal of negotiation. Matt continued his fake text, hovering nearby but far enough away to avoid any direct involvement with the conversation.

"Another great show this evening, Una," the first manager began. He reached for his collar, releasing the tie ever so slightly from its knot.

"I'm Don," he said. "I wanted to thank you all for the tremendous performance you are putting on each evening here at the casino."

"Thank you, Don," Una said, looking for the other manager to follow suit. *Suit* was the optimal word, as the second gentleman shifted in his seat, looking exhausted.

"And you are?" she finally asked him.

"Steven, ma'am," he said, giving her a slight nod before looking down toward the floor, not even bothering to acknowledge her outstretched hand.

"What brings you to the suite at this late hour?" she asked, hoping to move the meeting along. "My makeup?"

"No, ma'am, uh, Una," Don said, extending his body forward. "You looked beautiful as always tonight. The audience continues to respond very positively to the show, and the numbers continue to reflect that."

"I'm glad to hear it," she said, glancing at the brothers before returning her gaze to the uncomfortable duo there to represent Pyrus.

"Why are we meeting tonight?" she asked again, this time with a more direct tone. "We only have a few more performances."

"Well, it has to do with what's happening outside the show," Steven picked up, sensing Don's unease. "There has been a precipitous drop in the other business inside the casino since the start of the show."

That was Matt's cue to return to the living room. They were speaking his language now.

"Precipitous drop?" Matt asked, entering the room and taking a seat next to Una. "From all I see, your casino is at maximum capacity, and the floor is packed before and after the show."

"We are seeing a decline in numbers with our regular financial drivers," Don said before clearing his throat. "Bar business is down, and our casino dollars are drying up."

"And what would that have to do with us?" Jaxson asked. "We handed out those vouchers like you asked."

"It's a rather unexpected outcome that we are attributing to your shows," Steven said, shifting uncomfortably and looking awkwardly at Don before continuing.

"It seems that people aren't doing what they usually do after a show in Vegas," he said, hoping the room would pick up on what he was trying to say. They didn't.

"They are, well, leaving," Don finally added. "We seem to have a problem keeping them within the walls here, and that's become a big problem for the casino and Mr. Payne specifically."

Don looked over at Steven, the two communicating on a level that the rest of the group couldn't quite read, except for Una.

"I thought he wanted the show and all that came with it: the crowds, the performance, the money. What exactly is the problem?" she asked, knowing the answer but wondering if they would respond with bald-faced lies or some half-truth.

"No, no, everyone loves the show, Una," Don responded quickly. "Seriously, you have done everything you said you would do, and that's wonderful. But the unspoken part of our agreement is that the show would drive more business, not take it away. We're here to make up for lost business and ask you to continue on with the shows. You have broken the contract, per section nine, and we are here to recoup the losses and are extending the shows for another ninety days as per the agreement."

Matt did everything in his power to stop himself from grabbing Don by the neck. Jayden saw it happening and quickly diverted Matt, directing him to a seat furthest away from the group. He gave Matt a stern, yet reassuring look, turning his attention back to Una. She gave Matt a knowing glance, calming him immediately with her energetic presence.

Una could tell that deep down, Don was a loving, caring individual. It was just a set of circumstances that led him to work for the most ruthless man on the strip, if not the entire nation. She was almost afraid to tell him how it would all work out for him in the end if he continued on this path.

"I appreciate that Don, but—"

"What Don is trying to say is that we need this show to be profitable overall, not just in the auditorium," Steven said. "If it isn't profitable, we are all out of jobs, and that's a problem. For Mr. Payne. For me. We need to fix this, and we need to fix it now."

"We have a couple of shows left," Matt said. "There's no point in talking about it now. It's going to be over soon enough."

"Well, that's why we are here," Steven said, leaning forward in his chair and fully taking the reins away from Don. "As Don said, Mr. Payne would like to extend the contract for the performances." He turned to Una, his eyes clouding over as me made his demand.

"You are signing this now, or we are suing you and the show for all the losses we've incurred."

The group glanced at each other, then simultaneously turning to Una for direction. It was her show. They were merely support. They weren't going to answer for her, but the man's claim was ridiculous. Matt immediately reached for his phone, pulling up the agreement and the section they were referring to. Una raised her hand to stop him.

"Matt, it's fine. And you all know you are far more than

support to me. You are part of this. Don't think anything less," she said, giving each face in the room a reassuring nod.

"But the others aren't here, Steven," she said, turning her attention to the suits. "I need their input as well."

"We need your signature tonight," Don said sternly. "The paperwork has already been prepared." He reached inside his suit pocket to retrieve the papers. Matt grabbed them, quickly scanning the details before responding.

"He's not kidding. They want us to continue on for another ninety days!" he exclaimed. "If you're as troubled as you say, gentlemen, then tell us how ninety days will possibly make a difference?"

"We believe ninety days is more than enough time to push the vouchers and help us with other promotions for the show," Don said. "You know, meet and greets, autographs, one-on-one sessions, that sort of thing. This is your chance to turn around the situation before Mr. Payne gets involved directly," Don said, looking directly at Una. "Payback."

"If you need a response now, then the answer is no. I think we all agree that the show ends as planned. We have other work to do."

"We would offer you compensation, of course," Steven said, ignoring Una's answer. "I mean, when we set up the deal, we had no idea that it was going to do as well as it's doing, in the auditorium at least. Besides, you don't want to face Mr. Payne in court, and that's where this is headed if you don't do as we ask."

Una said nothing, allowing the silence in the room to stifle the men. Sometimes no answer was the best answer. The two didn't seem bothered and continued. She waited for the truth to spill from Don's lips.

"Truth be told, it's the only thing we have going right now at the Neo, outside of the room revenue," Don said. Steven's eyes filled with rage as he stared his colleague down.

"I guess he wasn't supposed to mention that?" Una asked.

Steven tried to get the conversation back on track. He gave Don a "don't say a goddamn thing" look before laying out the plans for the additional performances. He smirked a little as he sat back in the chair, confident about what he was about to propose.

"As for the shows, we need to add more music," he said to the group.

"Music," Jaxson said. "That's what you propose?"

"Stay with me here," Steven said, beads of sweat forming at his temples. "It needs to have more pizzazz. We need to get the crowd on their feet, chanting, clapping. It needs to be like one of those big Tony Robbins shows, you know? I went to one last year, and it was amazing: people jumping up and down, crazy loud music playing. It was the shit!"

The trio looked at one another, confused at the idea.

"Una," Don jumped in, "there is no reason in the world why you couldn't do the same. 'Bridge Over Troubled Water' when you heal one person, a little Nickelback 'Savin' Me' when you bring a new one onto the stage. 'Don't Stop Believin'' will just kill it at the end. I mean, that crowd will be totally rocking by the time you leave the stage."

"Woo!" Steven said excitedly, clapping his hands together for effect.

"If we add a few more elements—merch, promotions, alcohol flowing during the performance, casino chips as people are leaving the theater—we could get them all loosened up and back on the floor after the show," Steven encouraged. "There's no limit as to what we could do with a two- or three-year residency. It's fucking exhilarating, man!"

"I get what you are proposing, Steven, but it sounds like a sick marketing ploy," Jaxson finally said.

"It's never been about the money," Petra said, entering the room with Tia, placing a hand on Una's shoulder for reassurance and support. "We are here to make a difference, and that's exactly what we have done."

"Even if just one person was healed, that would have been enough for Una," Tia affirmed to the suits. "I mean, she's healed us, and that's a damn miracle, at least as far as I'm concerned."

"Healed you?" Steven asked with a snort. "That will be the day."

"That's enough for tonight, gentlemen," Una said, pointing toward the door. "You may leave."

"I can't believe you would want to profit off of people's pain and tragedy," Jayden said, escorting them to the door. "Do you hear what you're saying?"

"Who the hell is saying—"

Don placed his arm in front of Steven, this time ordering him to stop.

"I've got this one," he said sternly to his colleague. "Listen, all we are saying is that we have to make money off of this. There are expenses, a cost to each performance. That cost has to be covered with a reasonable return on investment. What Steven was proposing would allow us to continue the show and help even more people. If that's truly what this is about, why wouldn't you want it to continue? It's giving you the opportunity to have a major impact, far beyond what you've already accomplished."

"And what exactly is that, Don?" Una asked, stepping forward in interest.

"The shows are sold out!" he exclaimed. "People are thrilled with what you are doing. You have amassed a major following online, like…thousands?" Don said, reaching for his phone to confirm the exact number.

"77,023,515 to be exact," Petra said, having just confirmed the number following the last show.

"See? Over seventy-seven million people. Jeez, that's a lot!" Don nearly screamed, dabbing away the sweat on his forehead. "Is the air on in here? Anyway, if you don't do it, then Mr. Payne will be expecting you and all of the crash victims to return the settlement checks in full, and he'll sue you for the losses we've incurred. That was the deal, if you read the fine print."

"I read the fine print, Don, and there's no way that will hold up in court," Matt said defiantly. "You have no proof that the show has directly impacted the entire Vegas economy. There are many other factors at play, and that cannot be Una's fault."

"This is ridiculous!" Jaxson screamed, fury building inside of him. Una signaled him to stop.

"Don, you are feeling this way because your values are not aligned with your work," Una said, parting the two men and ushering them back to the seating area. "You are doing one thing with your actions while believing another. It's a terrible place to be, like a cancer for the soul."

She took Don's hand into hers and looked deep inside him, pulling forth a truth she knew he should have spoken years ago.

"Mr. Payne sees what's happening with your work here in Vegas," said Don, the truth starting to drip from his lips. Steven looked at his coworker in disgust.

"Don't do this, man!" Steven shouted. "You're gonna fuck it all up!"

"I don't give a shit!" Don snapped back, turning his full attention to Una.

"Listen, your work here on the strip has greatly impacted the economic foundation of this city," Don began. "It's built on addictive, compulsive, even destructive behaviors, but you already know this. Now, people are leaving your shows seemingly healed, not only the ones up on the stage, but also those in the audience. But they are not leaving to gamble, drink, fuck, or fantasize about one or all three. They are simply pouring into the streets and going back to the airport or car to flee this place. Problem is, they are taking their money with them. We can't survive this the way it's going. We need people gambling, drinking, snorting, and fucking. It's the economic engine that has propelled Vegas to become one of the top vacation destinations in the world. Millions of people flock to this desert oasis in search of an escape from their pathetic lives. Now, there's no telling what they want to do. All I know is that they want out of this place. They are no longer compelled to engage in the things that make us money. And that's why we are here: to extend your show, to create some marketing tactics to bring people back to the behaviors that have become the gasoline for our economic engine. So, if you have any humanity inside you, I am asking… no, more like begging you, to please stop doing whatever it is you're doing to make them leave the casino and do everything in your power to keep them here."

Steven slapped his forehead in disgust and leapt up from his chair in a rage.

"You. Fucking. MORON!" he screamed, grabbing for Don's throat, shoving Una to the side in the process. Don struggled to break free from his clutch, gasping for air.

Jayden and Jaxson rushed to separate the men, using brute strength to pull them apart.

"I am not doing this anymore!" Don shouted to the room. "This is pathetic!"

He shook away Jaxson's hold, then turned toward Una.

"Thank you!" he shouted, reaching for her hand and allowing his lips to gently touch her skin. He noted how radiant it appeared, an ethereal glow moved from her hand to his, gliding up his arm and filling him with a warmth he had never known. He smiled at her before turning his attention back to his colleague.

"You can do whatever you want, Steven," he said. "I quit. I think I'll finally teach at the college. I've wanted to do that for years!"

He was out the door in seconds, leaving Steven stunned, eyes darting wildly around the room.

"Steven," Una said, nodding to Jayden to release him. "What Don was proposing is something I cannot do. I am bound to complete our agreement—conditions that your employer and I came to after the crash in Seattle. I have fulfilled it to the letter, providing you with an entertaining performance that promises the same healing powers that saved those on board the bus and all the people in this room. Except you, of course."

"Yes, but it's not enough to—"

"We cannot interfere with the concept of freewill," Una said, interrupting Steven's singular motive. "People are free to make decisions for themselves. If that decision involves not engaging in 'behaviors' as you call them within these walls, I cannot control that, nor would I ever interfere. I show them the path, but I cannot walk it for them. Do you understand?"

Steven's entire face began to turn red, not out of embarrassment but total rage. Blood began to boil underneath his artificially tanned skin.

Matt had seen Steven lose it before over some random technicality—a broken light, the makeup, and myriad small things that he would build up to be the end of the world. The man did not like to lose, and he certainly wouldn't accept he was wrong. But Don's departure had taken his blood pressure to the next level. He knew Una had about thirty seconds to make her point before he called Payne. If that happened, then all hell would break loose. He jumped in, hoping to buy them some time.

"Your casino has received an enormous amount of publicity," Matt began. "Petra could easily show you how many posts and comments have included the name of this resort from our own account, as well as the thousands of others who have walked through these doors to see the performance in person. People are talking about you. That is a level of advertising that would have cost you thousands, if not millions, of dollars to purchase. And that's going to continue after the show. You can take all your ideas and continue them if you want to, after we close the show."

Matt's tactic was working. He could see Steven's anger receding as his rational mind kicked in. He knew Steven was analyzing his comments, the logical side of his brain taking over, the emotional part losing its fervor.

"I know that was Mr. Payne's goal when we first talked," Steven said, emphasis on the word *first*. Like many of the lawyers turned businessmen Matt worked with in the past, Matt understood this guy. This was asshole Steven, the guy he usually saw across the table. Matt didn't necessarily blame him. The guy worked for Pyrus Payne. It was nearly impossible to clock in day after day and work for that level of evil without some sort of side effect.

"Mr. Payne wanted the casino to be viewed in a more positive light, given its aging interior and overall concept," Matt said. "He wanted to put off making an investment that would have involved literally blowing it up and starting over."

The room was silent except for Steven's breath. Matt could hear the pace slowing as Steven grasped what he was saying.

"The company has saved millions and millions of dollars, Steven," Matt said. "You have benefited greatly from us being here. It isn't as bad as you're making it out to be, I assure you."

"But our accounts are not reflecting the positive numbers you are talking about. We are losing money with this show. People aren't sticking around or even staying in the casino after the performance is over. They are leaving!" Steven would have thrown his fist through a wall for emphasis if one were within proximity. Una placed a hand on his shoulder, but he quickly shook it off.

"Look, I know that we aren't the only ones on the strip suffering as a result of this show," Steven said more calmly. Matt wondered what Una had done to affect his demeanor. "The streets are flooded, but no one is going inside. Like Don said, they are walking, marveling, holding hands, singing, and doing just about every other damn thing that doesn't involve spending money in Vegas. This city is going to collapse if we don't do something!"

"Maybe it's exactly as it should be, Steven," Una said, looking at him for a long moment. He struggled to respond, finally sighing in disgust before lowering his eyes. "Maybe it's time for a new attraction."

"If everything you are saying is true and it relates to Una's performance, why wouldn't you have us go?" Matt asked, stepping back into his lawyer form for a moment. "I mean, wouldn't that ensure the business would return immediately? Replace us at the end of the run, and you get your business back."

Steven studied Matt's face for a moment, attempting to form a rebuttal.

"Mr. Payne doesn't compromise," Steven replied coldly. "It's up to him what happens from here."

"Did you not listen to what I said earlier about freewill?" Una asked. "We are going at the end of the agreement, and that's final. Please have Mr. Payne talk to me directly if he has any other concerns."

Steven made a motion to leave, brushing away the wrinkles in his suit.

"This is not how this meeting was supposed to go," he said to the room. "You have no idea how much destruction you are causing to this city. You're affecting lives and fucking people over. You're all a bunch of assholes!" He stomped toward the exit, turning to flip off the group before slamming the door behind him.

"Well, that was fun," Matt said, looking bewilderedly at the group around him. "We need to leave immediately after the final show. We need a plan. Pyrus Payne is not going to let us go easily."

"I agree," Tia said nervously. "I think we have a major problem on our hands. I know what his people do to nobody makeup artists and showgirls. I can't image what he would do to us."

The group simultaneously turned to Una and searched for answers on her face. She had shared some visions before but nothing compared to what was about to happen.

"It will be fine," Una said, shooing their worries away with a wave of her hand. "Mr. Payne is distracted with other projects right now. We will fulfill the contract as promised. Then it's time to take this show on the road. Let's discuss the plan in full after a good night's rest."

Una watched as the group dispersed, arms around one another in support and encouragement. She could see how close they had become in this experience, and it brought her great comfort to know they had each other. It wouldn't be long now before the world knew. Sleep tonight was more important than ever. She needed it to refresh and replenish the energy that allowed her work to happen. She gazed out the window at the moonless night. She had truly timed their departure perfectly to coincide with the cycle. The city below was dropped in a veil of darkness, save a few beacons of light weaving in and out of the lost souls Pyrus preyed upon. She wanted to free them all. Getting out of the desert was just the start. The real work of lifting the veil of darkness that had covered so many souls that walked the earth was about to begin.

CHAPTER THIRTY-TWO

Tia retrieved the concealer from the makeup case, careful not to show concern. She had noticed Una's complexion after the last two shows. She seemed to be more translucent, almost as if she were sinking into her flesh. Her once glowing appearance was now sallow, her cheeks sunken. She looked gaunt and exhausted when she dropped into the chair that afternoon. Tia knew she'd have to work some magic to pull off a look presentable for the last performance.

"Everything OK, sweetie?" Tia asked, working to locate the right shade of concealer.

"Yes," Una said, sinking further into the director's chair, crossing her legs properly, and struggling to find her smile. It was obvious she was trying to hide the fact she was fading. Tia raised an eyebrow as she gently applied the coverup, working the liquid into the skin under the eye. "I'm just a little tired. I didn't rest very well last night."

"Maybe that has something to do with those thugs disguised as businessmen who visited us the other night."

"That was expected," Una said with a sigh. "I told you all that they were unhappy with the declining revenue at the hotel since the show started."

"But aren't the shows sold out?" Tia asked, carefully applying the cinnamon foundation. "Why do you have to do anything more than you are already doing? They are turning you into some sort of snake oil salesperson if you ask me."

"It's not so bad," Una replied defeatedly. "They seemed to think those promotion vouchers would drive business at the restaurants and bars on site. Matt told me it has had little effect, if any. Not that it matters now."

"What exactly were those promotions and gift cards they talked about? Like people are gonna go to some janky hotel gift shop or something? That shit is way too expensive."

"No," Una said laughing. "The gift cards are five-dollar credits for the casino games."

"Five dollars? Five dollars can't even buy you a water in this town! That money is just going back into their pockets. It's a damn shame. Those guys are shady as hell."

"Well, we are going to do what we have to do tonight and keep a very low profile after the show," Una said firmly. "I don't want us to stay here any longer than we have to."

"I gotta say, the plan is pretty flawless girl," Tia said, gliding the shimmering color across Una's eyelids. "Kind of like your skin. We are gonna need some *Ocean's Eleven* timing tonight if we are gonna pull this shit off like you plan it. I mean, I'm down for whatever, but I just hope I can do everything at the right time."

"Well, timing is everything, Tia," Una said, "and I have all the faith in the world in you."

"I'll do my best," she said, adding on another layer of foundation. "Frankly, you look like shit right now, and I don't know where you're gonna find the energy to do that final show and pull off that stunt of yours, but whatever. You have the music in you, girl. Don't need any 5-hour Energy to help you with those miracles you have to pull out of yourself every night. Me on the other hand…"

Tia whipped out the energy drink and drank it in one gulp.

Una laughed out loud at Tia's honesty and props. She hadn't shared with anyone just how much it took to read people each night. She would work to identify the issues, pull the darkness into her own body, and then ground the energy into the earth, recycling it anew. In the beginning it was easier. She was like a fully charged battery. But as time wore on, she found herself depleted of the reserves needed to recharge each night. She wondered how much longer she could continue, especially on the road ahead.

"I appreciate your concern, Tia, but I assure you that I'm fine. Sometimes, I just need good vibes from those around me to fully recharge and continue to do the work."

Tia nodded half-heartedly. She really wanted Una to look at herself closely in the mirror and see what she saw: a tired, shadow of a woman in desperate need of a vacation.

"I'll take a vacation as soon as the shows are done," Una said, reaching for the mirror on the table beside her. "We all will."

She observed herself closely, marveling at Tia's work to transform her each night. At first, she had resisted the idea, but working with her and seeing the result was a welcome relief. It also hid from the audience and the group at large what Tia had already seen. She was starting to fade but knew she could power through tonight and move on to the next phase. She had to, for her as much as the group.

"Another show, another seven or eight miracles," Petra said, as she walked through the door. It was amazing to see Petra's own transformation. Fitted clothing, swept back hair. She looked the part of any powerful CEO. Una smiled at her appearance, grateful to have her on the team.

"Anyone in particular you want me to watch out for in line tonight?" Petra asked.

"I think you'll have plenty to choose from," Una said, enjoying the sensation of Tia combing her hair into place.

"As the show gets underway, I know we will be overwhelmed with desperate, broken people," Petra said. "It's the last one, after all. These are the ones who paid upwards of a thousand dollars a ticket."

Una shook her head at the thought. "I wish I could just heal the world for free, but I'm pretty sure I wouldn't survive it."

"Speaking of which, is there something we should know about the process?" Petra asked, retrieving her phone, ready to take Una's order. "It seems like you've been very tired lately. We are all concerned about your health and ability to continue at this pace. We are also concerned about your plan tonight, but if you believe, then so shall we."

"Don't mind me," Una said, attempting a real smile in the process. "I'm just fine. A little positive reinforcement from you all goes a long way in helping me perform the shows."

"Girl, are you losing it?" Tia asked with a head tilt. "You just said that to me like two seconds ago. It's like you are stuck on repeat or something."

Una just shrugged off the comment. She studied them both, so grateful for their energy and support.

"Well, if it's praise you need, I can send Jaxson in to read the latest comments or…" Petra said, retrieving the phone from her pocket, "you can check them here."

She pulled up the app and with a few taps read the most relevant comments. Una scrolled her way through for a few moments, a genuine smile slowly breaking onto her full lips.

"These are wonderful," Una said. "I'm so glad that the stories have incited a genuine reaction. All of the people we've welcomed on stage have been so open and honest up there and even after the show." She scrolled through a few more before handing the phone back to Petra.

"Listen," Petra said, pulling up a chair next to Una as Tia packed up her case. "I think we need to talk about the plan tonight."

"Go on," Una encouraged.

"Don't you think it's a little risky? I mean, not the parts we are handling, but your part. Do you have the energy to pull something like that off?"

"That's what I was gonna say, but you beat me to it," Tia said. "It all is gonna have to go down like some Seal Team Six! Where's Jayden?"

"I have it all under control," Una said, patting their hands. "Besides, the crowd tonight is going to be amazing, not to mention the comments online. It helps when—"

"We know, positive vibes and all that," Tia said with a sigh.

"No to repeat myself yet again, but yes. And I tapped in a little longer this morning during my meditation. I believe I can do it. I trust the process, and I trust the spirit that moves me. Now you have to trust me."

"Oh, we trust you, girl," Tia said. "It's those shady people who run this place we're all worried about. They got eyes and ears everywhere in this desert hole."

"Yes, and believe me, I know shady," Petra said, glancing between the two. "We can't have you doing another ninety shows, Una. It's going to drain you or worse."

"I agree," Una said. "We need to get out of here. But these guys aren't going to let us out of here easily, hence the plan.

I know they will not let go until their ledger improves, and I don't see it improving. Ever."

"Then we need to get the hell out of here and trust we can all do what you're asking," Petra said.

"I'm not leaving without the group intact," Una said firmly. "I need you together. For the next phase, at least."

"What next phase?" Petra asked, looking at Tia to see if she had any clue. "Why won't you share where we're headed from here?"

"As I mentioned before, we need to take the show on the road after this. The people want more, and we are going to give it to them."

"How are you going to continue doing this day and night when you are barely holding it together as it is?" Petra asked.

"That's what I have Tia for," Una said.

"And that little vacation you promised a moment ago," Tia said with a raised eyebrow. "I'm good, but I do have my limits. At this point, we both be performing miracles."

Petra laughed at the comment and Una's humble reaction. "Don't sell yourself short, my dear," the healer said, performing a small stretch as she stood. "I'll be in my room if anyone needs me."

Petra and Tia watched their leader leave before giving each other a knowing look.

"I don't know how much longer she can do this, Petra," Tia said, turning to retrieve her case. "She's looking dead-ass tired under all that spackle I've been putting on each night. I think we need to do something when we get clear of this place. She could barely sit up in the chair at first. It's like she's not sleeping or something. I know the visit from those corporate thugs the other night didn't help."

"Well, we have reason to be concerned," Petra said, looking toward the window. "Even if we escape without notice, they are going to track us down. One thing I know for sure is that we are not leaving her to face those devils in suits alone, especially Jaxson. He owes her his life. In fact, we all do to some extent."

"Hey now, this is just another job for me," Tia chimed in. "I like you all, but I'm gonna do what's best for Tia. Full-stop."

"I get it, but we need you, Tia," Petra said, staring out the window. A long silence dropped between them, as Petra waited for an answer.

"If you all are hitting the road, then you can count me in," Tia finally said. "Besides, what the hell am I gonna do in this wasteland besides make some showgirls look better for the night? You know, those girls work harder than strippers for less money. If it were me, I'd be wrapping myself around a pole before I'd be dropping twelve pounds of rhinestones on my head every night. Less clothes means more money, honey. That's just the way the world works. Not even Una can change that one."

"I think she already has," Petra said. "And that's the problem, at least for the people who run this place." She turned and embraced Tia. Even at her own impressive height, Petra felt dwarfed in Tia's presence.

"I'm grateful you'll stay," Petra said. "We need you. You're part of this now."

"Well, I sure have made you sorry group of followers look better and that was nothing short of a miracle," Tia said with a chuckle. "You see what Matt was wearing when he pulled up in here? Thank the lord that man found me to make him the man he is today. I know, no judgment. Una's finally getting through to me."

The two laughed for a moment, remembering the Matt who showed up in Vegas and the remarkable transformation that had taken place since then. He was barely recognizable now—slimmed down, casual style, stubble on his face for effect. It was an unlikely group Una had assembled, but as different as they were, they all shared one important thing in common: true love, admiration, and support for the woman who brought them together.

CHAPTER THIRTY-THREE

Marco woke to the sound of sirens blaring out the window. The loud noise filled his ears as he struggled to separate dream from reality. Coming off a high was like that sometimes, a disoriented state of wonderment, usually ending with him grasping for the corners of his mind that occupied the dream over the stark reality that was his life now.

At least he still had his mother's memory. For now, anyway. He was starting to forget the sound of her voice, the delicate outline of her face. But as he walked room to room, inhaling deeply, he would sometimes pick up a faint scent of her. Other times, he would remember conversations in the kitchen or watching a movie together in the family room. He would relish the memory to the point of tears, the process going from warmth to stone cold in a matter of minutes. He was truly alone now. Why did she choose that moment to let go? Couldn't she hold on long enough to see her son emerge into the man she always wanted him to be?

His mother always knew him at a depth few others had ever reached. He rarely allowed a deep dive into who he truly was as a person—waves of emotion tumbling onto his shores, saturating all who dared to walk with him there. Some waves appeared docile and even inviting, but they could quickly turn to a tumultuous display of power and resentment. He always loved the Pacific and would often stare at the photo in the living room his mother had taken all those years ago. It showed the waves at a crest, the exact moment before they give in to gravity and pour forth a force no man could contain. That's what his grief had become, endless waves of sadness upon the barren shores of his soul.

Drugs allowed him to slow the waves. He started with an occasional pill here and there, the ones he would sneak from his mother's stash to help with the pain. It was truly incredible how many the pharmacy doled out once she was confirmed terminal. It was as if she was allowed to escape on a magic carpet known by the names of Vicodin and morphine. She resisted at first, but eventually gave into the relief it provided, even if it was at the expense of a sound mind.

It didn't matter now. His mother was long buried, and he was left with the aftermath: a new sea of indecision, fueled by angry waves he tried to corral at first but eventually let pulse freely in his veins, bubbling up into a nonsense rant that scared his friends and terrified his professors.

Perhaps it was his father's mistreatment of him. Mistreatment was an understatement. The man was a wall of negative emotions. Marco was never able to climb it, no matter how well he behaved or what grades he brought home on those early report cards. They bore little resemblance to one another, a bone of contention with his mother who was constantly accused of taking a lover to conceive their only son. Marco was never immune to the wrath his father's tongue would unleash on a regular basis.

"You are such a waste of space, son," his father would say to him at the dinner table, scanning the random artwork assignments he completed in the second and third grade.

"You think that drawing trees and sunshine is a show of strength? And look at this?" He pointed violently toward the picture, punching a hole with his manicured finger. "You drew a picture of your mother holding your hand!"

He crumpled the paper into his fist, tossing it onto the floor. It was his mother's turn to take the punishment.

"You need to STOP coddling our son!" His fist pounded onto the table, sending the plates into a mini-flight upward, contents spilling onto the table. "Clean up this fucking mess!"

Marco shuddered at the memory, shaking off the feelings of inadequacy his father had instilled in him from the moment of his birth. He would never, in all of his twenty-one years on the planet, live up to the image the man had of what a son should be. All Marco knew was that it wasn't him and never would be. His own name became synonymous with pussy, wimp, and loser. If not for his mother, Marco would have taken his life long ago. But she championed him, reinforcing his existence and purpose in the world.

"Marco, you are such a gentle soul. I swear you heal me just by holding my hand," she had told him countless times through treatment.

His mother had a way of finding the good in him, even with the words of his father swirling in his head. The collection of hateful phrases through the years had turned into a cesspool of despair that he could never seem to escape.

He stared at himself in the mirror, annoyedly brushing over the patches that made up some sad, half-assed five o'clock shadow. He couldn't even grow a beard right. That's what his father would say. He was tempted to keep it as it was but thought better of it. He didn't need to give his father another reason to throw verbal punches. He was perfectly capable of doing that himself now.

Besides, he needed money if he had any hope of avoiding the painful withdrawals that would follow after last night's hit. He was down to the dregs of his supply and knew if he groveled enough, his father would eventually give in. He always did, if only to dole out the endless cascade of insults Marco had to endure just to reach the point of reloading the syringe that would make him forget.

He took a rideshare to his father's penthouse, landing on the door at a little past seven in the evening. By now, dear old dad was well into his fourth or fifth drink, the perfect time to reach him before he dropped deeper into the bottle, summoning up phrases and words that no man should utter to his son. He knocked before entering the code to the door. The system beeped as he entered the foyer. It was an opulent space—a glimpse into his father's warped sense of style. The lavish apartment was filled with superficial artifacts that had been collected by some random designer who passed off junk as trend.

He heard his father's voice from the living area, not quite a slur of words but certainly on their way in an onslaught of directives and insults. He always found comfort in those moments, knowing that his father wasn't just singling him out with his wrath, but rather spreading the wealth to everyone in his long, narrow path. His father caught his eye through the mirror, brow furrowing as he motioned for his only son to sit in the uncomfortable chair beside him.

"You tell that fucker that he is going to do this deal on my terms or no deal," Pyrus said, taking a sip of his scotch before continuing. "I don't negotiate."

Marco could hear the man on the other end responding, but his father didn't give him the opportunity to make the point. He simply ended the call with a touch and a toss of the phone to the sofa across from them.

"These young men today don't know how to be men, Marco! Sound familiar?" He took another sip, staring directly into his son's eyes as he savored the liquid, then gently placing the glass onto the side table between them.

"What's up?" he asked almost cheerfully. "You here to leach off of me some more or actually do something with your pathetic life?"

Marco considered how to respond, wondering whether admitting defeat or challenging his father would be the best course of action.

"Once I make up my mind, I'm full of indecision. That's a quote son, if you ever bothered to learn or do anything other than spend my money."

He took another sip of scotch, watching his son carefully. Pyrus had a way of pushing his buttons, reminding him at every turn what a pathetic person he was and how he would never amount to anything.

"I, I…" Marco began.

"I? I? See, yet another example of how selfish you are," Pyrus said. "Only thinking of yourself, son. That's a mistake. Why don't you start with 'you'?"

"You are a piece of shit, Dad," Marco blurted out, not even knowing where the words came from. But he felt immense relief upon saying them, though he was afraid to look over and see his father's reaction.

"I'm a what?" Pyrus asked before bursting into laughter. "Are you actually making an attempt to stand up for yourself? Piece of shit? That's all you got?" He laughed for a long moment and grabbed for the bottle in the process.

"Son, this piece of shit has provided for you, taken care of you, given you everything you could have ever wanted."

"Except LOVE, Dad!" Marco screamed into the air. "You NEVER gave me love. Not once! Not even when Mom died! I'm fucking alone, and you have done nothing to show me compassion or—"

"Compassion?" Pyrus countered, rising to his feet. "I don't owe you anything, son! YOU owe ME a great deal of respect, admiration, and blind devotion for what my hard work has provided you!"

"You have never spoken a kind word to me, Dad," Marco said, tears forming in his eyes. "I'm nothing more than a burden to you. You only—"

"You only, you only," Pyrus repeated, dabbing fake tears from his eyes. "I only what? Please, you motherfucker. The world we live in is cruel, son! The sooner you toughen up and learn that no one has your back and your successes and failures are entirely your own, the faster you will become a man instead of the miserable, sniveling piece of shit I see before me!"

Marco had nothing to say. He was officially surrendering in the cruel, relentless emotional game of chess his father had played with him his entire life: his father, the king, completely controlling the board. And Marco, the rook. No, a pawn. This time, he was left wandering the board in a desperate attempt to checkmate his opponent. But even pawns had power. And the queen? Another level. He channeled his mother in that moment, pulling himself into a standing position. He remembered the videos he saw in his feed—the ones of the woman performing in his father's hotel, healing people like him, people worse than him, in a matter of seconds. If he wanted revenge now, he would march out of the penthouse and find his way into the theater and be healed of all the pain and damage his father had caused. Healed of the gaping wound his mother had left in his heart. And healed of the emptiness and void the drugs were filling in his soul.

"Fuck this," Marco said, making his way toward the door.

"And where the fuck do you think you're going, son? Ain't nobody gonna give you money out there! They work for me, remember? You haven't worked for anything a day in your life!"

"Watch me," Marco said under his breath, walking through the door and toward his future.

The woman he saw would heal him tonight. He would be free of the mess his father had created, or free to join his mother in eternity. Either way, he would be away from this place and free from the clutches of his father.

The anger bubbled up inside of him as he weaved his way across the casino floor. He was pretty sure Brian was still in charge of the box office. He had heard his father scream at him numerous times on the phone in the last as many months during one of their so-called "family" dinners he insisted Marco take part in. There was nothing familial between them other than resentment and seething hatred. On both sides. Come to think of it, maybe that was what family really was, Marco thought, as he approached the box office window.

"Hey, Bill, is Brian working tonight?" Marco asked through the window speaker.

"Hi-ya, Marco! What have you been up to?" Bill asked cheerfully, though Marco didn't really have much time to make small talk right now.

"I'm good, man," Marco said to his former supervisor. He had worked in the box office a couple summers ago, when his father made a feeble attempt to show him the family business.

"Brian is out tonight, but can I help you with something?" Bill asked, motioning for him to come through the side door. Marco followed suit, and Bill greeted him with a bear hug for the ages, squeezing the last bit of air from his lungs. "What are you doing over here? Can't get enough of the old man's winning personality?" Bill belly laughed, but the joke left little impression on Marco. He looked nervously at his phone and considered how to move the conversation along without hurting Bill's feelings.

"Listen, man, I'm wondering if you have tickets to the show that woman is putting on? The healer or whatever?"

"No, no," Bill said, waving his hand to dismiss the request. "That show was sold out within minutes of announcement, and besides, tonight is the final performance. I'm already dealing with all the crazies out there demanding more shows." Bill's eyes widened as he looked out the ticket window at the thousands of people pacing outside the auditorium doors. Security was on high alert.

"Look, I really need to get in that theater, man," Marco said with desperation in his voice.

He was starting to feel the effects of withdrawal whisper in his veins, physically manifesting in the form of sweat and shakes just under the skin. He didn't have much time now before full withdrawal set in. If this was the final performance, it was his only chance to fix this once and for all.

"You know I can't do that," Bill said, dropping his gaze and shaking his head in the process. "Rules are rules, and besides, every seat in the place is filled."

"I NEED to get in there, Bill!" Marco said, panic washing over his face.

He knew he sounded like a crazy person, but he didn't care. He wanted to be free of the effects his addiction had caused. He was ready to get off the train he had been riding for the last five years.

"Dude, rules. And I have a family to support. I can't fuck that up because I let you waltz in here and sweet talk your way into the biggest show on the strip."

Marco pleaded with him for another minute or so, just long enough for the beads of sweat to begin to seep out of his pores. He had to look like a real junky now: mood swings, beads of sweat on the forehead, shaking from the core. It was now or never.

"Look, I already told you, I—"

Marco made a break for the back room, dodging Bill's weak attempt to capture him before he pushed open the door and made a run for it through the office space within. He slipped past the offices to the back door. His arms and legs felt like lead as he pulled open the metal door, glancing both directions before remembering the stage was to the right. Bill's extra pounds made the escape much easier, though Marco would still have to sprint down the long corridor if he had any hope of hiding. He was just about to the stage door when he heard Bill shout behind him, his booming voice bouncing off the walls and echoing its way toward him.

"Marco! Stop!"

He slowed to a fast walk after bolting up the stairs, listening for Bill's Clydesdale feet before determining just how close he was behind him. He took a sharp right off the wing and entered the prop room, searching frantically for a place to hide. A trunk of wigs sat in the middle of the room. He quickly dove in and covered himself. He heard Bill enter the room a few seconds later before stomping out and heading back the way he came. Marco caught his breath for a moment, spitting out bits of synthetic hair that had fallen into his mouth.

Marco watched the performance from off-stage and marveled when Una reached for the woman in front of her and hovered her hands over her body. He arrived too late to know exactly what the deal was, but he was pretty sure it was a tragic story, given the woman's disheveled look and wild eyes. A soft, sparkling light began to emit from the woman's arms, neck, and other exposed skin. A warmth entered her expression as she let out an enormous sigh of relief.

He looked for strings, holograms, special lighting, or anything else that could possibly indicate some form of trickery or illusion, but he couldn't find any. The healer appeared to be the real deal and even more so in person.

After watching several videos online in the last couple of weeks, he was surprised that more people weren't out to discredit her. Most of the threads had at least a few trolls spewing venom, especially if they had the kind of following she did. But the few who did attempt to shame the woman were met with an onslaught of loving support from her followers. Her credibility, it seemed, only grew stronger with each performance. He found it interesting that those in support of the healer didn't snap back with the usual negative comments; instead, their reactions were more like rays of sunshine sent to erase the shadows. Most of the trolls gave up before any real debate could begin.

He wasn't sure what to think about it all as he watched the lights fall on the performance and the audience members rise to their feet. He was about to lose his courage and disappear backstage when he slammed right into a man who could have passed for a small tank.

"What are you doing back here, man? You working

on that broken light grid up there?" The man raised his massive arm and pointed to the structure above the stage. Marco's experience in the theater before kicked in instead of his sheer panic.

"I, uh, yes," Marco said, gathering his composure. "I wanted to watch the performance to see if there were any other lights affected, but all good." He tried to move around the man but was blocked at each step.

"Hold on," Jayden said, staring down Marco in the hope the truth would emerge before he had to call security. The kid sounded convincing but didn't look the part like the others he had seen over the last month. "I thought they said there were a couple of lights burned out," he said, raising an eyebrow.

"Oh, um, I guess I didn't get the email about that," Marco said hurriedly, looking around for any opportunity to exit the situation.

"You're not part of the crew, are you?" Jayden said lowering his voice.

Marco considered lying to him but realized that would only make the situation worse. The guy in front of him was a Mack truck, and it was pretty obvious he didn't suffer fools gladly. He muttered something under his breath, then thought the better of it and just let it all go.

"Listen, I am a...junkie. And I need to get on that stage tonight."

Marco's emotional well was so vast and deep that he couldn't quite fish out the right words to express what was going on inside of him. Everything he had felt about his mother, his father, his life had been tossed in through the years. He was beginning to doubt if the woman out there could even help him.

"I feel…" He closed his eyes, realizing that he hadn't really stopped to consider how he had really felt beyond the obvious. He dove deep into the feeling, trying to identify it, and finally finding the right word.

"I feel…lost," he said with a defeated sigh.

Jayden nodded, touching his shoulder for reassurance. He wanted him to continue but could see the young man before him struggling to break free from immense pain and darkness. He held his breath, almost willing him to speak.

"I don't really want to get into the specifics of how it all started, but let me just say that my mother died a couple of years ago, and I haven't exactly gotten over that."

"You never get over that, believe me," Jayden said.

"You lost your mom too?" Marco asked.

"Yes, many years ago. My father too. They were burned inside their church. It was a ruled a hate crime, but I'll tell you, it was aptly named because I was the one who was left with the hate in my heart for a very, very long time."

"Oh my God. I'm sorry."

"Thank you for saying that," Jayden said, keeping a watchful eye backstage just in case this was some sort of setup or elaborate scheme. "Seems like a lifetime ago now. I waged my own war with addiction along the way."

Marco perked up at the comment. Jayden observed him for a moment, looking for the physical signs of withdrawal. He could see the sweat beading on his forehead, color drained from his face.

"I'm sorry that's the path you're on right now. But it doesn't have to be that way forever. You know that, right?"

"That's why I'm here," Marco said, wiping the sweat from his brow. The shakes were upon him now. He didn't have any choice but to push through it. "I want the woman on stage to heal me," he blurted out in desperation. "Can she heal me now?"

"I don't know, man. There are others already picked out for tonight, and this is the last show." Jayden looked around, making sure this situation wasn't going to become a problem. His eyes scanned all the exits, considering how he could get the guy out of there if things turned.

"Look, I know I'm some strange guy who appeared out of nowhere, but I swear to you I am not here to ruin the show or blow up the place or—"

Jayden instinctively pulled him into a headlock. Marco gasped for air as Jayden leaned into his ear.

"What are you doing here, friend?"

"I'm…I…" Marco struggled for air. Jayden loosened his grip enough for the young man to speak. "I worked here a couple years ago," he said with the breath of a small child.

Jayden stared at him for a long moment before dropped his grip. He watched him for another moment after, trying to figure out how long it had been since his last high.

"Please, get me on that stage," Marco pleaded.

Jayden searched frantically for one of the others, but the entire backstage was clear save an older woman waiting in the wings for a rebirth into a life she had yet to achieve. He marched his way toward her and mumbled something in her ear. Within moments, the woman stepped back, gesturing Marco to take her place on deck.

Marco stumbled his way toward the wings, watching Una do her work on the stage. If he had any hope of releasing himself from his father, this was it. He would finally be rid of all the shame, guilt, and sadness. He realized in that moment that he had not once associated his father with love, acceptance, and compassion. Healed or not tonight, he knew he would never treat his son or daughter that way.

Jayden nodded to the woman on stage and then motioned for Marco to step out before the crowd. The applause was brief. It was something that had been common with most of the shows so far: people judging who was chosen and who wasn't, mostly based on appearances rather than by the circumstances that brought them there. Marco was shaking too badly to care, partly out of nerves, but mostly because of withdrawal.

"What brings you to the show today, Marco?" the woman asked after a brief introduction.

"I'm an addict, and I want to be healed once and for all from the pain of my addiction," he said, dropping his eyes to the stage floor.

"What do you think caused your addiction, Marco?"

"A shoulder injury to start. My mother's illness was definitely a trigger. She was battling cancer for a number of years."

"I'm so sorry to hear that. I take it she lost her battle?"

"Yes, she did. Two years ago, last month."

"And where was the rest of your family during that difficult time, Marco?"

"It was just me taking care of my mom," Marco said with a tremor in his voice. "She, uh," he paused to gather his thoughts, tears forming in the corners of his eyes. "She was such a positive force in my life. I didn't quite know how to move on once that voice was gone. She was my champion, you know? Always cheering me on, even when I sucked at something."

"That must have been so terrible for you," Una said, taking his hand in hers. A calm came over him, and the tremors instantly stopped. She looked him directly in the eyes, beautiful amber reflected back to him. He could see his own reflection in the iris almost inviting him to open his soul. He couldn't remember later how he began, but in that moment, he poured his heart and hurt onto the stage in a way no other had before. Several in the audience openly sobbed as he shared his story of pain, love of his mother, abuse by his father, and the addiction that followed. As his last words escaped his lips, a hush fell over the crowd.

"I guess I forgive my father," he said. A look of serenity swept across his face as Una took his hands in hers.

"Oftentimes, addictions mask themselves as temporary comfort in desperate situations. Their medicinal properties, while helpful when used temporarily, can be so destructive when used consistently. I want you to know I understand why you did it in the first place. Please forgive yourself for making that choice."

The tears began to flow from his eyes as he felt the words seep into his system. The feeling was like the drug he had craved just minutes before. The feeling the word *forgive* evoked poured through the crown of his head, rushed toward his face and neck, then slowly and deliciously dropped down into every surface and cell of his being. He couldn't believe the transformation. Every ache, pain, and craving designed to hold back the flood of guilt, shame, and hurt he had shouldered for years lifted immediately from his system. Suddenly, all was clear; even his ears and vision were renewed. The crowd cheered as the magic entered his body, feeling their own rushes of exhilaration and healing.

As the crowd's reaction dissipated, Marco dropped into the shadows along the side of the stage and marveled at the encounter. He had never known such an instant relief. It was even more powerful than the first time he shot up.

The thought made him shudder. He would never go back to using after such an experience. The craving and desire were gone. It would seem like the most awful betrayal to Una and whatever universal power she called upon to make his human experience suddenly bearable.

Above all, he marveled at the feeling of forgiveness. He pictured the man now, somewhere in the suite several stories up. He bet the monster was feeling an unease in his belly but not knowing why. His father no longer controlled his destiny. And once destiny took hold, Marco knew it would be impossible to escape its grip.

CHAPTER THIRTY-FOUR

L ucas stared at the envelope for several minutes before opening it. It was a feeling he remembered from high school, staring at the return address in the left corner from the so-called school of his "choice." But it wasn't a choice. An error in judgment his sophomore year of high school put the Ivy League colleges of his dreams out of contention on an ordinary Saturday night.

In his freshman year, Lucas moved from group to group like a couch surfer working for a startup in the Bay Area. Much like the couch that turned into a temporary bed, high school was agony. He had come to this conclusion about twenty-five minutes into his first day upon realizing his best friend, Matt, had moved to a new city. Lucas hoped he was joking but quickly realized his friend had been serious when his messages were merely delivered and not read. He remembered his friend commenting about school starting much earlier in Las Vegas. But for Lucas, denial ran long and deep. He and Matt had been inseparable since first grade when the two were paired up on an art project. Instead of the normal family pictures, they both drew sad and disturbing images that bonded them immediately. It wasn't until that moment that he fully comprehended the reality of his social situation. Without Matt, he was alone.

He glanced at his student ID in first period. The only thing he had going for himself was an early autumn birthday, a trivial detail until he considered the cut-off to enter school and the prospect of driving earlier than the others in the class at the time. He remembered waiting out the entry to kindergarten as he watched the other kids in the neighborhood boarding the yellow bus toward something other than home. He watched from the front window, longing to dart out the door and climb the steps to join his friends in the seats and stare out the window at people like him staring back.

A decade and a year had passed, and now he was a sophomore with a driver's license in hand. The beat-up Honda left behind by his older brother was like an extra life in the video game of his boring, socially pathetic life without his best friend. Driving to school on that late September day made him feel like a god. He watched as his fellow classmates stepped off the yellow buses, heads down in despair in the thought of another year going to and from school without any freedom.

That Honda Civic was the closest he had ever come to popular status in school. Even if the general consensus was that the guys who welcomed him in were geeks and stoners, they were a big step up from the theater kids and chess club dorks he had surrounded himself with after Matt moved away.

His new friends, donned in ghoulish costumes, passed the weed as he drove the half mile to the Halloween party to end all parties, or at least that's how he thought of it at the time. A cop saw the crazy costumes swaying in the backseat as the smoke escaped the tiny crack in the passenger window. His Ivy League dreams went up in the smoke that filled the inside of his ride as police lights filled his rearview mirror.

His parents shouted at first, then tortured him with the silent treatment for the better part of the fall semester. It wasn't until his father needed help hanging Christmas lights that the two finally talked about what happened and the plan to fix it.

When he looked back on it now, some fifteen-plus years later, Lucas realized that on that fateful day, he didn't just receive a traffic ticket for speeding. He had received a ticket to freedom. He was no longer forced to walk the path his parents had paved for him long before he was conceived. He was no longer expected to hold the weight of his family's hopes and dreams or to be a shining example of all the sacrifices his parents made just to call him an American. Leaving medical school was the final straw for them. He was finally his own man.

And here he was, on the precipice of the greatest story of his career—not just birthing the story of an extraordinary event, but piecing together a jigsaw puzzle of facts, deciphering them to bring the detail in focus, and presenting a masterpiece for all of humanity to consider.

What he now held in his hands was the answer to a question he had asked Una's mother a few weeks before. The response to an email to the hospital where Una was born was now wrapped up in the contents of a simple manila envelope. The evidence would confirm if Marisol was, in fact, Una's mother and if the story she told him about her own medical history was true.

He hadn't included the answer to his simple question in the initial interview. It was the question about how Una could possibly be conceived by a woman born without fallopian tubes. Medically, Lucas knew it was impossible. He followed up on the information she had given him, along with her letter of consent, and called the hospital to request the record on file. He was told it could take months, but with a little begging and pleading, he was able to convince the clerk on the phone to take the FedEx account number, grateful for his Spanish minor in that moment.

He knew he could be fired for what he did. It was the most important part of the interview, and the truth was he withheld the information. From everyone. But he wanted to be sure. He knew the station bosses would go nuts for a nugget that big. The scientist inside of him told him to fact-check first. It could be a simple mistake. Una could have been adopted. Marisol could have been confused by the doctor's findings. Whatever the case, the details in the envelope would be the start or finish to a vital question in the sea of a much larger conversation.

At the same time, the ego inside of him screamed to reveal all, no matter where the facts stood. Facts could be sorted out later. The question and subsequent answer could literally catapult his career as a journalist to a level he had only dreamed of. He longed for the recognition but knew if he allowed the scientist to take over, he would know definitively what to do. No guesswork. He stuffed his ego deep down inside him, bombarding it with the facts inside his head. There would be time for recognition later. And if his gut was right, he wouldn't just be a pretty face with a good question. He would be the journalist he craved to become.

He ripped open the envelope, fingers diving down to retrieve the documents with the answer. He pulled the pages inches from his face, scanning every line and detail, mulling over the meaning inside his head. He knew what to do now, silently thanking the scientist that lurked inside and allowing his ego a small step forward. With the information about to be released—the information that was dominating the editorial meeting and all the major outlets—these new findings would be the definitive proof. His phone chirped, causing him to jump. The news was about to break across the world, the story they talked about in the editorial meeting an hour earlier. Now the proof was in his hands.

In that moment, Lucas made the decision. If he caught the next flight to Vegas, he just might be there in time to catch the healer after her last show. Maybe he would even look up Matt while he was there. The two hadn't spoken in years, but he still wondered about his childhood friend.

He grabbed his bag and headed for the back door, sliding the letter of resignation he had prepared earlier under Stein's door. He was thankful Stein was already gone for the day. He knew Stein and the big bosses at the station would be unhappy with his decision to leave so abruptly, but the world would be different after the story came out. It was much bigger than any of them. He didn't need the station anymore. He had a phone, social pages, a YouTube page, and a decent following. This was his story now, and he was going right to the source.

CHAPTER THIRTY-FIVE ────────

The sound of the television could be heard through the door. He knew Jade would be watching for the report. He had asked her to meet him in the suite. His son's dramatic departure left him seething earlier. He knew the little fucker wouldn't last long in the jungle. He would be back in a matter of hours, begging for money. He relished the thought of beating him to a pulp when he did. He used the time to check the casino floor. Money was flowing like mud. He called his legal team, barking orders between swear words, demanding the suit be filed immediately. He wouldn't bother begging her to sign. Better to let the dogs fight over the remains of her pathetic life. Pyrus waved his hand over the keypad, and the door opened.

"You're late, darling," Jade said, muting the volume and slinking over to him in a gown that hugged her every curve. It was obvious she was putting in the workouts. He didn't bother to compliment her, rather dismissing her affection and reaching for the drink she offered. He downed it immediately. She revealed the second glass from behind her back like a magician in one of the many shows in the Neo over the years. She raised an eyebrow as he took the glass from her, offering the smallest of pecks on her cheek before finding his usual spot in the living room.

"The moment we've been waiting for," he said, sitting down in the chair."

"The governor really did come through," Jade said, sitting on the couch opposite of him. She tried to get his attention with an alluring pose, but he didn't bother rewarding her with his gaze. Rather, he kept his focus intently on the screen before him, then checked his watch for the time.

"Any moment now," he said, swirling the glass in his hand before taking a long, thoughtful sip of the golden elixir. Damn, it was good to feel the bittersweet taste on his tongue. The day had truly been a shit show until he received word the news was about to break. He watched as the graphics appeared on the screen and then reached to blast the volume.

"Unbelievable news this afternoon out of CIA headquarters, where the agency's director has just disclosed undeniable proof that a healer currently headlining a popular Las Vegas show at the Neo Hotel Resort and Casino could, in fact, be the second coming."

"See how they worked the name in there," he said, raising a glass to her. "Here we go."

The announcer continued. "Religious groups around the world have worked with the agency to provide relics, objects, and other items believed to be associated with Jesus Christ."

"What do they mean, 'undeniable proof'?" Jade asked, sitting forward in interest.

"Oh, just you wait," he said, eyes never leaving the screen.

"We are just learning that sophisticated technology was used to determine if the healer, who has been exhibiting many of the gifts and talents of Christ in biblical times, is a descendant of, or otherwise biologically linked to, the prophet that Christians believe to be the son of God. We go to our science contributor, Jason Howell, who has just read the report in our DC bureau. Lila Lorenzo is standing by at the Vatican, awaiting the response from the Pope. Jason, we will start with you. What exactly did the report say, and why is it so significant?"

"John, the 162-page report outlines the reasons why certain relics were identified to be tested for DNA links to the mysterious healer known by her followers as Una. Teams of scientists, DNA experts, and religious leaders worked together to secure the most protected items—ones that have been under constant protection for millennia— that had concretely been linked to Jesus Christ in his time. What the report concluded is that the DNA of the healer, secured from a drinking glass and other personal items in a suite she is occupying at the Neo Hotel, matched the DNA found on nine of the relics. Eleven in total were tested. The archeological findings of the two items that did not prove to have a link had been in question before, with several scientists believing the items were off by as much as two hundred years from the time of Christ. What the report doesn't show is the notarized documents that allegedly prove the items taken from the hotel suite are in fact from the mysterious healer. Right now, all we can do is wait and see what transpires as more of the report is released in the next week. Back to you."

"Una isn't going anywhere after this," Pyrus said, a dark expression washing over his face.

Jade wasn't sure how to respond. She knew there was breaking news about the show, but this story was nothing short of unbelievable. She thought of Jayden in the moment, his searing eyes bearing into her soul. The show would be ending soon downstairs. She had to go to him but wondered if she would have time now to make her escape. The crowds would be enormous. She turned her attention back to the screen, careful not to draw attention from Pyrus.

"Thank you, Jason. Lila Lorenzo reports now from the Vatican, where the Pope is preparing a statement soon to be released to the public."

"We are just moments away from the Pope's words on the matter. Several thousand have gathered in St. Peter's Square to hear the opinion of the Catholic Church on the report. Sources say that the church's supreme leader contemplated the findings for several hours and sought the advice of his council before preparing his speech."

Pyrus sat quietly, taking a sip from his glass. Jade knew he was considering the weight of the words the Pope would release onto the world. If he confirmed the findings, Pyrus's power would grow exponentially, the stress of a new property would be gone in an instant, and his hopes of reaching the highest level of government would be all but secured. Jade had never seen his fate wrapped up in the words and actions of another before. She almost enjoyed watching him squirm in his seat, reaching for the bottle to refill his glass. She could see his eyes beginning to glaze over, a sheer sign he hadn't eaten and the liquor's effect was even more potent than usual.

"The Pope is now stepping out onto the balcony. Let's listen in." Pyrus took in a large breath and paused a moment before slowly allowing it to escape his lungs. He looked older to Jade in that moment. Perhaps she was seeing more of his flaws now that Jayden had captured her heart.

Somewhat of a relic himself, the Pope emerged through the columns, waving enthusiastically at the crowd below. The cheers seemed to lift him even higher into the heavens.

He outstretched his arms, as if to embrace his followers, and pulled the presence toward him as it settled deeply in his soul. He closed his eyes to draw the spotlight upon him, relishing the love and light that his flock provided. He took a deep breath then, a gesture so strong it picked up on the microphone positioned at his heart. He held his arms above him, lifting his face to the sky. The crowd amped up the volume with thunderous applause. He waited a moment before lowering his arms slowly toward the earth, the sound dissipating with every inch of movement downward. It was a move Catholics around the world had come to know in his seven years of leadership. A silence fell on the crowd below.

"Grazie, grazie," the Pope said loudly into the crackling microphone. A servant nearby rushed to his side, positioning the microphone upward to capture the man's every word. He quickly transitioned to English, considering the many American Catholics who may be watching.

"This is a momentous occasion. A moment the world has waited for!"

The crowd erupted in applause. The Pope put his arms up, gesturing for them to quiet down before he continued. Silence fell on the crowd in an instant.

"Today, we learned that a number of relics, objects that are dated to the time of Jesus Christ, our Lord and Savior, and believed to be in His possession in the time He walked the earth, have matched to one walking this earth among us." He paused to give a sign of the cross, looking upward for another moment before continuing.

"With technology such as it is today, this is a profound discovery—one that could have a tremendous impact on the nearly one billion Christians who have prayed for this day. But who is this person who matches the one we follow?"

He glanced down at his notes then, absorbing the words in front of him before continuing.

"She..." He paused again, dropping his head. Silence kept its hold on the crowd, who were waiting with bated breath for him to continue. "She is an enigma, first to rise like a phoenix from the ashes of a deadly crash in Seattle, Washington, a city in the far Northwest corner of the United States. We understand that she is currently performing miracles on a nightly basis in a hotel casino in Las Vegas, Nevada, a city known for its ties to sin!"

Rumbles rippled through the crowd, faces turning toward each other for confirmation of the confusion they were feeling from the message coming from the balcony above.

"I understand that this woman has healed the sick, the addicted, the dregs of a broken society. She continues to use her gifts, night after night, amusing the crowd before her as she transforms individuals, not only from broken to healed, but also from obscurity to notoriety. This begs an important question: why would this woman make a spectacle of her gifts?"

Pyrus shifted uncomfortably in his seat. His fate depended on the words that were about to follow.

"That's a low blow," Jade said partly under her breath. Pyrus glared at her, as if the interruption would somehow alter the outcome.

"How could this *woman*, a so-called human descendant of Jesus Christ, our Lord and Savior, make a scene of such gifts? Why would she not quietly go along and perform miracles, just as he did in his time? Why would she choose to draw crowds, or worse, profit from her God-given gifts?" The crowd turned in an instant, growling, grunting, and shouting disdain for the suggestions from above. The Pope once again gestured for them to stop.

"But then I considered this: the times we live in. A time when technology and media allow for such gifts to be shared instantly across the world. If Jesus Christ had walked the earth in this modern time, would He not do the same?"

The crowd stayed silent, expressions pleading, begging the man to continue.

"I am not a man of technology or media. I live a simple life and have for many years in service to God. The science tells us that this woman is a descendant of Christ in body. But let it be known that through the miracles she is performing in another part of the world, far from the Vatican walls, she is certainly showing promise to possess the same gifts that He did in his time."

The silence in the crowd remained, as the Pontiff gathered his thoughts. The aide from before emerged with a glass of water. The Pope quickly gulped the contents before continuing.

"I have prayed for an answer today," he said, lifting his head toward the heavens. "For days and days, I have sat in silence, in quiet prayer, begging for an answer to come."

Whispers turned to a low roar in the crowd as the bystanders considered the Pontiff's words. It was unusual for him to say something so raw in regard to his relationship to God. The evidence that the findings were significant began to emerge from the masses who, like the Pope, had prayed to know and understand how Una came to be.

"It wasn't until this morning that the answer emerged," he continued. "God whispered quietly in my ear, and I strained to listen. His answer wasn't one of question or doubt. It was quite clear and one that I believe we should all see to conclusion. He asked this woman, Una, to display a sign so significant that there would be no doubt. Until she produces this sign, we will consider her a gifted healer, a prophet in her own right. The sign will be the proof we need to concretely stand by the claims of these reports and declare Una as the Second Coming!"

A deafening sound exploded from the square below, as the people cheered, danced, and shouted in agreement, reaching for their phones in the process.

Pyrus let out a sigh a relief, dropping his head for a moment before throwing a fist in the air.

"Yes!" he shouted. "Thank you, governor!"

Jade sat quietly across from him, eager to say what was weighing so heavily on her heart.

"How is Una going to produce proof beyond what she has already done?"

"What?" Pyrus said, his expression turning cold. "Why the fuck would you be worried about that? God, you really don't trust me, do you? What the fuck are you doing here then?" Jade ducked as the glass flew past her head, smashing into the wall behind her. "We'll make the shit up if we have to. It doesn't matter! I'm Pyrus Payne! I'll do whatever it takes to make it happen."

He smirked as she stared back at him, fear filling her eyes. She had to get out of there.

"Baby, of course you will," she said, shoving her fear deep down and pulling forth a game face for the ages. She waltzed over to him, stroking his hair before refilling his glass.

"Let's celebrate, baby," she purred into his ear.

"I don't have time now," he said, quickly downing the drink, the effects of which were starting to show on his tired face. She could see the wrinkles forming around his eyes; his forehead was like a piece of leather in the light. The drink was advancing his age. He leaped out of the chair, pushing her aside and stumbling before regaining his balance.

"I need to eat something," he said, making his way toward the kitchen.

Within seconds, she was dashing toward the bedroom, slipping out of the elegant gown and pulling on a pair of faded jeans, an old T-shirt, and sneakers before retrieving the backpack out of the closet. It was an outfit he wasn't used to seeing her in and would help her blend in with the thousands of tourists flooding the strip. She tiptoed into the hallway, stopping briefly just outside the kitchen to catch what she hoped would be a final glimpse of the man who had simultaneously loved and tortured her for the last few years.

He was sitting at the counter, gloating about the news to a caller on the phone, laughing obnoxiously as he stuffed roast beef into his mouth. He was oblivious to her, drinking in his power and making plans to capitalize on Una and the moment. It made Jade sick to her stomach to think what would happen to her and the healer if the plan didn't work.

Jayden had revealed all to her earlier that afternoon. He had invited her to the suite, pulling her into his bedroom and quickly locking the door behind him. He nuzzled her neck for a moment, breathing in the smell of her—lilac with a hint of citrus. The had made love in the heat of the afternoon, drinking in one another, finding solace in each other's arms.

Afterward, he held her tightly against his chest, kissing the nape of her neck and the tops of her shoulders. When she asked about the future beyond the show, she expected him to say the extension was already signed, and he would be there for some time. But something made him reveal the plan to her. He knew deep inside that Jade was one of them now. He explained how important her logistical knowledge would be as they headed out on the road and all the work they would be doing over the next as many weeks and months. She didn't think of Pyrus in that moment. She was relishing the fact that Jayden trusted her enough to share the plan, but more importantly, he wanted her beside him. Her heart almost burst at the notion; a grin spread across her face as she listened to his soulful voice, pouring over every detail of the plan after the show and how they would escape the city without as much as a stir from Pyrus and his hired hands.

She felt a twinge of guilt as the last of it was revealed, considering just how badly Pyrus would respond to the news. It was true he was a bad man, the worst she had ever encountered. But he had provided for her in a way she had never known. She paid the price dearly, but she didn't wish him ill will. She wanted to walk away cleanly. As if he had heard her thought, Jayden proposed the idea for her escape. She listened intently, taking a deep breath before turning to face him and respond.

"I'll be there," she said, kissing him lightly on the lips. "You're right. I'm one of you now."

He pulled her into a warm, soft embrace, wondering how the heavens had opened up in the theater that day and placed a living angel before him. She was his better half, the yin to his yang, the feminine to balance his masculine. She was a vision of light who held the missing piece of his heart, the one that was still left empty even after Una had penetrated his soul. He knew he had craved this woman into creation, long before they had walked this human existence.

Jade ducked down as she passed the opening to the kitchen, picking up the pace as she crossed the living room, the main entrance in her sight. Her sneaker caught in the foyer, a screech piercing the air as she reached for the door handle.

"Jade?" Pyrus yelled out, still talking to the party on the phone.

She disengaged the alarm and slowly opened the door, closing it softly behind her before bolting for the stairwell down the hall.

"Sure, sure," Pyrus said, downing the last of the roast beef slices and washing it down with a bottled water before pouring another glass of scotch. "We'll be down there around midnight. We need to celebrate!"

"Mr. Payne?" Steven's voice rang out from the foyer.

"OK I have to go," he said, ending the call and walking out of the kitchen to find Steven in the living room.

"How did you get in here?" Pyrus asked. "I didn't hear the door ring."

"Sorry, ," Steven said, eyes darting wildly. "You need to come out here, sir. It's important." He didn't bother to wait for Pyrus to follow but instead walked briskly toward the balcony, his arm outstretched pointing down at the Bellagio fountain.

"What are we looking at here, Steven?" Pyrus asked, squinting his eyes to see.

"She's down there, sir," Steven said, voice trembling, pointing wildly at the masses gathered in the middle of Las Vegas Boulevard.

"Who the hell is that?" Pyrus asked. In his drunken state, all he could make out clearly was the usual fountain show. Then, the subject of Steven's concern came quickly in view a few hundred yards way. He could see the woman, dressed in white, parting the crowds in the middle of the boulevard.

"Una," Steven said, bracing for the man's reaction.

CHAPTER THIRTY-SIX ───────────

Una untied her laces, studying each shoe for a moment before slipping off her sneakers. It was the same faded pair she had worn on the day of the crash, the ones that brought her to her destiny. She had packed them for Vegas but had not put them on since she arrived, not even to walk the strip. Now, before her was the very center of the city she had hoped to heal. She looked up to see the lights of the boulevard pouring onto the pavement in a kaleidoscope of colors, distorted and shimmering, much like the energy of so many souls who came up on the stage over the past forty days. She looked down at her left shoe, noticing a faint blood stain. She closed her eyes, reaching for its origin, but nothing came through.

She was ready to leave now.

When she reflected back on the experience—the crash, the settlement, the formation of the group, the shows and the healing that followed—she felt a sense of calm and peace like she had never known before. Walking off the stage for the last time with thunderous applause behind her, she was ready to step forward into a future that would provide the kind of freedom she had craved from the beginning. She would no longer be beholden to Pyrus and the contract. This was her chance to leave her true mark on the world.

Jamie J. Kemp

A passing shower less than an hour before had dampened the pavement, only adding to the spectacle of light that danced before her. She set her right foot down, feeling the droplets of cool water before taking the next step. Una savored the moment, noticing the tingling in her heel as the left foot joined the right in what would be the walk of her life.

Everything had to go perfectly if she had any hope of continuing her work and healing beyond the lights of Vegas. She was certain the others were already in place, ready to put into motion the plan they had so carefully crafted a few days before. She knew they would wait for the right moment, working together like the elegant inner workings of a clock. Time would be on their side tonight. They had no other choice.

She stood now, grounding herself into the earth. The breeze picked up, sweeping the white dress she had worn during her last performance behind her. The front of the dress clung to her shimmering form, her skin appeared almost iridescent underneath the garment. Those around her gasped upon recognizing her, reaching for their phones to record her every move.

She made her way from the front of the Mirage hotel, not bothering to follow the sidewalk in front of her but rather opting to walk her fate in the middle of Las Vegas Boulevard. She moved slowly and with intention, fully grounding her feet with each step forward.

Una ignored the signal changing from red to green, only raising her hands to stop the oncoming traffic in her path. There were fewer cars on the road now that Vegas was collapsing, so the dozen or so in her way simply halted. Like so many others following her along the sidewalks, the drivers stopped, stepped out of the vehicles, and began to film the healer's path. She didn't look far in front of her. She focused fully on each intentional step along the strip. The boulevard was now a wind tunnel, as others braced themselves against the desert fury. Una was unphased, stepping into the headwind, her dress now flowing freely behind her. Each footprint revealed a shiny imprint as she passed, almost inviting others to follow in her steps.

She drifted along the strip, not bothering to engage with the large crowds now forming on either side of her. Each member of the crowd struggled for a position to capture her walk. Some whispered ideas of where she may be headed. None seemed clear of the answer. Their bewildered looks only added to the chaos building around her. Several began to run, hoping to catch her in full view somewhere further down the strip. The crowds poured into the boulevard in front of her. Her outstretched arms invited them to part, revealing a small trail for her to follow. Many shouted and cried out for help, but her focus was undeterred.

Una continued on, passing the neon lights and nearly empty casinos along the way. Workers were now joining the others to capture a glimpse of the healer, shielding themselves from the gusts of wind, which seemed to grow stronger with each step. She continued on for nearly a mile, stopping herself in front of the Bellagio fountains. She turned to face the shimmering water, watching the tiny waves dance to the delight of the howling wind. She raised her arms and parted the crowd, making her way toward the most dazzling spectacle along the strip.

While she never allowed her eyes to leave the path straight in front of her, she could see thousands of phones pointed directly at her, subbing for the faces she so desperately longed to see. She wanted their expressions now, not just the anxious energy that spilled onto her as she passed by. She could feel the waves of love building as she made her way to the water's edge, stopping at the concrete façade before her.

From a distance, she could hear him shouting, not bothering to grace him with acknowledgment of his existence. Within moments, the cameras turned to the man barreling down the strip, his screams muffled by the crowds, insulating her from his vile insults. Pyrus Payne pushed and shoved his way onto the boulevard, shouting at full sprint, a testament to his phenomenal fitness despite the liquor swimming in his veins.

"UNA!" he shouted, the upper half of his body barely keeping up with the lower. "STOP!"

She ignored his distant plea, turning her attention to the water below.

"YOU OWE ME!" he screamed. "YOU WORK FOR ME!"

The sea of people seemed to part for the tyrant, most so shocked by the dramatic scene and his comments that they would do almost anything to have it unfold on their screens, only to collect shares, comments, and followers en mass after releasing their experiences to the world.

Una pulled herself onto the concrete ledge, swinging her legs around and jumping into the pool below with a splash. The masses followed her movements with their devices for a moment, only to be distracted by the demented man following her to the water's edge.

"GET OUT OF THE FOUNTAIN, UNA!" he screamed, stopping himself after seeing the hundreds of screens pointed directly at his face. "YOU ARE A LIAR! YOU ARE A FRAUD!"

The crowd gasped, considering his words before turning their screens back to Una like a fast and furious tennis match. Una continued her path through the pool's center, wading along in the waist-deep water. The white dress revealed her human form, now sparkling in an iridescent light. Pyrus spotted a few guards nearby, ordering them to enter the pool and retrieve her. They ignored his demands with a shrug.

"YOU ARE PAYING ME BACK FOR THE ALL THE DAMAGE YOU HAVE DONE!" Pyrus shouted, dripping in sweat now that his sprint had reached its conclusion. His heart raced as he contemplated swimming after her, only to remember he hated water and never learned to dog paddle, much less freestyle his way to the healer.

"THESE PEOPLE KNOW YOU'RE A FRAUD!" he screamed, looking around for confirmation from a few faces in the crowd. Only screens filled his views, capturing his desperate expression, eyes darting to find a solution to reach the healer and drag her back to the casino. He'd lock her away for this. She had no fucking idea who she was dealing with, he thought. He would make her pay with everything short of her life. He would work her pathetic ass to the bone if he had to. The embarrassment alone was enough to justify calling upon the biggest goons on the strip to take care of it, old-world style. Una and her entire gang of cheating, lying assholes would be turned to dust.

"NO!" he shouted. It was the only word he could retrieve in that moment, as he watched her make her way to the fountain's center. He glanced at his watch, noting the time. Luckily, the resort's fountain show had ended for the night. He reached for his phone and called Steven.

"Get her out of there!" he shouted into the speaker, before smashing it into the pavement.

"Get the fuck out of my way!" he shouted to the people around him, pulling himself up onto the concrete fence and watching as the healer appeared to rise out of the water, as if standing on a fountain base. From above the crowd, he took a moment to see the thousands gathered to watch his pathetic cry for her attention. He would kill her for this, he decided. Her life wasn't worth all the embarrassment caused tonight. He'd sue her, then write it off as a loss, and in a few months, people wouldn't even remember.

He watched the healer turn around slowly, revealing herself to the adoring crowd. They cheered as she revealed her face to them, a noise so deafening, Pyrus had to plug his ears to regain his sanity. The sweat continued to pour from his skin, the drunken feeling left behind the moment he heard she had escaped.

The two locked eyes then, even from such a distance. He could feel her presence piercing his shields, attempting to penetrate his soul. He'd never allow it. She was nothing more than a devil to him now; he just needed time to prove it. He knew people. He made her. He could just as easily destroy her.

"YOU WILL GET DOWN FROM THERE! RIGHT NOW!" he screamed.

Without a second thought, he plunged into the fountain waters, shocked at the shallow depth as his knees absorbed the impact. His limbs struggled to keep him afloat, but he was determined to reach the healer ahead of the authorities. He stopped briefly to catch his breath, whipping his head out of the water to find thousands of phones pointed at him, waiting for his next move. He whisked the chlorinated water from his eyes, desperately searching for Una's shimmering form. Lights suddenly flooded the fountain waters, as if setting the stage for some epic finale that the final show was yet to produce.

The phones flashed from him to Una, almost willing the two to duel in the middle of the fountain waters. Una lowered her head, looking down at the grate below. She could see Jaxson and Jayden below and knew full well that her escape route was secured. But something inside called her to change the plan.

"Una!" Jaxson shouted, his arms waving to get her attention. "Let's do this! We're running out of time!"

She smiled sweetly at him, giving him a knowing nod before returning her gaze to the crowds in front of her. The sound of the roaring crowd was only amplified by the water below. The Pope had asked for proof. There was no better moment than this.

The healer closed her eyes and centered herself, ignoring the desperate orders of her loyal team below. Pyrus was nearly upon her now, arms flailing with each tired stroke. She tried desperately to ignore his advancing form, wanting no part in a future that involved his ruthless attempt at absolute power. She had no choice but to proceed now, ignoring the possibility he may not survive the force building around her.

She raised her hands along her sides, willing an aura of golden light to surround her as she slowly unfolded her wingspan, raising her arms up high above her. The thousands before her turned on their phone flashlights, a gesture of support that revealed a glittering sea of light. The cheers continued as she pulled her hands into tight fists, arms outstretched as her body formed into the sign of a cross.

Jamie J. Kemp

She held the pose calmly for a few moments, drinking in the energy of the transformed. She was ready to make her mark on this world and the one beyond it.

As Una slowly opened her fists and closed her eyes, she whispered a silent mantra to herself. It was a prayer for the ages. A gust of wind swept along the water's surface toward her as clouds formed overhead. She could hear the distant thunder and knew that her moment had finally arrived. The lightning bolt appeared from above, a call from a universal source so strong no human being could ever survive its force and power. The energy force entered the crown of her head and blazed through her bodily form, conducting with the waters below. With a flash, the healer was gone. Pyrus, now motionless in the water, slowly sank into the shimmering shallow waters. A faint smile emerged on his colorless face as he settled onto the concrete surface below. Only shimmers of the phone lights remained, a parting sorrow to the millions of followers who prayed Una would heal them and the world she had seemingly left behind.

Made in the USA
Middletown, DE
20 April 2021